THIS ROUGH MAGIC

When Lucy Waring, a young actress temporarily out of a job, comes to stay in Corfu with her sister, she finds the peace of the idyllic island rudely broken by a series of tragic and frightening events . . .

" . . . an effective thriller . . . keeps one awake through the long night's journey into day."

The Guardian

"An animated adventure story in which suspense and romance are expertly intermingled."

The Observer

"A splendid book at any time."

News of the World

**Also by the same author,
and available in Coronet Books:**

This Rough Magic

Mary Stewart

CORONET BOOKS
Hodder and Stoughton

First published 1964
by Hodder and Stoughton Ltd

Coronet edition 1966
Seventeenth impression 1986

Printed in Great Britain for
Hodder and Stoughton Paperbacks, a
division of Hodder and Stoughton Ltd,
Mill Road, Dunton Green, Sevenoaks,
Kent (Editorial Office: 47 Bedford
Square, London, WC1 3DP) by
Richard Clay (The Chaucer Press) Ltd,
Bungay, Suffolk

ISBN 0 340 02202 7

for
John Attenborough

AUTHOR'S NOTE

Among the many debts I have incurred while writing this book, two are outstanding. I should like to thank especially Mr. Michael Halikiopoulos, Director of the Corfu Tourist Services, 5 Arseniou Street, Corfu, for all his kindness, and for the help he gave me. My other debt is to Mr. Antony Alpers, whose enchanting *Book of Dolphins* (John Murray, 1960) provided not only the inspiration, but also a great deal of information for this book.

M.S.

CHAPTER ONE

...A relation for a breakfast.
The Tempest. Act V. Scene 1.

"AND if it's a boy," said Phyllida cheerfully, "we'll call him Prospero."

I laughed. "Poor little chap, why on earth? Oh, of course... Has someone been telling you that Corfu was Shakespeare's magic island for *The Tempest*?"

"As a matter of fact, yes, the other day, but for goodness' sake don't ask me about it now. Whatever you may be used to, I draw the line at Shakespeare for breakfast." My sister yawned, stretched out a foot into the sunshine at the edge of the terrace, and admired the expensive beach sandal on it. "I didn't mean that, anyway, I only meant that we've already got a Miranda here, and a Spiro, which may not be short for Prospero, but sounds very like it."

"Oh? It sounds highly romantic. Who are they?"

"A local boy and girl: they're twins."

"Good heavens. Papa must be a literary gent?"

Phyllida smiled. "You could say so."

Something in her expression roused my curiosity, just as something else told me she had meant to; so I—who can be every bit as provoking as Phyllida when I try—said merely: "Well, in that case hadn't you better have a change? How about Caliban for your unborn young? It fits like a glove."

"Why?" she demanded indignantly.

" 'This blue-eyed hag was hither brought with child,' " I quoted. "Is there some more coffee?"

"Of course. Here. Oh, my goodness, it's nice to have you here, Lucy! I suppose I oughtn't to call it luck that you were free to come just now, but I'm awfully glad you could. This is heaven after Rome."

"And paradise after London. I feel different already. When I think where I was this time yesterday ... and when I *think* about the rain ..."

I shuddered, and drank my coffee, leaning back in my chair

7

to gaze out across pine tops furry with gold towards the sparkling sea, and surrendering myself to the dreamlike feeling that marks the start of a holiday in a place like this when one is tired, and has been transported overnight from the April chill of England to the sunlight of a magic island in the Ionian Sea.

Perhaps I should explain (for those who are not so lucky as I) that Corfu is an island off the west coast of Greece. It is long and sickle-shaped, and lies along the curve of the coast; at its nearest, in the north, it is barely two miles off the Albanian mainland, but from the town of Corfu, which is about half-way down the curve of the sickle, the coast of Greece is about seven or eight miles distant. At its northern end the island is broad and mountainous, trailing off through rich valleys and ever-decreasing hills into the long, flat scorpion's tail of the south from which some think that Corfu, or Kerkyra, gets its name.

My sister's house lies some twelve miles north of Corfu town, where the coast begins its curve towards the mainland, and where the foothills of Mount Pantokrator provide shelter for the rich little pocket of land which has been part of her husband's family property for a good many years.

My sister Phyllida is three years older than I, and when she was twenty she married a Roman banker, Leonardo Forli. His family had settled in Corfu during the Venetian occupation of that island, and had managed somehow to survive the various subsequent 'occupations' with their small estate more or less intact, and had even, like the Vicar of Bray, contrived to prosper. It was under the British Protectorate that Leo's great-grandfather had built the pretentious and romantic Castello dei Fiori in the woods above the little bay where the estate ran down to the sea. He had planted vineyards, and orange orchards, including a small plantation (if that is the word) of the Japanese miniature oranges called *koùm koyàt* for which the Forli estate later became famous. He even cleared space in the woods for a garden, and built—beyond the southern arm of the bay and just out of sight of the Castello—a jetty and a vast boat-house which (according to Phyllida) would almost have housed the Sixth Fleet, and had indeed housed the complicated flock of vessels in which his guests used to visit him. In his day, I gathered, the Castello had been the scene of one large and continuous house-party: in summer they sailed and fished, and in the fall there were hunting-parties, when thirty or so guests

8

would invade the Greek and Albanian mainlands to harry the birds and ibexes.

But those days had vanished with the first war, and the family moved to Rome, though without selling the Castello, which remained, through the twenties and thirties, their summer home. The shifting fortunes of the Second World War almost destroyed the estate, but the Forlis emerged in post-war Rome with the family fortunes mysteriously repaired, and the then Forli Senior—Leo's father—turned his attention once more to the Corfu property. He had done something to restore the place, but after his death three years ago his son had decided that the Castello's rubbed and faded splendours were no longer for him, and had built a pair of smallish modern villas—in reality twin bungalows—on the two headlands enclosing the bay of which the Castello overlooked the centre. He and Phyllida themselves used the Villa Forli, as they called the house on the northern headland; its twin, the Villa Rotha, stood to the south of the bay above the creek where the boat-house was. The Villa Rotha had been rented by an Englishman, a Mr. Manning, who had been there since the previous autumn working on a book. ("You know the kind," said my sister, "all photographs, with a thin trickle of text in large type, but they're *good*.") The three houses were connected with the road by the main drive to the Castello, and with each other by various paths through the woods and down into the bay.

This year the hot spring in Rome, with worse promised, had driven the Forlis early to Corfu. Phyllida, who was pregnant, had been feeling the heat badly, so had been persuaded to leave the two older children (whose school term was still running) with their grandmother, and Leo had brought her over a few days before I arrived, but had had to go back to his business in Rome, with the promise to fly over when he could at weekends, and to bring the children for Easter. So Phyllida, hearing that I was currently at a loose end, had written begging me to join her in Corfu and keep her company.

The invitation couldn't have been better timed. The play I was in had just folded after the merest face-saver of a run, and I was out of a job. That the job had been my first in London—my 'big chance'—accounted partly for my present depression. There was nothing more on the cards: the agencies were polite, but evasive: and besides, we had had a dreadful winter and I was tired, dispirited, and seriously wondering, at twenty-five, if

9

I had made a fool of myself in insisting against all advice on the stage as a career. But—as everyone knows who has anything to do with it—the stage is not a profession, but a virus, and I had it. So I had worked and scraped my way through the usual beginnings until last year, when I had finally decided, after three years of juvenile leads in provincial rep., that it was time to try my luck in London. And luck had seemed at last to be with me. After ten months or so of television walk-ons and the odd commercial, I had landed a promising part, only to have the play fold under me like a dying camel, after a two-months run.

But at least I could count myself luckier than the other few thousand still fighting their way towards the bottom rung of the ladder: while they were sitting in the agents' stuffy offices here was I on the terrace of the Villa Forli, with as many weeks in front of me as I cared to take in the dazzling sunshine of Corfu.

The terrace was a wide, tiled platform perched at the end of the promontory where wooded cliffs fell steeply to the sea. Below the balustrade hung cloud on cloud of pines, already smelling warm and spicy in the morning sun. Behind the house and to either side sloped the cool woods where small birds flashed and twittered. The bay itself was hidden by trees, but the view ahead was glorious—a stretch of the calm, shimmering Gulf that lies in the curved arm of Corfu. Away northward, across the dark blue strait, loomed, insubstantial as mist, the ghostly snows of Albania.

It was a scene of the most profound and enchanted peace. No sound but the birds; nothing in sight but trees and sky and sun-reflecting sea.

I sighed. "Well, if it isn't Prospero's magic island it ought to be ... Who are these romantic twins of yours, anyway?"

"Spiro and Miranda? Oh, they belong to the woman who works for us here, Maria. She has that cottage at the main Castello gate—you'd see it last night on your way in from the airport."

"I remember a light there ... A tiny place, wasn't it? So they're Corfu people—what's the word? Corfusians?"

She laughed. "Idiot. Corfiotes. Yes, they're Corfiote peasants. The brother works for Godfrey Manning over at the Villa Rotha. Miranda helps her mother here."

"Peasants?" Mildly intrigued, I gave her the lead I thought she wanted. "It does seem a bit odd to find those names here. Who was this well-read father of theirs, then? Leo?"

10

"Leo," said his loving wife, "has to my certain knowledge read nothing but the Roman *Financial Times* for the last eight years. He'd think 'Prospero and Miranda' was the name of an Investment Trust. No, it's even odder than you think, my love..." She gave her small cat-and-canary smile, the one I recognised as preceding the more far-fetched flights of gossip that she calls 'interesting facts that I feel you ought to know' ... "Actually, Spiro's officially called after the island saint—every second boy's called Spiridion in Corfu—but since our distinguished tenant at the Castello was responsible for the christening—and for the twins as well, one gathers—I'll bet he's down as Prospero in the parish register, or whatever they have here."

"Your 'distinguished tenant'?" This was obviously the *bonne bouche* she had been saving for me, but I looked at her in some surprise, remembering the vivid description she had once given me of the Castello dei Fiori: 'tatty beyond words, sort of Wagnerian Gothic, like a set for a musical version of *Dracula*'. I wondered who could have been persuaded to pay for these operatic splendors. "Someone's rented Valhalla, then? Aren't you lucky. Who?"

"Julian Gale."

"*Julian Gale?*" I sat up abruptly, staring at her. "You can't mean—*do* you mean Julian Gale? The actor?"

"As ever was." My sister looked pleased with the effect she had produced. I was wide awake now, as I had certainly not been during the long recital of our family affairs earlier. Sir Julian Gale was not only 'an actor', he had been one of the more brilliant lights of the English theatre for more years than I could well remember. And, more recently, one of its mysteries.

"Well!" I said. "So this is where he went."

"I thought you'd be interested," said Phyl, rather smugly.

"I'll say I am! Everyone's still wondering, on and off, why he packed it in like that two years ago. Of course I knew he'd been ill after that ghastly accident, but to give it up and then just quietly vanish ... You should have heard the rumours."

"I can imagine. We've our own brand here. But don't go all shiny-eyed and imagine you'll get anywhere near him, my child. He's here for privacy, and I mean for privacy. He doesn't go out at all—socially, that is—except to the houses of a couple of friends, and they've got *Trespassers Will Be Shot* plastered at intervals of one yard all over the grounds, and the gardener throws all callers over the cliff into the sea."

"I shan't worry him. I think too darned much of him for that. I suppose you must have met him. How is he?"

"Oh, I—he seems all right. Just doesn't get around, that's all. I've only met him a couple of times. Actually it was he who told me that Corfu was supposed to be the setting of *The Tempest*." She glanced at me sideways. "I—er—I suppose you'd allow him to be 'a literary gent'?"

But this time I ignored the lead. "*The Tempest* was his swansong," I said. "I saw it at Stratford, the last performance, and cried my eyes out over the 'this rough magic I here abjure' bit. Is that what made him choose Corfu to retire to?"

She laughed. "I doubt it. Didn't you know he was practically a native? He was here during the war, and apparently stayed on for a bit after it was over, and then I'm told he used to bring his family back almost every year for holidays, when the children were young. They had a house near Ipsos, and kept it on till quite recently, but it was sold after his wife and daughter were killed. However, I suppose he still had ... connections ... here, so when he thought of retiring he remembered the Castello. We hadn't meant to let the place, it wasn't really fit, but he was so anxious to find somewhere quite isolated and quiet, and it really did seem a godsend that the Castello was empty, with Maria and her family just next door; so Leo let it go. Maria and the twins turned to and fixed up a few of the rooms, and there's a couple who live at the far side of the orange orchards; they look after the place, and their grandson does the Castello garden and helps around, so for anyone who really only wants peace and privacy I suppose it's a pretty fair bargain ... Well, that's our little colony. I won't say it's just another St. Trop. in the height of the season, but there's plenty of what you want, if it's only peace and sunshine and bathing."

"Suits me," I said dreamily. "Oh, how it suits me."

"D'you want to go down this morning?"

"I'd love to. Where?"

"Well, the bay, of course. It's down that way." She pointed vaguely through the trees.

"I thought you said there were notices warning trespassers off?"

"Oh, goodness, not literally, and not from the beach, anyway, only the grounds. We'd never let anyone else have the bay, that's what we come here for! Actually it's quite nice straight down from here on the north side of the headland where our own little jetty is, but there's sand in the bay, and it's heaven for lying about, and quite private . . . Well, you do as you like. I might go down later, but if you want to swim this morning, I'll get Miranda to show you the way."

"She's here now?"

"Darling," said my sister, "You're in the lap of vulgar luxury now, remember? Did you think I made the coffee myself?"

"Get you, Contessa," I said, crudely. "I can remember the day——"

I broke off as a girl came out on to the terrace with a tray, to clear away the breakfast things. She eyed me curiously, with that unabashed stare of the Greeks which one learns to get used to, as it is virtually impossible to stare it down in return, and smiled at me, the smile broadening into a grin as I tried a "Good morning" in Greek—a phrase which was, as yet, my whole vocabulary. She was short and stockily built, with a thick neck and round face, and heavy brows almost meeting over her nose. Her bright dark eyes and warm skin were attractive with the simple, animal attraction of youth and health. The dress of faded red suited her, giving her a sort of dark, gentle glow that was very different from the electric sparkle of the urban expatriate Greeks I had met. She looked about seventeen.

My attempt to greet her undammed a flood of delighted Greek which my sister, laughing, managed at length to stem.

"She doesn't understand, Miranda, she only knows two words. Speak English. Will you show her the way down to the beach when you've cleared away, please?"

"Of course! I shall be pleased!"

She looked more than pleased, she looked so delighted that I smiled to myself, presuming cynically that it was probably only pleasure at having an outing in the middle of a working morning. As it happened, I was wrong. Coming so recently from the grey depressions of London and the backstage bad tempers of failure, I wasn't able as yet to grasp the Greek's simple delight in doing anyone a service.

She began to pile the breakfast dishes on her tray with clattering vigour. "I shall not be long. A minute, only a minute . . ."

"And that means half an hour," said my sister placidly, as the girl bustled out. "Anyway, what's the hurry? You've all the time in the world."

"So I have," I said, in deep contentment.

*   *   *

The way to the beach was a shady path quilted with pine needles. It twisted through the trees, to lead out suddenly into a small clearing where a stream, trickling down to the sea, was trapped in a sunny pool under a bank of honeysuckle.

Here the path forked, one track going uphill, deeper into the woods, the other turning down steeply through pines and golden oaks towards the sea.

Miranda paused and pointed downhill. "That is the way you go. The other is to the Castello, and it is private. Nobody goes that way, it is only to the house, you understand."

"Whereabouts is the other villa, Mr. Manning's?"

"On the other side of the bay, at the top of the cliff. You cannot see it from the beach because the trees are in the way, but there is a path going like this"—she sketched a steep zigzag —"from the boat-house up the cliff. My brother works there, my brother Spiro. It is a fine house, very beautiful, like the Signora's, though of course not so wonderful as the Castello. *That* is like a palace."

"So I believe. Does your father work on the estate, too?"

The query was no more than idle; I had completely forgotten Phyllida's nonsense, and hadn't believed it anyway, but to my intense embarrassment the girl hesitated, and I wondered for one horrified second if Phyllida had been right. I did not know, then, that the Greek takes the most intensely personal questions serenely for granted, just as he asks them himself, and I had begun to stammer something, but Miranda was already answering:

"Many years ago my father left us. He went over there."

'Over there' was at the moment a wall of trees laced with shrubs of myrtle, but I knew what lay beyond them; the grim, shut land of Communist Albania.

"You mean as a prisoner?" I asked, horrified.

She shook her head. "No. He was a Communist. We lived then in Argyrathes, in the south of Corfu, and in that part of the island there are many such." She hesitated. "I do not know why this is. It is different in the north, where my mother comes from." She spoke as if the island were four hundred miles long instead of forty, but I believed her. Where two Greeks are

14

gathered together, there will be at least three political parties represented, and possibly more.

"You've never heard from him?"

"Never. In the old days my mother still hoped, but now, of course, the frontiers are shut to all, and no one can pass in or out. If he is still alive, he must stay there. But we do not know this either."

"D'you mean that no one can travel to Albania?"

"No one." The black eyes suddenly glittered to life, as if something had sparked behind their placid orbs. "Except those who break the law."

"Not a law I'd care to break myself." Those alien snows had looked high and cold and cruel. I said awkwardly: "I'm sorry, Miranda. It must be an unhappy business for your mother."

She shrugged. "It is a long time ago. Fourteen years. I do not even know if I remember him. And we have Spiro to look after us." The sparkle again. "He works for Mr. Manning, I told you this—with the boat, and with the car, a wonderful car, very expensive—and also with the photographs that Mr. Manning is taking for a book. He has said that when the book is finished—a real book that is sold in the shops—he will put Spiro's name in it, in print. Imagine! Oh, there is nothing that Spiro cannot do! He is my twin, you understand."

"Is he like you?"

She looked surprised. "Like me? Why, no, he is a man, and have I not just told you that he is clever? Me, I am not clever, but then I am a woman, and there is no need. With men it is different. Yes?"

"So the men say." I laughed. "Well, thanks very much for showing me the way. Will you tell my sister that I'll be back in good time for lunch?"

I turned down the steep path under the pines. As I reached the first bend something made me glance back towards the clearing.

Miranda had gone. But I thought I saw a whisk of faded scarlet, not from the direction of the Villa Forli, but higher up in the woods, on the forbidden path to the Castello.

15

CHAPTER TWO

Sir, I am vex'd.
IV. 1.

The bay was small and sheltered, a sickle of pure white sand holding back the aquamarine sea, and held in its turn by the towering backdrop of cliff and pine and golden-green trees. My path led me steeply down past a knot of young oaks, straight on to the sand. I changed quickly in a sheltered corner, and walked out into the white blaze of the sun.

The bay was deserted and very quiet. To either side of it the wooded promontories thrust out into the calm, glittering water. Beyond them the sea deepened through peacock shades to a rich, dark blue, where the mountains of Epirus floated in the clear distance, less substantial than a bank of mist. The far snows of Albania seemed to drift like cloud.

After the heat of the sand, the water felt cool and silky. I let myself down into the milky calm, and began to swim idly along parallel to the shore, towards the southern arm of the bay. There was the faintest breeze blowing off the land, its heady mixture of orange-blossom and pine, sweet and sharp, coming in warm puffs through the salt smell of the sea. Soon I was nearing the promontory, where white rocks came down to the water, and a grove of pines hung out, shadowing a deep, green pool. I stayed in the sun, turning lazily on my back to float, eyes shut against the brilliance of the sky.

The pines breathed and whispered; the tranquil water made no sound at all . . .

A ripple rocked me, nearly turning me over. As I floundered, trying to right myself, another came, a wash like that of a small boat passing, rolling me in its wake. But I had heard neither oars nor engine; could hear nothing now except the slap of the exhausted ripples against the rock.

Treading water, I looked around me, puzzled and a little alarmed. Nothing. The sea shimmered, empty and calm, to the turquoise and blue of its horizon. I felt downwards with my feet, to find that I had drifted a little further out from shore, and could barely touch bottom with the tips of my toes. I turned back towards the shallows.

This time the wash lifted me clear off my feet, and as I plunged clumsily forward another followed it, tumbling me over, so that I struggled helplessly for a minute, swallowing water, before striking out, thoroughly alarmed now, for shore.

Beside me, suddenly, the water swirled and hissed. Something touched me—a cold, momentary graze along the thigh—as a body drove past me under water . . .

I gave a gasp of sheer fright, and the only reason I didn't scream was because I gasped myself full of water, and went under. Fighting back, terrified, to the surface, I shook the salt out of my eyes, and looked wildly round—to see the bay as empty as before, but with its surface marked now by the arrowing ripples of whatever sea-creature had brushed by me. The arrow's point was moving fast away, its wake as clear as a vapour-trail across the flat water of the bay. It tore on its way, straight for the open sea . . . then curved in a long arc, heading back . . .

I didn't wait to see what it was. My ignorant mind, panic-stricken, screamed 'Sharks!' and I struck out madly for the rocks of the promontory.

It was coming fast. Thirty yards off, the surface of the water bulged, swelled, and broke to the curved thrust of a huge, silver-black back. The water parted, and poured off its sides like liquid glass. There was a gasping puff of breath; I caught the glimpse of a dark bright eye, and a dorsal fin cusped like a crescent moon, then the creature submerged again, its wash lifting me a couple of yards forward towards my rock. I found a handhold, clung, and scrambled out, gasping, and thoroughly scared.

It surely wasn't a shark. Hundreds of adventure stories had told me that one knew a shark by the great triangular fin, and I had seen pictures of the terrible jaws and tiny, brutal eye. This creature had breathed air, and the eye had been big and dark, like a dog's—like a seal's, perhaps? But there were no seals in these warm waters, and besides, seals didn't have dorsal fins. A porpoise, then? Too big . . .

Then I had the answer, and with it a rush of relief and delight. This was the darling of the Aegean, 'the lad who lives before the wind', Apollo's beloved, 'desire of the sea', the dolphin . . . the lovely names went rippling by with him, as I drew himself up on to the warm rock in the shade of the pines, clasped my knees, and settled down to watch.

Here he came again, in a great curve, smooth and glistening,

17

dark-backed and light-bellied, and as graceful as a racing yacht. This time he came right out, to lie on the surface watching me.

He was large, as dolphins go, something over eight feet long. He lay rocking gently, with the powerful shoulders waiting curved for the plunge below, and the tail—crescent-shaped, and quite unlike a fish's upright rudder—hugging the water flatly, holding the big body level. The dark-ringed eye watched me steadily, with what I could have sworn was a friendly and interested light. The smooth muzzle was curved into the perpetual dolphin-smile.

Excitement and pleasure made me light-headed. "Oh, you darling!" I said foolishly, and put out a hand, rather as one puts it out to the pigeons in Trafalgar Square.

The dolphin, naturally, ignored it, but lay there placidly smiling, rocking a little closer, and watching me, entirely unafraid.

So they were true, those stories . . . I knew of the legends, of course—ancient literature was studded with stories of dolphins who had befriended man; and while one couldn't quite accept all the miraculous dolphins of legend, there were also many more recent tales, sworn to with every kind of modern proof. There was the dolphin called Pelorus Jack, fifty years ago in New Zealand, who saw the ships through Cook Straight for twenty years; the Opononi dolphin of the fifties, who entertained the holiday-makers in the bay; the one more recently in Italy, who played with the children near the shore, attracting such large crowds that eventually a little group of business-men from a near-by resort, whose custom was being drawn away, lay in wait for the dolphin, and shot her dead as she came in to play. These, and others, gave the old legends rather more than the benefit of the doubt.

And here, indeed, was the living proof. Here was I, Lucy Waring, being asked into the water for a game. The dolphin couldn't have made it clearer if he'd been carrying a placard on that lovely moon's-horn fin of his. He rocked himself, watching me, then half-turned, rolled, and came up again, nearer still . . .

A stray breeze moved the pines, and I heard a bee go past my cheek, travelling like a bullet. The dolphin arched suddenly away in a deep dive. The sea sucked, swirled, and settled, rocking, back to emptiness.

So that was that. With a disappointment so sharp that it felt like a bereavement, I turned my head to watch for him moving out to sea, when suddenly, not far from my rock, the sea burst apart as if it had been shelled, and the dolphin shot upwards on a steep slant that took him out of the water in a yard-high leap, and down again with a smack of the tail as loud as a cannon-shot. He tore by like a torpedo, to fetch up all standing twenty yards out from my rock, and fix me once again with that bright, humorous eye.

It was an enchanting piece of show-off, and it did the trick. "All right," I said softly, "I'll come in. But if you knock me over again, I'll drown you, my lad, see if I don't!"

I lowered my legs into the water, ready to slide down off the rock. Another bee shot past above me, seawards, with a curious, high humming. Something—some small fish, I supposed—splashed a white jet of water just beyond the dolphin. Even as I wondered, vaguely, what it was, the humming came again, nearer ... and then another white spurt of water, and a curious thin, curving whine, like singing wire.

I understood then. I'd heard that sound before. These were neither bees nor fish. They were bullets, presumably from a silenced rifle, and one of them had ricocheted off the surface of the sea. Someone was shooting at the dolphin from the woods above the bay.

That I was in some danger from the ricochets myself didn't at first enter my head. I was merely furious, and concerned to do something quickly. There lay the dolphin, smiling at me on the water, while some murderous 'sportsman' was no doubt taking aim yet again ...

Presumably he hadn't yet seen me in the shadow of the pines. I shouted at the top of my voice: "Stop that shooting! Stop it at once!" and thrust myself forward into the water.

Nobody, surely, would fire at the beast when there was the chance of hitting me? I plunged straight out into the sunlight, clumsily breasting the water, hoping that my rough approach would scare the dolphin away from the danger.

It did. He allowed me to come within a few feet, but as I lunged further, with a hand out as if to touch him, he rolled gently away from me, submerged, and vanished.

I stood breast-deep, watching the sea. Nothing. It stretched silent and empty towards the tranquil, floating hills of the mainland. The ripples ran back to the shore, and flattened, whispering. The dolphin had gone. And the magic had gone with him. This was only a small—and lonely—bathing-place, above which waited an unpleasant and frustrated character with a gun.

I turned to look up at the enclosing cliffs.

The first thing I saw, high up above the bay's centre, was what must be the upper storeys of the Castello dei Fiori, rearing their incongruously embattled turrets against a background of holm-oak and cedar and Mediterranean cypress. The house was set well back, so that I could not see the ground-floor windows, but a wide balcony, or terrace, edged with a stone balustrade, jutted forward right to the cliff's edge over the bay. From the beach directly below nothing of this would be visible through the tangle of flowering shrubs that curtained the steep, broken cliff, but from where I stood I could see the full length of the balustrade with its moss-grown statues at the corners, a stone jar or two full of flowers showing bright against the dark background of cypress, and, a little way back from the balustrade, a table and chairs set in the shadow of a stone-pine.

And a man standing, half invisible in the shade of the pine, watching me.

A moment's study convinced me that it could not be Sir Julian Gale. This man was too dark, and even from this distance looked quite unfamiliar—too casual in his bearing, perhaps—and certainly too young. The gardener, probably; the one who threw the trespassers over the cliff. Well, if Sir Julian's gardener had the habit of amusing himself with a bit of shooting-practice, it was high time he was stopped.

I was out of the water before even the dolphin could have dived twice, had snatched up shoes and wrap, and was making for a dilapidated flight of steps near the cliff which, I assumed, led up to the terrace.

From above I heard a shout, and looked up. He had come forward to the balustrade, and was leaning over. I could barely see him through the thick screen of hibiscus and bramble, but he didn't look like a Greek, and as I paused, he shouted in English: "That way, please!" and his arm went out in a gesture towards the southern end of the bay.

I ignored it. Whoever he was—some guest of Julian Gale's, presumably—I was going to have this out with him here and now, while I was hot with temper; not wait until I had to meet him at some polite bun-fight of Phyllida's ... 'But you really mustn't shoot at dolphins, Mr. Whosit, they do no harm ...'

The same old polite spiel, gone through a thousand times with stupid, trigger-happy men who shot or trapped badgers, otters, kestrels—harmless creatures, killed because some man wanted a walk out with his dog on a fine day. No, this time I was white-hot, and brave with it, and I was going to say my piece.

I went up those steps like a rocket leaving the launching-pad.

They were steep and crooked, and wound up through the thickest of the wood. They skirted the roots of the cliff, flicked up and round thickets of myrtle and summer jasmine, and emerged into a sloping glade full of dappled sunlight.

He was there, looking annoyed, having apparently come down from the terrace to intercept me. I only realised, when I stopped to face him, how very much at a disadvantage I was. He had come down some fifty feet; I had hurtled up a hundred or so. He presumably had a right to be where he was; I had not. He was also minding his own business, which was emphatically none of mine. Moreover, he was fully dressed, and I was in swimming costume, with a wet wrap flying loose round me. I clutched it to me, and fought for breath, feeling angrier than ever, but now this didn't help at all, as I couldn't get a word out.

He said, not aggressively but not politely: "This is private ground, you know. Perhaps you'd be good enough to leave by the way you came? This only takes you up to the terrace, and then more or less through the house."

I got enough breath to speak, and wasted neither time nor words. "Why were you shooting at that dolphin?"

He looked as blank as if I had suddenly slapped his face. "Why was I what?"

"That was you just now, wasn't it, shooting at the dolphin down in the bay?"

"My dear g——" He checked himself, and said, like someone dealing with a lunatic: "Just what are you talking about?"

"Don't pretend you don't know! It must have been you! If you're such death on trespassers, who else would be there?" I was panting hard, and my hands were shaking as I clutched the wrap to me clumsily. "Someone took a couple of pot-shots at it, just a few minutes ago. I was down there, and I saw you on the terrace."

"I certainly saw a dolphin there. I didn't see you, until you shouted and came jumping out from under the trees. But you

21

must be mistaken. There was no shooting. I'd have been bound to hear it if there was."

"It was silenced, of course," I said impatiently. "I tell you, I was down there when the shots came! D'you think I'd have come running up here for the fun of the thing? They were bullets all right! I know a ricochet when I hear it."

His brows snapped down at that, and he stared at me frowningly, as if seeing me for the first time as a person, and not just a nuisance to be thrown down the cliff as quickly as possible.

"Then why did you jump into the water near the dolphin?"

"Well, obviously! I wanted to drive it away before it got hurt!"

"But you might have been badly hurt yourself. Don't you know that a bullet ricochets off water the way it does off rock?"

"Of course I do! But I had to do something, hadn't I?"

"Brave girl." There was a dryness in his voice that brought my cooling temper fizzing to the boil again. I said hotly:

"You don't believe me, do you? I tell you it's true! They *were* shots, and *of course* I jumped in to stop you! I knew you'd have to stop if someone was there."

"You know," he said, "you can't have it both ways. Either I did the shooting, or I don't believe there was any shooting. Not both. You can take your pick. If I were you, I'd choose the second; I mean, it's simply not credible, is it? Even supposing someone wanted to shoot a dolphin, why use a silencer?"

"*I'm* asking *you*," I said.

For a moment I thought I had gone too far. His lips compressed, and his eyes looked angry. There was a short silence, while he stared at me frowningly, and we measured one another.

I saw a strongly built man of about thirty, carelessly dressed in slacks and a sleeveless Sea Island shirt which exposed a chest and arms that might have belonged to any of the Greek navvies I was to see building the roads with their bare hands and very little more. Like theirs, too, his hair and eyes were very dark. But something at once sensual and sensitive about the mouth contradicted the impression of a purely physical personality; here, one felt, was a man of aggressive impulses, but one who paid for them in his own private coinage.

What impression he was getting of me I hated to think— damp hair, flushed face, half-embarrassed fury, and a damned wrap that kept slipping—but of one thing I could feel pretty

22

sure: at this very moment he was having one of those aggressive impulses of his. Fortunately it wasn't physical ... yet.

"Well," he said shortly, "I'm afraid you'll have to take my word for it. I did not shoot at the beast, with a rifle or a catapult or anything else. Will that do? And now if you'll excuse me, I'll be obliged if you would——"

"Go out by the way I came in? All right. I get the message. I'm sorry, perhaps I was wrong. But I certainly wasn't wrong about the shooting. I don't see any more than you do why anyone should do it, but the fact remains that they did." I hesitated, faltering now under his indifferent eye. "Look, I don't want to be any more of a nuisance, but I can't just leave it at that ... It might happen again ... Since it wasn't you, have you any idea who it could have been?"

"No."

"Not the gardener?"

"No."

"Or the tenant at the Villa Rotha?"

"Manning? On the contrary, if you want help in your protection campaign I suggest you go to the Villa Rotha straight away. Manning's been photographing that beast for weeks. It was he who tamed it in the first place, he and the Greek boy who works for him."

"Tamed it? Oh ... I see. Well, then," I added, lamely, "it wouldn't be him, obviously."

He said nothing, waiting, it seemed, with a kind of neutral patience for me to go. I bit my lip, hesitating miserably, feeling a fool. (Why did one always feel such a fool when it was a matter of kindness—what the more sophisticated saw as sentimentality?) I found that I was shivering. Anger and energy had drained out of me together. The glade was cool with shadows.

I said: "Well, I imagine I'll see Mr. Manning some time soon, and if he can't help, I'm sure my brother-in-law will. I mean, if this is all private land, and the shore as well, then we ought to be able to stop that kind of trespasser, oughtn't we?"

He said quickly: "We?"

"The people who own the place. I'm Lucy Waring, Phyllida Forli's sister. I take it you're staying with Sir Julian?"

"I'm his son. So you're Miss Waring? I hadn't realised you were here already." He appeared to be hesitating on the brink of some apology, but asked instead: "Is Forli at home now?"

23

"No," I said shortly, and turned to go. There was a trail of bramble across my shoe, and I bent to disengage it.

"I'm sorry if I was a little abrupt." His voice had not noticeably softened, but that might have been due to awkwardness. "We've had rather a lot of bother with people coming around lately, and my father ... he's been ill, and came here to convalesce, so you can imagine that he prefers to be left to himself."

"Did I look like an autograph hunter?"

For the first time there was a twitch of amusement. "Well, no. But your dolphin has been more of an attraction even than my father: the word got round somehow that it was being photographed hereabouts, and then of course the rumour started that a film was being made, so we got a few boat-loads of sightseers coming round into the bay, not to mention stray parties in the woods. It's all been a bit trying. I wouldn't mind, personally, if people wanted to use the beach, if it weren't that they always come armed with transistor radios, and that I cannot stand. I'm a professional musician, and I'm here to work." He added, dryly: "And if you're thinking that this gives me the best of reasons for wanting to get rid of the dolphin, I can only assure you again that it didn't occur to me."

"Well," I said, "it seems there's no more to be said, doesn't it? I'm sorry if I interrupted your work. I'll go now and let you get back to it. Good-bye, Mr. Gale."

My exit from the clearing was ruined by the fact that my wrap caught on the bramble, and came clean off me. It took me some three horrible minutes to disentangle it and go.

But I needn't have worried about the threat to my dignity. He had already gone. From somewhere above, and alarmingly near, I heard voices, question and answer, so brief and idle as to be in themselves an insult. Then music, as a wireless or gramophone let loose a flood of weird atonal chords on the still air.

I could be sure I was already forgotten.

CHAPTER THREE

This gallant which thou seest
Was in the wrack: and but he's something stain'd
With grief (that's beauty's canker) thou might'st call him
A goodly person.

I. 2.

BY the time I had showered and dressed I felt calmer, and very
ready to tell Phyllida all about it, and possibly to hear her
barbed comments on the unaccommodating Mr. Gale. But
when I looked on the terrace she was not to be seen, only the
table half-laid for lunch, with the silver thrown down, as if
hastily, in the middle of the cloth. There was no sign of
Miranda or her mother.

Then I heard the door from the kitchen premises swing open
and shut, and the quick tap of my sister's steps crossing the hall,
to enter the big living-room she called the *salotto*.

"Lucy? Was that you I heard?"

"I'm out here." I made for the french windows as I spoke,
but she had already hurried out to meet me, and one look at her
face drove all thoughts of my morning's adventure from my
head.

"Phyl! What's the matter? You look ghastly. Is it Caliban?"

She shook her head. "Nothing so simple. There's been bad
news, an awful thing. Poor Maria's boy's been drowned. Spiro,
the boy I told you about at breakfast."

"*Phyl!* Oh, my dear, how frightful! But—how? When?"

"Last night. He was out with Godfrey in the boat—Godfrey
Manning, that is—and there was an accident. Godfrey's just
come over with the news, and I've been breaking it to Maria and
Miranda. I—I've sent them home." She put a hand to her head.
"Lucy, it was so awful! I simply can't tell you. If Maria had
even *said* anything, but she didn't, not one single word ... Oh
well, come on in. Godfrey's still here, you'd better come and
meet him."

I drew back. "No, no, don't you bother about me: I'll go to
my room, or something. Mr. Manning won't want to have to do
the polite. Poor Phyl; I'm sorry ... Look, would you like me to

25

take myself right away for the rest of the day? I'll go and get lunch somewhere, and then——"

"No, please, I'd rather you stayed." She dropped her voice for a moment. "He's taking it pretty hard, and quite honestly I think it might do him good to talk about it. Come on in ... God! I could do with a drink! Caliban'll have to lump it, for once." She smiled a bit thinly, and led the way in through the long window.

The *salotto* was a long, cool room, with three big windows opening on the terrace with its dazzling view. The sun was tempered by the wistaria that roofed the terrace, and the room was cool and airy, its duck-egg blue walls and white paint setting off to perfection the gilt of the Italian mirrors and the pale-gold polished wood of the floor. A calm room, with the kind of graceful simplicity that money and good taste can produce. Phyllida had always had excellent taste. It was a good thing, I sometimes reflected, that she, and not I, had married the rich man. My own taste—since I had outgrown the gingham-and-Chianti-bottle stage—had been heavily conditioned by the fact that I had lived for so long in a perpetual welter of junk-shop props picked up cheaply and licked into stage-worthiness for the current show. At best, the effect was a kind of poor man's Cecil Beaton; at worst, a cross between sets designed by Emmett and Ronald Searle for a stage version of Samuel Becket's *Watt*. That I enjoyed my kind of life didn't stop me from admiring my sister's undoubted talent for elegance.

There was a table at the far end of the room, laden with bottles. A man stood with his back to us, splashing soda into a glass. He turned as we came in.

My first quick impression was of a mask of rather chilly control held hard down over some strong emotion. Then the impression faded, and I saw that I was wrong; the control was not a mask; it was part of the man, and was created by the emotion itself, as a Westinghouse brake is slammed on automatically by the head of steam. Here was something very different from Mr. Gale. I looked at him with interest, and some compassion.

He was tall, and toughly built, with brown hair bleached by the sun, a narrow, clever face, and grey eyes which looked tired and dragged down at the corners, as if he had had no sleep. I put his age somewhere in the middle thirties.

Phyllida introduced us, and he acknowledged me civilly, but

26

all his attention was on my sister. "You've told them? Was it very bad?"

"Worse than bad. Get me a drink, for heaven's sake, will you?" She sank into a chair. "What? Oh, Scotch, please. What about you, Lucy?"

"If that's fruit juice in the jug, may I have that, please? Is there ice?"

"Of course." He handed the drinks. "Look, Phyl, ought I to go and talk to them now? There'll be things they'll want to ask."

She drank, sighed, and seemed to relax a little. "I'd leave it for now, if I were you. I told them they could go home, and they didn't say a word, just picked up their things. I suppose the police'll be there to see them ... Later on they'll want to hear every last detail from you, but just at the moment I doubt if Maria's fit to take anything in at all, except that he's dead. As a matter of fact, I don't think she even took *that* in, I don't think she believes it, yet." She looked up at him. "Godfrey, I suppose ... I suppose there couldn't be any doubt?"

He hesitated, swirling the whisky in his glass, frowning down at it. The lines of fatigue were deep in his face, and made me wonder if he were older than I had thought.

"Well, yes. That's rather the hell of it, don't you see? That's why I didn't come over till now ... I've been phoning around all over the place, trying to find out if he could possibly have got ashore either here or on the mainland, or if he'd been ... well, found. If his body had been washed ashore, that is." He looked up from the drink. "But I'm morally certain there's no chance. I mean, I saw him go."

"And how far out were you?"

He grimaced. "About dead centre."

"From here?"

"Further north, out from Kouloura, right in the strait. But that's still a mile each way."

I said: "What happened?"

They both started as if they had forgotten my presence completely. Godfrey Manning straightened his shoulders, and smoothed back his hair in a gesture I was to know well.

"Do you know, I'm still hardly sure. Does that sound incredibly stupid? It's no more than the truth. I've been over it so many times in my mind since it happened that I'm beginning to wonder now how much I really do remember. And, of course, a night without sleep doesn't help." He crossed to the table to pour himself another drink, saying over his shoulder: "The worst of it is, I can't get rid of the feeling that there must have been something I could have done to prevent it."

Phyllida cried out at that, and I said quickly: "I'm sure that's not true! I'm sorry, I shouldn't have asked. You won't want to talk about it any more."

"It's all right." He came back to a chair, but didn't sit in it, just perched rather restlessly on the arm. "I've already been through it with the police, and given Phyl a sketch of a sort. You might say the worst part is over ... except, God help me, that I'll have to talk to the boy's mother. She'll want to know rather more than the police were concerned with ... As a matter of fact, it would be quite a relief to talk it out." He took a pull at the whisky as if he needed it, and looked at me straight for the first time. "You hadn't met Spiro?"

"I only came last night."

His mouth turned down at the corners. "What a start to your visit. Well, he was Miranda's twin—I take it you'll have met her and her mother?—and he works, or rather worked, for me."

"Phyl told me."

"I was lucky to have him. He was a clever mechanic, and that's something not so easy to find in these parts. In most of the villages the only 'machines' are donkeys and mules, and there's no work for a mechanically-minded boy. They move to the towns. But of course Spiro wanted work near home; his father's dead, and he wanted to live with his mother and sister. I came here last year, and he's worked for me all that time. What he didn't know about boats wasn't worth knowing, and when I tell you that I even let him loose on my car, you'll realise he was pretty good." He nodded towards the window, where a big portfolio lay on a table. "I don't know if Phyl told you, but I'm working on a book, mainly photographs, and even with that Spiro was invaluable. He not only picked up enough to help me technically—with the processing and so on—but I actually got him to model for a few of them."

"They're marvellous, too," Phyllida told me warmly.

He smiled, a tight, meaningless little smile. "They are good, aren't they? Well, that was Spiro. Not a world-beater, whatever poor Miranda says about him. What brains he had were in his hands, and he was slow, and as stubborn as a blind mule—but he was tough, and you could trust him. And he had that one

28

extra, priceless quality which was worth the earth to me—he photographed like a dream. He was a 'natural' for the camera—you simply couldn't miss." He swallowed the last of his whisky, and stooped to set the glass down. The click of glass on wood sounded oddly final, like the full stop after the valediction. "Which brings me to last night."

There was a little pause. The tired grey eyes came back to me.

"I've been doing some experiments in night photography—fishing-boats at night, moonscapes, that kind of thing ... and I wanted to try my hand at the sunrise over the mainland, while there's still snow on the mountains. Spiro and I took my boat out last night. There was a stiffish breeze, but it was nothing to worry about. We went up the coast. You'll know, perhaps, that Mount Pantokrator lies north of here? Well, the coast curves right out, running almost due east under the shelter of the mountain. It's only when you come to the end of this, and turn north through the open strait, that you get the weather. We got there within half an hour or so of dawn, and turned up about opposite Kouloura—that's the narrowest bit between here and the mainland. The sea was choppy, but nothing a sailor would call rough, though the wind was still rising from the north ... Well, I was in the cabin, busy with my camera, and Spiro was aft, when the engine suddenly stopped. I called to ask what was wrong, and he shouted that he thought something was fouling the screw, and he'd have it clear in a minute. So I went on with my job, only then I found he'd let the boat's head fall away, and she'd turned across the wind, and was rolling rather too much for comfort. So I went out to see what was going on."

He lifted one hand in a slight, but oddly final gesture. "Then it happened. I saw Spiro in the stern, leaning over. The boat was heeling pretty steeply, and I think—I can't be sure—that I yelled to him to take care. Then a gust or a wave or something got her on the beam, and she kicked over like a mule. He'd had hold of the toe-rail, but it was slippery, and he lost it. I saw him grab again as he went over, but he missed. He just disappeared. By the time I got to the stern I couldn't even see him."

"He couldn't swim?"

"Oh, yes, but it was very dark, and the boat was drifting fast, with a fair sea on by that time. The wind must have got up more than I'd realised while I was working in the cabin, and we must have been driven yards apart in as many seconds. Even if

29

he'd stayed afloat it would have been hard to find him . . . and I don't think he can have done, or he'd have shouted, and I'd surely have heard something. I yelled myself hoarse, as it was, and there was no answer . . ."

He got up again, restlessly, and prowled over to the window. "Well, that's all. I threw a lifebelt out, but we were being blown away at a fair speed, and by the time I'd got the engine started, and gone back to where I thought he'd gone overboard, there wasn't a sign. I must have been somewhere near the right place, because I found the lifebelt. I cruised about for a couple of hours —rather stupidly, I suppose, but then one can't somehow give up and go. A fishing-boat came within hail, and helped, but it was no use."

There was a pause. He stood with his back to us, looking out.

Phyllida said drearily: "It's a horrible thing to happen. Horrible."

"And was the propeller fouled after all?" I asked.

He turned. "What? No, it wasn't. At least, I saw nothing there. It was a choked jet. It only took a few seconds to put right. If he'd looked there first . . ." He lifted his shoulders, letting the sentence hang.

"Well," said Phyl, with an attempt at briskness, "I honestly don't see why you should reproach yourself at all. What could you have done more?"

"Oh, it's not that I blame myself for what happened, I know that's absurd. It's my failure to find him that I find so hard to live with. Casting round for two hours in that black windy sea, and knowing all the time that at any minute it would be too late . . . Don't misunderstand me, but it would be a lot easier if I'd had to bring the boy's body home."

"Because his mother can't believe he's gone?"

He nodded. "As it is, she'll probably hope against hope, and sit waiting for him to turn up. And then when—if—his body is washed ashore, this will all be to go through again."

Phyllida said: "Then all we can do is hope the body will turn up soon."

"I doubt if it will. The wind and tide were setting the other way. And if he went ashore on the Albanian coast, we may never hear about it. She may wait for years."

"The way she did for his father," I said.

He stared at me, as if for some seconds he hardly saw me. "His father? Oh, God, yes, I forgot that."

30

Phyllida stirred. "Then go on forgetting it, for heaven's sake, Godfrey! You're not to flay yourself over this any more! The situation's horrible enough without your trying to blame yourself for something you couldn't help, and couldn't have prevented!"

"As long as his mother and sister understand that."

"Of course they will! Once the shock's over, and you can talk to them, you'll have to tell them the whole story, just as you've told us. You'll find they'll accept it, without even thinking of praise or blame—just as they'd accept anything fate chose to hand out to them. These people do. They're as strong as their own rocks, and so's their faith."

He was looking at her in some surprise. People who only see the everyday side of Phyllida—the volatile, pretty-butterfly side —are always surprised when they come up against her core of solid, maternal warmth. He also looked grateful, and relieved, as if she had somehow excused him from blame, and this mattered.

She smiled at him. "Your trouble is, you've not only had a rotten experience and a bad shock, but now you're dreading having to face Maria, and stand a scene; and I don't blame you one bit." Her frankness was as comfortable as it was devastating. "But you needn't worry. There'll be no scenes, and it won't even occur to them to ask you questions."

"You don't quite understand. Spiro wasn't to have gone with me last night—he had a date of some sort in the town. I persuaded him to break it. His mother didn't even know till the last minute."

"So what? No doubt you were paying him overtime of a sort, the way you always did? I thought as much ... oh, yes, I knew all about it, Maria told me. Believe me, they were terribly grateful for the work you gave him, *and* for the way you paid, always so generous. Spiro thought the world of you, and so does Maria. Good heavens, *you*, to worry what they'll say to you?"

"Could I offer them anything, do you think?"

"Money?" She knitted her brows. "I don't know. I'll have to think. I don't know quite what they'll do now ... But don't let's worry about that yet. I'll ask a tactful question or two, and let you know, shall I? But I'll tell you one thing, you'd better take those pictures home with you when you go. I've not looked at them properly, but it'd be a pity if Maria saw them just now."

"Oh. Yes, of course. I'll take them."

31

He picked up the portfolio, and stood holding it irresolutely, as if he didn't quite know what to do next. One habit my profession has taught me is to watch faces and listen to voices; and if the people concerned are under some kind of stress, so much the better. As an actress I shall never be in the top class, but I am fairly good at reading people, and I felt here, in Godfrey Manning's hesitation and hunger for reassurance, something not quite in character: the contrast between the man as one felt he should be, and what shock had made of him, was obscurely disquieting, like watching an actor badly miscast. It made me say hastily, and not very tactfully—almost as if any diversion were better than none:

"Are those the photographs for your book?"

"Some of them, prints I brought the other day for Phyl to look at. Would you care to see them?"

He came quickly across the room, and laid the portfolio on a low table beside my chair. I wasn't sure that I wanted, at this moment, to look at the prints, among which were presumably some of the dead boy, but Phyl made no protest, and to Godfrey Manning, quite obviously, it was some kind of a relief. So I said nothing as he pulled the big prints from between the guard sheets and began to spread them out.

The first ones he showed me were mainly of scenery; bold pieces of cliff and brilliant sea, with the bright tangled flowers splashing down over sunlit rock, and pictures of peasant women with their goats and donkeys passing between hedgerows of apple blossom and purple broom, or stooping over a stone cistern with their piles of coloured washing. And the sea; this was in most of the pictures; sometimes just the corner of a pool laced with seaweed, or the inside of a curling wave, or the pattern of withdrawing foam over damp sand; and one marvellous one of a rocky inlet where, smiling and with bright intelligent eye, the dolphin lay watching the camera.

"Oh, look, the dolphin!" I cried, for the first time remembering my morning's adventure. Godfrey Manning looked curiously at me, but before I could say anything further Phyllida had lifted the print aside, and I found myself staring down at a picture of the dead boy.

He was very like his sister; there was the round face and wide smile, the sunburned skin, the thick black hair as springy as heather. I saw at once what Godfrey had meant when he called the boy a 'natural model'; the sturdy body and thick neck which gave Miranda her heavy, peasant look, were translated in the boy into a kind of classical strength, the familiar, deliberately thickened lines of sculpture. He fitted into the background of rock and sea as inevitably as the pillars of the temple at Sunium.

Just as I was wondering how to break the silence, my sister broke it quite easily.

"You know, Godfrey, I'm quite sure that later on, when things ease off a bit, Maria would love to have one of these. Why don't you do one for her?"

"If you think she would ... It might be an idea. Yes, and I could frame it for her." He began to put the prints back into the portfolio. "Some time, perhaps, you'd help me choose the one you think she'd like?"

"Oh, there's no question," said Phyllida, and pulled one out of the pile. "This. It's the best I've seen in years, and exactly like him."

He gave it a brief glance. "Oh, yes. It was a lucky one." His voice was quite colourless.

I said nothing, but stared and stared.

There was the dolphin, arching gently out of a turquoise sea, its back streaming silver drops. Standing thigh-deep beside the animal, laughing, with one hand stretched out to touch it, was the boy, bronzed and naked, his arrow-straight body cutting the arc made by the silver dolphin at the exact point known to painters as golden section. It was one of those miracles of photography—skill and chance combining to throw colour, light and mass into a flawless moment caught and held for ever.

I said: "It's marvellous! There's no other word for it! It's a myth come true! If I hadn't seen the dolphin myself, I'd have thought it was faked!"

He had been looking down at the picture without expression. Now he smiled. "Oh, it's genuine enough. Spiro tamed the beast for me, and it would come right in to play when he went swimming. It was a most co-operative creature, with a lot of personal charm. Did you say you'd seen it?"

"Yes. I've just been down for a swim, and it came to take a look at me. What's more, I may tell you, you nearly lost your dolphin for good and all this morning."

"Lost the dolphin?" said Phyl. "What on earth d'you mean?"

"Someone was shooting at it," I said crisply. "I came panting up here to tell you about it, but then your news knocked it clean out of my head till now." I glanced up at Godfrey. "When I was down in the bay, there was somebody up in the woods above, with a rifle, taking pot-shots. If I hadn't been there, and shooed the dolphin away, he'd probably have got it."

"But ... this is incredible!" This, at least, had broken through his preoccupation with Spiro's death. He stared at me frowningly. "Someone up in these woods, shooting? Are you sure?"

"Quite sure. And, which makes it worse, the rifle was silenced —so it wasn't just some sportsman out after hares or something, amusing himself by sniping at the dolphin. It was a deliberate attempt to kill it. I was sitting up under the trees, and I suppose he hadn't seen me. But when I yelled and jumped in beside the dolphin, the shooting stopped."

"But, *Lucy*!" Phyllida was horrified. "You might have been hurt!"

"I didn't think," I confessed. "I was just so blazing mad, I had to stop him somehow."

"You never do think! One of these days you *will* get hurt!" She turned, with a gesture half of exasperation, half of amusement, to Godfrey. "She's always been the same. It's the only thing I've ever seen her really fly off the handle about—animals. She even rescues drowning wasps, and spiders out of the bath, and worms that come out when it rains and get caught crossing the road. The funny thing is, they see her coming. She once put her hand down on an adder, and it didn't even bite her."

"It was probably knocked cold," I said curtly, as embarrassed under Godfrey's amused look as if I was being accused of some odd perversion. I added, defiantly: "I can't stand seeing anything hurt, that's all. So from now on I'll keep my eye on it if I have to bathe there every day. That dolphin of yours has got itself a one girl guard, Mr. Manning."

"I'm delighted to hear it."

Phyl said: "I still can't believe it. Who in the world could it have been, up in those woods with a gun?"

I thought for a moment he was going to answer, but he turned back to his task of stowing away the photographs, shutting the portfolio on the last of them with a snap. "I can't imagine." Then, to me: "I suppose you didn't see anyone?"

"Oh, yes."

This produced a gratifying amount of sensation. Phyllida gave a little squeak, and clapped a hand to where, roughly, one imagined Caliban to be. Godfrey Manning said quickly: "You did? Where? I suppose you didn't get near enough to see who it was?"

"I did indeed, in the wood below the Castello terrace, and he was utterly beastly!" I said warmly. "He said he was Julian Gale's son, and——"

"*Max Gale!*" This from Phyllida, incredulously. "Lucy, you're not trying to tell me that Max Gale was running round in the woods with a rifle, loosing it off at all and sundry? Don't be silly!"

"Well, he did say it wasn't him," I admitted, "and he'd got rid of the gun, so I couldn't prove it was, but I didn't believe him. He *looked* as if he'd be capable of anything, and anyway, he was quite foully rude, and it wasn't a bit necessary!"

"You were trespassing," said Godfrey dryly.

"Even so, it couldn't have been him!" said my sister positively.

"Probably not," said Godfrey.

She looked at him sharply. "What is it?"

"Nothing."

But she had obviously understood whatever it was he hadn't said. Her eyes widened. "But why in the world——?" She caught her breath, and I thought she changed colour. "Oh, my God, I suppose it could be...! But Godfrey, that's frightful! If *he* got his hands on a gun——!"

"Quite. And if he did, naturally Gale would cover up."

"Well, but what can we do? I mean, if there's any danger——"

"There won't be, now," he said calmly. "Look, Phyl, it'll be all right. If Max Gale didn't know before, he does now, and he'll have the sense to keep anything like that out of the old man's hands."

"How?" she demanded. "Just tell me how? Have you ever *been* in that ghastly museum of a place?"

"No. Why? Is there a gun-room or something?"

"Gun-room!" said Phyllida. "Give me strength! Gun-room! The Castello walls are just about *papered* with the things! Guns, daggers, spears, assegais, the lot. I'll swear there's everything there from carbines to knuckle-dusters. There's even a

35

cannon at the front door! Good heavens, Leo's grandfather *collected* the things! Nobody's going to know if a dozen rifles or so go missing!"

"Now isn't that nice?" said Godfrey.

"Look," I said forcibly, "one minute more of this, and I shall scream. What's all the mystery? Are you two talking about Julian Gale? Because if you are I never heard anything so silly in my life. Why in the world should *he* go round getting savage with a rifle? He might pick off a few theatre critics—I can think of one who's been asking for it for years—but not that dolphin! It's just not possible."

"D'you know him?" Godfrey Manning's tone was abrupt and surprised.

"I've never met him, he's way out of my star. But I've known stacks of people who've worked with him, and they all adored him. I tell you, it's not in character. And if you ask how I know that, let me tell you I've seen every play he's been in for the last ten years, and if there's one kind of person who can't hide what sort of man he is under everything he has to do and say, it's an actor. That's a paradox, I suppose, but it's true. And that Julian Gale could kill a living creature straight out of a Greek myth— no, it simply isn't *on*. Unless he was drunk, or went raving mad——"

I stopped. The look that had flashed between them would have wrecked a geiger-counter. There was a silence that could be felt.

"Well?" I said.

Godfrey cleared his throat awkwardly. He seemed uncertain of how to begin.

"Oh, for goodness' sake, if she's going to be here for a few weeks she'd better know," said my sister. "She's almost certain to meet him sooner or later. I know he only goes to the Karithis' place, and to play chess with someone in Corfu, and they never leave him alone the rest of the time, but I met him myself at the Karithis', and she may come across him any day in the grounds."

"I suppose so."

She turned to me. "You said this morning that you wondered why he disappeared like that after he'd retired. You knew about the car smash three or four years ago, when his wife and daughter were killed?"

"Oh, lord, yes. It happened just the week before he opened in

Tiger Tiger. I saw it after it had been running about a month. Lucky for him it was a part to tear a cat in, so he was better than ever, if possible, but he'd lost a couple of stones' weight. I know he was ill after he left the cast, and rumours started going round then that he was planning to retire, but of course nobody really believed them, and he seemed quite all right for the Stratford season; then they suddenly announced *The Tempest* as his last appearance. What happened, then? Was he ill again after that came off?"

"In a way. He finished up in a nursing home with a nervous breakdown, and he was there over a year."

I stared at her, deeply shocked. "I never knew that."

"Nobody knew," said my sister. "It's not the sort of thing one advertises, especially if one's a public person like Julian Gale. I only knew myself because Max Gale said something to Leo when they rented the house, and then a friend of mine told me the rest. He's supposed to be better, and he does go out sometimes to visit friends, but there's always someone with him."

I said flatly: "You mean he has to be watched? You're trying to tell me that Julian Gale is——" I paused. Why were all the words so awful? If they didn't conjure up grotesque images of Bedlam, they were even worse, genteel synonyms for the most tragic sickness of all. "—Unbalanced?" I finished.

"I don't know!" Phyllida looked distressed. "Heaven knows one doesn't want to make too much of it, and the very fact that he was discharged—if that's the word—from the home must mean that he's all right, surely?"

"But he *must* be all right! Anyway, you said you'd met him. How did he seem then?"

"Perfectly normal. In fact, I fell for him like a ton of bricks. He's very charming." She looked worriedly across at Godfrey. "But I suppose these things can recur? I never thought ... the idea wasn't even raised ... but if I'd thought, with the children coming here for their holidays and everything——"

"Look," said Godfrey briskly, "you're making altogether too much of this, you know. The very mention of a gun seems to have blown everything up right out of proportion. The man's not a homicidal maniac or anything like it—and never has been, or he wouldn't be here at all."

"Yes, I suppose you're right. Silly of me to panic." She gave a sigh, and subsided in her chair. "In any case Lucy probably dreamed it! If she never even *saw* a gun, and never heard it, either ...! Oh, well, let's forget it, shall we?"

I didn't trouble to insist. It no longer mattered. What I had just learned was too fresh and too distressing. I said miserably: "I wish I'd been a bit nicer to Mr. Gale, that's all. He must have had a foul time. It's bad enough for other people, but for his son——"

"Oh, honey, don't look so stricken!" Phyl, her worry apparently gone, was back in the role of comforter. "We're all probably *quite* wrong, and there's nothing the matter at all, except that the old man needs a bit of peace and quiet to recuperate in, and Max is seeing he gets it! If it comes to that, I wouldn't be surprised if it's Max who insists on the quarantine for his own sake; he's writing the score for some film or other, so the story goes, and *he* never appears at all. Hence all the 'trespassers will be shot' stuff, and young Adonis playing bodyguard."

"Young *who*?"

"Adonis. The gardener."

"Good heavens! Can anyone get away with a name like that, even in Greece?"

She laughed. "Oh, he does, believe you me!"

She turned to Godfrey then, saying something about Adonis, who had apparently been a close friend of Spiro's. I caught Miranda's name again, and something about a dowry, and difficulties now that the brother was dead; but I wasn't really listening. I was still caught up unhappily in the news I had just heard. We do not take easily to the displacing of our idols. It was like making a long and difficult journey to see Michelangelo's David, and finding nothing there but a broken pedestal.

I found I was re-living, as clearly as if it had been yesterday, that 'last appearance' in *The Tempest*; the gentle, disciplined verses resigning Prospero's dark powers, and with them, if this story were true, so much more:

> "... *This rough magic*
> *I here abjure: and when I have requir'd*
> *Some heavenly music (which even now I do)*
> *To work mine end upon their senses, that*
> *This airy charm is for, I'll break my staff,*
> *Bury it certain fathoms in the earth,*
> *And deeper than did ever plummet sound*
> *I'll drown my book ...*"

I stirred in my chair, pushed my own distress aside with an effort of will, and came back to the *salotto*, where Godfrey Manning was taking his leave.

"I'd better go. I meant to ask you, Phyl, when's Leo coming over?"

"He may manage this next weekend, I'm not sure. But definitely for Easter, with the children. D'you have to go? Stay to lunch if you like. Maria's done the vegetables, thank goodness —how I hate potatoes in the raw!—and the rest's cold. Won't you stay?"

"I'd like to, but I want to get back to the telephone. There may be news."

"Oh, yes, of course. You'll phone me straight away if you hear anything, won't you?"

"Certainly." He picked up the portfolio. "Let me know as soon as you think Maria would like to see me."

He said his good-byes, and went. We sat in silence till the engine of his car faded among the trees.

"Well," said my sister, "I suppose we'd better find something to eat. Poor Godfrey, he's taking it hard. A bit surprising, really, I never thought he'd be knocked endways quite like that. He must have been fonder of Spiro than he cares to admit."

"Phyl," I said abruptly.

"Mm?"

"Was that true, or was it just another of your stories, when you said Julian Gale was probably Miranda's father?"

She looked at me sideways. "Well ... Oh, damn it, Lucy, you don't have to take everything quite so literally! Heaven knows —but there's *something* in it, only I don't know what. He christened the girl 'Miranda', and can you imagine any Corfiote hatching up a name like that? And then Maria's husband deserted them. What's more, I'll swear Julian Gale's been supporting the family. Maria's never said a word, but Miranda's let things drop once or twice, and I'm sure he does. And why, tell me that? Not just because he happened to know the husband during the war!"

"Then if Miranda and Spiro were twins, he's Spiro's father, too?"

"The facts of life being what they are, you might even be right. Oh!" She went rigid in her chair, and turned large eyes on me. "You mean—you mean someone ought to go and break the news to *him*?" All at once she looked very uncertain and

39

flustered. "But, Lucy, it's only a rumour, and one could hardly *assume* it, could one? I mean, think if one went over there, and——"

"I didn't mean that," I said. "In any case, it's not our job to tell him, Maria'll tell him herself. He'll hear soon enough. Forget it. Where's this lunch you were talking about? I'm starving."

As I followed her out to the kitchen, I was reflecting that Julian Gale had almost certainly had the news already. From my chair facing the *salotto* windows, I had seen Maria and her daughter leave the house together. And not by the drive that would take them back to their own cottage. They had taken the little path that Miranda had showed me that morning, the path that led only to the empty bay, or to the Castello dei Fiori.

CHAPTER FOUR

He is drown'd
Whom thus we stray to find, and the sea mocks
Our frustrate search on land: well, let him go.
                                        III. 3.

DAYS went by, peaceful, lovely days. I kept my word, and went down daily to the bay. Sometimes the dolphin came, though never near enough for me to touch him, and, although I knew that for the animal's own sake I ought to try to frighten him and drive him away, his friendly presence delighted me so much that I couldn't bring myself to what would seem an act of betrayal.

I did keep a wary eye on the Castello terrace, but there was no further shooting incident, nor had there been any rumour that a local man might have been trespassing with a rifle. But I swam every day, and watched, and never left the bay until the dolphin had finally submerged and headed for the open sea.

There had been no news of Spiro. Maria and her daughter had come back to the Villa Forli the morning after the boy's death, and had gone stoically on with their work. Miranda had lost the plump brightness that characterised her; she looked as if she cried a lot, and her voice and movements were subdued. I saw little of Maria, who kept mostly to the kitchen, going silently about her work with the black head-kerchief pulled across her face.

The weather was brilliant, and hot even in the shade. Phyllida was rather listless. Once or twice she went with me on my sightseeing trips, or into the town of Corfu, and one evening Godfrey Manning took us both to dine at the Corfu Palace Hotel, but on the whole the week slipped quietly by, while I bathed, and sat on the terrace with Phyllida, or took the little car and drove myself out in the afternoons to explore.

Leo, Phyllida's husband, hadn't managed to get away for the weekend, and Palm Sunday came without a visit from him. Phyllida had advised me to go into the town that morning to watch the Palm Sunday procession, which is one of the four occasions in the year when the island Saint, Spiridion, is brought out of the church where he lies the year round in a dim shrine all smoky with taper-light, and is carried through the streets in his golden palanquin. It is not an image of the Saint, but his actual mummified body which is carried in the procession, and this, somehow, makes him a very personal and homely kind of patron saint to have: the islanders believe that he has Corfu and all its people in his personal and always benevolent care, and has nothing to do but concern himself deeply in all their affairs, however trivial—which may explain why, on the procession days, just about the whole population of the island crowds into the town to greet him.

"What's more," said my sister, "it's a *pretty* procession, not just a gaggle of top brass. And St. Spiro's golden chair is beautiful; you can see his face quite clearly through the glass. You'd think it would be creepy, but it's not, not a bit. He's so tiny, and so ... well, he's a sort of *cosy* saint!" She laughed. "If you stay long in Corfu you'll begin to get the feeling you know him personally. He's pretty well in charge of the island, you know, looks after the fishing, raises the wind, watches the weather for the crops, brings your boys safe home from sea ..." She stopped, then sighed. "Poor Maria. I wonder if she'll go today? She doesn't usually miss it."

"What about you?" I asked. "Are you sure you won't come with me?"

She shook her head. "I'll stay at home. You have to stand about for rather a long time while the procession goes past, and there'll be a bit of a crush. Caliban and I take up too much room. Home for lunch? Good. Well, enjoy yourself."

41

The little town of Corfu was packed with a holiday crowd, and the air was loud with bells. Caught up in the river of people which flowed through the narrow streets, I wandered happily along under the sound of the bells, which competed with the subdued roar of voices, and the occasional bursts of raucous brass from some upper window, where a village band was struggling with some last-minute practice. Shops were open, selling food and sweets and toys, their windows crammed with scarlet eggs ready for Easter, cockerels, dolls, baskets of tiny crystallised oranges, or enormous rabbits laden with Easter eggs. Someone tried to sell me a sponge the size of a football, and someone else to convince me that I must need a string of onions and a red plush donkey, but I managed to stay unburdened, and presently found my way to the Esplanade, which is Corfu's main square. Here the pavements were already packed, but when I tried to take my place at the back, the peasants—who must have come into town in the early morning, and waited hours for their places—made way for me with insistent gestures, almost forcing me forward into the place of honour.

Presently, from somewhere, a big bell struck, and there came the distant sound of the bands starting up. The vast crowd fell almost silent, all eyes turned to watch the narrow mouth of Nikephoros Street, where the first banners glinted, slowly moving up into the sunlight of the square. The procession had begun.

I am not sure what I had expected—a spectacle at once quaint and interesting, because 'foreign'—something to take photographs of, and then forget, till you got them out to look at, some evening at home. In fact, I found it very moving.

The bands—there were four of them, all gorgeously uniformed—played solemnly and rather badly, each a different tune. The village banners with their pious legends were crudely painted, enormous, and cruelly heavy, so that the men carrying them sweated and trembled under the weight, and the faces of the boys helping them wore expressions of fierce and dedicated gravity. There were variations in the uniforms of the school-children that were distinctly unconventional, but the standard of personal beauty was so high that one hardly noticed the shabby coats of the boys, or the cheap shoes the girls wore; and the young servicemen in their reach-me-down uniforms, with their noticeable absence of pipeclay and their ragged timing, had still about them, visibly, the glamour of two Thermopylaes.

And there was never a moment's doubt that all this was done in honour of the Saint. Crowded along the pavements in the heat, the people watched in silence, neither moving nor pushing. There were no police, as there would have had to be in Athens: this was their own Spiridion, their island's patron, come out into the sunlight to bless them.

And here he came. The Archbishop, a white-bearded ninety-two, walked ahead, followed by Church dignitaries, whose robes of saffron and white and rose shone splendidly in the sun, until, as they passed nearer, you saw the rubbed and faded patches, and the darns. Then came the forest of tall white candles, each with its gilt crown and wreath of flowers, and each one fluttering its long ribbons of white and lilac and scarlet. Then finally, flanked by the four great gilded lanterns, and shaded by its canopy, the gold palanquin approached, with the Saint himself inside it, sitting up for all to see; a tiny, withered mummy, his head sagging on to his left shoulder, the dead features flattened and formless, a pattern of shadows behind the gleaming glass.

All around me, the women crossed themselves, and their lips moved. The Saint and his party paused for prayer, and the music stopped. A gun boomed once in salute from the Old Fort, and as the echo died a flight of pigeons went over, their wings whistling in the silence.

I stood watching the coloured ribbons glinting in the sun, the wreaths of flowers fading already, and hanging crookedly from the crowned candles; the old, upraised hand of the Archbishop, and the faces of the peasant-women near me, rapt and shining under the snowy coifs. To my own surprise I felt my throat tighten, as if with tears.

A woman sobbed, in sudden, uncontrollable distress. The sound was loud in the silence, and I had glanced round before I could prevent myself. Then I saw it was Miranda. She was standing some yards from me, back among the crowd, staring with fiercely intent eyes at the palanquin, her lips moving as she crossed herself repeatedly. There was passion and grief in her face, as if she were reproaching the Saint for his negligence. There was nothing irreverent in such a thought; the Greek's religion is based on such simplicities. I suppose the old Church knew how great an emotional satisfaction there is in being able to lay the blame squarely and personally where it belongs.

The procession had passed; the crowd was breaking up. I saw Miranda duck back through it, as if ashamed of her tears, and

43

walk quickly away. The crowds began to filter back again down the narrow main streets of the town, and I drifted with the tide, back down Nikephoros Street, towards the open space near the harbour where I had left the car.

Half-way down, the street opens into a little square. It chanced that, as I passed this, I saw Miranda again. She was standing under a plane tree, with her back to me, and her hands up to her face. I thought she was weeping.

I hesitated, but a man who had been hovering near, watching her, now walked across and spoke. She neither moved, nor gave any sign that she had heard him, but stood still with her back turned to him, and her head bowed. I couldn't see his face, but he was young, with a strong and graceful build that the cheap navy blue of his Sunday best suit could not disguise.

He moved up closer behind the girl, speaking softly and, it seemed, with a sort of urgent persuasion. It appeared to me from his gestures that he was pressing her to go with him up one of the side streets away from the crowd: but at this she shook her head, and I saw her reach quickly for the corner of her kerchief, and pull it across to hide her face. Her attitude was one of shy, even shrinking, dejection.

I went quickly across to them.

"Miranda? It's Miss Lucy. I have the car here, and I'm going back now. Would you like me to take you home?"

She did turn then. Above the kerchief her eyes were swollen with tears. She nodded without speaking.

I hadn't looked at the youth, assuming that he would now give up his importunities and vanish into the crowd. But he, too, swung round, exclaiming as though in relief:

"Oh, thank you! That's very kind! She ought not to have come, of course—and now there's no bus for an hour! Of course she must go home!"

I found myself staring, not at his easy assumption of responsibility for the girl, or even at the near-perfect English he spoke, but simply because of his looks.

In a country where beauty among the young is a common-place, he was still striking. He had the fine Byzantine features, with the clear skin and huge, long-lashed eyes that one sees staring down from the walls of every church in Greece; the type which El Greco himself immortalised, and which still, recognisably, walks the streets. Not that this young man conformed in anything but the brilliant eyes and the hauntingly perfect

44

structure of the face: there was nothing to be seen here of the melancholy and weakness which (understandably) tends to afflict the saintly persons who spend their days gazing down from the plaster on the church walls—the small-lipped mouths, the meekly slanted heads, the air of resignation and surprise with which the Byzantine saint properly faces the sinful world. This youth had, indeed, the air of one who had faced the sinful world for some years now, but had obviously liked it enormously, and had cheerfully sampled a good deal of what it had to offer. No church-plaster saint, this one. And not, I judged, a day over nineteen.

The beautiful eyes were taking me in with the frank appraisal of the Greek. "You must be Miss Waring?"

"Why, yes," I said, in surprise; then suddenly saw who, inevitably, this must be. "And you're—Adonis?"

I couldn't for the life of me help bringing out the name with the kind of embarrassment one would feel in labelling one's own compatriot 'Venus' or 'Cupid'. That in Greece one could meet any day a Pericles, an Aspasia, an Electra, or even an Alcibiades, didn't help at all. It was the looks that did it.

He grinned. He had very white teeth, and eyelashes at least an inch long. "It's a bit much, isn't it? In Greek we say 'Adoni'." (He pronounced it A-thoni.) "Perhaps you'd find that easier to say? Not quite so cissy?"

"You know too much by half!" I said, involuntarily, and quite naturally, and he laughed, then sobered abruptly.

"Where is your car, Miss Waring?"

"It's down near the harbour." I looked dubiously at the crowded street, then at the girl's bent head. "It's not far, but there's a dreadful crowd."

"We can go by a back way." He indicated a narrow opening at the corner of the square, where steps led up into the shadow between two tall houses.

I glanced again at the silent girl, who waited passively. "She will come," said Adoni, and spoke to her in Greek, briefly, then turned to me, and began to usher me across the square and up the steps. Miranda followed, keeping a pace or so behind us.

He said in my ear: "It was a mistake for her to come, but she is very religious. She should have waited. It is barely a week since he died."

"You knew him well, didn't you?"

45

"He was my friend." His face shut, as if everything had been said. As, I suppose, it had.

"I'm sorry," I said.

We walked for a while in silence. The alleys were deserted, save for the thin cats, and the singing-birds in cages on the walls. Here and there, where a gap in the houses laid a blazing wedge of sunlight across the stones, dusty kittens baked themselves in patches of marigolds, or very old women peered from the black doorways. The smell of charcoal-cooking hung in the warm air. Our steps echoed up the walls, while from the main streets the sound of talk and laughter surged back to us, muted like the roar of a river in a distant gorge. Eventually our way opened into a broader lane, and a long flight of shallow steps, which dropped down past a church wall straight to the harbour square where I had left Phyl's little Fiat.

There were crowds here, too, but these were broken knots of people, moving purposefully in search of transport home, or the midday meal. Nobody paid any attention to us.

Adoni, who apparently knew the car, shouldered his way purposefully through the groups of people, and held out a hand to me for the keys.

Almost as meekly as Miranda (who hadn't yet spoken a word) I handed them over, and our escort unlocked the doors and ushered her into the back seat. She got in with bent head, and sat well back in a corner. I wondered, with some amusement, if this masterful young man intended to drive us both home—and whether Phyl would mind—but he made no such attempt. He shut the driver's door on me and then got in beside me.

"You are used to our traffic now?"

"Oh, yes." If he meant was I used to driving on the right-hand side, I was. As for traffic, there was none in Corfu worth mentioning; if I met one lorry and half a dozen donkeys on an average afternoon's excursion it was the most I had had to contend with. But today there was the packed and teeming harbour boulevard, and possibly because of this, Adoni said nothing more as we weaved our way through the people and out on to the road north. We climbed a steep, badly cambered turn, and then the road was clear between high hedges of judas trees and asphodel. The surface was in places badly pitted by the winter's rain, so I had to drive slowly, and the third gear was noisy. Under cover of its noise I said quietly to Adoni:

"Will Miranda and her mother be able to keep themselves, now that Spiro has gone?"

"They will be cared for." It was said flatly, and with complete confidence.

I was surprised, and also curious. If Godfrey Manning had made an offer, he would surely have told Phyllida so; and besides, whatever he chose to give Maria now, he would hardly feel that he owed this kind of conscience-money. But if it was Julian Gale who was providing for the family, as Phyllida had alleged, it might mean that her story of the twins' parentage was true. I would have been less than human if I hadn't madly wanted to know.

I put out a cautious feeler. "I'm glad to hear that. I didn't realise there was some other relative."

"Well," said Adoni, "there is Sir Gale, in a way, but I didn't mean him or Max. I meant that I would look after them myself."

"You?"

He nodded, and I saw him throw a half-glance over his shoulder at Miranda. I could see her in the driving-mirror; she was taking no notice of our soft conversation in English, which in any case may have been too rapid for her to follow, but was staring dully out of the window, obviously miles away. Adoni leaned forward and put a finger on the radio button, a gadget without which no Greek or Italian car ever seems to take the road. "You permit?"

"Of course."

Some pop singer from Athens Radio mooed from under the dash. Adoni said quietly: "I shall marry her. There is no dowry, but that's no matter, Spiro was my friend, and one has obligations. He had saved to provide for her, but now that he is dead her mother must keep it; I can't take it."

I knew that in the old Greek marriage-contract, the girl brought goods and land, the boy nothing but his virility, and this was considered good exchange; but families with a crop of daughters to marry off had been beggared before now, and Miranda, circumstanced as she was, would hardly have had a hope of marriage. Now here was this handsome boy calmly offering her a contract which any family would have been glad to accept, and one in which, moreover, he was providing all the capital; of the virility there could certainly be no doubt, and besides, he had a good job in a country where jobs are scarce,

47

and, if I was any judge of character, he would keep it. The handsome Adoni would have been a bargain at any reckoning. He knew this, of course, he'd have been a fool not to; but it seemed that he felt a duty to his dead friend, and from what I had seen of him, he would fulfil it completely, efficiently, and to everyone's satisfaction—not least Miranda's. And besides (I thought, prosaically), Leo would probably come through with a handsome wedding present.

"Of course," added Adoni, "Sir Gale may give her a dowry, I don't know. But it would make no difference; I shall take her. I haven't told her so yet, but later, when it's more fitting, I shall tell Sir Gale, and he will arrange it."

"I—yes, of course. I hope you'll both be very happy."

"Thank you."

I said: "Sir Julian is ... he makes himself responsible for them, then?"

"He was godfather to the twins." He glanced at me. "I think you have this in England, don't you, but it is not quite the same? Here in Greece, the godfather, the *koumbàros*, is very important in the child's life, often as important as the real father, and it is he who arranges the marriage contract."

"I see." As simple as that. "I did know Sir Julian had known the family for years, and had christened the twins, but I didn't know he—well, had a responsibility. The accident must have been a dreadful shock to him, too." I added, awkwardly: "How is he?"

"He is well. Have you met him yet, Miss Waring?"

"No. I understood he didn't see anyone."

"He doesn't go out much, it's true, but since the summer he has had visitors. You've met Max, though, haven't you?"

"Yes." There had been nothing in Adoni's voice to show what he knew about that meeting, but since he called him 'Max', without prefix, one might assume a relationship informal enough for Max to have told him just what had passed. Anyway, this was the faithful watch-dog who threw the callers over the cliff. No doubt he had heard all about it—and might even have had orders regarding further encroachments by Miss Lucy Waring ...

I added, woodenly: "I understood he didn't see anyone, either."

"Well, it depends," said Adoni cheerfully. He pulled a duster out from somewhere under the dashboard, and began to polish

48

the inside of the screen. "Not that this helps much, it's all the insects that get squashed on the outside. We're nearly there, or you could stop and I'd do it for you."

"It doesn't matter, thanks."

So that was as far as I'd get. In any case, Miranda seemed to be coming back to life. The back seat creaked as she moved, and in the mirror I could see that she had put back her kerchief, and was watching the back of Adoni's head. Something in her expression, still blurred though it was with tears, indicated that I had been right about the probable success of the marriage.

I said, in the brisk tone of one who changes the subject to neutral ground: "Do you ever go out shooting, Adoni?"

He laughed, undeceived. "Are you still looking for your criminal? I think you must have been mistaken—there's no Greek would shoot a dolphin. I am a sailor, too—all Corfiotes are sailors—and the dolphin is the beast of fair weather. We even call it 'dolphin weather'—the summer time, when the dolphins go with the boats. No, me, I only shoot people."

"*People?*"

"That was a joke," explained Adoni. "Here we are. Thank you very much for bringing us. I'll take Miranda to her mother now, then I've promised to go back to the Castello. Max wants to go out this afternoon. Perhaps I shall see you there soon?"

"Thank you, but I—no, I doubt if you will."

"That would be a pity. While you are here, you should see the orange orchards; they are something quite special. You have heard of the *koùm koyàts*—the miniature trees? They are very attractive." That quick, enchanting smile. "I should like to show them to you."

"Perhaps some time."

"I hope so. Come, Miranda."

As I put the car into gear, I saw him usher the silent girl through her mother's door as if he already owned the place. Suppressing a sharp—and surely primitive—envy for a woman who could have her problems simply taken out of her hands and solved for her, willy-nilly, I put down my own independent and emancipated foot, and sent the little Fiat bucketing over the ruts of the drive, and down the turning to the Villa Forli.

At least, if Max Gale was to be out, I could have my afternoon swim in peace.

*　　*　　*

I went down after tea, when the heat was slackening off, and the cliff cast a crescent of shade at the edge of the sand.

Afterwards I dressed, picked up my towel, and began slowly to climb the path back to the villa.

When I reached the little clearing where the pool lay, I paused to get my breath. The trickle of the falling stream was cool and lovely, and light spangled down golden through the young oak-leaves. A bird sang somewhere, but only one. The woods were silent, stretching away dim-shadowed in the heat of the late afternoon. Bee-orchises swarmed by the water, over a bank of daisies. A blue tit flew across the clearing, obviously in a great hurry, its beak stuffed with insects for the waiting family.

A moment later the shriek came, a bird's cry of terror, then the rapid, machine-gun swearing of the parent tit. Some other small birds joined the clamour. The shrieks of terror jagged through the peaceful wood. I dropped my towel on the grass, and ran towards the noise.

The blue tits met me, the two parent birds, fluttering and shrieking, their wings almost brushing me as I ran up a twisting path, and out into the open stretch of thin grass and irises where the tragedy was taking place.

This couldn't have been easier to locate. The first thing I saw as I burst from the bushes was a magnificent white Persian cat, crouched picturesquely to spring, tail jerking to and fro in the scanty grass. Two yards from his nose, crying wildly, and unable to move an inch, was the baby blue tit. The parents, with anguished cries, darted repeatedly and ineffectually at the cat, which took not the slightest notice.

I did the only possible thing. I dived on the cat in a flying tackle, took him gently by the body, and held him fast. The tits swept past me, their wings brushing my hands. The little one sat corpse-still now, not even squeaking.

I suppose I could have been badly scratched, but the white cat had strong nerves, and excellent manners. He spat furiously, which was only to be expected, and wriggled to be free, but he neither scratched nor bit. I held him down, talking soothingly till he was quiet, then lifted him and turned away, while behind me the parent birds swooped down to chivvy their baby out of sight.

I hurried my captive out of the clearing before he got a chance to see where the birds were making for, and away at random through the bushes. Far from objecting to this, the cat seemed now rather pleased at the attention than otherwise; having had to surrender to *force majeure* he managed—in the way of his species—to let me know that he did in fact prefer to be carried ... And when, presently, I found myself toiling up a ferny bank which grew steeper, and steeper yet, he even began to purr.

This was too much. I stopped.

"I'll tell you something," I said to him, "you weigh a ton. You can darned well walk, Butch, as from now! And I hope you know your way home from here, because I'm not letting you go back to those birds!"

I put him down. Still purring, he stropped himself against me a couple of times, then strolled ahead of me up the bank, tail high, to where at the top the bushes thinned to show bright sunlight. There he paused, glancing back and down at me, before stalking forward out of view.

He knew his way, no doubt of that. Hoping there was a path there that would take me back clear of the tangled bushes, I clambered up in his wake, to find myself in a big clearing, full of sunshine, the hum of bees, and a blaze of flowers that pulled me up short, gaping.

After the dappled dimness of the wood, it took some moments before one could do more than blink at the dazzle of colour. Straight ahead of me an arras of wistaria hung fully fifteen feet, and below it there were roses. Somewhere to one side was a thicket of purple judas-trees, and apple blossom glinting with the wings of working bees. Arum lilies grew in a damp corner, and some other lily with petals like gold parchment, transparent in the light. And everywhere, roses. Great bushes of them rampaged up the trees; a blue spruce was half smothered with sprays of vivid Persian pink, and one dense bush of frilled white roses must have been ten feet high. There were moss roses, musk roses, damask roses, roses pied and streaked, and one old pink rose straight from a mediæval manuscript, hemispherical, as if a knife had sliced it across, its hundred petals as tightly whorled and packed as the layers of an onion. There must have been twenty or thirty varieties there, all in full bloom; old roses, planted years ago and left to run wild, as if in some secret garden whose key is lost. The place seemed hardly real.

I must have stood stock still for some minutes, looking about me, dizzied with the scent and the sunlight. I had forgotten roses could smell like that. A spray of speckled carmine brushed my hand, and I broke it off and held it to my face. Deep among the leaves, in the gap I had made, I saw the edge of an old metal label, and reached gingerly for it among the thorns. It was thick with lichen, but the stamped name showed clearly: Belle de Crécy.

I knew where I was now. Roses: they had been another hobby of Leo's grandfather's. Phyl had some of his books up at the Villa, and I had turned them over idly the other night, enjoying the plates and the old names which evoked, like poetry, the old gardens of France, of Persia, of Provence ... Belle de Crécy, Belle Isis, Deuil du Roi de Rome, Rosamunde, Camaïeux, Ispahan ...

The names were all there, hidden deep in the rampant leaves where some predecessor of Adoni's had lovingly attached them a century ago. The white cat, posing in front of an elegant background of dark fern, watched benevolently as I hunted for them, my hands filling with plundered roses. The scent was heavy as a drug. The air zoomed with bees. The general effect was of having strayed out of the dark wood into some fairy-tale. One almost expected the cat to speak.

When the voice did come, suddenly, from somewhere above, it nearly startled me out of my wits. It was a beautiful voice, and it enhanced, rather than broke, the spell. It spoke, moreover, in poetry, as deliberately elegant as the white cat:

> "*Most sure, the goddess*
> *On whom these airs attend: vouchsafe my prayer*
> *May know if you remain upon this Island?*"

I peered upwards, at first seeing no one. Then a man's head appeared at the top of the wistaria—and only then did I realise that the curtain of blossom hung in fact down some kind of high retaining wall, which it had hidden. I saw, between the thick trusses of flowers, sections of the stone balustrading. The terrace of the Castello. The rose garden had been planted right up beside it.

I wanted to turn and run, but the voice held me. Needless to say it was not Max Gale's; this was a voice I had heard many times before, spinning just such a toil of grace as this in the stuffy darkness of London theatres.

"*My prime request,*" added Sir Julian Gale, "*Which I do last pronounce, and which in fact you may think impertinent, Is, O you wonder, If you be maid, or no?*"

I suppose if I had met him normally, on our common ground of the theatre, I might have been too overawed to do more than stutter. But here at least the answer was laid down in the text, and had, besides, the advantage of being the truth. I narrowed my eyes against the sun, and smiled up at the head.

"No wonder, sir,
But certainly a maid."

"My language! Heavens!" The actor abruptly abandoned the Bard, and looked delighted. "I was right! You're Max's trespasser!"

I felt myself flushing. "I'm afraid I am, and I seem to be trespassing again. I'm terribly sorry, I didn't realise the terrace was quite so near. I wouldn't have dreamed of coming so far up, but I was rescuing a bird from Butch there."

"From whom?"

"The cat. Is he yours? I suppose he's called something terribly aristocratic, like Florizel, or Cosimo dei Fiori?"

"As a matter of fact," said Julian Gale, "I call him Nit. I'm sorry, but it's short for Nitwit, and when you get to know him, you'll see why. He's a gentleman, but he has very little brain. Now you're here, won't you come up?"

"Oh, no!" I spoke hastily, backing a little. "Thanks all the same, but I've got to get back."

"I can't believe there's all that hurry. Won't you please take pity on me and break the deadly Sabbath peace up a little? Ah!" He leaned further over. "Not only trespass, I see, but theft as well! You've been stealing my roses!"

This statement, uttered in the voice whose least whisper was clearly audible in the back row of the gallery, had all the force of an accusation made before the High Praesidium. I started guiltily, glanced down at the forgotten blooms in my hands, and stammered:

"Well, yes, I—I have. Oh, murder ... I never thought ... I mean, I took it they were sort of wild. You know, planted ages ago and just left ..." My voice faltered, as I looked round me and saw what I hadn't noticed before, that the bushes, in spite of their riotous appearance, were well shaped, and that the edges of the mossed paths were tidily clipped. "I—I suppose this is your garden now, or something? I'm most terribly sorry!"

" 'Or something?' By heaven, she picks an armful of my beloved Gallicas, and then thinks they come out of my garden 'or something'! That settles it, young woman! By all the rules you have to pay a forfeit. If Beauty strays into the Beast's garden, literally loaded with his roses, she's asking for trouble, isn't she? Come along, now, and no arguments! There are the steps. Nit'll bring you up. Nitwit! Show the lady the way!"

The white cat rose, blinked at me, then swarmed in an elaborately careless manner up the wistaria, straight into Julian Gale's arms. The latter straightened, smiling.

"Did I say he hadn't much brain? I traduced him. Do you think you could manage something similar?"

His charm, the charm that had made Phyllida fall for him 'like a ton of bricks', was having its effect. I believe I had completely forgotten what else she had told me about him.

I laughed. "In my own plodding way, I might."

"Then come along."

The way up was a flight of shallow steps, half hidden by a bush of York and Lancaster. It curved round the base of some moss-green statue, and brought me out between two enormous cypresses, on to the terrace.

Julian Gale had set the cat down, and now advanced on me.

"Come in, Miss Lucy Waring. You see, I've heard all about you. And here's my son. But of course, you've already met..."

CHAPTER FIVE

You do look, my son, in a mov'd sort,
As if you were dismay'd: be cheerful, sir.
IV. 1.

MAX GALE was sitting there under the stone-pine, at a big table covered with papers. As he got to his feet, I stopped in my tracks.

"But I thought you weren't here!" I hadn't thought I could have blurted out anything quite so naïve. I finished the performance by blushing furiously and adding, in confusion: "Adoni said ... I thought ... I'm sure he said you'd be out!"

"I was, but only till tea-time. How do you do?" His eyes, indifferent rather than hostile, touched mine briefly, and dropped to the roses in my hands. It was possibly only to fill the sizzling pause of embarrassment that he asked: "Was Adoni down in the garden?"

I saw Sir Julian's glance flick from one to the other of us. "He was not, or he might have stopped her pillaging the place! She's made a good selection, hasn't she? I thought she should be made to pay a forfeit, *à la* Beauty and the Beast. We'll let her off the kiss on such short acquaintance, but she'll have to stay and have a drink with us, at least!"

I thought I saw the younger man hesitate, and his glance went down to the littered table as if looking there for a quick excuse. There wasn't far to look; the table was spread with scribbled manuscript scores, notebooks, and papers galore, and on a chair beside it stood a tape-recorder with a long flex that trailed over the flags and in through an open french window.

I said quickly: "Thank you, but I really can't——"

"You're in no position to refuse, young lady!" Sir Julian's eyes held a gleam of amusement, whether at my reluctance or his son's it was impossible to guess. "Come now, half an hour spent entertaining a recluse is a small price to pay for your loot. Have we some sherry, Max?"

"Yes, of course." The colourlessness of his voice might after all only be in comparison with his father's. "I'm afraid we've no choice, Miss Waring. Do you like it dry?"

"Well ..." I hesitated. I would have to stay now. I could hardly snub Sir Julian, who was after all my host, and besides, I had no wish to pass up the chance to talk to a man who was at the head of my own profession, and whom I had admired and loved for as long as I could remember. "Actually, if there is one, I'd love a long drink, long and cold ...? I've just been swimming, and I'm genuinely thirsty. Would there be any orange juice, or something like that?"

"You ask that here? Of course." Max Gale smiled at me suddenly, and with unexpected charm, and went into the house.

As at the Villa Forli, there were long windows opening from the terrace into some big room, all of them shuttered against the sun except the one through which Max Gale had vanished. Through this dark opening I thought I could make out the shapes of a grand piano, what looked like a huge gramophone, and a revolving bookcase. The tops of the two last were stacked with books and records.

"Sun or shade?" asked Sir Julian, pulling up a gaudy camp

chair for me. I chose sun, and he settled himself beside me, the sombre wall of cypresses beyond the balustrade making as effective a backcloth for him as the ferns had for the white cat. The latter, purring, jumped up on to the actor's knee, turned carefully round twice, and settled down, paws going.

The pair of them made a striking picture. Sir Julian was not—had never been—handsome, but he was a big man, of the physical type to which the years can add a sort of heavy splendour. (One remembered his Mark Antony, and how after it all other attempts at the part seemed to be variations of his; attempts, in fact, to play *him*.) He had the powerful breadth of chest and shoulder that runs to weight in middle age, and his head was what is commonly called leonine—thick grey hair, a brow and nose in the grand manner, and fine grey eyes—but with some hint of weakness about the jaw from which the charm of the wide mouth distracted you. His eyes looked pouchy and a little strained, and there were sagging lines in his face which naturally I had never seen across the footlights, lines which might be those of petulance or dissipation, or merely a result of his illness and consequent loss of weight. It was difficult to tell just where his undeniable attractiveness lay; it would, indeed, be hard to give any definite description of him: his face was too familiar for that, melting as one watched him into one character after another that he had made his own, as if the man only existed as one saw him on the stage—king, madman, insurance salesman, soldier, fop ... as if in leaving that lighted frame, he ceased to exist. It was a disquieting idea when one remembered that he had, in fact, left his frame. If he could not be himself now, he was nothing.

He glanced up from the cat, caught me staring, and smiled. He must be very used to it. What he cannot have realised is that I was trying to find in his face and movements some evidence of nervous strain that might justify Phyllida's fears. But he seemed quite self-contained and relaxed, his hands (those betrayers), lying motionless and elegantly disposed—perhaps just a bit too elegantly disposed?—over the cat's fur.

"I'm sorry," I said, "was I staring? I've never been so close to you before. It's usually the upper circle."

"With me tastefully disguised behind several pounds of false beard, and robed and crowned at that? Well, here you see the man himself, poor, bare forked creature that he is. I won't ask you what you think of him, but you must at least give me your

56

opinion of his setting. What do you think of our crumbling splendours?"

"The Castello? Well, since you ask ... I'd have said it wasn't quite *you*. It would make a marvellous background for a Gothic thriller—*Frankenstein,* or *The Mysteries of Udolpho,* or something."

"It would, wouldn't it? One feels it ought to be permanently shrouded in mist, with vampires crawling down the walls—not surrounded by flowers, and the peace and sunshine of this enchanted island. However, I suppose it's highly appropriate for a decayed actor to retire to, and it's certainly a haven of peace, now that Max has clamped down on the sightseers."

"I heard you'd been ill. I'm sorry. We—we miss you terribly in London."

"Do you, my dear? That's nice of you. Ah, Max, here you are. Miss Waring thinks the house is a perfect setting for Frankenstein and his monster."

"I did not! I never said—I certainly didn't put it like that!"

Max Gale laughed. "I heard what you said. You could hardly insult this kind of crazy baroque anyway. Loco rococo. This is fresh orange, is that all right for you?"

"Lovely, thank you."

He had brought the same for himself, and for his father. I noticed that the latter's hand, as he put it out for the glass, shook badly, and his son quickly lifted a small iron table within reach, set the glass down on that, and poured the iced juice in. Sir Julian dropped his hands back into the cat's fur, where they once more lay statue-still. I had been right about the self-consciousness of that pose. But it hadn't been vanity, unless it is vanity that conceals a weakness of which one is ashamed.

As Max Gale poured my drink, I made to lay the roses on the table, but he set the jug down and put out a hand.

"Give them to me. I'll put them in water for you till you go."

"So I'm to be allowed to keep them, after I've paid the forfeit?"

"My dear child," said Sir Julian, "you're welcome to the lot! I hope you don't take my teasing seriously, it was only an excuse to make you come up. I'm only glad you liked them so much."

"I love them. They look like the roses in old pictures—you know, *real* roses in old story-books. *The Secret Garden,* and Andrew Lang's *Sleeping Beauty,* and the *Arabian Nights.*"

"That's just what they are. That one was found growing on a pavilion in Persia, where Haroun al Raschid may have seen it. This is the one out of the Romance of the Rose. And this was found growing in Fair Rosamund's garden at Woodstock. And this, they say, is the oldest rose in the world." His hands were almost steady as he touched the flowers one by one. "You must come back for more when these die. I'd leave them in the music-room, Max, it's reasonably cool ... Now, pay up, Miss Lucy Waring. I'm told you're in the business, and one of the reasons I lured you up here was to hear all you can give me of the latest gossip. The facts I can get from the periodicals, but the gossip is usually a great deal more entertaining—and quite often twice as true. Tell me . . ."

I forget now just what he asked me, or how much I was able to tell him, but though I moved in very different theatrical circles from him, I did know a good deal of what was going on in Town; and I remember that in my turn I found it exciting to hear him using, casually and in passing, names which were as far above my touch as the clouds on Mount Pantokrator. He certainly gave me the impression that he found me good value as an entertainer, but how far this was due to his own charm I can't guess, even today. I know that when, finally, he turned the conversation to my affairs, you'd have thought this was the big moment towards which all the star-spangled conversation had been leading.

"And now tell me about yourself. What are you doing, and where? And why have we never met before?"

"Oh, heavens, I'm not anywhere near your league! I'd only just got to the West End as it was!"

I stopped. The last phrase had been a dead giveaway, not only of the facts, but of feelings which I had not discussed, even with Phyllida. I had my vanities, too.

"Play folded?" Where a layman's sympathy would have jarred, his matter-of fact tone was marvellously comforting. "What was it?"

I told him, and he nodded.

"Yes, that was McAndrew's pet pigeon, wasn't it? Not a very wise venture on Mac's part, I thought. I read the play. Who were you? What's-her-name, the girl who has those unlikely hysterics all over Act Two?"

"Shirley. Yes. I was rotten."

"There was nothing there to get hold of. That sort of fantasy

58

masquerading as working-class realism needs rigid selection and perfect timing—not merely uncontrolled verbal vomit, if you'll forgive the phrase. And he never can do women, haven't you noticed?"

"Maggie in *The Single End*?"

"Do you call her a woman?"

"Well ... I suppose you're right."

"I'm right in telling you not to blame yourself over Shirley. What comes next?"

I hesitated.

"Like that, is it?" he said. "Well, it happens. How wise of you to cut and run for Corfu while you could! I remember ..." and he turned neatly off into a couple of malicious and very funny stories involving a well-known agent of the thirties, and a brash young actor whom I had no difficulty in identifying as Sir Julian Gale himself. When he had finished, and we had done laughing, I found myself countering with some of my own experiences which I had certainly never expected to find funny —or even to tell anybody about. Now, for some reason, to talk about them was a kind of release, even a pleasure, while the crenellated shadow of the Castello advanced unheeded across the weedy flags, and Sir Julian Gale listened, and commented, and asked questions, as if he had 'lured' me to his terrace for no other reason than to hear the life story of a mediocre young actress who would never play anything but seconds in her life.

A slight sound stopped me, and brought me sharply round. I had forgotten all about Max Gale. I hadn't heard him come out of the house again, but he was there, sitting on the balustrade well within hearing. How long he had been there I had no idea.

It was only then that I realised how the light had faded. My forfeit was paid, and it was time to be gone, but I could hardly take my leave within seconds, as it were, of acknowledging Max Gale's presence. I had to make some motion of civility towards him first.

I looked across at him. "Did you go to watch the procession this morning, Mr. Gale?"

"I? Yes, I was there. I saw you in the town. Did you get a good place?"

"I was on the Esplanade, at the corner by the Palace."

"It's rather ... appealing, don't you think?"

"Very." I smiled. "Being a musician, you'd appreciate the bands."

He laughed, and all at once I saw his father in him. "Very much. And when all four play at the same time, it really is something."

"The leitmotive for your *Tempest*, Max," said his father, stroking the white cat. " '*The isle is full of noises.*' "

Max grinned. "Perhaps. Though even I might fight shy of reproducing some of them."

Sir Julian turned to me. "My son is writing a score for a film version of *The Tempest*."

"Is that what it's to be? How exciting! I gather you've come to the right place to do it, too. Is that why you chose Corfu after you'd drowned your book at Stratford, Sir Julian?"

"Not really; the thing's fortuitous. I've known the island on and off for thirty years, and I've friends here. But it's a pleasant chance that brought this work to Max when we happened to be marooned here."

"Do you really think this is Prospero's island?"

"Why not?" asked Julian Gale, and Max said, "That's torn it," and laughed.

I looked at him in surprise. "What have I said?"

"Nothing. Nothing at all. But if you will invite a man to explain a theory he's been brooding over for weeks, you must be prepared for a lecture, and by the gleam in my father's eye, nothing can save you now."

"But I'd love to hear it! Besides, your father could make the Telephone Directory sound like *War and Peace* if he tried, so his private theory about *The Tempest* ought to be *something*! Don't take any notice of him, Sir Julian! Why do you think this might be Prospero's island?"

"You are a delightful young lady," said Sir Julian, "and if you wish to dig my roses out by the roots and carry them away, I shall send Adoni to help you. No, on second thoughts, Max can do it. It would be good for him to do a little real work, instead of floating around in that lunatic fringe where musicians seem to live ... Who was it who said that the really wise man isn't the man who wants a thing proved before he'll believe in it, but the man who is prepared to believe anything until it's shown to be false?"

"I don't know, but it sounds to me like somebody's definition of a visionary or a genius."

"*All* the roses," said Sir Julian warmly. "Did you hear that, Max? My theories about *The Tempest* are those of a visionary and a genius."

"Oh, sure," said his son.

He was still sitting on the balustrade, leaning back against the stone urn that stood at the corner. I had been watching his face covertly for some resemblance to his father, but, except for his build, and an occasional chance expression, could see none. His eyes were dark, and more deeply set, the mouth straighter, the whole face less mobile. I thought the hint of the neurotic was there, too, in the faint lines between the brows, and somewhere in the set of the mouth. The careful under-emphasis in all he said and did might well be a deliberate attempt to control this, or merely to avoid profiting by his father's charm. Where Sir Julian seemed automatically, as it were, to make the most of his lines, Max threw his away. It seemed to me that he was even concerned not to be liked, where his father, consciously or not, had the actor's need to be loved.

"There is no evidence of any kind," Sir Julian was saying, "to connect this island with the island of the play, any more than we can prove it was the Scheria' of Odysseus and Nausicaa; but in both cases tradition is strong, and when traditions persist hard enough, it seems only sensible to conclude that there may be something in them worth investigating."

"Schliemann and Troy," murmured Max.

"Exactly," said Sir Julian. He gave me that sudden smile that was so like his son's. "So, being like Schliemann a genius and a visionary, and being determined to believe that Corfu *is* Prospero's island, I've been looking for evidence to prove it."

"And is there any?"

"Perhaps not 'evidence'. That's a strong word. But once you start looking, you can find all sorts of fascinating parallels. Start with the easiest, the description of the natural details of the island, if you can remember them."

"I think I can, fairly well. There's rather more physical description of the setting than you usually find in Shakespeare, isn't there?"

"I'd say more than anywhere, except *Venus and Adonis*. And what description one gleans from the play fits this island well enough; the pines, tilled lands, the fertility (not so many of the Mediterranean islands are really fertile, you know), the beaches

61

and coves, the lime groves outside Prospero's cave . . ." He lifted a hand to point where a group of trees stood golden-green beside the pines on the southern promontory. "There are young limes growing all down the cliff beyond Manning's villa, and the whole coast is honeycombed with caves. You might say these things are found on any island, but one thing isn't—the brine-pits that Caliban talks about, remember?"

"And there are some here?"

"Yes, down at Korissia, in the south. They've been there for centuries."

"What about the pignuts and filberts he promised to dig up? Do they grow here?"

"Filberts certainly, and pignuts, too, if he means the English sort. And if he means truffles—as I believe—yes, those too."

"And the marmosets?" I asked it diffidently, as one who puts a question in doubtful taste.

Sir Julian waved the marmosets aside. "A momentary confusion with the still-vex'd Bermoothes. No doubt Ariel had been shooting a nice line in travel-tales, and the poor monster was muddled."

Max said: "You can't argue with a man with an obsession. Humour him, Miss Waring."

"I'll do no such thing! If a theory's worth holding, it's worth fighting over! What about the *story*, then, Sir Julian? Take the start of it, the shipwreck. If the ship was on its way from Tunis to Naples, you'd think Corfu was just a little too far off course——"

"Ah, yes, you run up against the same thing in the Odysseus story, where they're supposed to have rowed—rowed, mark you —from Scheria to Euboea in a single night. But to my mind that does nothing to discount Corfu's claim to be Scheria. It's poetic truth, the kind of telescoping that you find in the seven days of Creation—one assumes that the gods helped them. The same with the Neapolitan ship in *The Tempest*. The storm was a tremendous one, an historic tempest. The ship was blown right off her course, and could have driven blindly along for days before fetching up on these coastal rocks. Can't you see that what makes the story plausible is its very unlikelihood?"

"Have a heart," said his son, "of course she can't."

"It's very simple. The fact that the ship did end up here, so fantastically off course, made it necessary later on to explain the storm as being magical, or somehow supernatural."

62

"Just a minute," I said quickly. " 'The fact?' Are you trying to say that the business of the shipwreck is *true*?"

"Only that like all legends it could be founded on the truth, just as there really was a Cretan labyrinth, and a Troy that burned. It's my guess—strictly as a visionary—that there was in fact some spectacular wreck here, that became the basis of a legend."

"No more than a guess? You haven't found any actual Corfiote story, or any real record?"

"No."

"Then why here? Why Corfu? Your geographical details don't prove a thing. They might confirm, but they're hardly a start."

Sir Julian nodded, smoothing the cat's head with a gentle finger. "I started at the wrong end. I should have begun, not with the 'facts', but with the play—the play's king-pin, Prospero. To my mind, the conception of his character is the most remarkable thing about the play; his use as a sort of summing-up of Shakespeare's essay on human power. Look at the way he's presented: a father-figure, a magician in control of natural forces like the winds and the sea, a sort of benevolent and supernatural Machiavelli who controls the island and all who are in it."

He finished on a faint note of inquiry, and looked at me with raised eyebrows, waiting for my reply.

"Saint Spiridion?"

"Saint Spiridion. Exactly!" He glanced up at Max, as if showing off the cleverness of a favourite pupil. I saw Max smile faintly. "Even the name ... you'll notice the similarity; and its abbreviation, Spiro, makes it even closer." The shadow which touched his face was gone immediately. "Saint Spiridion—his body, that is—was brought here in 1489, and in no time at all he had the reputation for all sorts of magic, miracles if you like, especially weather-magic. There was another saint, a female, brought with him. Her mummy is also in a church in the town, but she didn't catch the public imagination, so she doesn't get the outings. In fact, I can't even remember her name."

"I've never even heard she existed," I said.

He smiled. "It's a man's country. But she may well be the origin of the *idea* of Miranda, the magician's daughter. She would hardly survive into legend merely as a female companion, or even as a wife. Magicians don't have them, for reasons which

I suppose it would be fascinating to explore, but which you might disagree with, Miss Lucy Waring."

"I know, Delilah and Co. All right, I don't resent it, it's a man's world. If it comes to that, witches don't have husbands, not the real old fairy-story witches, anyway."

"Fair enough." Sir Julian leaned back in his chair. "Well, there you have your starting point, the fabulously fertile island of Corfu, guarded by a Saint who is believed to control the weather. Now we postulate a tempest, some historic humdinger of a storm, when some important ship—perhaps even with a few Italian V.I.P.'s on board—was driven far off course and wrecked here, but with her passengers saved from drowning by some apparent miracle that would be imputed to the Saint. So, a legend starts to grow. Later the Germanic elements of fairy-tale are added to it—the 'magic', the beautiful daughter, the fairy characters." He paused, with a mischievous gleam at me. "It would be nice if one could somehow equate the elementals with the facts of the island's history, wouldn't it? I've tried my hardest to see the 'foul witch Sycorax' from 'Argier', as a sort of personification of the Moslem rulers who penned the heavenly power—Ariel—in a cloven pine till the Saint-magician released him . . . But I'm afraid I can't quite make that one stick."

"What a pity!" I said it quite without irony: I was enjoying myself vastly. "And Caliban? Paganism or something?"

"If you like. There's the brutality, the sexuality, and the superbly sensitive poetry. And he was certainly a Greek."

"How d'you work that out?" I asked, startled.

He chuckled. "He welcomed Prospero to the island with 'water with berries in it'. Haven't you come across the Greek custom of giving you berried jam in a glass of water?"

"No, I haven't. But really, you can't have that! It could even be coffee! What would that make him? French?"

"All right," he said amiably, "We'll leave poor Caliban as an 'infernal' seeking for grace. Well, that's all." Here the white cat stretched, flexed its claws, and yawned, very loudly. Sir Julian laughed. "You shouldn't have encouraged me. Nitwit has heard it all before, and so, I'm afraid, has poor Max."

"Well, I hadn't, and it's fascinating. One could have endless fun. I must read it again and look for all these things. I wish I thought my sister had a copy here."

"Take mine," he said immediately. "It should be somewhere

64

on top of the bookcase, I think, Max ... Thanks very much."
This as his son went to get it.

I said quickly: "But if you're working on it——"

"Working?" The word, lightly spoken as it was, sounded
somehow out of tune. "You've just heard how seriously. In any
case I use a Penguin for working, one I can mark and cut up ...
Ah, thank you, Max; and here are your roses, too. That's my
own copy; it's a bit ancient, and I'm afraid it's been scribbled
in, but perhaps you can ignore that."

I had already seen the pencilled notes. Holding the book as if
it were the original Blackfriars prompt copy, with the author's
jottings in the margin, I got to my feet. Sir Julian rose with me,
and the white cat, displaced, jumped down and stalked with
offended dignity off the terrace and down the steps to the rose
garden.

"I'll really have to go," I said. "Thank you for the book, I'll
take great care of it. I—I know I've stayed far too long, but I've
really loved it."

"My dear child, you've done us both a kindness. I've enjoyed
your visit enormously, and I hope you'll come back soon. As
you see, there's a limit to the amount of my conversation that
Max and the cat will stand, and it's pleasant to have a good-
mannered and captive audience again. Well, if you must ..."

The woods were dark already with the quickly falling twi-
light. Mr. Gale, accompanying me politely to the edge of the
rose garden, pointed out the path which led down to the clearing where the pool lay. The beautiful Nitwit was there,
dreamily regarding a large moth which hovered near some
honeysuckle. Max Gale picked him up, said good-bye to me,
and went quickly back. A very few minutes later I heard the
sound of the piano. He had lost no time in getting back to work.
Then the woods closed in and I was out of hearing.

The woods were always quiet, but now, with the darkness
muffling their boughs, they seemed to hold a hushed and heavy
stillness that might be the herald of storm. The scent of flowers
hung like musk on the air.

As I picked my way carefully down the path I was thinking
of the recent interview; not of the 'theory' with which Sir
Julian had been beguiling his exile, but of Sir Julian himself,
and what Phyl and Godfrey had said about him.

That there had been—still was—something badly wrong
seemed obvious: not only was there the physical evidence that

even I could see, there was also that attitude of watchful tension in the younger man. But against this could be set the recent conversation, not the normal—and even gay—tone of it, but the use of certain phrases that had struck me. Would a man who had recently emerged from a mental home talk so casually and cheerfully about the 'lunatic fringe' inhabited by his son? A son had, after all, a big stake in his father's sanity. And would the son, in his turn, speak of his father's 'obsession', and the need to 'humour' him? Perhaps if the need were serious, this was Mr. Gale's way of passing off a potentially tricky situation? Perhaps that edgy, watchful air of his was on my behalf as much as his father's?

Here I gave up. But as for the idea of Sir Julian's roaming the countryside with a rifle to the danger of all and sundry, I could believe it no more than formerly. I would as soon suspect Phyllida, or Godfrey Manning himself.

And (I thought) I would suspect Max Gale a darned sight sooner than any.

I could hear the trickle of water now, and ahead of me was the break in the trees where the pool lay. At the same moment I became conscious of a strange noise, new to me, like nothing more nor less than the clucking and chattering of a collection of hens. It seemed to come from the clearing.

Then I realised what it was; the evening chorus at the pool—the croaking of the innumerable frogs who must live there. I had stopped at the edge of the clearing to pick up my towel, and some of them must have seen me, for the croaking stopped, and then I heard the rhythmic plopping of small bodies diving into the water. Intrigued, I drew back behind the bushes, then made a silent way round the outer edge of the clearing towards the far side of the pool, where there was cover. Now I was above the bank. I gently pressed the branches aside, and peered down.

At first, in the dusk I could see nothing but the dark gleam of the water where the sky's reflection struck it between the upper boughs, and the matt circles of the small lily leaves and some floating weed. Then I saw a frog, a big one, sitting on a lily-pad, his throat distended and pulsing with his queer little song. His body was fat and freckled, like a laurel leaf by moonlight, and the light struck back from eyes bright as blackberry-pips. Close by him sang another, and then another . . .

Amused and interested, I stood very still. Growing every moment in volume, the chorus gobbled happily on.

Silence, as sudden as if a switch had been pressed. Then my frog dived. All around the lily-pads the surface ringed and plopped as the whole choir took to the water. Someone was coming up the path from the bay.

For a moment I wondered if Phyllida had been down to the beach to find me; then I realised that the new-comer was a man. His steps were heavy, and his breathing, and then I heard him clear his throat softly, and spit. It was a cautious sound, as if he were anxious not to make too much noise. The heavy steps were cautious, too, and the rough, hurried breathing, which he was obviously trying to control, sounded oddly disquieting in the now silent woods. I let the bushes slip back into place, and stood still where I was, to wait for him to pass.

The dimming light showed him as he emerged into the clearing; Greek, someone I hadn't seen before, a young man, thick-set and broad-chested, in dark trousers and a high-necked fisherman's sweater. He carried an old jacket of some lighter colour over one arm.

He paused at the other side of the pool, but only to reach into a pocket for a cigarette, which he put between his lips. But in the very act of striking the match, he checked himself, then shrugged, and put it away again, shoving the cigarette behind his ear. He could not have indicated his need for secrecy more plainly if he had spoken.

As he turned to go on his way, I saw his face fairly clearly. There was a furtive, sweating excitement there that was disturbing, so that when he glanced round as if he had heard some noise, I found myself shrinking back behind my screen of leaves, conscious of my own quickened heart-beats.

He saw nothing. He drew the back of a hand over his forehead, shifted his coat to the other arm, and trod with the same hasty caution up the steep path towards the Castello.

Above me a sudden gust of wind ran through the treetops, and chilly air blew through the trunks with the fresh, sharp smell of coming rain.

But I kept quite still until the sound of the Greek's footsteps had died away, and beside me the frog had climbed out again on to his lily-pad, and swelled his little throat for song.

67

CHAPTER SIX

Methinks he hath no drowning mark upon him.
                                    I. 1.

FOR some reason that I never paused to examine, I didn't tell
my sister about my visit to the Gales, not even when next morning she decided that for once she would go down to the bay
with me, and, as we passed the pool, pointed out the path that
led up to the Castello.

The clearing looked very different this morning with the high
clear light pouring into it. There had been a sudden little snap
of storm during the night, with a strong wind that died with
the dawn, and this had cleared the air and freshened the woods.
Down in the bay the sand was dazzling in the morning sun, and
the wake of the wind had left a ripple at the sea's edge.

I spread a rug in the shade of the pines that overhung the
sand, and dumped our things on it.

"You are coming in, aren't you?"

"Sure thing. Now I'm down here, nothing will stop me from
wallowing in the shallow bit, even if I do look like a mother
elephant expecting twins. That's a smashing swimsuit, Lucy,
where'd you get it?"

"Marks and Spencer's."

"Good heavens."

"Well, I didn't marry a rich man," I said cheerfully, pulling
up the shoulder-straps.

"And a fat lot of good it does me in my condition." She
looked sadly down at her figure, sighed, and dropped her smart
beach coat down beside the hold-all containing all the sun-
lotions, magazines, Elizabeth Arden cosmetics and other para-
phernalia without which she would never dream of committing
herself to the beach. "It isn't fair. Just look at me, and these
things come from Fabiani."

"You poor thing," I said derisively. "Will they go in the
water? And for Pete's sake, are you going to bathe with that
Koh-i-noor thing on?"

"Heavens, *no!*" She slipped the enormous marquise diamond
off her finger, dropped it into the plastic bag that held her
cosmetics, and zipped the bag shut. "Well, let's go in. I only

hope your friend doesn't mistake me for the dolphin, and let fly. Much the same general shape, wouldn't you say?"

"You'll be all right. He doesn't wear yellow."

"Seriously, there *isn't* anyone watching, is there, Lucy? I'd just as soon not have an audience."

"If you keep near inshore they can't see you anyway, unless they come to the front of the terrace. I'll go and look."

The water in the shade of the pines was a deep, deep green, lighting to a dazzling pale blue where a bar of sand ran out into the bay. I walked out along this, thigh-deep, until I was about fifty yards from the shore, then turned and looked up towards the terrace of the Castello. There was no one visible, so I waved to Phyllida to follow me in. As we swam and splashed, I kept an eye open to seaward for the dolphin, but, though I thought once that I could see a gleaming wheel turning a long way out, the creature did not approach the bay. After a time we waded back to the beach, where we lay sunning ourselves and talking idly, until Phyl's remarks, which had been getting briefer and briefer, and more and more sleepy, ceased altogether.

I left her sleeping, and went back into the water.

Though I had kept a wary eye on the woods and the terrace every time I bathed, I had never seen anyone since the first day, so it was with a slight feeling of surprise that I now saw someone sitting there, at the table under the stone-pine. Grey hair. Sir Julian Gale. He lifted a hand to me, and I waved back, feeling absurdly pleased that he should have bothered. He turned away immediately, his head bent over a book. I caught the flutter of its pages.

There was no one with him on the terrace, but as I turned to let myself down into the deep water beyond the bar, something else caught my eye.

In one of the upper windows, which stood open, something had flashed. And behind the flash I saw movement, as whoever stood watching there lifted the binoculars again to focus them on the bay . . .

There is something particularly infuriating about being watched in this way. I should have dearly loved to return rudeness for rudeness by pulling a very nasty face straight at the Castello windows, but Sir Julian might have seen it, and thought it was meant for him, so I merely splashed back to the sand-bar, where I stood up, and, without another glance, stalked expressively (Drama School exercise; Outraged Bather driven from water) towards the rocks at the southern edge of the bay. I would finish my swim from the rocks beyond the point, out of range of the Castello.

I hadn't reckoned on its being quite so difficult to stalk with dignity through three feet of water. By the time I reached the end of the sand-bar and the deep pool near the rocks, I was furiously angry with Max Gale, and wishing I had gone straight out on to the beach. But I was damned if I would be driven back now. I plunged across the deep water, and was soon scrambling out under the pines.

A path ran through the tumble of rocks at the cliff's foot, leading, I supposed, to Godfrey Manning's villa, but its surface looked stony, so I stayed on the rocks below. These, scoured white by the sea and seamed with rock pools, stretched out from the cliff in stacks and ridges, with their roots in the calm, creaming water.

I began to pick my way along between the pools. The rocks were hot, and smooth to the feet. There were crevices filled with flowering bushes, running right down to the water's edge where the green swell lifted and sank, and here and there a jut of the living cliff thrust out into the water, with the path above it, and bushes at its rim hanging right out over the sea.

At the point I paused. Here the rocks were more broken, as if the tide was driven hard that way when there was a wind, and under the cliff was a pile of broken rock and sea-wrack, some of which looked fresh enough to have come up in last night's squall. Further round, beyond the next curve of the cliff, I could see where a cove or inlet ran in, deep and narrow and surrounded by thick trees which stretched right up the slopes of the cliff; there were pines and oaks and hollies, and among them the limes of which Sir Julian had spoken. Through the boughs of a young thicket at the cliff's foot I caught a glimpse of red tiling which must be the roof of Godfrey's boat-house.

There was nobody about. I decided to finish my bathe in the deep water off the point and then return by the path.

I made my way carefully through the piled rocks and the sea-wrack. Here and there a shallow pool barred the way, and I paddled across with caution, wondering uneasily about sea-urchins, which in these waters (I had read) can drive poisonous spines into your feet. *Like hedgehogs, which Lie tumbling in my barefoot way, and mount Their pricks at my foot-fall ...* Poor Caliban. Was Julian Gale right, I wondered? I had read

The Tempest late into the night, following up the fascinating game he had suggested, and I had even had a few ideas myself, things I must ask him when I went to the Castello again . . . If I ever went to the Castello again . . . But of course I would have to return the Shakespeare . . . If I could find out from Miranda or Adoni or someone when Max Gale was likely to be out . . .

I had come to the edge of a deep inlet, a miniature cove running back through the rocks. This would be as good a place as any. I paused, peering down into it, to see what the bottom was like.

The water was the colour of Imperial jade. Tiny, shrimp-like creatures scudded here and there among the olive and scarlet bladders, and shoals of small fish darted and nibbled. The shadows cast by the sun looked blue-black, and were alive with the movements of crabs which shuffled through the brown weed that clothed the bottom. The weed itself moved all the time, faintly and continuously, like rags in the swell. A cuttlefish bone showed white and bare. *Of his bones are coral made. These are pearls* . . .

The body was lying half in, half out, of the largest patch of shadow. The sun, shining straight into my eyes, had hidden it till now, the hump of flesh and clothes not holding any kind of human shape, just a lump of rags rolled over and over by the swell and dumped there, jammed somehow under an overhang at the base of the pool.

Even now, with the sun directly in my eyes, I could hardly be sure. Sick and shaken, I hesitated: but of course I would have to look. I sank to my knees at the edge of the pool, and shaded my eyes to peer downwards . . .

The rags moved in the faint swell like weed. Surely it was only weed . . .? But then I saw the head, the face, a shape blurred and bleached under dark hair. Some sea-creatures had already been at it. The tiny fish flicked to and fro, busily, in the green water.

Spiro, I thought, *Spiro* . . . And his mother would have to see this. Surely it would be better to say nothing, to let the tide carry it away again; let the busy sea-creatures purge and clean it to its sea-change, like the cuttlefish bone showing white beside the dark hair . . .?

Then reason threw its ice-water on my confusion. She would have to be told. It would be more cruel not to tell her. And there was no tide here. Without another storm, the thing could be held down here for days, for anyone to find.

Some freak current thrust a tentacle of movement through the pool. The water swayed, and the dead man moved his head. With the movement, I knew him. It wasn't specifically the face that I recognised; that would have been impossible: but somehow everything came together in the same moment to enforce recognition—the shape of face and head, the colours, better seen now, of the sodden lumps of rag that had been navy trousers and sweater and light grey jacket . . .

It wasn't Spiro, after all; not, that is, unless it had been Spiro in the woods last night, still alive, and making his way up towards the Castello.

There could be no doubt about it, no possible doubt. This was the man I had seen last night in the clearing. I found that I was sitting back on my heels, slumped to one side, with a hand out to the hot face of a boulder beside me. It was one thing to find a dead man; but to recognise him, and to know where he had been shortly before he had met his death . . .

I had my eyes shut, as tightly as the fingers that gripped the hot stone. The sunlight boiled and fizzed against the closed lids. I bit my lips, and breathed slowly and hard, and concentrated on not being sick. Phyllida: the thought was as bracing as sal volatile: Phyllida mustn't see this, or even be allowed to suspect the horror that lay just round the point from her. I must steady myself decently, then go back to Phyllida, and somehow persuade her to leave the beach soon. Then get quietly to the telephone, and get in touch with the police.

I opened my eyes, with a silly hope that somehow I had been wrong, and there was no dead man there in the water. But he still lay in his splash of inky shadow, grotesque and faintly moving and familiar. I got to my feet, held myself steady by the boulder for another full minute, then, without looking back, made my way through the tumble of rock towards the thicket that edged the cliff path. It was only when I had reached the bushes, and was wondering if I could pull myself up the eight feet or so to the path, that some sound, vaguely heard a few moments ago, and now repeated, made me pause and glance to my left, towards the boat-house. Someone had slammed a door. Something appeared to be wrong with the catch, because I heard, clearly now, an exclamation of irritation, and the slam was repeated. This time the door shut firmly, and a moment later I heard footsteps, and Godfrey Manning came briskly into view along the path.

I wasn't sure if he was coming my way, or if the path branched off above the trees somewhere for the Villa Rotha. I opened my mouth to call him, hoping that this wouldn't also bring Phyllida, but at the same moment Godfrey glanced up and saw me below him on the rocks. He lifted a hand in greeting, but before he could call out I put a finger to my lips, then beckoned urgently.

Not surprisingly, he looked startled, but his expression deepened sharply into concern as he approached and paused on the path above me.

"Lucy? Is something wrong? Are you feeling ill? The sun?" Then his voice changed. "It's not that damned lunatic again with the rifle?"

I shook my head. Infuriatingly, after I had so far controlled myself, I found I couldn't speak. I pointed.

He glanced over towards the pool, but at that distance nothing was visible. Then he swung himself lightly down through the bushes to where I stood, and his arm went round me, gently.

"You'd better sit down . . . There. Better? All right, don't try to talk any more. Something scared you, over there in the big pool? Relax a minute now; I'll go and take a look, but don't you move. Just sit there quietly, and don't worry. I won't be long."

I sat with my hands jammed tightly together between my knees, and watched my feet. I heard Godfrey's steps, quick and confident, cross the rocks towards the pool. Then there was silence, prolonged. The sea murmured, and some cliff-building swallows twittered shrilly as they cut in and out above the path.

I looked up. He was standing stock-still where I had stood, staring down. He was in profile to me, and I could see that he looked considerably shaken. It was only then that it occurred to me that he, too, must in the first moment of shock have expected it to be Spiro. If I had been capable of reasoned thought or speech, I should have known this, and spared him.

I cleared my throat. "It's not . . . Spiro, is it?"

"No."

"Do you know who it is?"

I thought he hesitated, then he nodded. "His name's Yanni Zoulas."

"Oh? You *do* know him?" Somehow this shook me, too,

73

though it was reasonable to assume that the man had been drowned locally. "Is he from near here, then?"

"Yes, from the village."

"What—what do you suppose happened?"

"God knows. Some accident at sea, that's obvious. He was a fisherman, and usually went out alone ... You must have seen his boat; it was always plying to and fro along this bit of shore —the rather pretty blue boat, with the dark brown sail. But in last night's sea ... I wouldn't have thought ..."

His voice trailed away as he stared frowningly down at the pool. Then he turned and made his way back across the rock to where I sat.

"Two in a week?" I said. It came out as a query, asked quite as if Godfrey could supply the answer. I hadn't meant even to say it aloud, and could have bitten my tongue with vexation as soon as it was out.

"Two in a week?" He spoke so blankly that it was evident my meaning hadn't registered. "Oh, I see."

"I'm sorry. It was stupid of me. I was thinking aloud. I shouldn't have reminded you. It's just one of those ghastly coincidences."

"Normally," he said, "I'd have said I didn't believe in co-incidence. In fact, if I hadn't seen with my own eyes what happened to Spiro, I'd certainly be starting to wonder what was going on around here." He paused, and his eyes went back to the pool. "As it is, all that has happened is that two young men from the same district have died this week by drowning, and in a community that lives largely by the sea, that's hardly sur-prising. Only ..." He stopped.

"Only what?"

He looked at me with troubled eyes. "One doesn't expect an epidemic of it in summer weather, that's all."

"Godfrey, what is it? You look as if you thought——" I, too, checked myself, biting my lip. He watched me bleakly, saying nothing. I finished, rather hoarsely: "Are you trying to tell me that this wasn't an accident?"

"Good God, no! Just that it poses problems. But none that you need worry about. In any case, they may never arise."

None that you need worry about ... Heaven knew what he'd have said if he had had even the slightest inkling of the problem it had set me ... Why I still said nothing about last night I am not quite sure. I think now that this last incident took its place

74

in a context of violence, felt rather than apprehended, that
made it unsurprising, and that forced me, through some instinct
of fear, to hold my tongue. It was as if the first shot from that
silenced rifle had been the signal for danger and fear to crowd
in; as if by my silence I could still detach myself from them,
and stay inside my own bubble of security, keep my own enchanted island free of invaders from the violent world I had
come here to escape.

So I said instead: "Has he any people?"

"A wife. They live with his parents. You probably know the
house, it's that pink one at the crossroads."

"Yes, I do. It's very pretty. I remember thinking that the folk
in it must be well off."

"They were. They're going to miss him."

I looked at him, startled, not by the words, which were trite,
but by the quite undue dryness of his tone.

"You *are* getting at something. You *know* something about
this, don't you? Why won't you tell me?"

He hesitated, then smiled suddenly. "I don't really know why
not. It hardly concerns me, and it certainly won't touch you.
It's only that when the police move in on this something might
crop up that could be awkward."

"Such as?"

He lifted his shoulders. "No plain and simple fisherman lived
as well as Yanni and his family. Rumour has it that he was a
smuggler, with a regular 'milk run' into Albania, and that he
made a good bit on the side."

"Well, but surely ... I'd have imagined that an awful lot of
men played around with that sort of thing hereabouts? And
Corfu's very well placed, just next door to the Iron Curtain. I
suppose any sort of 'luxury goods' would go well there? But
how could anyone like Yanni Zoulas get supplies of things like
that?"

"How do I know? He'd have his contacts; someone in Corfu
town, perhaps, who has connections with Athens or Italy ...
But I'm sure that Yanni Zoulas wouldn't be in it on his own
account. He wasn't exactly a master mind. He probably did it
for a salary."

I licked my lips. "Even so ... You wouldn't suggest that
there could be any connection—that he was *killed* because of
this? Is that what you're getting at? That—that would make it
murder, Godfrey."

"No, no. For goodness sake, I wasn't suggesting anything like that! Good God, no! Don't upset yourself. Why, you're as white as a sheet! Look, the idea's pure nonsense ... I doubt if poor Yanni would ever be important enough to get himself murdered! You can forget that. But it did occur to me to wonder if he could have run into trouble on the other side—coastguard trouble: I believe they're hot stuff over there, search-lights, machine-guns, the lot. If he did, and was wounded, and then ran for home, that might account for an accident happening on a night that wasn't particularly rough. He might have fainted and gone overboard."

"I see. But even if the police do find out something about it, his family won't be in trouble, will they?"

"I doubt it. It isn't that."

"Then what's worrying *you?*"

"It might bring them closer to young Spiro than would be quite pleasant," said Godfrey frankly. "I've a strong suspicion that he'd been out with Yanni more than once. It didn't worry me, and I asked no questions; the boy had a mother and sister to keep, and how he did it was his own affair. But I don't want them to find out about it now. It would serve no purpose, and might distress his mother. According to her, Spiro was *sans peur et sans reproche*, and a good Christian into the bargain. I'm sure she'd label smuggling as immoral, however lightly you or I might regard it."

"I didn't say I regarded it lightly. I think that if you live under a country's protection you should obey its laws. I just wasn't surprised. But, you know, even if the police do find out something discreditable about Spiro, I'm sure they'd never tell Maria. Police are human, when all's said and done, and the boy's dead."

"You're probably right. Ah, well ..." He stretched, and sighed. "Hell, what a wretched business. We'd better go and get it over. Do you feel as if you'd like to move now?"

"Oh, yes, I'm fine."

He took my arm, and helped me up the rough bank to the path.

"I'm going to take you up to my house now, to telephone," he said. "It's nearer, and there's no need to alarm your sister till you're feeling a bit more the thing yourself. The police will want to see you, and you can see them at my place if you like, then I'll take you home by road, in the car ... Now, did you have some clothes with you, or some sort of wrap and shoes? If you wait here a moment, I'll get them."

"They're back in the bay, but I'm afraid Phyl's there, too. I left her asleep on the beach. She's probably awake by now, and wondering where I am."

"Oh." He looked uncertain. "Well, that alters things, doesn't it? We'll have to tell her. I don't know much about these things, but will it—well, upset her, or anything?"

"I think she'll be okay as long as she doesn't see the body. She'll have to know soon enough ... Wait a minute, someone's coming, That'll be her."

A second later she appeared on the path, round the point of the cliff. She must have been awake for some time, for all traces of the sea had been removed; she was freshly made up, her hair was shining and immaculate, she had clipped a pretty beach skirt on over her bathing costume, and she wore her gay beach coat. As usual, the sight of her brought my own shortcomings immediately to mind. I was conscious for the first time of what I must look like, with the salt dried on my skin, my hair damp, and my face—I imagined—still sallow with shock.

She said gaily: "I thought I heard voices! Hullo, Godfrey! Were you on your way over to us, or did you just come down to swim?"

"Neither. I was down at the boat-house giving the boat a once-over, when I saw Lucy."

I said: "Are those my shoes you've brought? Thanks very much. How did you guess I'd be wanting them?"

"Well, dearie, knowing you," said Phyllida, "when I woke up and found you'd vanished, I knew you'd be straying along here poking around in the rock-pools, and heaven knew how far you'd get." She laughed up at Godfrey. "It wouldn't surprise me in the least to find her with a jam-jar full of assorted shrimps and things to take home. I remember once——" She stopped. There was a pause, in which she looked from one to the other of us. Then her voice sharpened. "Lucy. Godfrey. Something's wrong. What is it?"

He hesitated just that second too long. "Your sister was feeling the heat a bit, and I offered to take her up to my house and give her a drink. She told me you were on the beach, so I was just coming across for you. I hope you'll come up too?"

His tone was perfect, easy and natural, but my sister was

77

never anybody's fool. She had seen all she needed to see in my face, and in the fact that Godfrey's hand still supported my arm.

She said, more sharply still: "Something *is* wrong. Lucy, you look awful ... And it's not the heat, either; don't give me that; you never felt the heat in your life. What's happened? Have you hurt yourself, or something?"

"No, no. There's nothing the matter with me, honestly." I disengaged myself gently, and looked up at Godfrey. It struck me suddenly, irrelevantly, that he was better-looking than I had thought. The sunlight showed up the deep tan of his skin, and the crisp hair bleached fair at the front. Against the tan his eyes looked a very clear grey.

I said: "You may as well tell her straight away."

"Very well. Phyl, I'm afraid a beastly thing's happened. One of the local fishermen's been drowned, and washed ashore over there, and Lucy found the body."

"Oh, my God, how ghastly! Lucy, my dear ... you poor kid! I suppose it looked——" Then her eyes widened, and a hand went up to her face. "Did you *see*? Could you tell? I mean ... after a week ..."

"It's not Spiro." Godfrey spoke quickly, almost harshly.

"*It's not?*" The hand dropped, and she let out a long breath of relief. "Oh, I was so sure ... But does that mean *two*, in just a few days? Have you any idea who it is?"

"It's a local man called Yanni Zoulas. I doubt if you know him. Look, we were just going up to telephone. Will you come with us? If I just go back now to the bay for the rest of——"

He stopped abruptly, and turned. A shadow fell across me where I sat pulling on my sandals. Max Gale's voice said, just behind me:

"Is anything the matter?"

I know I jumped as if he had hit me. The other two were caught gaping, as if in some guilty act. He must be stones heavier than Phyllida, but we had none of us heard a sound. I thought: he must move like a cat.

For seconds, nobody replied. It was a queer, hair-pricking little pause, during which the men eyed each other like unfriendly dogs circling one another, and I sat with a sandal half on, watching them.

"The matter?" said Godfrey.

I knew then that he didn't want to tell Gale what had happened. The knowledge, somehow not surprising, came like a cold breath along my skin. Mr. Gale glanced from Godfrey to Phyl, then down at me, and I bent my head quickly, pulled the sandal on, and began to fasten the strap.

He said impatiently: "It's obvious there's something. I was watching the bay with glasses, and I thought I saw something odd—some debris or other floating, away out; I couldn't make it out. Then Miss Waring came this way, and I saw her on the rocks that run out from the point. She stopped and looked into one of the pools, and her reactions made it pretty obvious that there was something very wrong indeed. Then you went over and made it rather plainer. What is it? Or shall I go and see for myself?"

It was Phyllida who answered him. She must not have felt the overtones that had chilled me—but then she didn't know what I knew. She said, in a sort of rush: "It's a dead body. Drowned. In that pool, there. We were just going up to phone the police."

There was a moment in which I seemed to hear the cliff-swallows, very loud and shrill, just overhead. Then Max Gale said: "Who is it? Do you know?"

Godfrey still said nothing. He had not taken his eyes off the other man's face. It was Phyllida who answered.

"I forget the name. Godfrey says he's from the village. Yanni something."

"Yanni Zoulas," I said.

He looked down at me as if he was aware fully for the first time that I was there. I got the strong impression that he wasn't seeing me even now. He didn't speak.

"Did you know him?" I asked.

The dark eyes focused on me for a moment, then he looked away again, over towards the pool. "Why, yes, slightly."

Godfrey said: "You say you were watching something floating, some debris. You couldn't say what sort of thing? Could it have been flotsam from a sunk boat?"

"Eh? Well, I told you I couldn't see at that distance, but it could have been ... My God, yes, I suppose it could!" All of a sudden Gale was fully with us; his gaze sharpened, and he spoke abruptly. "I wonder what time he went out last night? I thought I heard a boat soon after midnight, bearing north-east." He looked at Godfrey. "Did you hear it?"

"No."

79

"Last night?" said Phyllida. "Did it happen as recently as that? Could you tell, Godfrey?"

"I'm not an expert. I don't know. I don't think he's been there long. However, it shouldn't be hard to find out when he was last seen."

I had been watching Max Gale's face. He was looking thoughtful now, grave—anything but the way I knew he ought to be looking. "It must have happened within the last forty-eight hours. I saw his boat myself on Saturday. It went past the bay at about three in the afternoon."

If I hadn't known what I did, I'd never have known that he was lying—or rather, implying a lie. For a moment I even wondered if perhaps Yanni had not been on his way to the Castello last night, then I remembered that Mr. Gale had, in the last few minutes, given me another reason for doubting his good faith. He looked down suddenly, and caught me watching him. I bent my head again, and fiddled with the second sandal.

"Well," said Godfrey, "it'll be easy enough to check with his family, and the sooner we let the experts get on the job, the better. Shall we go? One thing, nobody need stay with the body. There's no tide to shift it ... Where are you going?"

Max Gale didn't trouble to answer; he was already swinging himself down to the rocks below us. Godfrey made a quick, involuntary movement as if to stop him, then he shrugged, said softly to us: "Do you mind? We won't be long," and slithered in his turn down through the bushes.

Gale was bending over the pool. Like Godfrey, he stood looking down at the body for some time in silence, then he did what neither Godfrey nor I had done: he lay flat at the edge of the rock, and reached down through the water as if to touch the dead man. I saw Godfrey make another of those sharp involuntary movements, but he must have decided that what evidence there was could hardly be damaged further by a touch, for he said nothing, merely stooping down himself to watch with close attention.

"What in the world are they doing?" asked Phyl, rather petulantly.

I was clasping my knees, hugging myself together closely. In spite of the sun, I had begun to feel cold. "I don't know and I don't care. I hope they hurry, that's all. I want to get some clothes on and get the police over and done with."

"You poor lamb, are you cold? Here, have my coat." She

took it off and dropped it over my shoulders, and I hugged it gratefully round me.

"Thanks a lot. That's marvellous." I laughed a little. "At least it puts me in competition again! I wish you didn't always look as if you'd just got back from Elizabeth Arden, when I feel like a bit of Mr. Gale's debris. It was probably me he saw floating. If, that is, he saw anything."

She looked quickly down at me. "What does that mean? It sounds loaded."

"Not really."

She sat down beside me. "You don't often make remarks for nothing. What *did* you mean?"

"I'm not happy about this affair, that's all."

"Well, heavens, who is? But is it an 'affair'?"

"I don't know. There's a feeling ... a feeling that there's something going on. I can't put it better than that, and I'm probably wrong, but I think—I *think*—Godfrey feels it, too. Why don't he and Mr. Gale like one another?"

"I didn't know they didn't. They *were* a bit wary today, weren't they? I suppose Godfrey's more upset than he lets on ... after all, it's rather soon after the Spiro business ... And Max Gale doesn't just put himself out to be charming, does he?"

"He has things on his mind," I said.

The remark was intended merely as an evasion, to imply only that his personal worries—over his father—made him difficult to know or like, but she took it to refer specifically to what had just happened. She nodded.

"I thought so, too ... Oh, nothing special, just that he seemed to be thinking about something else. But what did *you* mean?" She shot me another look. "Something's really worrying you, isn't it?"

I hesitated. "Did it strike you as odd, the way Mr. Gale took the news?"

"Well, no, it didn't. Perhaps because I know him better than you. He's never very forthcoming. What sort of 'odd' did you mean?"

I hesitated again, then decided not to specify. "As if he wasn't surprised that a body should roll up here."

"I don't suppose he was. He'd be expecting it to be Spiro."

"Oh, of course," I said. "Look, they seem to be coming back."

81

Mr. Gale had finished whatever grisly examination he had been conducting, and had withdrawn his hand. He rinsed it in the salt water, then stood up, drying it on a handkerchief. As far as I could make out, the two men still hadn't spoken a word. Now Godfrey said something with a gesture towards Phyl and myself, and they turned together and started over to us.

"Thank goodness," I said.

"You'll feel better when you've had a drink, old dear," said my sister.

"Coffee," I said, "as hot as love and as sweet as hell."

"Godfrey might even run to that, you never know."

The men scrambled up to the path beside us.

"Well?" said Phyl and I, together.

They exchanged a glance, which might even be said to hold complicity. Then Gale said: "It should be interesting to hear what the doctor has to say. He seems to have been knocked about the head a bit. I was wondering if the neck was broken, but I don't think so."

Godfrey's eye met mine. I stood up. "Well, when the boat's found, there may be something there to show how it happened."

"For all we know," said Godfrey, "that's been done, and the hue and cry's on already. Let's go, shall we?"

"Thank goodness!" I said. "But I still want to get dressed. My things——"

"Good God, I was forgetting. Well, hang on another minute or two, I won't be long."

Max Gale said, in that abrupt, rather aggressive way of his: "You three start up the path. I'll go and pick your stuff up and bring it along."

He had so plainly not been invited to go with us, and just as plainly fully intended to hear all that was said to the police, that I thought Godfrey was going to demur. But Phyllida got eagerly to her feet.

"Yes, let's get away from here! It's giving me the grue. Mr. Gale, if you *would* be an angel ... I've left some things, too, they're under the pine trees."

"I saw where they were. I won't be long. Don't wait for me; I'll catch you up."

He went quickly. Godfrey looked after him, the grey eyes curiously cold. Then he caught me watching him, and smiled. "Well, this way."

The path followed the cliff as far as the boat-house, then

turned up a steep zigzag through the trees. We toiled up it, grateful for the shade. Godfrey walked between us, in a sort of awkwardly divided solicitude that might at any other time have been amusing; but just now all I could think of was a bit of solitude in his bathroom, then a comfortable chair, and—failing the coffee—a long, cool drink. I hoped Max Gale would hurry with the clothes. I thought he probably would: he wouldn't want to miss what was said to the police. It had surprised me that he had risked this by offering to go back.

Godfrey had paused to help Phyl negotiate a dry gully which the winter's rain had gouged across the path. I was a few paces ahead of them when I came to a corner where a sudden gap in the trees gave a view of the point below.

I might have known there would be a good reason for Max Gale's offer. He was back at the rock pool, lying flat as before, reaching down into the water. I could just see his head and shoulders. Just as I caught the glimpse of him he withdrew his arm and got quickly to his feet. As he turned, I drew back into the shade of the trees, and just in time, for he glanced up briefly before he vaulted up to the path, and out of sight.

"Tired?" asked Godfrey, just behind me.

I started. "No, not a bit. Just getting my breath. But I'll be glad when it's all over."

"So shall we all. I seem to have spent the whole week with the police as it is." He added, rather bitterly: "At least they know their way here, and most of the questions to ask."

Phyllida touched his arm gently. "Poor Godfrey. But we're terribly grateful. And at least this time it doesn't touch you . . . except as a rather ghastly sort of coincidence."

His eyes met mine. They held the bleak expression I was beginning to know.

"I don't believe in coincidence," he said.

CHAPTER SEVEN

What have we here, a man, or a fish? dead or alive?
II. 2.

EITHER she had been more distressed than she had allowed us to see, or else the trip down to the beach in the heat, with the bathe and the climb to the Villa Rotha, had been too much for Phyllida. Though we spent the rest of the day quietly, and she lay down after lunch for a couple of hours, by evening she was tired, fidgety, and more than somewhat out of temper, and very ready to be persuaded to go to bed early.

Maria and Miranda had gone as soon as dinner was over. By ten o'clock the house was very quiet. Even the pines on the hill behind it were still, and once I had shut the windows I could hear no sound from the sea.

I felt tired myself, but restless, with sleep still a long way off, so I went along to the scrubbed and empty kitchen, made myself more coffee, then took it through to the *salotto*, put my feet on a chair, some Mozart on the gramophone, and settled myself for a quiet evening.

But things didn't quite work out that way. The calm, beautiful room, even the music, did not manage to keep at bay the thoughts that had been knocking for admission since that morning. In spite of myself, my mind went persistently back to the morning's incidents; the discovery in the pool, the two men's raw antagonism, and the long, wearying aftermath of interrogation, with the fresh problems it had brought to light.

The police from Corfu had been civil, thorough, and kind. They had arrived fairly soon after we had reached Godfrey's house, and had gone straight down with the two men to see the body. Shortly after that a boat had arrived from somewhere, and presently departed with its burden. Another came soon afterwards, and cruised off out to sea—searching, one assumed, for the 'debris' which Mr. Gale insisted that he had seen. From the terrace of the Villa Rotha Phyl and I had watched it tacking to and fro some way out from land, but with what success it had been impossible—failing Mr. Gale's binoculars—to guess.

Then the men came back. The questions had been searching, but easy enough for my part to answer, because of course nobody imagined that I had ever seen Yanni before in my life, so the only questions I was asked were those touching on my finding of the body.

And when Max Gale reiterated to the police that he had not laid eyes on Yanni Zoulas since a possible glimpse of his boat on Saturday afternoon, I had not said a word.

It was this that bore on me now, heavily, as I sat there alone in the *salotto*, with darkness thickening outside the windows, and moths thumping against the lighted glass. And if I was beginning to get too clear an idea why, I didn't want to face that, either. I pushed that line of thought to one side, and concentrated firmly on the facts.

These were, in their own way, comforting. Godfrey had rung up in the late afternoon to give us the latest reports. It appeared that Yanni's boat had been found drifting, and on the boom were traces of hairs and blood where, as the boat heeled in a sudden squall, it must have struck him and sent him overboard. An almost empty bottle of ouzo, which had rolled away behind a pile of rope and tackle, seemed to provide a clue to the young fisherman's carelessness. The doctor had given it as his opinion (said Godfrey) that Yanni had been dead when he went into the water. The police did not seem inclined to press the matter further. Of the debris reported by Mr. Gale no trace had been found.

Finally—Godfrey was a little cryptic over this part of the message, as the telephone was on a party line—finally, no mention had been made of any illegal activities of the dead man. Presumably his boat had been searched, and nothing had come to light, so the police (who preferred to turn a blind eye to small offences unless action was forced on them) were satisfied that the fatal voyage had been a routine fishing trip, and that Yanni's death had been accidental. It was obvious that they had no intention of opening any further line of inquiry.

So much for Godfrey's anxiety. My own went a little further.

It had transpired, from police inquiries, that the last time Yanni's family had seen him alive was on Sunday: he had spent the day with them, they said, going with them to watch the procession, and returning home in the late afternoon. Yes, he had seemed in good spirits. Yes, he had been drinking a fair amount. He had had a meal, and then had gone out. No, he had not said where he was going, why should he? They had assumed he was going fishing, as usual. He had gone down to the boat. Yes, alone; he usually went alone. That was the last time they had seen him.

It was the last time anyone had seen him, according to the police report. And I had said nothing to make them alter it. Where Godfrey had been worrying about the inquiry's leading back to Spiro, I was worrying about its involving Julian Gale. That Max Gale was somehow implicated seemed obvious, but I had my own theories about that, and they hardly justified turning the police searchlight on Yanni's activities, and so wrecking Sir Julian's precarious peace. With Yanni's death an accident— and I saw no reason to doubt this—it didn't matter if he had indeed paid a furtive visit to the Castello before going out last night. So if Max Gale chose to say nothing about it, then it was none of my business. I could stay in my enchanted bubble and keep quiet. It didn't matter one way or the other . . .

But I knew quite well that it did, and it was this knowledge that kept me sleepless in my chair, while one record followed another, unheeded, and the clock crawled on towards midnight. For one thing, I had had information forced on me that I would rather not have owned. For another——

The record stopped. With its slow, deliberate series of robot clicks, the auto-changer dropped another on the turntable, moved a gentle arm down on it, and loosed Gervase de Peyer's clarinet into the room in a brilliant shower of gold.

I switched my own thoughts back into the groove of facts. One thing at a time. The best way of forgetting how you think you feel is to concentrate on what you know you know . . .

Godfrey had been sure that Yanni was a smuggler, and that he must have some 'contact' who was probably his boss. I was pretty sure now that the contact was Max Gale. It all tied up: it would explain that furtive visit just before Yanni's voyage, and Gale's silence on the subject. It would also account for the thing that had so much worried me this morning—Gale's reaction to the news of Yanni's death. He had not been surprised at the news that a body was on the rocks, and this was not, as Phyl had assumed, because he thought it was Spiro. To me it was obvious that Spiro had never entered his head. His first question had been "Who is it? Do you know?" though the obvious assumption would have been the one the rest of us had made, that this must be the body of the drowned boy.

If my guess about him was correct, then his actions were perfectly consistent. He had known Yanni was to make a trip the night before; he must know there was some risk involved. He would obviously not have expected Yanni to meet his death, but, once faced with a drowned body, he had had no doubts as to who it would be. His story of floating debris was nonsense, of that I was sure: what had happened was that he had seen me, and then Godfrey, at the rock-pool, had jumped to conclusions, and had made an excuse to come down to see for himself. There had been that sharp "Who is it?" and then the next, immediate, reaction—to examine the body as closely as he dared, presumably for any evidence of violence. No doubt if such evidence had been there, he would have had to come out with the truth, or part of it. As it was, he held his tongue, and no doubt shared Godfrey's relief that the matter need not be brought into the open.

Yes, it all tied up, even Gale's surreptitious return to the pool, presumably to examine the body more closely than he had dared with Godfrey there, and to remove anything Yanni might have been carrying which might link him with his 'contact'. And it was Gale's luck that the boat had proved innocent: either poor Yanni had been on his way home when the accident happened, or last night's trip had, in fact, merely been a routine one to the fishing-grounds. Even the attack on the dolphin took its place with the rest. I was certain, now, that Gale had shot at the creature because he was afraid it would attract the tourist crowds, and destroy his badly-needed privacy. But the anger that this action had roused in me didn't give me the right, I decided, to open up a field of inquiry that would probably hurt Spiro's people, and would certainly hurt Yanni's. The two bereaved families had already quite enough to bear. No, I would hold my tongue, and be thankful that I had been allowed to stay inside my enchanted bubble with a quiet conscience. And as for Max Gale——

The Clarinet Concerto came to an end, the bright pomp ascending jubilant into a triumph of golden chords. The player switched itself off. In the silence that followed I heard sounds from Phyllida's room. She was up and busy.

I glanced at the clock. Twenty past twelve. She should have been asleep long ago. I went across the hallway to her door.

"Phyllida?"

"Oh, come in, come in!"

She sounded thoroughly edgy and upset. I went in, to find her out of bed and rummaging through a drawer, dragging the contents out anyhow and strewing them on the floor. She was looking enchantingly pretty in some voluminous affair of yellow nylon, with her hair down, and her eyes wide and dark-shadowed. She also looked as if she were on the verge of tears.

"What's up? Are you looking for something?"

"Oh, God!" She jerked open another drawer and rummaged in it, and slammed it shut again. "Not that it'll be *there* ... I would do a damn fool thing like that, wouldn't I?"

I looked at her in some alarm. Phyllida hardly ever swears. "Like what? Lost something?"

"My ring. The diamond. The god-damned Forli blasted diamond. When we were down at the bay. I've only just this moment remembered it, what with everything. I had it on, didn't I? *Didn't* I?"

"Oh, my heaven, yes, you did! But don't you remember, you took it off before we went in the water? Look, stop fussing, Phyl, it's not lost. You put it in your make-up bag, that little zip thing covered with roses. I saw you."

She was at the wardrobe now, feeling in the pockets of the beach coat. "Did I or did I not put it on again after I'd left the water?"

"I don't think so. I don't remember ... No, I'm sure you didn't. I'd have noticed it on your hand. You didn't have it on when we were having coffee up at Godfrey's. But honey, it'll be in the little bag. I know you put it here."

She shoved the coat back, and slammed the wardrobe shut. "That's the whole blasted point! The beastly bag's still down on the beach!"

"Oh, no!"

"It must be! I tell you, it's not here, I've looked everywhere." The bathroom was ajar, and on the floor her beach bag lay in a heap with slippers and towel. She picked up the bag for what was obviously the umpteenth time, turned it upside down, shook it, and let it fall. She kicked over the towel with her foot, then turned to face me, eyes tragic, hands spread like a mourning angel invoking a blessing. "You see? I bloody *left* the thing, on the bloody *beach*!"

"Yes, but listen a minute ..." I thought back rapidly. "Perhaps you did put it back on. After all, you used the zip bag when you did your face. Did you put the ring on then, and take it off again when you washed at Godfrey's? Perhaps you left it in his bathroom."

"I'm sure I didn't. I can't remember a thing about it, and I know that if I *had* the thing on when I washed at Godfrey's, I'd have known it. You can't help knowing," she said ingenuously, "when you're flashing a thing like that about on your hand. Oh, what a *fool* I am! I didn't mean to bring it here at all, but I forgot to put it in the bank, and it's safer on my hand than off it ... Or so I thought! Oh hell, hell, *hell!*"

"Well, look," I said soothingly, "don't start to worry yet. If you didn't put it back on, it's still in the little bag. Where was that when you last saw it?"

"Just where we were sitting. It must have got pushed to one side under the trees or something, and when Max Gale went back for our things he just wouldn't see it. He'd just grab the things and chase after us."

"Probably. He'd be in a hurry."

"That's what I mean." She noticed nothing in my tone, but spoke quite simply, staring at me with those wide, scared eyes. "The wretched thing's just *sitting* there on the sand, and——"

"Well, for heaven's sake don't look like that! It'll be as safe as a house! Nobody'll be there, and if they were, who'd pick up a scruffy plastic bag with make-up in?"

"It's not scruffy, and Leo gave it to me." She began to cry. "If it comes to that, he gave me the beastly ring, and it belongs to his beastly family, and if I lose it——"

"You haven't lost it."

"The tide'll wash it away."

"There's no tide."

"Your foul dolphin'll eat it. *Something*'ll happen to it, I know it will." She had cast reason to the winds now, and was crying quite hard. "Leo had no *business* to give me anything like that and expect me to watch it *all the time!* Diamonds are hell, anyway—if they're not in the bank you feel as miserable as sin, and if they *are* in the bank you're all frustrated, so you simply can't *win*, they're not worth having, and that ring cost thousands and thousands, and it's worse in lire, *millions* of lire," wept Phyl unreasonably, "and there'll be his mother to face, not to mention that ghastly collection of aunts, and did I tell you his uncle's probably going to be a C-Cardinal——"

"Well, honey, this won't exactly wreck his chances, so take a pull at yourself, will you, and—hey! Just what do you think you're doing?"

She had yanked the wardrobe door open again, and was

pulling out a coat. "If you think I'll get a wink, a *single wink* of sleep, while that ring's lying out there——"

"Oh, no, you don't!" I said with great firmness, taking the coat from her and putting it back. "Now, don't be a nit! Of course you're worried stiff, who wouldn't be, but you're certainly not going down there tonight!"

"But I've got to!" Her voice thinned and rose, and she grabbed for the coat again. She was very near to real hysteria.

I said quickly: "You have not. I'll go myself."

"You can't! You can't go alone. It's after midnight!"

I laughed. "So what? It's a nice night, and I'd a darned sight rather take a walk out than see you work yourself into a fit of the screaming abdabs. I don't blame you, I'd be climbing the walls myself! Serves you right for flashing that kind of ice around, my girl!"

"But, Lucy——"

"I mean it. I'll go straight away and get the wretched thing, so for sweet Pete's sake dry your eyes or you'll be fretting yourself into a miscarriage or something, and then Leo *will* have something to say, not to mention his mother and the aunts."

"I'll come with you."

"You'll do no such thing. Don't argue. Get back into bed. Go on ... I know exactly where we were sitting, and I'll take a torch. Now mop up, and I'll make you some Ovaltine or something, and then go. Hurry up now, get *in*!"

I don't often get tough with Phyllida, but she is surprisingly meek when I do. She got in, and smiled shakily.

"You're an angel, you really are. I feel so ashamed of myself, but it's no use, I shan't rest till I've got it ... Look, I've had an idea, couldn't we just ring Godfrey, and ask him to go? Oh, no, he said he was going to be out late, didn't he? Well, what about Max Gale? It's his fault, in a way, for not seeing the thing ... We could ring him up to ask if he'd noticed it, and then he'd *have* to offer to go down——"

"I'm not asking favours of Max Gale."

This time she did notice my tone. I added, hastily: "I'd rather go myself. I honestly don't mind."

"You won't be scared?"

"What's there to be scared of? I don't believe in ghosts. Anyway, it's not so dark as it looks from in here; the sky's thick with stars. I suppose you've got a torch?"

"There's one in the kitchen, on the shelf beside the door. Oh,

90

Lucy, you *are* a saint! I shouldn't have slept a wink without that beastly thing safe in its box!"

I laughed at her. "You should be like me, and get your jewellery you-know-where. Then you could lose the lot down on the beach, and not worry about Leo's beating you."

"If that was all I thought would happen," said Phyllida, with a spice of her usual self, "I'd probably enjoy it. But it's his mother."

"I know. And the aunts. And the Cardinal. Don't come that one over me, my girl, I know darned well they all spoil you to death. Now, stop worrying. I'll bring you the Ovaltine, and you shall have the Grand Cham's diamond safe under your pillow 'or ere your pulse twice beat'. See you."

*   *   *

The woods were still and silent, the clearing full of starlight. The frogs had dived at my approach; the only sound now from the pool was the lap and stir of the lily-pads as the rings of water shimmered through them and set them rocking.

I paused for a moment. I had told Phyllida that I didn't believe in ghosts, and I knew I had no reason to be afraid, but for the life of me I couldn't help glancing towards the place where Yanni had appeared last night, while just for a moment I felt my skin prickle and brush up like a cat's fur.

Next moment, very faintly, I heard the piano. I tilted my head to listen to the thin, falling melodic line that crept down through the trees. I recognised phrases that I had heard last night. It was this, no doubt, that had unconsciously given me pause, and called up poor Yanni for me.

The ghost had gone. The pathway to the beach was just a pathway. But I didn't follow it yet: slowly, rather as if I were breasting water instead of air, I climbed the path to the Castello.

I paused at the edge of the rose garden, hanging back in shadow. The roses smelt heavy and sweet. The music was clear now, but muted, so that I guessed it came from the house rather than the terrace. I recognised another passage, a simple, almost lyrical line that suddenly broke and stumbled in the middle, like a step missed in the dark. I found it disquieting. After a while the pianist stopped, started again, played for another half-minute before he broke off to go back a few bars; then the same long phrase was played over several times before being allowed to flow on unchecked.

The next time he stopped I heard the murmur of voices. Julian Gale's tones carried beautifully; Max replied indistinguishably. Then the piano began again.

He was there, and working. They were both there. As if I had had something proved to me—whatever it was I had come for—I turned away and, with the help of the torch, followed the Castello's own path downhill, through the clearing where I had met Max Gale, and on down the broken steps to the bay.

After the heavy shade of the path, the open beach seemed as light as day. The white crescent of sand was firm and easy walking. As I left the wood I switched off the torch, and went rapidly across the bay to where we had been sitting that morning. The pines, overhanging, made a black pool of shadow, so black that for a moment it looked as if something was lying there. Another body.

But this time I didn't pause. I knew it for a trick of the shadows, no more; just another ghost to fur the skin with gooseflesh; an image painted on the memory, not of the living Yanni this time, but of the dead.

The music sounded faintly from above. I kept the torch switched off in case the flash attracted the Gales' attention, and approached the trees.

Something *was* lying there. Not shadows; it was solid, a long dark bundle-shape, like the thing in the rock-pool. And it was real.

This time the shock really did hit me. I still remember the kick over the heart, the sharp, frightening pain that knocked all the blood in my body into hammering motion, the way a kick starts a motor-cycle engine. The blood slammed in heavy, painful strokes in my head, my fingers, my throat. My hand tightened so convulsively on the torch that the switch went down and the light came on, pinpointing whatever it was that lay there under the pines.

It wasn't a body. It was a long, smoothly-wrapped bundle of something, longer than a man. It was lying just where we had been sitting that morning.

I had my free hand clamped tightly against my ribs, under the left breast. It is a theatrical gesture, but, like all the theatre's clichés, it is based soundly on truth. I believe I felt I must hold my terrified heart from battering its way out of the rib-cage. I must have stood there for several minutes, rigid, unable either to move forward or to run away.

The thing didn't move. There was no sound, other than the distant notes of the piano, and the soft hushing of the sea.

My terror slowly faded. Body or no body, it obviously wasn't going to hurt me, and, I thought grimly, I'd be better facing a dozen bodies than going back to Phyllida without the Forli diamond.

I pointed the torchlight straight at the thing under the trees, and approached it bravely.

The bundle stirred. As my breath whistled sharply in, I saw, in the torchlight, the gleam of a living eye. But then in the split half-second that prevented me from screaming, I saw what—not who—this was. It was the dolphin.

Apollo's child. Amphitryte's darling. The sea-magician. High and dry.

The eye moved, watching me. The tail stirred again, as if trying to beat movement out of the hard earth as it would from water. It struck the edge of the crisping ripples with a splash that seemed to echo right up the rocks.

I tiptoed closer, under the blackness of the pines. "Darling?" I said softly. "What's the matter? Are you hurt?"

The creature lay still, unblinking, the eye liquid and watchful. It was silly to look, as I did, for recognition, but at least I could see no fear of me. I shone the torch carefully over the big body. There seemed to be no wound, or mark of any kind. I examined the sand round about. There was no blood, only a wide, dragged wake where the animal had been hauled or thrown out of the water. Near a pine-root the torchlight caught the pale gleam of Phyllida's make-up bag; I snatched this up; I didn't even look inside, but rammed it into my pocket and then forgot it. Presumably the diamond was safe inside it, but more important now than any diamond was the dolphin, stranded and helpless, a prey for anyone who wanted to hurt him. And that someone did want to hurt him, I very well knew ... Moreover, unless he could be got back into the water, he would die as soon as the sun got up and dried his body out.

I straightened up, trying to force my thoughts into order, and to recall everything I had ever read or known about dolphins. It was little enough. I knew that, like whales, they sometimes stranded themselves for no obvious reason, but that if they were unhurt and could be re-floated fairly soon, they would suffer no ill effects. I knew, too, that they must be kept wet, or the skin cracked and went septic; and that they breathed through an air-hole on the top of the head, and that this must be kept clear.

I shone the torch again. Yes, there was the air-hole, a crescent-shaped, glistening nostril on top of the head. It was open, but half clotted with sand thrown up as the creature had ploughed ashore. I fixed the torch as best I could in the crotch of a pine bough, dipped my hands in the sea, and gently wiped the sand from the hole.

The dolphin's breath was warm on my hands, and this was somehow surprising: the creature was all at once less alien, his friendliness and intelligence at the same time less magical and more touching. It was unthinkable that I might have to watch him die.

I ran my hands over his skin, noticing with fear how rough this was; the breeze was drying it out. I tried to judge the distance I would have to drag him. Now and again a ripple, driven by that same breeze, washed right up to the dolphin's tail, but this was the thinnest film of water licking up from the shallows four yards away. Another few feet out, as I knew, the sand shelved sharply to deeper water beside the rocks. Once get him even half floating, and I should be able easily to manage his weight.

I switched off the torch, then put my arms round the dolphin as far as I could, and tried to pull him. But I couldn't get hold of him; my hands slipped over the faultless streamlining of his body. Nor could I grasp the dorsal fin, and when I tried tugging at his flippers he fidgeted for the first time, and I thought he was going to struggle, and work himself further up the shore. Finally, kneeling, I got my shoulder right against his, and tried to thrust him backwards with all the strength I could muster. But he never moved an inch.

I stood back at length, panting, sweating, and almost in tears. "I can't do it. Sweetie, I can't even *budge* you!" The bright liquid eye watched me silently. Behind him, four yards away, the sea heaved and whispered under the tail of the wind. Four yards; life or death.

I reached the torch down from the tree. "I'll go and get a rope. If I tie it round you, I could *pull* you. Get a leverage round a tree—anything!" I stopped to caress his shoulder, whispering: "I'll hurry, love, I'll run all the way."

But the feel of the dolphin's skin, dry and roughening, made me hesitate. It might take some time to find a rope, or get help. No good going for Godfrey; if he was still out, it would be time lost. And I couldn't go to the Castello. I would have to go all the way home. I had better throw some sea-water over the animal's skin before I left him, to keep him safe while I was away.

I kicked off my sandals and ran into the shallows. But the spray I splashed up barely reached beyond his tail, and (so shallow was the water here) came up full of sand and grit that would dry on him even more disastrously than before.

Then I remembered the plastic bag, stupidly small, but better than nothing. I ran out of the water, dragged the bag from my pocket, shone the torch down, and tipped Phyllida's make-up out on the sand. The Forli diamond fell into the torchlight with a flash and a shimmer. I snatched it up and pushed it on my finger, and dropped the rest of the things back into my pocket, along with the torch. Then I ran back to the sea's edge, and scooped up my pathetic pint of water to throw over the dolphin.

It seemed to take an age. Stooping, straightening, running, tipping, stooping, running, tipping ... When I reached the beast's shoulders I put a hand over the air-hole and poured the water carefully round it: unbelievably, dolphins could drown, and under the circumstances one couldn't expect the right reflexes to be working. When I poured water over his face the first time he blinked, which startled me a little, but after that he watched me steadily, the nearer eye swivelling as I moved to and fro.

At last he seemed wet enough to be safe. I dropped the dripping bag, wiped my hands on my coat, which was probably already ruined beyond repair, pulled on my sandals, and patted the damp shoulder again.

"I'll be back, sweetie, don't worry. I'll be as quick as I can. Keep breathing. And let's pray no one comes."

This was the nearest I had got to admitting, even to myself, why I had been whispering, and why, as soon as I no longer needed the light, I had snapped the torch out.

I ran back across the sand. The piano had stopped, but I could still see the faint glow of light from the open terrace window. Nothing moved on the terrace itself. Then I was in the shadow of the wood, where the path to the Villa Forli went up steeply. Using the torch once more, I clambered breathlessly. The breeze, steady now, had filled the wood with a rustling that drowned my steps.

And now the starlit clearing. The frogs plopped into the pool. The stream glittered in the flying edge of my torchlight. I switched off as I emerged from the trees, and crossed the open space quietly, pausing at the far side of it to get my breath, leaning up against a young oak that stood where the path tunnelled afresh into the black burrow of the woods.

As I came out from under the oak, something moved on the path.

I checked, fingers fumbling clumsily with the torch. It flashed on, catching the edge of a side-stepping figure. A man, only a yard or so away. I would have run straight into him.

The bushes rustled just beside me. Someone jumped. The torch was struck out of my hand. I whipped round, and I think I would have screamed to wake the dead, only he grabbed me, pulled me to him brutally, and his hand came down hard over my mouth.

CHAPTER EIGHT

Pray you tread softly, that the blind mole may not
Hear a foot fall: we now are near his Cell.

IV. 1.

HE was very strong. I struggled and fought, necessarily in silence, but I couldn't do a thing. I must have hurt him, though, in clawing at his hand, for he flinched, and I heard his breath go in sharply. He took the hand away with a hissed "*Keep quiet, will you?*" in English, and then made it certain by jamming my head hard into the front of his jacket, so that I was not only dumb, but blinded, too. His coat was damp, and smelt of the sea. I got the swift impression of other movement near by, but heard nothing above my own and my assailant's breathing, and the thudding of my heart. The pressure of his hand on the back of my head was hurting me, and a button scored my cheek. My ribs, held in the hard embrace of his other arm, felt as if they were cracking.

I stopped fighting and went slack, and straight away the cruel grip eased, but he still held me pressed to him, both arms caught now and firmly pinioned. As his hold relaxed I pulled my head free. If I screamed, they would hear me from the Castello terrace . . . they could be down here in a few seconds . . . surely, even Max Gale——

"Where have you been?" demanded my captor.

I gaped at him. As soon as he saw I had no intention of screaming, he let me go. "*You?*" I said.

"Where have you been?"

I had my hands to my face, rubbing the sore cheeks. "What's that got to do with you?" I asked furiously. "You go a bit far, don't you, Mr. Gale?"

"Have you been up at the Castello?"

"I have not! And if I had——"

"Then you've been to the beach. Why?"

"Is there any reason——?" I began, then stopped. Fright and fury, together, had let me forget for a moment what else had happened that day. Max Gale might have no business to demand an account of my movements, but he might well have the best of reasons for wanting to know them.

Nothing was to be gained by refusing to tell him. I said, rather sulkily: "I went down to get Phyl's ring. She left it on the beach this morning. You needn't look as if you don't believe me: it was in a little bag, and you missed it. There, see?" I flashed the diamond at him, then pushed the hand deep into my coat pocket, almost as if I expected him to grab it from me, and glared up at him. "And now perhaps you'll tell me what *you're* playing at? This game of yours is 'way beyond a joke, let me tell you! It'll be mantraps next, I suppose. You hurt me."

"I'm sorry. I didn't mean to. I thought you were going to scream."

"Good heavens, of course I was! But why should you have minded, if I had?"

"Well, I——" He hesitated. "Anyone might have heard . . . My father . . . It might have startled him."

"Thoughtful of you!" I said tartly. "It didn't matter, did it, if you scared *me* half out of my wits? What a model son you are, aren't you? I'm surprised you could bring yourself to go out so late and leave your father alone! If it comes to that, where've *you* been, that you don't want anyone to know about?"

"Fishing."

"Oh?" The heavily ironic retort that jumped to my lips

97

withered there and died. I said slowly: "But you were up there at the Castello half an hour ago."

"What do you mean? I thought you said you hadn't been near the Castello."

"The noise *you* make with that piano," I said nastily, "you could hear it from the mainland. I heard you from the beach."

"That's impossible." He spoke abruptly, but with a note of puzzlement.

"I tell you I did! You were playing the piano, and then talking to your father. I know your voices. It *was* you."

He was silent for a moment. Then he said slowly: "It sounds to me as if you heard a working session on tape being played through, comments and all. But I still don't see how that could be. My father isn't there. He's away staying the night at a friend's house."

"How far away?"

"If it's anything to do with you, Corfu."

"You must think I've a scream like a steam whistle," I said dryly.

"What? Oh, I . . ." he had the grace to stammer slightly . . . "I'm afraid I did rather say the first thing that came into my head. But it's true that he's not at home."

"And neither were you?" I said. "Well, whoever was playing the tape, it certainly made a wonderful alibi."

"Don't be silly." His laugh was excellently done. He must have some of his father's talent, after all. Possibly only someone as experienced with actors' voices as I could have told that the easy amusement was assumed over some urgent preoccupation. "Your imagination's working overtime, Miss Waring! Please don't go making a mystery out of this. All that'll have happened is that my father's decided for some reason to come home, and he was amusing himself with the tape-recorder. As for myself, I've been out fishing with Adoni . . . And if it's any satisfaction to you, *you* frightened *me* half out of my wits. I'm afraid my reactions were a bit rough. I'm sorry for that. But if someone suddenly breaks out of the dark and runs straight into you, you—well, you act according."

"According to what? Jungle law?" I was still smarting. "I wouldn't have said those reactions were exactly normal, unless you were expecting . . . Just what *were* you expecting, Mr. Gale?"

"I'm not sure." This, at any rate, sounded like the truth. "I thought I heard someone coming up from the beach, fast, and trying not to be heard, but the breeze was covering most of the sounds, and I couldn't be certain. Then the sounds stopped, as if whoever it was was hiding and waiting. Naturally that made me begin to wonder what they might be up to, so I waited, too."

"I only stopped to get my breath. Your imagination's working overtime, Mr. Gale."

"Very probably." I wasn't sure if he had even noticed the gibe. His head was bent, and he seemed to be studying one of his hands, turning it this way and that. "Well, just as I decided I'd been mistaken, you erupted from the trees like a deer on the run. I grabbed you. Pure reflex."

"I see. And I suppose it was pure reflex that you knocked the torch out of my hand before I could see anything?"

"Of course," he said woodenly.

"And that even when you saw who it was, you acted like a—a *Gestapo*?" No reply to that. I can only suppose that excitement and the moment's fright had pumped too much adrenalin into my bloodstream; I think I was a bit 'high' with it. I remember feeling vaguely surprised that I was not in the least afraid of him. At some level, I suppose, I was reasoning that the man (in spite of his dubious bit of adventuring in what Godfrey had called the 'milk run') was hardly a dangerous criminal, and that he obviously intended me no harm: on the conscious level I was damned if I went tamely home now without finding exactly what was going on around here. It had already touched me far too closely to be ignored. The enchanted bubble had never really existed. I was beginning to suspect that there was no such thing.

So I asked, as if it were a matter of purely academic interest: "I still want to know why it should have mattered to you where I'd been? Or that I might recognise you? Or was it the others I wasn't supposed to see?"

I thought for a moment that he wasn't going to answer. From somewhere further up in the wood, an owl called breathily once, and then again. In the pool, a frog tried his voice tentatively for a moment, lost his nerve, and dived again. Max Gale said, quietly: "Others?"

"The men who went past while you were holding me."

"You're mistaken."

"Oh, no, I'm not. There was somebody else there. I saw him beside the path, just as you jumped on me."

99

"Then you probably recognised him as well. That was Adoni, our gardener. You've met him, I believe?"

You wouldn't have thought he was admitting another lie, or even conceding a slight point. The tone was that of a cool, social brush-off. I felt the adrenalin soaring dangerously again as he added, calmly: "He usually comes with me when I go fishing. What's the matter? Don't you believe me?"

I managed to say, quite pleasantly: "I was just wondering why you didn't beach the boat in your own bay. This seems a funny way to come—if you've just been fishing."

"The wind was getting up, and it was easier to come in the other side of the point. And now, if you'll excuse me——"

"You mean," I said, "that you left your boat on *our* side of the point? Tied to our jetty, even? Now, isn't that too bad? I think you'd better go straight down again and move it, Mr. Gale. We don't like trespassers at the Villa Forli."

There was a short, sharp pause. Then, unexpectedly, he laughed. "All right. One to you. But not tonight. It's late, and I've got things to do."

"I suppose you ought to be helping Adoni to carry home the fish? Or would it be more correct to call it 'the catch'?"

That got through. You'd have thought I'd hit him. He made a sudden movement, not towards me, but I felt my muscles tighten, and I think I even backed a pace. I wondered why I had ever thought him a subdued edition of his father. And, quite suddenly, I was scared.

I spoke quickly: "You needn't worry. I don't mean to give you away! Why should I? It's nothing to me, but you must see it's awful to be in the middle of something and now know just what's going on! Oh, yes, I know about it, it was obvious enough. But I'll not say anything—I think too much of Miranda and her mother, and, if it comes to that, of your father, to drag the police back here with a lot more questions. Why should I care what you've got yourself into? But I *do* care about Adoni ... Did you know he's going to marry Miranda? Why did you have to involve him in this? Hasn't there been enough trouble?"

After that first, uncontrollable start, he had listened without movement or comment, but I could see his eyes on me, narrow and intent in the dim light. Now he said, very quietly: "Just what are you talking about?"

"You know quite well. I suppose poor Yanni never got the

100

job done last night, so you've been across there tonight, to the Albanian coast, to do it yourself. Am I right?"

"Where did you get this . . . fantasy?"

"Fantasy, nothing," I said roundly. "Godfrey Manning told me this morning."

"*What?*" If I had got through before, this was straight between the joints of the harness. The word alone sent me back another pace, and this time he followed. I felt my back come up against a tree, and turned aside blindly—I think to run away—but his hand shot out and took my wrist, not hard, but in a grip I couldn't have broken without struggling, and probably not even then. "Manning? *He* told you?"

"Let me go!"

"No, wait a minute. I'm not going to hurt you, don't be scared . . . But you've got to tell me. What did Manning say to you?"

"Let me go, please!"

He dropped the wrist immediately. I rubbed it, though it was not in the least hurt. But I was shaking now. Something had happened that had changed the whole pitch of the scene; in place of the slightly pleasurable bitchiness of the previous exchange, there was now something urgent, hard, and yes, threatening. And it was Godfrey's name that had done it.

Gale repeated: "What did he tell you?"

"About Yanni? That he was a smuggler, and that he would probably have a 'contact' or whatever you call it, who'd get his supplies for him, and that he hoped the police wouldn't tumble to it, because Spiro had been in it too, and it would hurt Maria if it came out."

"That was all?"

"Yes."

"When did he tell you all this?"

"This morning, at the point, before you came down."

"Ah." I heard his breath go out. "Then you weren't up at Manning's house just now?"

"Of course I wasn't! Have you any idea what time it is?"

"I—of course. I'm sorry. I didn't think. I wasn't trying to be offensive. Did Manning tell you that I was Yanni's 'contact'?"

"No. I worked that out for myself."

"You did? How?"

I hesitated. The feeling of fear had gone, and common sense had come back to tell me that I was in no danger. Smuggler or not, he would hardly murder me for this. I said: "I saw Yanni coming up to the Castello last night."

"I ... see." I could almost feel the amazement, the rapid reassessment of the situation. "But you said nothing to the police."

"No."

"Why not?"

I said carefully: "I'm not quite sure. To begin with, I kept quiet because I thought I might be mistaken, and Yanni possibly hadn't been going up to the Castello at all. If I'd thought you'd had anything to do with his death, I'd have told straight away. Then later I realised that there *was* some connection between you and Yanni, and that you'd known he was going out last night."

"How?"

"Because you weren't surprised when you heard he'd been drowned——"

"You noticed that, did you? My mistake. Go on."

"But you *were* shocked. I saw that."

"You see a darned sight too much." He sounded grim. "Was that what made you decide I hadn't killed him?"

"Good heavens, no! It wouldn't have occurred to me that you'd killed him! If I'd thought it was anything but an accident, I'd have told the whole thing straight away! It—it wasn't, was it?"

"Not that I'm aware of. Go on. What else did you see?"

"I saw you go back to the body, and have another look at it."

"Did you, by God? From the path? Careless of me, I thought I was out of view. Who else saw that?"

"Nobody."

"You're sure of that?"

"Pretty well."

"And you said nothing about that, either? Well, well. So it was entirely your own idea that I was smuggling along with Yanni?"

"Yes."

"And now you've found out for certain. Do you still propose to say nothing?"

I said, without challenge, but out of simple curiosity: "How would you make sure of it?"

He said, equally simply: "My dear, I couldn't begin to try. I

102

can only tell you that it's urgent that nobody should know I've been out tonight, nobody at all, and beg you to keep quiet."

"Then don't worry. I will."

There was a short pause. "As easy as that?" he said, in an odd tone.

"I told you—for your father's sake," I said, perhaps a little too quickly, "and for Maria's. The only thing is——"

"Yes?"

"Things go in threes, they say, and if anything should happen to Adoni——"

He laughed. "Nothing shall, I promise you! I couldn't take the responsibility for damaging a work of art like Adoni! We-ell . . ." There was a whole world of relief in the long-drawn syllable. Then his voice changed; it was brisk, easy, normal. "I mustn't keep you any more. Heaven knows what the time is, and you must get home with that treasure trove of yours. I'm sorry I missed it this morning, and gave your sister a bad half-hour . . . And I'm sorry I frightened you just now. To say that I'm grateful is the understatement of the year. You'll let me see you home?"

"There's no need, really, thank you. In any case, hadn't you better get up there to help Adoni?"

"He's all right. Didn't you hear the signal?"

"Signal? But there hasn't been——" I stopped as I saw him smile. "Not the owls? No, really, how corny can you get! Was that really Adoni?"

He laughed. "It was. The robber's mate is home and dry, complete with 'catch'. So come along now, I'll take you home."

"No, really, I——"

"Please. After all, these woods are pretty dark and you were nervous, weren't you?"

"Nervous? No, of course not!"

He looked down in surprise. "Then what in the world were you racing back like that for?"

"Because I——" I stopped dead. The dolphin. I had forgotten the dolphin. The breeze, riffling the treetops, breathed gooseflesh along my skin. I thought of the dolphin, drying in it, back there on the beach. I said quickly: "It was so late, and Phyl was worrying. Don't bother, please, I'll go alone. Good night."

But as I reached the tunnel of trees, he caught me up. "I'd sooner see you safely home. Besides, you were quite right about shifting the boat; I'd rather have her nearer to hand in the morning. I'll take her across into the lee of the pines."

For the life of me, I couldn't suppress a jerk of apprehension. He felt it, and stopped.

"Just a minute."

His hand was on my arm. I turned. It was very dark under the trees.

He said: "You've found out more about me than is quite comfortable. It's time you were a little bit honest about yourself, I think. Did you meet anyone down in the bay?"

"No."

"See anyone?"

"N-no."

"Quite sure? This is important."

"Yes."

"Then why don't you want me to go down there?"

I said nothing. My throat was stiff and dry as cardboard. Tears of strain, fear, and exhaustion were not very far away.

"Look," he said, urgently and not unkindly, "I have to know. Some day I'll tell you why. Damn it, I've got to trust *you*; what about your trusting me for a change? Something did happen down there to scare you, didn't it? It sent you running up here like a hare in front of a gun. Now, what was it? Either you tell me what it was, or I go down and look for myself. Well?"

I threw in my cards. I said shakily: "It was the dolphin."

"The dolphin?" he echoed, blankly.

"It's in the bay."

There was a pause, then he said, with a sharpness that was part exasperation, part relief: "And am I supposed to be going down there to shoot it in the middle of the night? I told you before that I'd never touched the beast!" He added, more kindly: "Look, you've had a grim sort of day, and you're frightened and upset. Nobody's going to hurt your dolphin, so dry your eyes, and I'll take you back home now. He can look after himself, you know."

"He can't. He's on the beach."

"He's what?"

"He's stranded. He can't get away."

"Well, my God, you don't *still* think I'd do him any harm——?" He stopped, and seemed for the first time to take in what I had been telling him. "*Stranded?* You mean the creature's actually beached?"

104

"Yes. High and dry. He'll die. I've been trying and trying to move him, and I can't. I was running just now to get a rope, that's why I was hurrying. If he's out of water too long the wind'll dry him, and he'll die. And all this time we've been wasting——"

"Where is he?"

"The other side, under the pines. What are you—oh!" This was an involuntary cry as his hand tightened on my arm and swung me round. "What are you doing?"

"Don't worry, this isn't another assault. Now listen, there's a rope in my boat. I'll go down and get it, and I'll be with you as soon as I can. Get away back to your dolphin now, and wait for me. Can you keep him going another twenty minutes? Good. We'll manage him between us, don't worry. But"—a slight pause—"be very quiet, do you mind?"

Before I could reply, he was gone, and I heard him making a swift but still stealthy way back the way he had come.

CHAPTER NINE

To the elements
Be free, and fare thou well.
v.1.

THERE was no time for doubt or questioning. That could come later. I obeyed him, flying back down the path to the beach, back across the pale sand to where the big bulk still lay motionless.

The dark eye watched. He was alive. I whispered: "It's all right now, he's coming," and went straight back to my scooping and tipping of sea-water. If I noticed that I hadn't bothered, even in my thoughts, to specify the 'he', that was another question that could wait till later.

He came, sooner than I had expected. A small motor-boat came nosing round the bay, without her engine, just with a dip and splash of oars as she was poled gently along. The breeze and the lapping of the sea on the rocks covered all sound until the boat was a rocking shadow within yards of me. I saw him stand up then, and lever it nearer the shore. Timber grated gently on rock, and he stepped out, making fast to a young pine, and then he was beside me on the sand, with a coil of rope over his arm.

"Good God. How did he get out here?"

"They do," I said, "I've read about it. Sometimes a storm blows them in, but sometimes they get their radar-beams fogged up, or something, and they come in at a fast lick and before they know where they are, they're high and dry. We're lucky there's only a foot or so of tide, or the water might have been miles away from him by now. Can you move him, d'you think?"

"I can try." He stooped over the animal. "Trouble is, you can't really get a hold. Didn't you have a torch?"

"I dropped it when you savaged me up in the wood."

"So you did. There's one in the boat—no, perhaps not, we'll do without. Now, can you get to his other side?"

Together we fought to grasp and lift the dolphin, and with some success, for we did drag and shove him a foot or so down-shore. But the dolphin himself defeated us; frightened, possibly, of the man's presence, or hurt by our tugging and by the friction of sand and pebbles, he began to struggle, spasmodically but violently; and at the end of the first strenuous minutes we had gained only a foot. I was exhausted, and Max Gale was breathing very hard.

"No good." He stood back. "He weighs a ton, and it's like trying to get hold of an outsize greased bomb. It'll have to be the rope. Won't it hurt him?"

"I don't know, but we'll have to try it. He'll die if he stays here."

"True enough. All right, help me get it round the narrow bit above the tail."

The dolphin lay like a log, his eye turning slowly back to watch us as we bent to tackle the tail-rope. Without the torch it was impossible to tell, but I had begun to imagine that the eye wasn't so bright or watchful now. The tail felt heavy and cold, like something already dead. He never flickered a muscle as we fought to lift and put a loop round it.

"He's dying," I said, on a sort of gulp. "That fight must have finished him." I dashed the back of my hand over my eyes, and bent to the job. The rope was damp, and horrible to handle, and the dolphin's tail was covered with coarse sand.

"You do tear yourself up rather, don't you?"

I looked up at him as he worked over the loop. His tone was

not ungentle, but I got the impression from it that half his mind was elsewhere: he cared nothing for the dolphin, but wanted merely to get this over, and get back himself to whatever his own queer and shady night's work had been.

Well, fair enough. It was good of him to have come at all. But some old instinct of defensiveness made me say a little bitterly:

"It seems to me you can be awfully happy in this life if you stand aside and watch and mind your own business, and let other people do as they like about damaging themselves and each other. You go on kidding yourself that you're impartial and tolerant and all that, then all of a sudden you realise you're dead, and you've never been alive at all. Being alive hurts."

"So you have to break your heart over an animal who wouldn't even know you, and who doesn't even recognise you?"

"Someone has to bother," I said feebly. "Besides, he does recognise me, he knows me perfectly well."

He let that one pass, straightening up from the rope. "Well, there it is, that's the best we can do, and I'm hoping to heaven we can get it off again before he takes off at sixty knots or so ... Well, here goes. Ready?"

I dropped my coat on the sand, kicked off my sandals, and splashed into the shallows beside him. We took the strain of the rope together. It didn't even strike me as odd that we should be there, hands touching, working together as naturally as if we had done it every day of our lives. But I was very conscious of the touch of his hand against mine on the rope.

The dolphin moved an inch or two; another inch; slid smoothly for a foot; stuck fast. This way, he seemed even heavier to haul, a dead weight on a rope that bit our hands and must surely be hurting him abominably, perhaps even cutting the skin ...

"Easy, now," said Max Gale in my ear.

We relaxed. I let go the rope, and splashed shorewards. "I'll go and take a look at him. I'm so afraid he's——"

"*Blast!*" This from Gale, as the dolphin heaved forward suddenly, beating with his tail, slapping up water and sand. I heard the rope creak through Gale's hands, and another sharp curse from him as he plunged to keep his footing.

I ran back. "I'm sorry ... Oh! What is it?" He had twisted the rope round his right hand and wrist, and I saw how he held his left arm up, taut, the fingers half clenched as if it had hurt him. I remembered how he had examined it, up in the glade. This must be why he had made such heavy weather of fixing the rope, and had been unable to shift the dolphin.

"Your hand?" I said sharply. "Is it hurt?"

"No. Sorry, but I nearly went in then. Well, at least the beast's still alive. Come on, we'll have another go before he really does take fright."

He laid hold once more, and we tried again. This time the dolphin lay still, dead weight again, moving slowly, slowly, till the lost ground was regained; but then he stuck once more, apparently immovable.

"There must be a ridge or something, he sticks every time." Gale paused to brush the sweat out of his eyes. I saw him drop his left hand from the rope and let it hang.

"Look," I said tentatively, "this'll take all night. Couldn't we possibly—I mean, could the *boat* tow him out ... with the engine?"

He was silent for so long that I lost my nerve, and said hurriedly: "It's all right, I do understand. I—I just thought, if Adoni really had got safe in, it wouldn't matter. Forget it. It was marvellous of you to bother at all, with your hand and everything. Perhaps ... if I just stay here all night and keep him damp, and if you could ... *do* you think you could ring Phyl for me and tell her? You could say you saw me from the terrace, and came down? And if you could come back in the morning, when it doesn't matter, with the boat, or with Adoni ..." He had turned and was looking down at me. I couldn't see him except as a shadow against the stars. "If you wouldn't mind?" I finished.

"We'll use the boat now," he said, abruptly. "What do we do—make the rope fast to the bows, and then back her out slowly?"

I nodded eagerly. "I'll stay beside him till he's floated. I'll probably have to hold him upright in the water till he recovers. If he rolls, he'll drown. The air-hole gets covered, and they have to breathe terribly often."

"You'll be soaked."

"I'm soaked now."

"Well, you'd better have my knife. Here. If you have to cut the rope, cut it as near his tail as you can."

I stuck the knife in my belt, pirate-wise, then splashed back to where the dolphin lay. It wasn't my imagination, the lovely dark eye was duller, and the skin felt harsh and dry again. I put a hand on him, and bent down.

"Only a minute now, sweetheart. Don't be frightened. Only a minute."

"Okay?" called Max softly, from the boat, which was bobbing a few yards from shore. He had fixed the rope; it trailed through the water from the dolphin's tail to a ring on the bows.

"Okay," I said.

The engine started with a splutter and then a throbbing that seemed to fill the night. My hand was on the dolphin's body still ... Not even a tremor; boats' engines held no terrors for him. Then the motor steadied down to a mutter, and the boat began to back quietly out from shore.

The rope lifted, vibrated, with the water flying from it in shining spray; then it tightened. The engine's note quickened; the rope stretched, the starlight running and dripping along it. The loop, fastened just where the great bow of the tail springs out horizontally from the spine, seemed to bite into the beast's flesh. It was very tight; the skin was straining; it must be hurting vilely.

The dolphin made a convulsive movement, and my hand clenched on the knife, but I kept still. My lip bled where I was biting on it, and I was sweating as if I was being hurt myself. The boat's engine beat gently, steadily; the starlight ran and dripped along the rope ...

The dolphin moved. Softly, smoothly, the huge body began to slide backwards down the sand towards the water. With my hand still on the loop of the tail-rope, I went with it.

"It's working!" I said breathlessly. "Can you keep it very slow?"

"Right. That okay? Sing out as soon as he's afloat, and I'll cast off here."

The dolphin slithered slowly backwards, like a vessel beginning its run down the launching-ramp. The grating of sand and broken shells under his body sounded as loud to me as the throbbing engine a few yards out to sea. Now, at last, he touched water ... was drawn through the crisping ripples ... was slowly, slowly, gaining the sea. I followed him as he slid deeper. The ripples washed over my feet, my ankles, my knees; the hand that I kept on the loop of rope was under water to the wrist.

And now we had reached the place where the bottom shelved

109

more steeply. All in a moment I found myself standing nearly breast-deep, gasping as the water rose round me in the night chill. The dolphin, moving with me, rocked as the water began to take his weight. Another few seconds, and he would be afloat. He only moved once, a convulsive, flapping heave that twanged the rope like a bow-string and hurt my hand abominably, so that I cried out, and the engine shut to a murmur as Max said sharply:

"Are you hurt?"

"No. Go on. It held him."

"How far now?"

"Nearly deep enough. He's quiet now, I think he's . . . Oh, God, I think he's dead! Oh, Max . . ."

"Steady, my dear, I'll come. Hold him, we'll float him first. Say when."

"Nearly . . . *Right! Stop!*"

The engine shut off, as suddenly as if a soundproof door had slammed. The dolphin's body floated past me, bumping and wallowing. I braced myself to hold him. Max had paid out the rope, and was swiftly poling the boat back to her mooring under the pines. I heard the rattle of a chain as he made fast, and in another few moments he was beside me in the water, with the slack of the rope looped over his arm.

"How goes it? Is he dead?"

"I don't know. I don't know. I'll hold him up while you get the rope off."

"Turn his head to seaward first, just in case . . . Come along, old chap, round you come . . . There. Fine. Now hang on, my dear, I'll be as quick as I can."

The dolphin lay motionless in my arms, the air-hole flaccid and wide open, just out of water, his body rolling heavily, like a leaky boat about to founder. "You're all right now," I told him, in an agonised whisper that he certainly couldn't hear, "you're in the sea . . . the *sea*. You can't die now . . . you can't . . ."

"Stop worrying." Max's voice came, cheerfully brisk, from the other end of the dolphin. "St. Spiridion looks after his own. He is a bit sub., poor beast, isn't he? However, heaven keep him so till I've got this damned rope off him. Are you cold?"

"Not very," I said, teeth chattering.

As he bent over the rope again, I thought I felt the dolphin stir against me. Next moment I was sure. The muscles flexed under the skin, a slow ripple of strength ran along the powerful back, a flipper stirred, feeling the water, using it, taking his weight . . .

"He's moving!" I said excitedly. "He's all right! Oh, Max—quick—if he takes off now——"

"If he takes off now, we'll go with him. The rope's wet, I can't do a thing. I'll have to cut it. Knife, please."

As he slid the blade in under the rope and started to saw at it, the dolphin came to life. The huge muscles flexed smoothly once, twice, against me, then I saw the big shoulders ripple and bunch. The air-hole closed.

I said urgently: "Quick! He's going!"

The dolphin pulled out of my arms. There was a sudden surge of cold water that soaked me to the breast, as the great body went by in a splendid diving roll, heading straight out to sea. I heard Max swear sharply, and there was a nearer, secondary splash and swell, as he disappeared in his turn, completely under the water. The double wash swept over me, so that I staggered, almost losing my footing, and for one ghastly moment I thought that Max, hanging grimly on to the rope, had been towed straight out to sea in the dolphin's wake, like a minnow on a line. But as I regained my own balance, staggering back towards shallower water, he surfaced beside me, waist-deep and dripping, with the cut loop in his hand, and the rope trailing.

I gripped his arm, almost crying with relief and excitement. "Oh, Max!" I staggered again, and his soaking arm came round me. I hardly noticed. I was watching the dark, starry sea where, far out, a trail of sea-fire burned and burst in long, joyous leaps and curves, and vanished into the blackness . . .

"Oh, Max . . . Look, there he goes, d'you see the light? There . . . he's gone. He's gone. Oh, wasn't it *marvellous*?"

For the second time that night I felt myself gripped, and roughly silenced, but this time by his mouth. It was cold, and tasted of salt, and the kiss seemed to last for ever. We were both soaked to the skin, and chilled, but where our bodies met and clung I could feel the quick heat of his skin and the blood beating warm against mine. We might as well have been naked.

He let me go, and we stood there staring at one another.

I pulled myself together with an effort. "What was that, the forfeit for the roses?"

"Hardly. Call it the climax of a hell of a night." He pushed

111

the soaking hair back off his forehead, and I saw him grin. "The recreation of the warrior, Miss Waring. Do you mind?"

"You're welcome." *Take it lightly, I thought, take it lightly.* "You and Adoni must have had yourselves quite a time out fishing."

"Quite a time." He was not trying to take it any way at all; he merely sounded cheerful, and decidedly pleased with himself. "As a matter of fact, that was the pent-up feelings of a hell of a week. Didn't you see it coming? My father did."

"Your father? After that first meeting? I don't believe you. You looked as if you'd have liked to lynch me."

"My feelings," he said carefully, "could best be described as mixed. And damn it, if you will persist in being half naked every time you come near me——"

"Max Gale!"

He laughed at me. "Didn't they ever tell you that men were only human, Lucy Waring? And some a bit more human than others?"

"If you call it human. You flatter yourself."

"All right, darling, we'll call it the forfeit for the roses. You took a fair number, didn't you? Splendid. Come here."

"Max, you're impossible ... Of all the complacent—this is ridiculous! What a time to *choose* ..."

"Well, my love, since you spark like a cat every time I come near you, what can I do but duck you first?"

"Shows what a lot you know about electricity."

"Uh-huh. No, keep still a minute. You pack a pretty lethal charge, don't you?"

"You could blow a few fuses yourself, if it comes to that ... For pity's sake, we must be mad." I pushed him away. "Come on out. I'd love to die with you and be buried in one grave, but not of pneumonia, it's not romantic ... *No*, Max! I admit I owe you anything you like, but let's reckon it up on dry land! Come on *out*, for goodness' sake."

He laughed, and let me go. "All right. Come on. Oh, God, I've dropped the rope ... no, here it is. And that's to pay for, too, let me tell you; a brand new sisal rope, sixty feet of it——"

"You're not the only one. This frock cost five guineas, and the sandals were three pounds ten, and I don't suppose they'll ever be quite the same again."

"I'm perfectly willing to pay for them," said Max cheerfully, stopping in eighteen inches of water.

"I'm sure you are, but it's not your bill. Oh, darling, don't be *crazy*, come *out*!"

"Pity. Who do you suppose settles the dolphin's accounts? Apollo, or the Saint? I think I'd opt for Apollo if I were you. Of course, if you've lost your sister's diamond it'll step the bill up quite a lot."

"*Murder!* Oh, no, here it is." The great marquise flashed blue in the starlight. "Oh, Max, seriously, thank you most awfully—you were so wonderful . . . I've been such a fool! As if you could ever——"

His hand tightened warningly on my arm, and in the same moment I saw a light, a small dancing light, like that of an electric torch, coming round the point along the path from the Villa Rotha. It skipped along the rocks, paused on the moored boat, so that for the first time I saw her name, *Ariel*; then it glanced over the water, and caught us, dripping and bedraggled, splashing out of the shallows. We were also, by the time it caught us, at least four feet apart.

"Great God in heaven!" said Godfrey's voice. "What goes on? Gale—Lucy . . . you're soaked, both of you! Is this another accident, for heaven's sake?"

"No," said Max. "What brought you down?"

His tone was about as informative, and as welcoming, as a blank wall with broken glass on the top. But Godfrey seemed not to have noticed. He had already jumped lightly down from the rocks to the sand beneath the pines. I saw the torchlight pause again, then rake the place where the dolphin had lain, and the wide, gouged track where he had been dragged down to the sea. My coat lay there in a huddle, with the sandals kicked off anyhow.

"For pity's sake, what gives?" Godfrey sounded distinctly alarmed, and very curious. "Lucy, you haven't had trouble, have you? Did you get the diamond?"

"How did you know that?" I asked blankly.

"Good God, Phyl rang up, of course. She said you'd come down hours ago, and she was worried. I said I'd come and look for you. I'd only just got in." The torchlight fingered us both again, and rested on Max. "What's happened?"

"Don't flash that thing in my face," said Max irritably. "Nothing's happened, at least not in the sense you mean. That dolphin of yours got itself stranded. Miss Waring was trying to heave it back into the water, and couldn't manage, so I brought

113

the boat along and towed the beast out to sea. We got drenched in the process."

"You mean to tell me"—Godfrey sounded frankly incredulous—"that you brought your boat out at this time of night to rescue *a dolphin?*"

"Wasn't it good of him?" I put in eagerly.

"Very," said Godfrey. He hadn't taken his eyes off Max. "I could have sworn I heard you go out some time ago."

"I thought you were out yourself?" said Max. "And had only just come in?"

Here we were again, I thought, the stiff-backed dogs warily circling. But it might be that Max's tone was repressive only because he was talking through clenched teeth—owing to cold, rather than emotion—because he added, civilly enough: "I said 'along', not 'out'. We went out, as it happened, some time after ten. We got in a few minutes ago. Adoni had just gone up when Miss Waring came running. I was still in the boat."

Godfrey laughed. "I'm sorry, I didn't mean to belittle the good deed! What a piece of luck for Lucy and the dolphin!"

"Yes, wasn't it?" I said. "I was just wondering what on earth to do, when I heard Mr. Gale. I'd have come for you, but Phyl had said you wouldn't be there."

"I wasn't." I thought he was going to say something further, but he changed it to: "I went out about ten-thirty, and I'd only just got into the house when the telephone rang. *Did* you find the ring?"

"Yes, thank you. Oh, it's been quite a saga, you've no idea!"

"I'm sorry I missed it," he said, "I'd have enjoyed the party."

"I enjoyed it myself," said Max. "Now, look, to hell with the civilities, you'll have to hear it all some other time. If we're not to die of pneumonia, we've got to go. Where are your shoes, Miss Waring? Oh, thanks," this as Godfrey's torch picked them out, and he handed them to me. "Get them on quickly, will you?"

"What's this?" Godfrey's voice altered sharply.

"My coat." I paid very little attention to his tone; I was shivering freely now, and engaged in the very unpleasant struggle to get my sandals on over wet and sandy feet. "Oh, and there's Phyl's bag. Mr. Gale, would you mind——?"

"That's blood!" said Godfrey. He was holding the coat up, and his torch shone, powerful as a headlamp, on the sleeve. I looked up, startled.

It was indeed blood. One sleeve of the coat was streaked with it.

I felt, rather than saw, Max stiffen beside me. The torch beam started its swing towards him. I said, sharply, "*Please* put the torch out, Godfrey! I don't feel decent in this sopping dress. Give me the coat, please. Yes, it's blood ... The dolphin had got a cut from a stone or something; it bled all over me before I saw it. I'll be lucky if I ever get the stain out."

"Hurry up," said Max brusquely, "you're shivering. Put this round you. Come on, we'll have to go."

He slung the coat round my shoulders. My teeth were chattering now like a typewriter; the coat was no comfort at all over the soaked and clinging dress. "Y-yes," I said, "I'm coming. I'll tell you about it when I see you, Godfrey. Th-thanks for coming down."

"Good night," said Godfrey. "I'll come over tomorrow and see how you are."

He turned back into the shadow of the pines. I saw the torch-light move slowly over the ground where the dolphin had lain, before it dodged once again up on to the rocks.

Max and I went briskly across the sand. The wind blew cold on our wet clothing.

"The coat cost nine pounds fifteen," I said, "and *that* bill's yours. That dolphin wasn't bleeding. What have you done to your hand?"

"Nothing that won't mend. Here, this way."

We were at the foot of the Castello steps and I would have gone past, but he put out a hand and checked me.

"You can't go all the way home in those things. Come on up."

"Oh, no, I think I'd better——"

"Don't be silly, why not? Manning'll telephone your sister. So can you, if it comes to that. And I'm not going to escort you all the way over there and then tramp back myself in these. What's more, these blasted boots are full of water."

"You might have drowned."

"So I might. And how much would that have been to Apollo's account?"

"You know how much," I said, not lightly at all, but not for him to hear.

CHAPTER TEN

He is drunk now; where had he wine?
v. 1.

THE terrace was empty, but one of the long windows stood open, and Max led the way in through this.

The room was lit only by one small shaded lamp on a low table, and looked enormous and mysterious, a cave full of shadows. The piano showed its teeth vaguely near a darkened window, and the unlit stove and the huge gramophone loomed like sarcophagi in some dim museum.

Sir Julian sat in an arm-chair beside the lamp, which cast an almost melodramatic slant of light on the silver hair and emphatic brow. The white cat on his knee, and the elegant hand that stroked it, completed the picture. The effect was stagey in the extreme. Poe's *Raven*, I thought appreciatively; all it needs is the purple drapes, and the croaking from the shadows over the door . . .

In the same moment I became aware of other, even less comfortable stage effects than these. On the table at his elbow, under the lamp, stood a bottle of Turkish gin, two-thirds empty, a jug of water, and two glasses. And Sir Julian was talking to himself. He was reciting from *The Tempest*, the speech where Prospero drowns his book; he was saying it softly, an old magician talking half to himself, half to the heavenly powers from whose kingdom he was abdicating. I had never heard him do it better. And if anyone had wanted to know how much sheer technique —as opposed to nightly sweat and blood in front of the lights— was worth, here was the answer. It was doubtful if Sir Julian Gale even knew what he was saying. He was very drunk indeed.

Max had stopped dead just inside the window, with me close behind him, and I heard him make some sort of sound under his breath. Then I saw that Sir Julian was not alone. Adoni detached himself from the thicker darkness beyond the lamp, and came forward. He was dressed, like Max, in a fisherman's sweater and boots, rough clothing which only served to emphasise his startling good looks. But his face was sharp with anxiety.

"Max——" he began, then stopped abruptly as he saw me, and the state we were both in. "It was *you*? What's happened?"

"Nothing that matters," said Max shortly.

This wasn't the time to choose words, or, certainly, to resent them. So much was made more than ever obvious as he advanced into the light, and I saw him clearly for the first time that night. Whatever aggressive high spirits had prompted the little interlude there in the sea had vanished abruptly; he looked not only worried now, but angry and ashamed, and also very tired indeed. His left hand was thrust deep into his trouser-pocket, and there was some rag—a handkerchief, perhaps—twisted round the wrist, and blotched with blood.

Sir Julian had turned his head at the same time.

"Ah, Max . . ." Then he, too, saw me, and the hand which had been stroking the cat lifted in a graceful, practised gesture that looked as natural as breathing. "*Most sure, the goddess, On whom*—no, we had that before, didn't we? But how delightful to see you again, Miss Lucy . . . Forgive me for not getting up; the cat, as you see . . ." His voice trailed away uncertainly. It seemed he was dimly realising that there was need of more excuse than the cat would provide. A smile, loose enough to be disturbing, slackened his mouth. "I was having some music. If you'd care to listen . . ."

The hand moved, not very steadily, to the switch of the tape-recorder which stood on a chair beside him, but Adoni stooped quickly and laid a hand over it, with a gentle phrase in Greek. Sir Julian gave up the attempt, and sank back in his chair, nodding and smiling. I saw with horrified compassion that the nod had changed to a tremor which it cost him an effort to check.

"Who's been here, father?" asked Max.

The actor glanced up at him, then away, with a look that might, in a less distinguished face, have been called shifty. "Been here? Who should have been here?"

"Do you know, Adoni?"

The young man lifted his shoulders. "No. He was like this when I got in. I didn't know there was any in the house."

"There wasn't. I suppose he was alone when you got in? You'd hardly have given me the 'all clear' otherwise." He glanced down at his father, who was taking not the slightest notice of the conversation, but had retreated once more into some private world of his own, some gin-fumed distance apparently lit by strong ambers and swimming in a haze of poetry. "Why did he come back, I wonder? He hasn't told you that?"

117

"He said something about Michael Andiakis being taken ill, but I haven't had time to get anything more out of him. He's not been talking sense ... he keeps trying to switch that thing on again. It was going when I got up to the house. I got a fright; I thought someone was here with him."

"Someone certainly has been." Max's voice was tight and grim. "He didn't say how he got back from town?"

Adoni shook his head. "I did think of telephoning Andiakis' house to ask, but at this time of night ..."

"No, you can't do that." He bent over his father's chair and spoke gently and clearly. "Father. Who's been here?"

Sir Julian, starting out of his dreams, glanced up, focused, and said, with dignity: "There were matters to discuss."

His enunciation was as faultless as ever; the only thing was, you could hear him working to keep it so. His hands lay motionless now on the cat's fur, and there, again, you could see the controls being switched on. The same with Max, who had himself well in hand now, but I could hear the effort that the patient tone was costing him. Watching them, I felt myself so shaken with compassion and love that it seemed it was that, and not my wet clothes, which made me shiver.

"Naturally," said Sir Julian clearly, "I had to ask him in when he had driven me home. It was very good of him."

Max and Adoni exchanged glances. "Who had?"

No reply. Adoni said: "He won't answer anything straight. It's no use."

"It's got to be. We've got to know who this was and what he's told him."

"I doubt if he told him much. He wouldn't say anything to me, only tried to turn the tape on, and talked on and on about the story you are writing the music for, you know, the old story of the island that he was telling Miranda and Spiro."

Max pushed the damp hair off his brow with a gesture almost of desperation. "We've got to find out—now, before he passes out. He knew perfectly well where we were going. He agreed to stay out of the way. My God, I was sure he could be trusted now. I thought he'd be safe with Michael. Why the *hell* did he come home?"

"Home is where the heart is," said Sir Julian. "When my wife died, the house was empty as a lord's great kitchen without a fire in it. Lucy knows, don't you, my dear?"

"Yes," I said. "Shall I go, Max?"

"No, please . . . if you don't mind. If you'll please stay. Look, father, it's all right now. There's only me and Adoni and Lucy. You can tell us about it. Why didn't you stay at Michael's?"

"Poor Michael was playing a very interesting game, Steinitz gambit, and I lost a rook in the first few minutes. Do you play chess, my dear?"

"I know the moves," I said.

"Five moves would have done it. White to play, and mate in five moves. A foregone conclusion. But then he had the attack."

"What sort of attack?" asked Max.

"I had no idea that his heart wasn't all it should be, for all he never drinks. I am quite aware that this is one reason why you like me to visit Michael, but a drink occasionally, for purely social reasons, never does the least harm. My heart is as strong as a bell. As strong as a bell. One's heart," added Sir Julian, with the air of one dismissing the subject, "is where the home is. Good night."

"Just a minute. You mean Michael Andiakis has died of a heart attack? I *see*. I'm sorry, father. No wonder you felt you needed——"

"No, *no*! Who said he had died? Of course he didn't, I was there. They have no telephone, so it was a good thing, the doctor said so, a very good thing. But then if I hadn't been there, I doubt if Michael would have had the attack at all. He always did get too excitable over our little game. Poor Michael."

"You went to fetch the doctor?"

"I told you," said his father impatiently. "Why can't you listen? I think I'd like to go to bed."

"What happened when the doctor came?"

"He put Michael to bed, and I helped him." It was the first direct answer he had given, and he seemed to feel obscurely that something was wrong, for he gave that sidelong look at his son before going on: "It's as well that I'm as sound as a bell myself, though I have never understood why bells should be particularly—particularly sound. Sweet bells jangled, out of tune and harsh. Then I went to get the doctor." He paused. "I mean the daughter. Yes, the daughter."

Adoni said: "There's a married daughter who lives in Capodistrias Street. She has three children. If she had to bring them with her, there would be no room for Sir Gale to stay."

"I see. How did you get the lift back, father?"

"Well, I went to Karamanlis' garage, of course." Sir Julian

119

suddenly sounded sober, and very irritable. "Really, Max, I don't know why you talk as if I'm incapable of looking after myself! Please try to remember that I lived here before you were born! I thought Leander might oblige me, but he was away. There was only one boy on duty, but he offered to get his brother to take me. We had a very interesting chat, very interesting indeed. I knew his uncle, Manoulis was the name. I remember once, when I was at Avra——"

"Was it Manoulis who brought you home?"

Sir Julian focused. "Home?"

"Back here?" amended Max quickly.

The older man hesitated. "The thing was, I had to ask him in. When he came in for petrol and saw me there, you might say he had to offer the lift, but all the same, one has to be civil. I'm sorry, Max."

"It's all right, I understand. Of course one must. He brought you home, and you felt you'd have to ask him in, so you bought the gin?"

"Gin?" Sir Julian was drifting again. I thought I could see something struggling in his face, some intelligence half drowned with gin and sleep, holding on by a gleam of cunning. "That's Turkish gin, too, terrible stuff, God knows what they put in it. It was what he said he liked ... We stopped at that taverna— Constantinos' it used to be, but I forget the name now—two miles out of Ipsos. I think he must have guessed there wouldn't be any in the house."

Max was silent. I couldn't see his face.

Adoni broke the pause. "Max, look." I had seen him stoop to pick something up, and now he held out a hand, with some small object on the palm; a cigarette stub. "It was down there, by the stove. It's not one of yours, is it?"

"No." Max picked the thing up, and held it closer to the light. Adoni said: "It is, isn't it?"

"Obviously." Their eyes met again, over the old man's head. There was a silence, in which the cat suddenly purred. " '*Thing to discuss.*' " Max quoted it softly, but with a new note in his voice that I found frightening. "What the sweet hell can *he* have wanted to discuss with my father?"

"This meeting," said Adoni, "could it be accidental?"

"It must have been. He was driving by, and picked my father up. Pure chance. Who could have foreseen that? Damn and damn and damn."

"And getting him . . . like this?"

"Letting him get like this. There's a difference. That can't have been deliberate Nobody knew he was like this except us, and Michael and the Karithis'."

Adoni said: "Maybe he's been talking this sort of nonsense all evening. Maybe *he* couldn't get any sense out of him, either."

"He couldn't get any sense out of me," said Sir Julian, with intense satisfaction.

"Oh, my God," said Max, "let's hope he's right." He flicked the cigarette butt back towards the stove, and straightened his shoulders. "Well, I'll get him to bed. Be a good chap and look after Miss Lucy, will you? Show her the bathroom—the one my father uses is the least repulsive, I think. Find her a towel and show her a spare bedroom—the one Michael sleeps in. There's an electric fire there."

"All right, but what about your hand? Haven't you seen to it at all?"

"Not yet, but I will in a moment . . . Go on, man, don't fuss. Believe me, I'd fuss plenty if I thought it was serious; I'm a pianist of a sort, don't forget! Lucy, I'm sorry about this. Will you go with him now?"

"Of course."

"This way," said Adoni.

The massive door swung shut behind us, and our steps rattled across the chequer-board marble of the hall floor.

It would have taken Dali and Ronald Searle, working overtime on alternate jags of mescal and Benzedrine, to design the interior of the Castello dei Fiori. At one end of a hall was a massive curved staircase, with a wrought-iron banister and bare stone treads. The walls were panelled in the darkest possible oak, and what small rugs lay islanded on the marble sea were (as far as I could judge in the gloom) done in uniform shades of drab and olive-green. A colossal open fireplace, built for roasting oxen whole, by men who had never roasted, and would never roast, an ox whole in their lives, half-filled one wall. The hearth of this bristled with spits and dogs and tongs and cauldrons and a hundred other mediæval kitchen gadgets whose functions I couldn't even guess at; they looked like—and probably were—instruments of torture. For the rest, the hall was cluttered like a bargain basement: the Gales must have thrown most of the furniture out of their big living-room to clear the acoustics—or perhaps merely in the interests of sane living—

and as a result the hall was crammed full of enormous, over-stuffed furniture in various shades of mud, with innumerable extras in the way of bamboo tables, Chinese screens, and what-nots in spindly and very shiny wood. I thought I glimpsed a harmonium, but might have been wrong, because there was a full-sized organ, pipes and all, in the darkness beyond a fret-work dresser and a coat-rack made of stags' antlers. There was certainly a harp, and a small forest of pampas grass stuck in what I am sure was the severed foot of an elephant. These riches were lit with a merciful dimness by a single weak bulb in a torch held by a fully armed Javanese warrior who looked a bit like a gila monster in rut.

Adoni ran gracefully up the wide stairs in front of me. I followed more slowly, hampered by my icily clinging clothes, my sandals leaving horrible wet marks on the treads. He paused to wait for me, eyeing me curiously.

"What happened to you and Max?"

"The dolphin—Spiro's dolphin—was stranded on the beach, and he helped me to float it again. It pulled us both in."

"No, did it really?" He laughed. "I'd like to have seen that!"

"I'm sure you would." At least his spirits didn't seem to have been damped by the recent scene in the music-room. I wondered if he were used to it.

"When you ran into Max, then, you were coming for help? I see! But why were you out on the beach in the dark?"

"Now don't *you* start!" I said warmly. "I had plenty of that from Max! I was down there picking up a ring—this ring—that my sister had left this morning."

His eyes and mouth rounded at the sight of the diamond. "*Po po po!* That must be worth a few drachs, that one! No wonder you didn't mind making a journey in the dark!"

"Worth more than your journey?" I asked innocently.

The beautiful eyes danced. "I wouldn't say that."

"No?" I regarded him uneasily. What on earth—what in heaven—could they have been up to? Drugs? Surely not! Arms? Ridiculous! But then, what did I know about Max, after all? And his worry in case his father might have 'talked' hadn't just been worry; it had been fear. As for Adoni—I had few illusions as to what my young Byzantine saint would be capable of . . .

He asked: "When you first went out through the wood, you saw nobody?"

"Max asked me that. I heard Sir Julian playing the tape-recorder, but I've no idea if his visitor was still there. I gather you know who it was?"

"I think so. It's a guess, but I think so. Sir Gale may tell Max when they are alone, I don't know."

"Max doesn't normally have drink in the house at all?"

"None that his—none that can be found."

"I see."

I did indeed see. I saw how the rumours had arisen, and just how false Phyl's picture of the situation had been. Except in so far as this sort of periodic 'bender' was a symptom of mental strain, Sir Julian Gale was sane enough. And now that I thought even further back, there had been whispers in the theatre world, possibly strong ones among those who knew him, but on my level the merest breath ... rumours scotched once and for all by Sir Julian's faultless performances right up to the moment of retirement. Well, I had had a personal demonstration tonight of how it had been done.

"We thought he was better," said Adoni. "He has not done this for, oh, a long time. This will make Max very ..." He searched for a word and came up with one that was, I felt, not quite adequate ... "unhappy."

"I'm sorry. But he does seem to have been pushed into it this time."

"Pushed in? Oh, yes, I understand. That is true. Well, Max will deal with it." He gave a little laugh. "Poor Max, he gets everything to deal with. Look, we had better hurry, or you will get cold, and then Max will deal with *me*!"

"Could he?"

"Easily. He pays my wages."

He paused, and pressed a switch in the panelling, invisible except to its intimates. Another dim light faltered into life, this time held aloft by a startling figure in flesh-pink marble, carved by some robust Victorian with a mind above fig-leaves. A wide corridor now stretched ahead of us, lined on one side by massive, iron-studded doors, and on the other by what would, in daylight, be stained-glass windows of a peculiarly repulsive design.

"This way."

He led the way quickly along the corridor. To either side the light glimmered yellow on the pathetic heads of deer and ibexes, and case after case where stuffed birds stood enthroned and moth-eaten. Every other available foot of wall-space was filled with weapons—axes, swords, daggers, and ancient firearms which I (who had furnished a few period plays in my time) identified as flintlocks and muskets, probably dating from the Greek War of Independence. It was to be hoped that Sir Julian and his son were as blind to the murderous décor as Adoni appeared to be.

"Your bathroom is along there." He pointed ahead to a vast door, opposite which hung a tasteful design in crossed whips and spurs. "I'll just show you where everything is, then I must go and dress his wrist."

"How badly is he hurt? He wouldn't say."

"Not badly at all. I think it's only a graze, for all it bled a lot. Don't worry, Max is sensible, he'll take all the care he should."

"And you?" I said.

He looked surprised. "I?"

"Will you take care of yourself as well? Oh, I know it's nothing to do with me, Adoni, but ... well, be careful. For Miranda's sake, if not for your own."

He laughed at me, and touched a thin silver chain at his neck which must have held a cross or some sort of medal. "Don't you worry about me, either, Miss Lucy. The Saint looks after his own." A vivid look. "Believe me, he does."

"I take it you did well tonight?" I said, a little dryly.

"I think so. Here we are." He shoved the door wide, and found another switch. I glimpsed the splendours of marble and mahogany beyond him. "The bedroom is the next one, through there. I'll find you a towel, and later I shall make you something hot to drink. You can find the way down?"

"Yes, thank you."

He rummaged in a cupboard the size of a small garage, and emerged with a couple of towels. "Here you are. You have everything now?"

"I think so. The only thing is—do I have to touch that thing?"

'That thing' was a fearsome contraption which, apparently, heated the water. It looked like a stranded mine, and sat on a panel of dials and switches that might have come straight off the flight deck of an air-liner designed by Emmett.

"You are as bad as Sir Gale," said Adoni indulgently. "He calls it Lolita, and refuses to touch it. It's perfectly safe, Spiro made it."

"Oh."

"It did go on fire once, but it's all right now. We re-wired it only last month, Spiro and I."

Another dazzling smile, and the door shut gently. I was alone with Lolita.

You had to climb three steps to the bath, which was about the size of a swimming-pool, and fairly bristling with gadgets in blackened brass. But I forgave the Castello everything when I turned the tap marked C, and the water rushed out in a boiling cloud of steam. I hoped poor Max wouldn't be long before he achieved a similar state of bliss—it was to be assumed there was another bathroom, and another Lolita as efficient as mine—but just at the moment I spared Max no more than the most passing of thoughts, and none whatever for the rest of the night's adventures. All I wanted was to be out of those dreadful, sodden clothes, and into that glorious bath . . .

By the time I was languidly drying a body broiled all over to a glowing pink, my underclothing, which was mostly nylon, was dry. The dress and coat were still wet, so I left them spread over the hot pipes, put on the dressing-gown which hung behind the door, then padded through into the bedroom to attend to my face and hair.

I had what I had salvaged of Phyl's make-up, which included a comb, so I did the best I could with the inevitable dim light, and a cheval-glass, swinging between two mahogany pillars, that seemed designed to hang perpetually facing the carpet, until I found on the floor and replaced the wedge of newspaper that had held it in position since, apparently, July 20th, 1917.

In the greenish glass my reflection swam like something that might well have startled the Lady of Shalott out of her few wits. The dressing-gown was obviously one of Sir Julian's stagier efforts; it was long, of thick, dark red silk, and made one think of Coward comedies. With Phyl's lipstick, and my short, damply curling hair, and the enormous diamond on my hand, it made a pretty high camp effect.

Well, it was no odder than the other guises he had seen me in up to now. I wondered if this, too, would qualify as 'half-naked'. Not that it mattered, just now he would have other things very much on his mind.

I grimaced briefly at the image in the glass, then went out, back along Murder Alley, and down the stairs.

125

CHAPTER ELEVEN

The very instant that I saw you, did
My heart fly to your service, there resides
To make me slave to it.

III. 1.

THE music-room door was standing open, but, though the lamp
still burned, there was no one there. The gin had vanished, too,
and in its place was something that looked like the remains of a
stiff Alka-Seltzer, and a cup that had probably contained coffee.

As I hesitated in the doorway, I heard a quick step, and the
service door under the stairway opened with a swish of chilly air.

"Lucy? Ah, I thought I heard you. You're all right? Warm
now?"

"Lovely, thank you." He himself looked a different person. I
noticed that there was a fresh white bandage on his wrist, and
that his dry clothes—another thick sweater and dark trousers—
made him look as tough as before, but younger, rather nearer
Adoni's league. So did the look in his face; he looked tired still,
but with a tautness that now seemed to have some sort of
affinity with Adoni's dark glow of excitement. A worthwhile
trip, indeed . . .

I said quickly: "Your clothes . . . You're surely not planning
to go out again?"

"Only to drive you home, don't worry. Come along to the
kitchen, will you? It's warm there, and there's coffee. Adoni
and I have been having something to eat."

"I'd adore some coffee. But I don't know if I ought to stay—
my sister really will have the wind up by now."

"I rang her up and told her what had happened . . . more or
less." He grinned, a boy's grin. "Actually, Godfrey Manning
had already called up and told her about the dolphin, and that
her ring was safe, so she's quite happy, and says she'll expect
you when she sees you. So come along."

I followed him through the service door and down a bare,
echoing passage. It seemed that the Castello servants could not
be allowed to share the glories which fell to their betters, for
'below stairs' the Castello was unadorned by dead animals and
lethal weapons. Personally I'd have traded the whole building,

organ pipes and all, for the kitchen, a wonderful, huge cavern of a place, with a smaller cave for fireplace, where big logs burned merrily in their iron basket, adding their sweet, pungent smells to the smells of food and coffee, and lighting the big room with a living, beating glow. Hanging from the rafters, among the high, flickering shadows, bunches of dried herbs and strings of onions stirred and glimmered in the updraught of warm air.

In the centre of the kitchen was about an acre of scrubbed wooden table, and in a corner of the room Adoni was frying something on an electric cooker which had probably been built, or at any rate wired, by himself and Spiro. There was a wonderful smell of bacon and coffee.

"You can eat some bacon and eggs, surely?" asked Max.

"She will have to," said Adoni briefly, over his shoulder. "I have done them already."

"Well ..." I said, and Max pulled out a chair for me at the end of the table nearest to the fire, where a rather peculiar assortment of plates and cutlery were set in a space comprising about a fiftieth of the table's total area. Adoni put a plate down in front of me, and I realised that I was suddenly, marvellously hungry. "Have you had yours?" I asked.

"Adoni has, and I've just reached the coffee stage," said Max. "Shall I pour some for you straight away?"

"Yes, please." I wondered whether it would be tactful to ask after Sir Julian, and this made me remember my borrowed finery. "My things were still wet, so I borrowed your father's dressing-gown. Will he mind, do you think? It's a terribly grand one."

"*Present Laughter*," said Max. "Of course he won't. He'd be delighted. Sugar?"

"Yes, please."

"There. If you can get outside that lot I doubt if the pneumonia bugs will stand a chance. Adoni's a good cook, when pushed to it."

"It's marvellous," I said, with my mouth full, and Adoni gave me that heart-shaking smile of his, said, "It's a pleasure," and then, to Max, something that I recognised (from a week's painful study of a phrase book) as, "Does she speak Greek?"

Max jerked his head in that curious gesture—like a refractory camel snorting—that the Greeks use for "No", and the boy plunged forthwith into a long and earnest speech of which I caught no intelligible word at all. It was, I guessed, urgent and excited rather than apprehensive. Max listened, frowning, and without comment, except that twice he interrupted with a Greek phrase—the same one each time—that checked the flow and sent Adoni back to speak more slowly and clearly. I ate placidly through my bacon and eggs, trying not to notice the deepening frown on Max's face, or the steadily heightened excitement of Adoni's narrative.

At length the latter straightened up, glancing at my empty plate. "Would you like some more? Or cheese, perhaps?"

"Oh, no, thank you. That was wonderful."

"Some more coffee, then?"

"Is there some?"

"Of course." Max poured it, and pushed the sugar nearer. "Cigarette?"

"No, thanks."

He was returning the pack to his pocket when Adoni, who had been removing my plate, said something quickly and softly in Greek, and Max held the pack out to him. Adoni took three cigarettes, with the glimmer of a smile at me when he saw that I was watching, then he said something else in Greek to Max, added "Good night, Miss Lucy", and went out through a door I hadn't noticed before, in a far corner of the kitchen.

Max said easily: "Forgive the mystery. We've been putting my father to bed."

"Is he all right?"

"He will be." He threw me a look. "I suppose you knew about his—difficulty?"

"No, how could I? I'd no idea."

"But if you're in the business ... I thought it must surely have got round."

"It didn't get to me," I said. "I suppose there must have been rumours, but all I ever knew was that he wasn't well. I thought it was heart or something. And honestly, nobody knew here—at least, Phyl didn't, and if there's been any talk you can bet she'd be the first to hear it. She just knew what you told Leo, that he'd been ill, and in a nursing home. Does it happen often?"

"If you'd asked me that yesterday," he said, a little bitterly, "I'd have said it probably wouldn't happen again."

"Did he talk when you took him upstairs?"

"A little."

"Tell you who it was?"

"Yes."

"And what they'd talked about?"

"Not really, no. He just kept repeating that 'he hadn't got anything out of him'. That, with variations. He seemed rather more pleased and amused than anything else. Then he went to sleep."

I said: "You know, I think you can stop worrying. I'd be willing to bet that your father's said nothing whatever."

He looked at me with surprise. I hadn't realised before how dark his eyes were. "What makes you so sure?"

"Well . . ." I hesitated. "You were a bit upset, in there, but I had nothing to do but notice things. I'll tell you how it struck me. He was certainly drunk, but I think he was hanging on to something he knew . . . he'd forgotten *why*, but just knew he had to. He knew he hadn't to say anything about—about whatever you and Adoni were doing. He was so fuddled that he couldn't sort out who was safe and who wasn't, but he wasn't parting with anything: he even kept stalling you and Adoni because I was there, and even about things that didn't matter, like what happened at Mr. Andiakis'." I smiled. "And then the way he was reciting, and fiddling with the tape-recorder . . . you can't tell me he normally gives private renderings of Shakespeare in his own drawing-room? Actors don't. They may go on acting their heads off off-stage, but they aren't usually bores. It struck me—look, I'm sorry, am I speaking out of turn? Perhaps you'd rather I didn't——"

"God, no. Go on."

"It struck me that he was reciting because he knew that once he'd got himself—or the tape—safely switched into a groove, he could just go on and on without any danger of being jumped into saying the wrong thing. When I heard it, he was probably playing the tape to his visitor."

His mouth twitched in momentary amusement. "Serve him right. What's more, I'm certain that the meeting at the garage was an accident. If Adoni and I had been suspected, we'd have been watched, and perhaps followed . . . or intercepted on our way home."

"Well, there you are; and it stands to reason that if your father had told him anything, or even dropped a hint where you both were, there's been masses of time to have the police along, or . . . or anything."

"Of course." The look he gave me was not quite easy, for all that.

I hesitated. "Worrying about your father, though—that's a

129

different thing. I don't know about these things. Do you think it may have, well, started him drinking again?"

"One can't tell. He's not an alcoholic, you know; it wasn't chronic, or approaching it. It's just that he started to go on these periodic drunks to get out of his jags of depression. We can only wait and see."

I said no more, but turned my chair away from the table to face the fire, and drank my coffee. The logs purred and hissed, and the resin came bubbling out of one of them, in little opal globes that popped and swelled against the charring bark. The big airy room was filled with the companionable noises of the night; the bubbling of the resin, the spurt and flutter of flames, the creak of some ancient wooden floor settling for the night, the clang of the old hot-water system. As I stretched Sir Julian's bedroom slippers nearer the fire a cricket chirped, suddenly and clearly, about a yard away. I jumped, then, looking up, caught Max watching me, and we smiled at one another. Neither of us moved or spoke, but a kind of wordless conversation seemed to take place, and I was filled with a sudden, heart-swelling elation and happiness, as if the sun had come out on my birthday morning, and I had been given the world.

Then he had turned away, and was looking into the fire again. He said, as if he was simply going on from where we had left off:

"It started just over four years ago. Father was rehearsing at the time for that rather spectacular thing that Hayward wrote for him, *Tiger Tiger*. You'll remember it; it ran for ever. Just eight days before the play was due to open, my mother and sister were both killed together in a motor accident. My sister was driving the car when it happened; it wasn't her fault, but that was no comfort. My mother was killed instantly; my sister regained consciousness and lived for a day—long enough to guess what had happened, though they tried to keep it from her. I was away at the time in the States, and, as bad luck would have it, was in hospital there with appendicitis, and couldn't get home. Well, I told you, it was only eight days before *Tiger Tiger* was due to open, and it did open. I don't have to tell you what a situation like that would do to someone like my father ... It would damage anybody, and it half killed him."

"I can imagine." I was also imagining Max himself, chained to his alien hospital bed, getting it all by telephone, by cable, through the mail ...

"That was when he started drinking. It was nearly two months before I got home, and a lot of the damage had been done. Of course, I had realised how it would hit him, but it took the shock of actually coming home to make me realise . . ." He paused. "You can imagine that, too; the house empty, and looking lost, almost as if it hadn't even been dusted for weeks, though that was silly, of course it had. But if felt deserted—echoing, almost. Sally—my sister—had always been a bit of a live-wire. And there was Father, as thin as a telegraph post, with his hair three shades whiter, drifting about that damned great place like a dead leaf in a draughty barn. Not sleeping, of course, and drinking." He shifted in his chair. "What was that he said about the house being like a lord's kitchen without a fire?"

"It's from a play, Tourneur's *Revenger's Tragedy*. 'Hell would look like a lord's great kitchen without fire in't.'"

" 'Hell'?" he quoted. "Yes, I see."

I said quickly: "It wasn't even relevant. It only occurred to him as a sort of image."

"Of emptiness?" He smiled suddenly. "Sweet of you, but don't worry, things pass." He paused. "That was the start. It got better, of course; shock wears off, and with me at home he didn't drink so much, but now and again, when he was tired or over-strained, or just in one of those damned abysmal depressions that his sort of person suffers—they're as real as the measles, I don't have to tell you that—he would drink himself blind, 'just this once'. Unhappily, it takes remarkably little to do it. Well, if you remember, the play ran for a long time, and he stayed in it eighteen months. In all that time I only got him away for three weeks, then back he'd go to London, and after a while the house would get him down, and 'just this once', he'd go on another drunk."

"You couldn't get him to sell the house and move?"

"No. He'd been born there, and his father. It was something he wouldn't even begin to think about. Well, a couple of years of that, and he was going downhill like something on the Cresta Run. Then the 'breakdowns' started, still, thanks to his friends, attributed publicly to strain and overwork. He had the sense to know what was happening to him, and the integrity and pride to get out while he could still do it with his legend intact. He did what he could . . . went into a 'home' and was 'cured'. Then I got him to come away here, to make quite sure he was all

131

right, and to rest. Now he's breaking his heart to get back, but I know he won't do it while there's any danger of its starting again." He gave a quick sigh. "I thought he was through with it, but now I don't know. It isn't just a question of will-power, you know. Don't despise him."

"I know that. And how could I despise him? I love him."

"Lucy Waring's speciality. Given away regardless and for no known reason. No, I'm not laughing at you, heaven forbid ... Will you tell me something?"

"What?"

"Did you mean what you said down there on the beach?"

The abrupt, almost casual question threw me for a moment. "On the beach? When? What did I say?"

"I realise I wasn't meant to hear it. We were just starting up the steps."

There was a pause. A log fell in with a soft crash and a jet of hissing light.

I said, with some difficulty: "You don't ask much, do you?"

"I'm sorry, that was stupid of me. Skip it. My God, I choose my moments, as you say."

He leaned down, picked a poker up from the hearthstone, and busied himself with rearranging the pieces of burning wood. I stared at his averted face, while a straitjacket of shyness gripped me, and with it a sort of anger at his obtuseness in asking this. I couldn't have spoken if I'd tried.

A jet of flame, stirred by the poker, leaped up and caught the other log. It lit his face, briefly highlighting the traces of the night's excitement and pain and tension, the frowning brows so like his father's, the hard, exciting line of his cheek; his mouth. And the same brief flash lit something else for me. I was the one who was stupid. If one asks a question, it is because one wants to know the answer. Why should he have to wait and wrap it up some other way when the 'moment' suited me?

I said it quite easily after all. "If you'd asked me a thing like that three hours ago, I think I'd have said I didn't even like you, and I ... I think I'd have believed it ... I think ... And now there you sit looking at me, and all you do is look—like that—and my damned bones turn to water, and it isn't fair, it's never happened to me before, and I'd do anything in the world for you, and you know it, or if you don't you ought to—No, look, I—I didn't mean ... you *asked* me ..."

It was a better kiss this time, no less breathless, but at least we were dry and warm, and had known each other nearly two hours longer . . .

From somewhere in the shadows came a sharp click, and a whirring sound. Instantly, we were a yard apart.

A small, fluting voice said: "*Cuckoo, cuckoo, cuckoo, cuckoo,*" and clicked back into silence.

"That damned clock!" said Max explosively, then began to laugh. "It always frightens me out of my wits. It sounds like someone sneaking in with a tommy-gun. I'm sorry, did I drop you too hard?"

"Right down to earth," I said shakily. "Four o'clock, I'll have to go."

"Wait just a little longer, can't you? No, listen, there's something you've got to know. I'll try not to take too long, if you'll just sit down again . . .? Don't take any notice of that clock, it's always fast." He cocked an eyebrow. "What are you looking at me like that for?"

"For a start," I said, "men don't usually jump sky-high when they hear a noise like a tommy-gun. Unless they could be expecting one, that is. Were you?"

"Could be," he said cheerfully.

"Goodness me! Then I'll certainly stay to hear all about it!" I sat down, folding my silk skirts demurely about me. "Go on."

"A moment, I'll put another log on the fire. Are you warm enough?"

"Yes, thank you."

"You won't smoke? You never do? Wise girl. Well . . ."

He leaned his elbows on his knees, and stared once more at the fire.

". . . I'm not quite sure where to start, but I'll try to make it short. You can have the details later, those you can't fill in for yourself. I want to tell you what's happened tonight, and especially what's going to happen tomorrow—today, I mean—because I want you to help me, if you will. But to make it clear I'll have to go back to the start of the story. I suppose you could say that it starts with Yanni Zoulas; at any rate that's where I'll begin."

"It was true, then? He was a smuggler?"

"Yes, indeed. Yanni carried stuff regularly—all kinds of goods in short supply—over to the Albanian coast. Your guess was right about the 'contacts': he had his 'contact' on the other side, a man called Milo, and he had people over here who

133

supplied the stuff and paid him. But not me. Your guess was wrong there. Now, how much d'you know about Albania?"

"Hardly a thing. I did try to read it up before I came here, but there's so little to read. I know it's Communist, of course, and at daggers drawn with Tito's Yugoslavia, *and* with Greece on the other border. I gather that it's a poor country, without much workable land and no industries, just peasant villages perched on the edge of starvation, like some of the Greek ones. I don't know any of the towns except Durres on the coast, and Tirana, the capital, but I gathered that they were still pretty Stone Age at the end of the war, but trying hard, and looking round for help. That was when the U.S.S.R. stepped in, wasn't it?"

"Yes. She supplied Albania with tools and tractors and seeds and so forth, all it needed to get its agriculture going again after the war. But it wasn't all plain sailing. I won't go into it now—in fact I'm not at all sure that I've got it straight myself—but a few years ago Albania quarrelled with Russia, and broke with the Cominform, but, because it still badly needed help (and possible support against Russia) it applied to Communist China; and China, which was then at loggerheads with Russia, jumped happily in to play fairy godmother to Albania as Russia had done before—and presumably to get one foot wedged in Europe's back door. The situation's still roughly that, and now Albania's closed its frontiers completely, except to China. You can't get in, and by heaven, you certainly can't get out."

"Like Spiro's father?"

"I suspect he didn't want to. But you might say he brings us to the next point in the story, which is Spiro. I suppose you've heard about our connection with Maria and her family?"

"In a way. Adoni told me."

"My father was here in Corfu during the war, and he was working in with Spiro's father for a time—a wild type, I gather, but rather picturesque and appealing. He appealed to the romantic in my father, anyway." Max grinned. "One gathers they had some pretty tearing times together. When the twins were born, father stood godfather to them. You won't know this, but over here it's a relationship that's taken very seriously. The godfather really does take responsibility—he has as much say in the kids' future as their father does, sometimes more."

"I gathered that from Adoni. It was obvious he had a say in the christening, anyway!"

134

He laughed. "It certainly was. The isle of Corfu went to his head even in those days. Thank God I was born in London, or I've a feeling nothing could have saved me from Ferdinand. Would you have minded?"

"Terribly. Ferdinand makes me think of a rather pansy kind of bull. What is your name, anyway? Maximilian?"

"Praise heaven, no. Maxwell. It was my mother's name."

"I take it you had a godfather with no obsessions."

He grinned. "Too right. In the correct English manner, he gave me a silver teaspoon, then vanished from my life. But you can't do that in Corfu. When Spiro's own father did actually vanish, the godfather was almost literally left holding the babies."

"He was still over here when that happened?"

"Yes. He was here for a bit after the European war finished, and during that time he felt himself more or less responsible for the family. He would have been if he'd been a Greek, since Maria had no relatives, and they were as poor as mice, so he took the family on, and even after he'd gone home sent money to them every month."

"Good heavens! But surely, with children of his own——"

"He managed." Max's voice was suddenly grave. "We're not rich, heaven knows ... and an actor's life's a darned uncertain one at best ... but it's rather frightening how little a Greek family can manage on quite cheerfully. He kept them completely till Maria went out to work, and even after that he more or less kept them until the children could work, too." He stretched out a foot and shoved the log deeper on its bed of burning ash. "We came over here for holidays most years; that's where I learned my Greek and the kids their English. We had a whale of a time, and father always loved it. I was thankful I had somewhere like this to bring him when the crash came ... it was like having another family ready-made. It's helped him more than anything else could have done. Being wanted does."

"Good heavens, the thousands that want him! But I know it's different. So he came back here for peace to recover in, and then Spiro was killed. It must have hit him terribly."

"The trouble was," said Max, "that Maria wouldn't believe the boy could be dead. She never stopped begging and praying my father to find out what really happened to him, and to bring him back. Apparently she'd made a special petition to St. Spiridion for him, so she simply wouldn't believe he could have

135

drowned. She got some sort of idea that he'd gone after his father, and must be brought home."

The second cigarette stub went after the first. It hit a bar of the fire, and fell back on the hearthstone. He got up, picked it up and dropped it on the fire, then stayed on his feet with a shoulder propped against the high mantel.

"I know it wasn't reasonable, not after Manning had told her what had happened, but mothers don't always listen to reason, and there was always the faint chance that the boy *had* survived. My father didn't feel equal to handling it, and I knew that neither he nor Maria would have any peace of mind till they found what had become of his body, so I took it on. I've been having inquiries made wherever I could, here and on the mainland, to find out in the first place if he'd been washed ashore, dead or alive. I've also had someone in Athens trying to get information from the Albanian side. Where Spiro went in, the current sets dead towards the Albanian coast. Well, I did manage to get through in the end, but with no results. He hadn't been seen, either on the Greek coast or the Albanian."

I said: "And I read you a lesson on helping other people. I'm sorry."

"You couldn't know it was any concern of mine."

"Well, no, it did rather seem to be Godfrey's."

"I suppose so; but the local Greeks at any rate assumed that it was my father's job—or mine—to do it. So the police kept in touch with us, and we knew we'd get any information that was going. And when Yanni Zoulas went across on his routine smuggling trip on Saturday night, and did actually get some news of Spiro through his Albanian 'contact', he came straight to us. Or rather, as straight as he could. You saw him on his way up to see us, on Sunday evening."

I was bolt upright in my chair. "*News of Spiro?* Good news?"

I knew the answer before he spoke. The gleam in his eyes reminded me suddenly, vividly, of the way Adoni had looked at me on the staircase, glowing.

"Oh, yes. He came to tell us Spiro was alive."

"*Max!*"

"Yes, I know. You can guess how we felt. He'd been washed ashore on the Albanian side, with a broken leg, and in the last stages of exhaustion, but he'd survived. The people who found him were simple coast folk, shepherds, who didn't see any reason to report things to the People's Police, or whatever it's called over there. Most people know about the smuggling that goes on, and I gather that these folk assumed that Spiro was mixed up in something of the sort, so they kept quiet about him. What's more, they informed the local smuggler, who—naturally —knew Milo, Yanni's 'contact', who in turn passed the news along to Yanni on Saturday."

"Oh, Max, this is marvellous! It really is! Did Yanni actually see him?"

"No. It all came at rather third hand. Milo hasn't much Greek, so all that Yanni got from him were the bare facts, and an urgent message that Spiro somehow managed to convey that no one, no one at all—not even Maria—had to be told that he was still alive, except myself, my father, and Adoni ... the people who'd presumably get him out somehow." He paused, briefly. "Well, obviously we couldn't go to the police and get him out by normal channels, or the people who'd rescued him would be in trouble, not to mention Yanni and Milo. So Yanni fixed up a rendezvous to bring the boy off by night."

"And he went back last night after he'd seen you, and ran into the coastguards and got hurt?"

But he was shaking his head. "He couldn't have gone back alone; getting that boy off wasn't one man's job—don't forget he was strapped to a stretcher. No, when Yanni came up on Sunday night, he came to ask me to go across with him. The rendezvous was fixed for tonight; Milo and his friend were to have Spiro there and Yanni and I were to take him off. So you see——"

I didn't hear what he was going to say. It had all come together at last, and I could only wonder at my slowness in not seeing it all before. My eyes flew to his bandaged wrist, as the events of the night came rushing back: the secrecy of his journey through the woods, the impression I had had of more than one man passing me there, the owl's call, Adoni's vivid face ...

I was on my feet. "The catch! Adoni and the catch! You took Adoni, and went over there yourself tonight! You mean it's *done*? You've actually *brought Spiro home*?"

His eyes were dancing. "We have indeed. He's here at this moment, a bit tired, but alive and well. I told you our night's work had been worth while."

I sat down again, rather heavily. "I can hardly take it in. This is ... wonderful. Oh, Maria will be able to light herself a lovely candle this Easter! Think of it, Maria, Miranda, Sir Julian, Godfrey, Phyl ... how happy everyone's going to be! I can hardly wait till daylight, to see the news go round!"

The glow faded abruptly from his face. It must have been only imagination, but the gay firelight seemed dimmer, too.

He said sombrely: "I'm afraid it mustn't go round yet, not any further."

"But——" I stared, bewildered—"not to his mother or sister? Why on earth not, if he's safely home? Surely, once he's out of Albania he has nothing to fear? And Milo needn't be involved at all—no one need even know Spiro was ever on Albanian soil. We could invent some story——"

"I'd thought of that. The story will be that he was thrown ashore on one of the islands in the strait, the Peristeroi Islands, and that he managed to attract our attention when we were out fishing. It won't fool the Greek police, or the doctor, but it'll do for general release, as it were. But that's not the point."

"Then what is?"

He hesitated, then said, slowly: "Spiro may still be in danger ... Not from the other side, but here. What touched him, touched Yanni, too. And Yanni died."

Something in his face—his very reluctance to speak—frightened me. I found myself protesting violently, too violently, as if by protesting I could push the unwanted knowledge further away. "But we *know* what happened to Spiro! He went overboard from Godfrey's boat! How *can* he be in any danger now? And Yanni's death was an accident! You *said* so!"

I stopped. The silence was so intense that you could hear the crazy ticking of the cuckoo clock, and the scrape of silk on flesh as my hands gripped together in my lap.

I said quietly: "Go on. Say it straight out, you may as well. You're insinuating that Godfrey Manning——"

"I'm insinuating nothing." His voice was curt, even to rudeness. "I'm telling you. Here it is. Godfrey Manning threw Spiro overboard, and left him to drown."

Silence again, a different kind of silence.

"Max, I—I can't accept that. I'm sorry, but it isn't possible."

"It's fact, no more nor less. Spiro says so. Yes, I thought you were forgetting that I've talked to him. He says so, and I believe him. He has no reason to lie."

Seconds were out with a vengeance. Now that he had decided

he must tell me, he hurled his facts like stones. And they hit like stones.

"But—*why?*"

"I don't know. Neither does the boy. Which, when you come to think about it, makes it the more likely that he's telling the truth. It's something he'd have no reason to invent. He's as stunned by it as you are." He added, more gently: "I'm sorry, Lucy, but I'm afraid it's true."

I sat in silence for a minute or two, not thinking, but looking down at my hands, twisting and turning the great diamond, and watching the firelight break and dazzle among its facets. Slowly, the stunned feeling faded, and I began to think . . .

"Did you suspect Godfrey before?"

"No," he said, "why should I? But when I got that message from Yanni, I did wonder why Godfrey hadn't to be told. After all, it seemed reasonable to keep the news from Spiro's mother and sister, because they'd be so elated that they might give everything away before Yanni had done the job; but Godfrey was a different matter. He would presumably be worrying about Spiro, and he has by far the best boat. What's more, he's an experienced seaman, and I'm not. I'd have expected him to be in on the rescue, rather than me and Adoni. It wasn't much, but it did make me wonder. Then when Yanni was found dead next day, on top of Spiro's odd warning, I wondered still more."

I said: "You're not suggesting now—you *can't* be suggesting that Godfrey killed Yanni Zoulas? Max——"

"What I've told you about Spiro is fact: what happened to Yanni is guesswork. But to my mind the one murder follows the other as the night the day."

"*Murder* . . ." I don't think I said it aloud, but he nodded as if I had.

"I'm pretty sure of it. Same method, too. He'd been hit hard on the head and thrown into the sea. The bottle of ouzo was a nice touch, I thought."

"He was hit by the boom. The police said there were hairs——"

"He could also have been hit *with* the boom. Anyone can crack an unconscious man's head on a handy chunk of wood like that, hard enough to kill him before you throw him overboard—and hard enough to hide the crack you knocked him out with. I'm not bringing this out as a theory: I'm only saying it could have been done."

"Why did you go back to the body after we'd left?"

"After Yanni left us on Sunday night I heard his boat go out, and I did wonder if he'd been stupid enough to go back on his own, and had run into trouble with the coastguards. From all that we'd been able to see he might have had a bullet hole in him somewhere, or some other evidence that would start a serious investigation. I was pretty anxious in case they started patrolling local waters before I'd got Spiro safely home."

"I see. And your own wrist—was that the coastguards?"

"Yes, a stray bullet, and a spent one at that. It's honestly only a graze; I'll get it looked at when I get Spiro's leg seen to. They must have heard something, and fired blind. We were just about out of range, and well beyond their lights."

I said, rather wearily: "I suppose you do know what you're saying, but it all seems so ... so impossible to me. And I don't understand even the start of it."

"My God, who does? But I told you, it's all guesswork about Yanni, and there's no future in discussing that now. The first thing is to talk to Spiro again. I've only had time to get the barest statement from him, and I want to hear the rest before I decide what's best to do. He should be fit enough by now to tell us exactly what happened and, whether he knows it or not, he may have some clue as to why Manning tried to kill him. If he has, it may be a pointer to Yanni's death. And whatever it is that makes two murders necessary ..." He straightened abruptly, his shoulder coming away from the mantel. "Well, you can see that we have to get the boy safely into the hands of the authorities with his story, before Godfrey Manning has even a suspicion that he's not as dead as Yanni. Will you come with me now and see him?"

I looked up in surprise. "Me? You want me to?"

"If you will. I told you I wanted you to help me, and—if you'll agree—you'd better know as much as we do about it."

"Of course, whatever I can."

"Darling. Come here. Now, stop looking like that, and stop worrying. It's all impossible, as you say, but then this sort of situation is bound to be, when one gets mixed up in it oneself. All we can do is play for safety, and that means, for the moment, believing Spiro. All right?"

I nodded, as best I could with my head comfortably against his shoulder.

"Then listen. What I've got to do, as I see it, is get the boy straight off to Athens in the morning, to the hospital, then to the police. Once he's told his story there, he'll be safe to come home." He loosed me. "Well, shall we go?"

"Where is he?"

He laughed. "Right below our feet, in a very Gothic but reasonably safe dungeon, with Adoni standing guard over him with the one efficient rifle in this damned great arsenal of Leo's. Come along, then. Straight under the cuckoo clock, and fork right for the dungeons!"

CHAPTER TWELVE

My cellar is in a rock by th' sea-side,
where my wine is hid.

II. 2.

A WIDE flight of stone steps led downwards from just beyond the door. Max touched a switch, and a weak yellow light came on to show us the way. He shut the ponderous door, and I heard a key grate in the lock behind us.

"I'll go first, shall I?"

I followed him, curiously looking about me. The rest of the building had led me to expect goodness knew what horrors down here: it would hardly have come as a surprise to have found mouldering skeletons dangling in chains from the walls. But the underground corridor into which the stairs led us was innocent of anything except racks for wine—largely empty— which lined the wide passage-way. The floor was clean, and the walls surprisingly free of the dust and webs which would have accumulated in a similar place in England. The air smelt fresh, and slightly damp.

I said as much to Max, who nodded. "You'll see why in a minute. This is the official wine-cellar, but it leads off into a natural cave further along. I don't know where the opening is—it's probably no bigger than a chimney—but the air's always fresh, and you can smell the sea. There are more wine racks down there. In the last century, when one drank one's four bottles a day, rather a lot of room was needed. Anyway, it must have seemed natural to use the caves in the cliff when they built the Castello."

"It's rather exciting. I suppose these are the caves your father was talking about."

"Yes. Most of the cliffs along this coast have caves in them, but, as you can imagine, he'd love to think the Castello cave was the original Prospero's cell. When I point out that it doesn't look as if it had ever been open to the outside air, he says that doesn't matter. I gather it's more 'poetic truth', like the marmosets."

"Well, it's a lovely romantic theory, and I'm all for it! After all, what are facts? We get those every day ... Whereabouts are we now, in relation to 'outside'?"

"At present we're still moving along under the foundations of the house. The cave itself is in the southern headland, fairly deep down. We go down more steps in a moment, and then there's a natural passage through to the cave. Wait, here we are."

He had stopped two-thirds of the way along the corridor, and put a hand up to the empty racks. I watched him, puzzled. He laid hold of what looked like part of the wall of racks, and pulled. Ponderously, and by no means silently, a narrow section swung out into the corridor. Beyond where it had been was a gap in the wall, opening on blackness.

"Goodness me!" I exclaimed, and Max laughed.

"Marvellous, isn't it? I tell you, the Castello's got everything! As a matter of fact, I have a suspicion that old Forli kept the better vintages down here, out of the butler's reach ... Careful, now, there's no light from here on. I've brought a torch —here, take it for a moment, will you, while I shut this behind us. Don't look so scared!"

"It won't stay shut and trap us here for ever, till our bones bleach?"

"Not even till morning, I'm sorry to say. There. The torch, please. I'll go ahead."

The second flight sloped more steeply down, and, instead of being made of smooth slabs, seemed to be hacked out of solid rock. At the foot of the flight a rock-hewn passage curved away into darkness, still descending. Max went ahead, shining the beam for me. Here and there the walls showed a glint of damp, and the fresh smell was stronger, and perceptibly salty, while the hollow rock seemed—perhaps only in imagination—to hold a faint, echoing hum like the shushing of the sea through the curves of a shell. A moment I thought I heard it, then it was gone, and there was only the still, cold air, and the sound of our footsteps on the rock.

The yellow torchlight flung sharp lights and shadows on Max's face as he turned to guide me, sketching in, momentarily, the face of a stranger. His shadow moved, distorted and huge on the rough walls.

"Is it much further?" My voice sounded unfamiliar, like a whisper in an echo-chamber.

"Round this corner," said Max, "and down five, no, six steps —and there's the watch-dog."

A flash of the torch showed the pale blur of a face upturned, and a gun barrel gleaming blue.

"Adoni? It's Max, and I've brought Miss Lucy along. Is he all right?"

"He's fine now. He's awake."

Behind Adoni hung a rough curtain of some material like sacking, from beyond which came a dim, warm glow. Adoni drew the curtain aside for me and stood back. Max put the torch out and motioned me past him. I went into the cave.

This was large, with a great arched roof lost in shadows where stalactites hung like icicles; but the walls had been white-washed to a height of six feet or so, and were lined with wine racks and crates and the comfortable, bulging shapes of barrels. On one of these, up-turned to make a table, stood an old-fashioned lantern, a coach-lamp of about 1850 vintage, probably borrowed from the museum upstairs, which dispensed a soft orange light and the cheerful twinkle of brass. The air was warmed by a paraffin stove which stood in the middle of the floor, with a pan of coffee on it. Somewhere in the shadows a drip of water fell regularly—some stalactite dripping fresh water into a pocket of rock; the sound was as homely as a dripping tap. The unexpected effect of cosiness was enhanced by the smell of cigarettes and coffee and the faint fumes of the paraffin stove.

The injured boy lay at the far side of the cave, on a bed pushed up against a row of crates. The bed was a makeshift affair which nevertheless looked extremely comfortable—a couple of spring mattresses laid one above the other, with blankets galore, and feather pillows, and a vast eiderdown. Some sort of cage had been rigged up under the bedclothes to keep their weight off the injured leg.

Spiro, lying there in what looked like a pair of Sir Julian's pyjamas (pale blue silk with crimson piping), looked comfortable enough, and not at the moment particularly ill. He was propped up on his pillows, drinking coffee.

He looked up across the cup, a little startled at the sight of me, and threw a quick question at Max, who answered in English:

"It's Kyria Forli's sister. She's my friend, and yours. She's going to help us, and I want her to hear your story."

Spiro regarded me steadily, without noticeable welcome, the round dark eyes, so like his sister's, wary and appraising. I could recognise the boy in the photographs, but only just; there was the thick, springing hair and the stocky body, with obvious strength in the shoulders and thick neck; but the bloom of health and sunlight—and happiness—was gone. He looked pale, and—in the pyjamas—young and unprotected-looking.

Max pulled a box forward for me to sit on. "How do you feel?" he asked the boy. "Is it hurting?"

"No," said Spiro. That this was a lie was quite obvious, but it was not said with any sort of bravado. It was simply that one did not admit to weakness, and pain was weakness.

"He has slept," said Adoni.

"Good." Max perched himself half sitting against the cask which held the lantern. His shadow, thrown hugely up the walls, arched brooding and gigantic across the cave. He studied the younger boy for a minute or two, then said, briskly:

"If you're feeling better, I want you to tell us exactly what happened to you. All the details this time, please."

"All the what?"

"Everything you can remember," said Max, and Adoni, from the head of the bed, added a soft gloss in Greek.

"All right." Spiro drained the coffee-cup and handed it up, without looking, to Adoni. The latter took it, set it quietly aside, then crossed back to the bed and sat down, curling up gracefully, naturally, like a cat, near the head of the bed away from the injured leg. He reached into a pocket for two of the cigarettes he had got from Max, stuck them in his mouth, lit them both, and handed one to Spiro. Spiro took it without word or glance, but there was no suggestion, as there had been with me, of anything withdrawn or unfriendly. It was obvious that these two young men knew each other almost too well to need words. They sat there side by side against the pillows, Adoni relaxed and graceful, Spiro square and watchful and smoking jerkily, with his hand cupped working-class fashion round the cigarette.

He sent one more wary glance at me, then took no more notice of me: all his attention was on Max, almost as if the latter were judging him—at once judge and saviour and final court of appeal. Max listened without moving, the huge, curved shadow thrown right up the wall and over half the ceiling of the cave.

The boy spoke slowly, with the signs of fatigue deepening in his face. I have no recollection now of what language he spoke; whether his English was good, or whether Max and Adoni eked it out with translation: the latter, I suspect; but whatever the case, the story came over vividly and sharply in that darkened cellar-cave, with the lantern light, and the smell of the cigarettes, and the two boys curled in the welter of bedclothes, and the faint tangy scent from the silk of Julian Gale's dressing-gown.

I suppose that the strange, secret surroundings, the time of night, my own weariness and recent emotional encounter with Max, had edged the scene somehow; but it seemed real now only as a dream is real. In the dream I found I had already accepted Godfrey's guilt; I only waited now to hear how he had done it. Perhaps in the light of morning things would take a different dimension; but now it seemed as if any tale could be true, even the old man's romantic theory that this was Prospero's cave, and that here on this rough floor the Neapolitan lords had waited to hear the story from the long-drowned Duke, as I now waited to hear Spiro's.

*   *   *

There had been nothing, he said, that had struck him as unusual about the trip that night. The only thing that had surprised him was that the sky was none too clear, and from what the wireless had said, it might well be stormy at dawn. He had pointed this out to Godfrey, but Godfrey had said, a little abruptly, that it would clear. They had got the boat out, and gone shortly before midnight. As Spiro had anticipated, the night was black and thick, but he had said nothing more to Godfrey, who had stayed in the cabin, allegedly busying himself with his camera and equipment.

"He seemed much as usual?" asked Max.

Spiro frowned, considering this. "I cannot say," he said at length. "He was quiet, and perhaps a bit sharp with me when I protested about the weather, but all day he had been the same. I thought he was still angry with me because I had gone into the boat-house that morning on my own to service the engine, so I said nothing, and thought nothing. He pays me, and that is that."

"All the same, that might be interesting," said Max slowly. "But go on now. You were out in the strait, and the night was black."

Spiro took a quick drag on the cigarette, and reached awkwardly, hampered by the leg, to tap the ash on to the floor. Adoni slipped the saucer from under the empty coffee-cup, and slid it within his reach.

"I reckoned we were about half-way over," said Spiro, "in the strait between Kouloura and the mainland. We had gone close to the Peristeroi Islands; there was enough of a sea running to see the white foam quite distinctly. I asked Mr. Manning if we should lie up a little in the lee of them, and wait for the cloud to clear; there were gaps under the wind, where you could see stars; but he said no, we would go further across. We went on for a time, till I reckoned we were about two miles out. He came out of the cabin then, and sent me in to make some coffee." The boy glanced up under his thick brows at Max. "The camera was there, on the table, but I did not think he could have been looking at it, because he had had no light on, only a storm lantern hardly lit. At the time I did not think of these things; while we took pictures at night, we always—naturally—ran without lights. But afterwards, when I had all that time lying in bed, and nothing to do but think, and wonder . . . then I remembered all the things that seemed strange. It was strange that we were going at all on that dark night to take pictures; it was strange that he lied to me about the camera; and the next thing that happened was more strange still."

Adoni grinned. "I know, the engine failed. And what was so strange about that, when you'd been taking it to bits that morning, my little genius?"

Spiro smiled for the first time, and said something in Greek which nobody bothered to translate for me. "If that had happened," he added, with fine simplicity, "it would indeed have been strange. But it did not."

"But you told us before——"

"I told you the engine stopped. I did not say that it failed. There was nothing wrong with the engine."

Max stirred. "You're sure, naturally."

The boy nodded. "And it didn't need a genius with engines to know there was nothing wrong. Even you"—a glint at Adoni—"even you would have known, my pretty one." He ducked aside from Adoni's feint, and laughed. "Go on, hit me, no doubt you could do it now."

"I'll wait," said Adoni.

Spiro turned back to Max. "No, the engine was all right. Listen. I heard it stop, then Mr. Manning called me. I put my head out of the door and shouted that I would take a look—the engine hatch is under the cabin steps, you understand. But he said, 'I don't think it's there, Spiro, I think something's fouled the screw and stalled it. Can you take a look?' I went to the stern. He was standing there, at the tiller. He said, 'Steady as you go, boy, she's pitching a bit. Here, I'll hold the torch for you.' I gave him the torch, and then I leaned over to see if the shaft was fouled. The boat was pitching, and the toe-rail was wet, but I was holding on tightly. I should have been quite safe."

He paused, and stirred in the bed, as if the leg was hurting him. Adoni slipped to the floor and padded across to where a bottle stood on a box beside two empty glasses. He slopped some of the wine—it looked like the dark, sweet stuff they called *demèstica*—into one of the glasses and took it to the other boy, then glanced inquiringly at Max, who shook his head. Adoni set the bottle down, and returned to his place on the bed, adjusting his body, cat-like, to the new position of the injured boy.

"It all happened very fast. The boat gave a lurch, very sharp, as if Mr. Manning had turned her across the wind too quickly. I was thrown against the rail, but still safe enough, because I had a good grip, but then something hit me from behind, on the head. It does not stun me, but I think I try to turn and put an arm up, then the boat pitches again, and before I know what has happened, I am falling. I try to grip the rail, but it slips from me. Something hits me across the hand—here—and I let go. Then I am in the water. When I come up, the boat is still near, and I see Mr. Manning in the stern, peering out for me in the darkness. I shout—not loudly, you understand, because I am full of water, and too cold, gasping for air. But he must have heard me."

He shot a look up at Max, all of a sudden vivid, alive with pure hatred.

"And if he did not hear me, then he saw me. He put the torch on, and shone it on me in the sea."

"Yes?" said Max. His voice was expressionless, but I got the impression of a cold wind stirring in the cellar. Adoni felt it, too. He glanced fleetingly up at Max before his eyes went back to Spiro.

"I was not afraid, you understand," said Spiro, "not of him. It did not occur to me that it was he who had hit me, I thought it had been some accident. No, I was not afraid. I am a good swimmer, and though he had no engine, the boat was drifting down towards me, and he could see me. In a moment he could pick me up again. I called out again and swam towards him. I saw he had the starting-handle in his hand, but I still did not imagine what this was for. Then as I came within reach, he leaned down and hit me again. But the boat was pitching and he had to hold the rail, so he could not point the torch properly. The blow touched me, but this time I saw it coming, and I ducked away, and he hit my arm and not my head. I think he felt the blow, but did not see, because the torch went out, and a big wave swept me away from the boat's stern and out of his sight. You can imagine that this time I let it take me. I saw the light go on again, but I made no sound, and let myself be carried away into the dark. Then I heard the engine start." He drained the glass, and looked up at Max. "He looked for me for a little while, but the current took me away fast, and the waves hid me. Then he turned the boat away, and left me there in the sea."

There was silence. Nobody moved. For me, the dreamlike feeling persisted. The cave seemed darker, echoing with the sounds of the sea, the mutter of the receding boat, the empty hissing of waves running under the night wind.

"But the Saint was with you," said Adoni, and the deep human satisfaction in his voice sent the shadows scurrying. The cave was warm again, and full of the soft light from the English Victorian lantern.

Spiro handed the empty glass to Adoni, pulled the bedclothes more comfortably round him, and nodded. "Yes, he was with me. Do you want the rest, Kyrie Max? You know what happened."

"I want Miss Lucy to hear it. Go on, but make it short. You're tired, and it's very late."

The rest of the story was pure classic, made predictable and

148

credible by half a hundred stories from Odysseus to St. Paul.

It was the murderer's bad luck that the wind that night had set a fast current in to the Albanian coast. Spiro was a fair swimmer, and the Ionian Sea is very salt, but even so he would have been hard put to it to survive if he had not gone overboard into the stream of the current. Between that, the buoyancy of the water, and his own stubborn efforts, he managed to keep afloat long enough for the sea-race to throw him ashore some time just before dawn.

By the time he neared the shore he was almost exhausted, all his energy taken by the mere effort of keeping afloat, and at the mercy of the tide. He was not even aware that he had come to shore, but when a driving swell flung him against the cruel coastal rocks, he found just enough strength to cling there, resisting the backward drag once, twice, three times, before he could pull himself clear of it and crawl further up the slimy rock.

And here the luck turned. St. Spiridion, having seen him ashore, and out of his own territory, abandoned him abruptly. Spiro slipped, fell back across a jut of sharp rock with a broken leg twisted under him, and at last fainted.

He had no recollection of being found—by an old shepherd who had clambered down a section of cliff after a crag-fast ewe. When Spiro woke he was bedded down, roughly but dry and warm, in the shepherd's cottage, and it appeared that the shepherd had some rough surgical skill, for the leg had been set and strapped up. The old woman produced a drink that sent him to sleep again, and when he woke for the second time, the pain was a good deal easier, and he was able to remember, and think . . .

"And the rest you know." He yawned suddenly, tremendously, like an animal, and lay back among the blankets.

"Yes, the rest we know." Max got to his feet, stretching. "Well, you'd better get some sleep. In the morning—my God, in about three hours!—I'm going to get you out of here, don't ask me how, but I'll do it somehow, with Mr. Manning none the wiser. I want to get that leg of yours properly seen to, and then you've got to tell your story to the right authorities."

The boy glanced up, weariness and puzzlement lending his face a sullen, heavy look. "Authorities? Police? You mean you are going to accuse Kyrios Manning of trying to drown me? On my word alone? They will laugh at you."

149

"It's not just a question of accusing Mr. Manning of throwing you overboard. What I want to know is why? There's something here that must be investigated, Spiro. You'll have to trust me. Now, just for a few minutes longer, I want you to think back. You must have thought about it a lot yourself, while you were lying in bed ... Why do you think he did it? Have you any idea at all? You surely don't imagine it was because he was irritated with you for overhauling the engine without being told?"

"Of course not."

"There was nothing else—nothing had happened at any other time?"

"No. I have thought. Of course I have thought. No."

"Then we come back to the morning of the trip. When one has nothing to go on, one looks for anything, however slight, that's out of pattern—out of the ordinary. Did you usually overhaul that boat by yourself?"

"No, but I have done so before." Spiro stirred, as if his leg hurt him. "And I have been alone on it before."

"You have always asked him first?"

"Of course."

"But this time you didn't ... Why did you go to work on the boat this time without asking him?"

"Because he had told me that he meant to go out, and he wanted the engine serviced. I was to go that morning after breakfast, and work on it. But I had got up very early, to swim, and when I had done, I thought I would go straight along and start work. I knew where he kept the extra key, so I let myself in, and made some coffee in the galley, then opened the big doors for the light and started work. It was a good morning, with the summer coming, and I felt good. I worked well. When Mr. Manning had finished his breakfast and came down, I was half finished already. I thought he would be pleased, but he was very angry and asked how I got in, and then I didn't like to tell him that I had seen where he hid the key, so I said the door was not locked properly, and he believed this, because the catch is stiff sometimes. But he was still very angry, and said he would have the lock changed, and then I was angry also, and asked if he thought I was a thief, and if he thought so he had better count the money in his wallet which he had left in the galley. As if I would touch it! I was very angry!" Spiro remembered this

150

with some satisfaction. "I told him also that I would mend his lock for him myself, and that I would never come to his house again. After that he was pleasant, and said he was sorry, and it was all right."

Max was frowning. "It was then that he asked you to go out that night?"

"I think ... Yes, it must have been. He had said, before, that he did not want me with him, but he changed his mind ... I thought because he was sorry he had spoken to me like that." He added, naïvely: "It was a way to give me extra money without offence."

"Then it looks as if that was when he decided to take you and get rid of you. You can see that it only makes sense if he thought you'd seen something you shouldn't have seen ... And that means in the boat, or the boat-house. Now, think hard, Spiro. Was there anything unusual about the boat? Or the boat-house? Or about anything that Mr. Manning said, or did ... or carried with him?"

"No." The boy repeated himself with a kind of weary emphasis. "I have thought. Nothing."

"The wallet. You say he'd left his wallet lying. Where did you find it?"

"Down beside the stove in the galley. It had slipped there and he had not noticed. I put it on the cabin table."

"Were there papers in it? Money?"

"How should I know?" Spiro ruffled up again, like a young turkey-cock, then subsided under Max's look with a grin. "Well, I did take a look, a very small one. There was money, but I don't know how much, I only saw the corners. It wasn't Greek money, anyway, so what use did he think it would have been to me? But if it had been a million drachmas, I would not have taken it! You know that, Kyrie Max!"

"Of course I know it. Did he leave you alone in the boat after this?"

"No. When I had finished there, he asked me to go up to the house and help him with some photographs. I worked there all day. He telephoned to the Forli house to tell my mother that I was to go with him that night."

"In fact, he made sure that you saw nobody all that day ... Did you ever have any suspicion that he did anything illegal on these expeditions?"

"No—and why should it matter? I would not have told the

151

police." Spiro's eyes glinted up at him. "He would not be the only one."

Max declined the gambit, merely nodding. "All right, Spiro, I'll not bother you any more now. Adoni, I'm going to lock the pair of you in while I take Miss Lucy home. I'll be back within the half-hour. You have the gun."

"Yes."

"And this." Spiro searched under his pillow and produced, with as much drama as if it had been a handkerchief, a Commando knife sharpened to a murderous glitter.

"That's the stuff," said Max cheerfully. "Now, you go to sleep, and very soon I'll get you away." He stooped, and dropped a hand for a moment on the boy's shoulder. "All will be well, *Spiro mou.*"

Adoni followed us to the door.

"And Sir Gale?" he asked softly.

"I'll look in on him," promised Max. "He'll sleep soundly enough, you can be sure of that. He's in no danger, so stop worrying, and get some sleep yourself. When I get back I'll spend the rest of the night in the kitchen. If you need me, you've only to come to the upper door and call me. Good night."

"Good night, Adoni," I said.

"Good night." Adoni gave me that smile again, perhaps a little frayed at the edges, then let the curtain fall into place across the cave entrance, lopping off the warm glow and shutting Max and me out into the darkness of the rocky passage.

He switched on the torch, and we started up the steps. The rough walls, the curving passage-way, the hewn flight of stairs, swam past in a sort of dream of fatigue, but a corner of my brain still felt awake and restless, alert to what he was saying.

"You can see now why I'm hiding that boy away till I can smuggle him out to Athens? It's not so much that he's in actual danger still—though he may well be—as simply that we stand a far better chance of finding out what Manning's up to if he has no idea that we suspect him. It's something big—that seems obvious ... And I'm pretty sure in my own mind where to start looking for it."

"The boat?"

"Either that or the boat-house. He's up to something involving that boat, and the damned good 'cover' that his photography gives him. If you accept Spiro's story, which I do, his little quarrel with Manning that morning provides the only faint clue... the only deviation from pattern that I can see ... and it could tie in with Yanni's death as well. I've been thinking about that. When Yanni brought Spiro's message here on Sunday night we discussed it pretty freely, and I let it be seen that I thought it very odd that Manning hadn't to be told. Yanni then said that he'd seen Manning's boat out at odd times and in odd places and that he'd thought for some time he was up to no good, and when I mentioned the photographs, he just shrugged and looked cynical. Well, that's nothing to go by—a man like Yanni would think that photography was a pretty queer occupation for anyone; but he could have very well been suspicious and curious enough after our conversation to go down that night and snoop around the boat-house, or, somewhere else he had no right to be, and so got himself murdered. It's my guess he was taken by surprise and knocked out from behind, then bundled into his own boat, with Manning's dinghy attached, taken out to sea, had his head smashed on the boom, and was dumped overboard. Manning then set the boom loose, emptied a bottle of ouzo around, turned the boat adrift, and rowed himself silently home. Oh, yes, it could have been done. He couldn't take him a great distance, since he'd have to row himself home, and then there was the squall which washed the body straight back—but it worked; he got away with it. An impulsive chap, our Godfrey ... and with one hell of a lot at stake, that's for sure. Yes, I could bear to know just what it is."

I said in quick apprehension: "You've got to promise me something."

"What's that?"

"You're not going there tonight? You wouldn't be so silly!"

He laughed. "You're dead right I would not, my love! I've got to see Spiro safe where he belongs before I go arguing with anyone with Manning's peculiar ideas on life and death. He must have shot at the dolphin, you'd realised that?" He nodded at my exclamation. "Who else? There's only one plausible reason, the one you imputed to me, that the word had gone round, and people were beginning to come to this piece of coast to see the creature. When Manning first saw you there in the bay, he may have thought you were one of them—a stranger, getting too close to whatever he was trying to keep secret. As Spiro and Yanni did."

"But ... those beautiful pictures! They really are beautiful, Max! He *couldn't* destroy it when he'd worked with it like that! He must have been fond of it!"

His smile was crooked. "And of Spiro, too?" I was silent. "Well, here we are. A moment while I push the racks back."

"What do you want me to do?"

"Something I know will be safe, and I hope will be easy. Cover my trip back from Athens with Spiro."

"Of course, if I can. How?"

"By keeping Manning away from Corfu harbour tomorrow at the time when I'm likely to be there. It would be quicker to go by plane, but I can't take the boy that way without the whole island knowing, so I'll have to take him in my car, hidden under a rug or something, across by the *Igoumenitsa*."

"The what?"

"The ferry to the mainland. I'll drive to Jannina and get the Athens plane from there. It means we can't get there and back in the one day, but I'll try to get home tomorrow, and I'll ring up this evening to let you know which ferry we'll get. The late one doesn't get in till a quarter to eleven; it's pitch dark then, and I doubt if he'd be around. But I'd like to get the earlier one if I can, and that gets in at five-fifteen ... So if you could bear to be having tea with him or something, till after six, to give me time to drive home ...?"

"Just at the moment I feel it would choke me, but I'll do my best," I said.

We were back in the kitchen. Its light and warmth and comfortable food-smells closed round us like memories from a real, but distant world, something safe and bright beyond the tossing straits of the night's dream. He pulled the great door shut behind us, and I heard the key drive the lock shut with a grating snap.

"There. Now you must go home. Come upstairs and get your things, and I'll look along to see if my father's safely asleep."

"Let's hope Phyl is, too, or heaven knows what story I'll have to cook up! Anything but the truth, I suppose!" I stared up at him. "I can't believe it. You realise that, don't you? I know it's true, but I can't believe it. And in the morning in daylight, it'll be quite impossible."

"I know. Don't think about it now. You've had yourself quite an evening, as they say; but you'll feel different when you've had some sleep."

"My watch has stopped. Oh hell, I suppose I got water in it. What's the time, Max?"

He glanced at his wrist. "So has mine. Blast. That little sea-bathe doesn't seem to have done either of us much good, does it?"

I laughed. "Things that might have been better expressed, Mr. Gale?"

He reached out, and pulled me to him. "Things that might have been better done," he said, and did them.

CHAPTER THIRTEEN

While you here do snoring lie,
Open-ey'd Conspiracy
His time doth take.

II. 1.

I SLEPT very late that day. The first thing I remember is the sound of shutters being folded back, and then the sudden hot blaze of sunlight striking across the pillow into my eyes.

Phyllida's voice said: "And high time, too, Rip Van Winkle!"

As I murmured something, dragging myself up out of the depths of sleep, she added: "Godfrey rang you up."

"Oh?" I blinked into the sunlight. "Rang *me* up? What did he want—did you say *Godfrey?*" The jerk of recollection brought me awake and up off the pillow so sharply that I saw her look of surprise, and it helped me to pull myself together.

"I was dreaming," I said, rubbing my eyes. "What on earth's the time?"

"High noon, my child."

"Goodness! What was he ringing about?"

"To know if you'd got safely home with the ring, of course."

"Did he expect Mr. Gale to steal it *en route?*"

Too late, I heard the tartness in my voice, and my sister looked at me curiously, but all she said was: "I woke you up too suddenly. Never mind, I brought some coffee. Here."

"Angel ... Thank you. Heavens, I must have slept like the dead ... Your ring's over there on the dressing-table. Oh, you've got it."

"You bet your sweet life I have. I came in a couple of hours ago and took it, but I couldn't bear to wake you, you were flat out, you poor kid." She turned her hand in the sunlight, and the diamond flashed. "Thank heaven for that! Bless you, Lucy, I'm really terribly grateful! I'd have gone stark ravers if I'd had to sit there all night, wondering if someone had wandered by and picked it up. And I wouldn't have dared go down myself! What on earth time did you get in?"

"I hardly know," I said truthfully. "My watch stopped. I thought I'd got water in it, but I'd only forgotten to wind it up. Some ghastly hour of the morning." I laughed. "There were complications, actually. Didn't Godfrey tell you about them?"

"I didn't quite get that bit. Something about the dolphin being up on the beach, and you and Max Gale wrestling about with it in the water. I must say it all sounded highly unlikely. What did happen?"

"More or less that." I gave her a rapid—and suitably expurgated—version of the dolphin's rescue, finishing with Godfrey's arrival on the beach. "And you'll find the wreck of your precious plastic bag in the bathroom, I'm afraid. I'm fearfully sorry, but I had to use something."

"Good heavens, that old thing! It couldn't matter less!"

"I'm relieved. The way you were talking last night I thought it was practically a holy relic."

She shot me a look as she disappeared through the bathroom door. "I was not myself last night, and you know it."

"Well, no." I reached for the coffee-pot which she had put down beside the bed, and poured myself more coffee.

She emerged from the bathroom, holding the bag between thumb and forefinger. " 'Wreck' was the word, wasn't it? I suppose you don't even know what happened to my Lizzie Arden lipstick?"

"Lord, I suppose that was a holy relic, too?"

"Well, it was gold."

I drank coffee. "You'll find it in Sir Julian Gale's dressing-gown pocket. I forgot it. I'm sorry again. You might say I was not myself last night either."

"Julian Gale's dressing-gown? This gets better and better! What happened?" She sat down on the edge of the bed. "I tried like mad to stay awake till you got in, but those beastly pills put me right out, once Godfrey'd phoned and I stopped worrying. Go on. I want to know what I've missed."

156

"Oh, nothing, really. We were both soaked, so I had to go up to the Castello to get dry, and they gave me coffee, and I had a bath ... Phyl, the bathroom! You'd hardly *believe* the ghastly —oh, sorry! I forgot, it's the Forli ancestral palace. Well, then, you'll know the bathroom."

"There are two," said Phyl. "Don't forget there are twenty bedrooms. One must have one's comforts. I'll say I know the bathrooms. Was it the one with the alabaster bath, or the porphyry?"

"You make it sound like the New Jerusalem. I don't know, I don't live at those levels. It was a rather nasty dark red with white spots, exactly like stale salami."

"Porphyry," said my sister. "Was the water hot?"

"Boiling."

"*Was* it? They must have done something, then. It never used to get more than warm, and in fact I seem to remember a tap for *sea*-water, which was pumped up in some weird way from the caves. There are caves under the Castello."

"Are there?"

"They used to use them to keep the wine in."

"Really. How exciting."

"Only, shrimps and things kept coming in, which was discouraging, and once a baby squid."

"It must have been."

"So Leo stopped it. It was supposed to be terribly health-giving, but there are limits."

"I'm sure there are," I said. "Shrimps in the wine would be one of them."

"Shrimps in the *wine*? What on earth are you talking about?"

I put down my empty cup. "I'm not quite sure. I thought it was the wine-cellars."

"The sea-water baths, idiot! Leo stopped them. Oh, I see, you're laughing at me ... Well, go on, anyway. You had a bath. But I still don't see how you got hot water; they *can't* have got the furnaces to work. They used to burn about a ton of coal a day, and it practically needed three slaves to stoke all round the clock."

"Adoni and Spiro invented a geyser."

"Dear God," said Phyl devoutly, "does it work?"

"Yes, I told you, the water was marvellous. What's more, there were hot pipes to dry my things on, *and* an electric fire in the bedroom next door. Well, while my things dried I wore Sir Julian's dressing-gown—which is why I left all your make-up in the pockets—and had coffee and bacon and eggs in the kitchen. Then Max Gale brought me home with the diamond, and that's the end of the saga." I leaned back and grinned at her. "As a matter of fact, it was rather fun."

"It sounds it! Was Max Gale civil?"

"Oh, yes. Very."

"I must say I'm surprised he helped you. I thought he was supposed to be trying to get rid of the dolphin."

"It can't have been him, after all. He helped me as soon as I asked him. And it wasn't his father, either, I'm certain of that. I think it must just have been some beastly local lad out for a bit of fun." I sat up and pushed back the coverlet. "I'd better get up."

My sister glanced at her wrist, and stood up with an exclamation. "Heavens, yes, I'll have to run if I'm to be ready."

"Where are you going?"

"To get my hair done, and I've got some shopping to do, so I thought I'd have lunch in town. I ought to have waked you before to ask if you'd like to come, but you looked so tired ... there's cold meat and a fruit flan if you stay home, but you're welcome to come if you like. Can you make it? I'll have to leave in about twenty minutes."

I hesitated. "Did Godfrey expect me to ring him back or anything?"

"Oh heavens, yes, I'd forgotten. He's pining to hear all about last night at first hand, I gather. I told him I'd be out to lunch, or I'd have asked him over, but I think he was going to ask you to lunch with him." She paused, a hand on the door. "There's the phone now, that'll be him. What shall I tell him?"

I reached for my stockings, and sat down to pull them on. The action covered some rapid thinking.

Godfrey would obviously be very curious to know what had passed at the Castello last night—what Sir Julian had told us, and what Max's reactions had been. If I could put him off till tomorrow, I might use this curiosity to keep him out of Max's way.

I said: "Say I'm in the bathroom or something, and can't come to the phone now, and tell him I'm going out with you, and I don't know when I'll be in, but I'll ring him ... No, he can ring me. Some time tonight."

158

Phyl raised an eyebrow. "Hard to get, huh? All right. Then you are coming with me?"

"No, I'll never make it, thanks all the same. I'll laze around and go down to the beach later."

"Okay," said my sister amiably, and went to silence the telephone.

I had no intention of going down to the beach, as it happened, it being more than likely that Godfrey would see me there and come down. But I did want to go over to the Castello to find out if Max and Spiro had got safely away. I hesitated to use the party telephone, and in any case I doubted if Sir Julian would want to talk to me this morning, but I had hopes of finding Adoni about in the garden, and of seeing him alone.

So I ate my cold luncheon early, and rather hurriedly, then, telling Miranda that I was going down to the beach for the afternoon, went to my room for my things.

But she was waiting for me in the hall as I came out, with a small package in her hand.

"For me?" I said. "What is it?"

"Adoni just brought it. It's some things you left there last night."

I took it from her. Through the paper I could feel the small hard shapes of Phyl's lipstick and powder-box. "Oh, that's good of him. I was thinking I'd have to go across to collect them. Is he still here?"

"No, miss, he wouldn't stay. But I was to say to you that all was well."

There was just the faintest lift of curiosity in her voice. I noticed then how bright her eyes were, and that the flush was back in her cheeks, and for a moment I wondered if Adoni had given her some hint of the truth.

"I'm glad of that. Did he tell you about the adventure we had last night?"

"The dolphin? Yes, he told me. It must have been strange." The strangest thing to her Greek mind was, I could see, that anyone should have gone to that amount of trouble. "But your coat, Miss Lucy! I don't know if it will ever come right!"

I laughed. "It did get rather a beating, didn't it? I thought you'd be wondering what I'd been doing."

"I knew you must have fallen in the sea, because of your dress and coat ... and the bathroom, po po po. I have washed the dress, but the coat must go to a proper cleaner."

"Oh, goodness, yes, you mustn't bother with it. Thanks very much for doing the dress, Miranda. Well, when you see Adoni, will you thank him for bringing these things? And for the message. That was all, that all was well?"

"Yes."

"That's fine," I said heartily. "I did wonder. Sir Julian wasn't feeling well last night, and I was worried."

She nodded. "He will be all right this morning."

I stared for a moment, then realised that she knew exactly what my careful meiosis meant, and was untroubled by it. The Greek mind again; if a man chose to get drunk now and again, what did it matter except to himself? His women would accept it as they accepted all else. Life here had its shining simplicities.

"I'm very glad," I said, and went out towards the pine woods.

As soon as I was out of sight of the house I left the path, and climbed higher through the woods, where the trees thinned, and a few scattered pines stood on top of the promontory. I spread my rug in the shade, and lay down. The ground was felted with pine needles, and here and there grew soft furry leaves of ground ivy, and the pretty, dull-pink orchids, and lilac irises flecked with white. The Castello was hidden from view by its trees, but from this height I could just see, on the southern headland, the roof of the Villa Rotha. The Forli house was visible below me. In the distance, beyond the sparkling sea, lay the mountains of Epirus. Their snow had almost gone, but further north the Albanian peaks still gleamed white. There, beneath them, would be the rocks where Spiro had gone ashore, and where Max had brought him off under the coastguards' guns. And there, a coloured cluster under the violet hills of Epirus, was Igoumenitsa, where the ferry ran . . .

I had brought a book, but couldn't read, and it was not long before I saw what I had been expecting: Godfrey, coming with an air of purpose along the path round the headland. He didn't descend into the bay; just stood there, as if looking for someone who might have been on the beach or in the sea. He waited a little while, and I thought at one point that he was going to cross the sand and climb to the Forli house, but he didn't. He hung around for a few minutes more, then turned and went back.

Some time later my eye was caught by a glimpse of moving white, a glint beyond the treetops that rimmed the sea; and presently a boat stole out under sail from beyond the further headland, cutting a curved path of white through the glittering blue.

I lay, chin on hand, watching her.

She was not unlike a boat that Leo had owned some years back, and on which I had spent a holiday one summer, the year I had left school. She was a powered sloop, perhaps thirty feet overall, Bermuda rigged, with—as far as I could make out—a mast that could be lowered. That this was so seemed probable, since from something Godfrey had said I assumed she was Dutch built, so might presumably be adapted for canal cruising, and negotiating low bridges. In any case I had gathered last night that she was customarily moored not in the bay, but in the boat-house; and even if this was built on the same lavish scale as the Castello, and designed to house several craft, it would have to be a vast place indeed to take the sloop's forty-odd-foot mast. Her hull was sea-grey, with a white line at the bows. She was a lovely craft, and at any other time I would have lain dreamily admiring her sleek lines and the beauty of her canvas, but today I merely wondered about her speed—seven or eight knots, I supposed—and narrowed my eyes to watch the small black figure at the tiller, which was Godfrey.

The sea raced glittering along the grey hull (grey for camouflage?); the white wake creamed; she turned, beautiful, between me and the sun, and I could see no more of her except as a winged shape heading in a long tack out to sea, and then south, towards Corfu town.

*   *   *

"Lucy?" said the telephone.

"Yes. Hullo. You're very faint."

"Did you get the message from Adoni?"

"Yes. Just that all was well, so I assumed you'd got away safely. I hope it still is?"

"So far, a bit discouraging, but I'm still hoping. What about you?"

"I'm fine, thank you, and all's well here. Calm and normal, as far as I can see. Don't worry about this end."

"Ah." A slight pause. Though I knew there was no one else in the house, I found myself glancing quickly around me. Max's voice said, distant in my ear: "You know this libretto I came over here to discuss with that friend of mine? We've been talking over the story all afternoon now, and he's not very keen on it. Says it's not plausible. I'm not sure if I'm going to be able to persuade him to do much about it."

"I get it," I said, "but look this line's all right. My sister's out, and so is the other party on the line; I saw his boat go out, with him in it, quite a bit ago, and it's not back yet. I've been watching till now. You can say what you like."

"Well, I'm not sure how good their English is at the Corfu Exchange," said Max, "but you'll have gathered it's not very good news in any language. We've been with the police all afternoon, and they've listened civilly enough, but they're not inclined to take it all that seriously—certainly not to take action against our friend without some solid proof."

"If he were to be watched——?"

"They're inclined to think it's not worth it. The general idea is that it's only another spot of illegal trading, and no one's prepared to take it seriously enough to spend money on investigating."

"Don't they believe the boy's story, then?"

He hesitated. "I can't quite make that out. I don't think they do. They think he may be mistaken, and they're favouring the idea of an accident."

"A nice, trouble-free verdict," I said dryly. "And was Y's death an accident, too?"

"They're inclined to stick to the first verdict there as well. The trouble is, you see, they're furious with me over last night's little effort, which I've had to tell them about, and which might have started some trouble. The Greek–Albanian frontier's always like a train of dynamite with a slow fuse crawling up to it. Oh, they did admit in the end that I could hardly have called the police in on a rendezvous with Milo and his pal, but I did also withhold evidence in the inquiry on Y.Z. after they'd been so helpful to Father and myself over Spiro ... I must say I rather see their point, but my name's mud for the moment, and they're simply not prepared to take action on my say-so, especially if it means coming in over the heads of the local coppers. You see, there's no possible motive."

"But if it was ... 'illegal trading'?"

"That would hardly have led to murder. As we know, it's barely even taken seriously from this side of the border."

"I see."

"So they look like accepting accident on both counts. And, of

162

course, damn it, we can't prove a thing. I simply don't know what's going to happen."

"Can you bring him back—the boy?"

"I don't know that either. As far as the hospital's concerned it's all right, but as to whether it's safe for him ... If only one could find even some shred of an idea why it happened, let alone proof that it did ... If I didn't know the boy so well, and if it weren't for Y's death, I'd take the same attitude as the police, I can tell you that. You were right last night when you said it was incredible. In the cold light of day the idea's fantastic—but still my bones tell me it's true ... Ah, well. I'm going to talk to them again later tonight, and there's still to-morrow. We may get something done yet."

"When will you come back?"

"Tomorrow. I'll try to manage the earlier time I gave you."

"All right. I'm fairly sure I can have that under control. You won't be met."

"Well, that's one load off my mind." I heard him laugh. "We managed fine on the way out, but the hospital's fitted a wonderful new cast that won't go in the boot, so it's the back seat and a rug—and a damned awkward situation if anyone were hanging about. Will it be hard to arrange?"

"Dead easy—I think. I'm not sure which is the spider and which is the fly, but I don't think I'll even have to try."

"Well, for pity's sake watch your step."

"Don't worry, he'll get nothing out of me. I may be a darned bad actress on the stage, but off it I'm terrific."

He laughed again. "Who's telling whom? But that's not what I meant."

"I know. It's all right, I'll be careful."

I heard him take a long breath. "I feel better now. I'll go and tackle this bunch of very nice but all too sensible policemen again. I must go. Bless you. Take care of yourself."

"And you," I said.

The receiver at the other end was cradled, and through the wire washed the crackling hiss of the miles of sea and air that lay between us. As I put my own receiver down gently, I found that I was staring out of the long glass pane of the door that led to the terrace. It framed an oblong of the empty evening sky, dusk, with one burning planet among a trail of dusty stars. I sat for a few minutes without moving, one hand still on the receiver, not thinking of anything, just watching that bright planet, and feeling in me all tensions stilled at once, as if some-one had laid a finger across a thrumming string.

When the telephone rang again, right under my hand, I hardly even jumped. I sat back in the chair and put the receiver to my ear.

"Yes?" I said. "Oh, hullo, Godfrey. Yes, it's Lucy. In Corfu, are you? No, I've been home a little while. I was wondering when you'd ring . . ."

CHAPTER FOURTEEN

He's safe for these three hours.
III. 1.

HE called for me next day immediately after lunch. He had suggested that I lunch with him, and certainly he had sounded flatteringly anxious for my company, but since I didn't imagine he really wanted anything from me but information, and I had no idea how long I could hold him, I pleaded an engagement for lunch, but allowed myself to be suitably eager for a drive in the afternoon.

I even managed to suggest the route. Not that there was much choice in the matter; the road north was barely navigable by a car one cared about, so I could hardly suggest that Godfrey took it. We would have to go south on the road by which Max and Spiro would eventually be driving home, but there was, happily, a road leading off this to Palaiokastritsa, a famous beauty-spot on the western coast which I could be legitimately anxious to visit. It was in fact true that I had looked the place up on the map, but had put off going there because the road seemed mountainous and I had been slightly nervous of tackling it in Phyl's little car. With me driving (I told Godfrey) it would be nerve-racking, and with Phyl driving it would be suicide . . . But if Godfrey would drive me, and if he had a car that would manage the gradients . . .

He had laughed, sounding pleased, and had professed himself delighted to brave any gradients I wished, and yes, he had a car that would manage it quite easily . . .

He certainly had. It was a black XK 150, blunt-nosed, power-ful, and about as accommodating on the narrow roads as a bull seal on his own bit of beach. It nosed its way impatiently along the drive, humming like a hive of killer bees, bucked on to the rutted sweep of the Castello's private road, and turned to swoop down to the gate where Maria's cottage stood.

Maria was outside, bending over a rusty tin with a stick, stirring what seemed to be hen food. When she heard the car she straightened up with the tin clutched to her breast, and the hens clucking and chattering round her feet. Godfrey, slowing down for the turn into the main road, raised a hand and called out a greeting, to which she returned a look of pleasure mingled with respect, as warm a look as I had seen on her face in the last week or so. I had noticed the same look, shy but pleased, in Miranda's face, as she had showed him into the *salotto* earlier, as if the two women were grateful to Spiro's employer for his continued kindness to them in their bereavement.

I stole a look at him as the car swerved—rather too fast, and with a blare of its twin horns that sent Maria's hens up in a squawking cloud—on to the main road. I don't know quite what I had expected to see this afternoon—some smooth-skinned monster, perhaps, with hoofs, horns, and tail all visible to the eye of knowledge—but he was just the same, an undeniably attractive man, who handled his exciting car with skill and obvious enjoyment.

And this man, I thought, was supposed to have brushed the boy—the beloved son and brother—off the stern of his boat as if he were a jellyfish, and then sailed on, leaving him to drown . . .

He must have felt me watching him, for he flicked me a glance, and smiled, and I found myself smiling back spontaneously, and quite without guile. In spite of myself, in spite of Max, and Spiro's story, I could not believe it. The thing was, as I had said to Max, impossible in daylight.

Which was just as well. If I was to spend the next few hours with him, I would have to shut my mind to all that I had learned, to blot out the scene in the cellar, drop Spiro out of existence as if he were indeed dead. And, harder than all, drop Max. There was a curiously strong and secret pleasure, I had found, in speaking of him as 'Mr. Gale' in the off-hand tones that Godfrey and Phyllida commonly used, as one might of a stranger to whom one is under an obligation, but whom one hardly considers enough to like or dislike. Once, as I had mentioned his name in passing, my eye, downcast, caught the faint mark of a bruise on my arm. The secret thrill of pleasure that ran up my spine startled me a little; I slipped my other hand over the mark to hide it, and found it cupping the flesh as if it were his, and not my own. I looked away, out of the car, and made some random remark about the scenery.

It was a very pretty road. To our left was the sea, blue and smooth, broken only by a tiny white crescent of sail thin as a nail-paring and almost lost in the heat haze. On the right was a high hedge of apple blossom and judas-trees, their feet deep in a vivid bank of meadow flowers, yellow and purple and white. Two little girls, in patched and faded dresses of scarlet, stood barefoot in the dust to watch us go by, one of them holding a bough of oranges as an English child might hold a stick of balloons, the fruit bulging and glowing among the green leaves.

The road straightened, and the XK 150 surged forward with a smooth burst of speed. My spirits lifted. This was going to be easy; in fact there was no reason why I shouldn't simply relax and enjoy it too. I sat back and chatted on—I hoped naturally —about nothings; the view, the people Phyl had met yesterday in Corfu, the prospect of Leo's coming with the children for Easter...

We flashed by a fork in the road.

I sat up sharply. "That was the turning, wasn't it? I'm sure the signpost said Palaiokastritsa!"

"Oh, yes, it was. I'm sorry, I wasn't thinking; I meant to have told you, I'm not taking you there today. It's a long way, and we've hardly time. We'll go another day if you like, when we don't have to be back early."

"*Do* we have to be back early?"

The question slipped out before I thought, ingenuous in its dismay. I saw the faint shadow of gratified surprise in his face, and reflected that after my evasions over the telephone he had every right to find provocation in it.

"I'm afraid so. I'm going out tonight. I don't say we couldn't do it, but it's a shame to go all the way for a short time; it's a lovely place, and there's a lot to see. Besides which, it's a damned waste to go there and not have lunch; there's a restaurant right on the beach where they keep crayfish alive in pots in the sea, and you choose your own and they take them out fresh to cook." A sideways look at me and a teasing smile. "I suppose you disapprove, but I can tell you, they're wonderful. I'll take you there soon, if you promise not to stand me up for lunch next time."

"I didn't—that would be lovely."

We flicked through a tiny village, one narrow street of houses and a baked white church with a red roof. The snarl of the engine echoed back in a quick blast from the hot walls, and we were through, nose down through a scatter of goats, children, a scraggy puppy, and a donkey trailing a frayed end of rope. The children stared after us, admiring and unresentful.

"One thing," said Godfrey cheerfully, "one doesn't have to plan one's outings here according to the weather. The sun's always on call in this blessed isle, and one day's as good as another."

That's what you think, I said savagely to myself. My hands were tight together in my lap now, as much because of his driving as in a panic-stricken attempt to think of the map. How to get him off this road, head him away from Corfu?

I said aloud: "I'll hold you to that one day, *and* I'll eat the crayfish! I can't feel strongly about fish, I'm afraid! Where are we going then, Pellekas?" For Pellekas one turned off just at the north end of Corfu—the only other turning before the town.

"No, the Achilleion."

"Oh? That's a wonderful idea!"

It was a bloody awful idea, as well I knew. To get there one went right through Corfu—not quite to the harbour, but near enough—and, of course, the whole way home we would be using the same road as Max. Well, I'd just have to see that we didn't head for home around five-thirty, and I could only hope there was plenty of scope for sightseeing to the south of Corfu town. I reached for my handbag and fished in it for the guide I had brought, adding with great enthusiasm: "I'd planned to visit it one day, but there was the same objection—Phyl told me it was on top of a hill with the most ghastly zigzag going up to it! Yes, here it is... 'The villa of Achilleion, erected for the Empress Elizabeth of Austria ... The villa, which is in Italian Renaissance style, was purchased in 1907 by the German Emperor. The gardens are open to visitors (admission one drachma, applied to charitable purposes).' "

"What? What on earth's that?"

"An ancient Baedeker I found on Phyl's shelves. It was my grandfather's—date 1909. It's really rather sweet. Listen to the bit at the beginning about the history of the island ... he says 'it came into the possession of' the Romans, then 'fell to the share of' the Venetians, then 'was occupied by' the French: then 'was under Turkish, then Russian sway', but—notice the *but*—from 1815 to 1863 it 'came under the protection of' the British. Rule, Britannia. Those were the days."

"They certainly were." He laughed. "Well, you can see the whole palace as well, today, and it will cost a damned sight more than a drachma, and I imagine the gate money'll go straight to the Greek Government. As usual, charity begins at home ... I wish there'd been some classical relics to take you to—Phyl told me you were interested—but I don't know any, apart from some temple or other inside the Mon Repos park, which is private. However, you might say Achilles is the patron saint of the Achilleion, so perhaps it'll do! There's some talk of turning it into a casino, so this may be the last chance of seeing it more or less in the original state. And the drive up there is very pretty, you'll enjoy it."

"You're very kind," I said. It was all I could do not to stare. He spoke so easily and charmingly, sitting there relaxed and handsome at the wheel, the sun throwing up fair highlights in his hair, and a dusting of freckles along the bare brown arms. He was wearing an open-necked shirt, with a yellow silk scarf tucked in at the neck—Top People summer uniform—which suited him very well. He looked calm and contented, and perfectly normal.

Well, why not? When a felon's not engaged in his employment, he has to look as ordinary as possible for his own skin's sake. I supposed it was perfectly possible for a man to drown two young men one week, and enjoy a pleasant day out with a girl the next, take a lot of trouble to plan an outing for her, and even enjoy the view himself ...

"And there's a marvellous view," he said. "The palace is set on a steep wooded hill over the sea. From the belvedere you can see practically the whole way from Vutrinto in Albania, to Perdika along the Greek coast. On a clear day the harbour at Igoumenitsa's quite plain."

"How splendid."

"And now supposing you tell me exactly what happened last night at the Castello?"

It took every scrap of discipline and technique I had not to jump like a shot rabbit. "What happened? Well ... nothing much—what should? I got home with the diamond, you know that."

"Oh, to hell with the diamond, you know quite well what I

168

mean." He sent me another sideways, amused look. "Did you see Julian Gale?"

"Oh. Yes, I did. Adoni was with him when we got up there."

"Ah, yes, the faithful watch-pup. He would be. How was Sir Julian?"

"He went to bed pretty soon," I said cautiously. I kept my eyes on the road, and in the windscreen I saw Godfrey glance at me again. "He was—tired," I said.

"Say what you mean," said Godfrey. "He was stoned."

"How do you know?" The question came out flatly and even accusingly, but since he himself had hit the ball into the open with the last phrase there was no reason why I shouldn't keep it there.

"Come off it, they knew who'd been with him, didn't they?"

"We-ll, it was mentioned." I leaned back in my seat and let a spice of mischievous amusement creep into my voice. It sounded so like Phyl as to be startling. "Mr. Gale wasn't awfully pleased with you, Godfrey."

"Damn it all, what's it got to do with me if he wants to get plastered? By the time I saw which way the land lay, he was halfway there. Do they imagine it was up to me to stop him?"

"I wouldn't know. But I'd watch out for Mr. Gale if I were you."

"So?" His mouth curved. "Pistols for two and coffee for one, or just a horsewhip? Well, maybe he does owe it me, after all."

I knew then. I'm not sure what it was, something in his voice, or the infinitesimal degree of satisfaction at the corners of his mouth; something at once cruel and gay and quite terrifying. All the daylight doubts fled, once and for ever. Of course he was a murderer. The man was a natural destroyer. *Evil be thou my Good* . . . And the instinct that had allowed him to create those pictures wasn't even incongruous: no doubt it had given him much the same pleasure to destroy Spiro as it had to photograph him. Destroying Sir Julian would hardly have cost him a moment's thought.

I dragged my eyes and thoughts away from the evil sitting beside me in the car, and concentrated on the idyll of silver olive and black cypress through which the XK 150 slashed its way in a train of dust.

"What a lovely road."

"I wish they'd do something about these pot-holes, that's all. Don't side-track, Lucy. Was it really horsewhips?"

"I wouldn't be surprised. I mean, Mr. Gale had had a trying evening. I'd had hysterics all over him and dragged him out to help with the dolphin, and he fell slap in the sea, and then on top of it all when we got up to the house we found his father drunk ... in front of me, too. You can't blame him if he's out for your blood."

"I suppose not." He didn't sound as if it worried him vastly. "Where is he today?"

"I believe he said he was going to Athens. It was just some remark to Adoni—I didn't take much notice. But you're probably safe for today."

He laughed. "I breathe again. Just look at the colour of that girl's frock, the one picking up olives over there, that dusty red against the rather acid green."

"Don't *you* side-track. I want to know what happened."

He raised his brows. "Heavens, nothing, really. I saw the old man at the garage on the harbour, and he was looking for a lift, so I took him home. I was rather pleased to have the chance to talk to him, as it happened—you can never get near him alone, and it was too good a chance to miss."

"What on earth did you want to get him alone for? Don't tell me you're looking for a walk-on in the next Gale play!"

He grinned. "That'll be the day—always providing there is one. No, there were things I wanted to know, and I thought he'd be the softest touch. Max Gale and I aren't just the best of friends, and the watch-pup dislikes me. I can't think why."

"Godfrey! Are you telling me you got him drunk on purpose?"

"Good God, no. Why should I? I wasn't trying to get State secrets out of him. But by the time he'd had a couple there was no stopping him, and it wasn't my business to stop him, was it? I admit I didn't try." That fleeting smile again, gone in an instant; a flash of satisfaction, no more. "It was quite entertaining up to a point."

"What on earth *were* you wanting to get out of him?"

"Only what the police were up to."

"Police?"

He glanced at me with a lifted eyebrow. "Don't sound so startled. What have you been doing? No, it's only that on this island everything gets to the Gales' ears and to no one else's. I had a hell of a job finding anything out about the Spiro affair—

nobody seemed to think it was my business, but I'm damned sure they tell the Gales everything that turns up."

"Well, I gather there's some sort of family connection."

"So I'm told. But I don't see why that gives them an 'exclusive' on a police inquiry that involved me as closely as Spiro's death did."

"I do so agree," I said sympathetically. "It must have been a terribly nerve-racking time for you."

"It still is." Certainly if I hadn't known what I knew, I'd have heard nothing in the grave rejoinder but what should properly be there. But, keyed as I was, the two brief syllables hid a whole world of secret amusement. I found that the hand in my lap was clenched tightly, and deliberately relaxed it.

"Did Sir Julian have any news? What has turned up about Spiro?"

"Search me. He wouldn't say a word. We had a couple of drinks at the *taverna*, and I thought his manner was a bit odd; I thought at first he was being cagey, and there was something he didn't want to tell me, but after a bit I realised that he was merely feeling his corn, and trying to hide it. It's my guess the poor old chap hasn't had anything stronger than half a mild sherry for a year." His mouth twitched. "Well, after that I'm afraid I did rather give the party a push along the right lines ... I wanted to lay in a few bottles for myself—I was out of ouzo, for one thing, and there was a new *koùm koyàt* liqueur I was wanting to try, so I bought them, but when I suggested we should go along to my place the old man wouldn't have it. He was mellowing a bit by that time, and insisted on taking me to the Castello, and buying a bottle of gin to treat me to. It didn't take much of that stuff to get him good and lit, but I'm afraid it finished any hope I'd had of getting sense out of him. He'd got it fixed in his head that the only reason I'd gone to the Castello was to hear the recording of their blasted film music." He gave a short laugh where the exasperation still lingered. "Believe you me, I got the lot, words and all."

"Oh, I believe you! Hunks of *The Tempest*?"

"Did he do that for you, too?"

I laughed. "He was reciting when Mr. Gale and I got up to the house. As a matter of fact I enjoyed it. He did it marvellously, gin or no gin."

"He's had plenty of practice."

The cruel words were lightly spoken, but I think it was at

that moment that I began to hate Godfrey Manning. I remembered Max's face, strained and tired; Sir Julian's, blurred and drowning, holding on to heaven knew what straw of integrity; the two boys curled close together on the makeshift bed; Maria's grateful humility. Until this moment I had been content to think that I was helping Max: this had franked a piece of deception whose end I had not let myself explore. But now I explored it, and with relish. If Godfrey Manning was to be proved a murderer, then presumably he was going to be punished for it; and I was going to help with everything I had. Something settled in me, cold and hard. I sat down in the saddle and prepared to ride him down.

I felt him glance at me, and got my face into order.

"What actually happened when you got to the house?" he asked. "What did he tell them, Max and the model-boy?"

"Nothing, while I was there. No, honestly, Godfrey!" I was pleased to hear how very honest I sounded. "They only guessed it was you who'd been with him because you'd thrown a Sobranie butt into the stove."

He gave a crack of laughter. "Detectives Unlimited! You did have an exciting night, didn't you? Did they let anything drop in front of you—about Spiro, I mean?"

"Not a thing."

"Nor Yanni Zoulas?"

I turned wide, surprised eyes on him. "Yanni—oh, the fisherman who was drowned. No, why?"

"I wondered. Pure curiosity."

I said nothing, letting the silence hang. Now we were getting somewhere ... It was obvious that he was still uncertain whether the police really had accepted 'accident' as the verdict on Spiro and Yanni; and I thought it was obvious, too, that he badly wanted to know. And since he wasn't the man to sweat about what he had done, it must be what he still had to do that was occupying him: he needed a clear field, and no watchers. His efforts with Sir Julian, and now with me, showed that he had no suspicion that he was being watched, just that he badly needed a green light, and soon.

Well, I thought cheerfully, leaning back in my seat, let him sweat a bit longer. He'd get no green light from me.

The road was climbing now, zigzagging steeply up a wooded hill clothed with vineyards and olive-groves, and the fields of green corn with their shifting grapebloom shadows.

He said suddenly: "Didn't you see him go back to the body after we'd left it?"

"What? See who?"

"Gale, of course."

"Oh, yes ... sorry, I was looking at the view. Yes, I did. Why?"

"Didn't you wonder why he did that?"

"I can't say I did. I suppose he just wanted another look." I gave a little shiver. "Better him than me. Why, did you think he saw something we didn't?"

He shrugged. "Nothing was said to you?"

"Nothing at all. Anyway, I hardly know the Gales; they wouldn't tell me things any more than you. You aren't beginning to think there was more in Yanni's death than met the eye?"

"Oh, no. Let's just say it's curiosity, and a little natural human resentment at having things taken out of my hands. The man was drowned on my doorstep—as Spiro was from my boat —and I think I should have been kept in the picture. That's all."

"Well," I said, "if anything had turned up about Spiro Maria would know, and she'd tell my sister and me straight away. If there is anything, I'll let you know. I realise how you must be feeling."

"I'm sure you do. And here we are. Shall we see if they'll let us in for one drachma?"

*   *   *

The gates were open, rusting on their seedy pillars. Huge trees, heavy already with summer, hung over the walls. A sleepy janitor relieved us of twenty drachmas or so and nodded us through.

The house was very near the gate, set among thick trees. The doors were open. I had vaguely expected a museum of some kind, a carefully kept relic of the past, but this was merely an empty house, a summer residence from which the owners had moved out, leaving doors and windows unlocked so that dead leaves and insects had drifted year by year into the deserted rooms, floorboards had rotted, paintwork had decayed, metal had rusted ... The place was a derelict, set in the derelict remains of formal gardens and terraces, and beyond the garden boundaries crowded the trees and bushes of a park run wild.

I remember very little now of my tour of the Achilleion. I am sure Godfrey was a good guide: I recollect that he talked charmingly and informatively all the time, and I must have made the right responses; but I was obsessed with my new hatred of him, which I felt must be bound to show as plainly as a stain; in consequence I was possibly even a little too charming back again. I know that as the afternoon went on his manner warmed perceptibly. It was a relief to escape at length from the dusty rooms on to the terrace.

Here at least the air was fresh, and it wasn't quite as hard to linger admiringly as it had been in the dusty rooms of the palace, with their unkempt and shabby grandeurs. The terrace was floored with horrible liver-coloured tiles, and the crowding trees below it obscured any view there might have been, but I did my best with the hideous metal statues at the corners and the row of dim-looking marble 'Muses' posing sadly along a loggia. I was a model sightseer. I stopped at every one. You'd have thought they were Michelangelos. Three-fifteen ... three-twenty ... even at three minutes per Muse it would only keep us there till three-forty-seven ...

There remained the garden. We went in detail round it; arum lilies deep in the weeds at the foot of palm-trees; a few unhappy paeonies struggling up in the dank shade; a dreadful statue of Achilles triumphant (six minutes) and a worse one of Achilles dying (four); some Teutonic warriors mercifully cutting one another's throats in a riot of brambles (one and a half). I would even have braved the thorny tangle of the wood to admire a statue of Heine sitting in a chair, if the gate hadn't been secured with barbed wire, and if I hadn't been afraid that I would wear out even Godfrey's patience.

I needn't have worried. It was unassailable. He had to put the time in somehow, and I am certain that it never once crossed his mind that a day out with him could be anything but a thrill for me from first to last.

Which, to be fair, it certainly was. The thrill that I got, quite literally, when he took me by the elbow to lead me gently back towards the gate and the waiting Jaguar went through my bone-marrow as if the bones had been electrically wired. It was only twenty past four. If we left for home now, and if Godfrey, as seemed likely, suggested tea in Corfu, we should just be in nice time to meet the ferry.

There was one more statue near the gate, a small one of a

174

fisher-boy sitting on the fragment of a boat, bare-legged, chubby, smiling down at something, and wearing a dreadful hat. It was on about the same level of genius as the Muses, but, of course, I stopped in front of it, rapt, with Baedeker at the ready and my eyes madly searching the tiny print to see if there were any other 'sights' between here and Corfu which I could use to delay my blessedly complacent guide.

"Do you like it?" Godfrey's tone was amused and indulgent. He laid the back of a finger against the childish cheek. "Do you notice? If this had been done seven years ago instead of seventy it might have been Spiro. One wonders if the model wasn't a grandfather or something. It's very like, don't you think?"

"I never knew Spiro."

"Of course not, I forgot. Well, Miranda, then."

"Yes, perhaps I do see it. I was just thinking it was charming."

"The face is warm," said Godfrey, running a light hand down the line of the cheek. I turned away quickly, feeling my face too naked. Half past four.

He dropped his hand. "You keep looking at your watch. I suppose you're like Phyl, always gasping for tea at this time? Shall we go and look for some in Corfu?"

"What's the other way? The coast looked so lovely from the belvedere."

"Nothing much, the usual pretty road, and a fishing village called Benitses."

"There'll be a *kafenèion* there, surely? That would be more fun for a change. Wouldn't there be tea there?"

He laughed. "The usual wide choice, Nescafé or lemonade. There might even be some of those slices of bread, cut thick and dried in the oven. I've never yet discovered who eats them or even how. I can't even break them. Well, on your head be it. Jump in."

We got tea after all at Benitses, at a plain, clean little hotel set right on the sea. It couldn't have been better placed—for me, that is. There were tables outside, and I chose one right on the dusty shore, under a pepper-tree, and sat down facing the sea. Just beside us a whole stable of coloured boats dozed at their moorings, vermilion and turquoise and peacock, their masts swaying gently with the breathing of the sea; but beyond them I saw nothing but one red sail dancing alone on the empty and glittering acres.

Godfrey glanced over his shoulder. "What's going on there that's so interesting?"

"Nothing, really, but I could watch the sea by the hour, couldn't you? Those boats are so pretty. Your own is a real beauty."

"When did you see her?"

"Yesterday afternoon. I saw you go out."

"Oh? Where were you? I'd been looking for you down on the beach."

"What a pity! No, I didn't go down after all, I stayed up in the woods and slept." I laughed. "I rather needed the sleep."

"You'd certainly had a strenuous time. I wish I'd seen your rescue act with the dolphin. Some pictures by flash would have been interesting." He stirred the pale tea, squashing the lemon slice against the side of the cup. "I read somewhere—I think it was Norman Douglas—that while dolphins are dying they change colour. I believe it can be a remarkable display. Fascinating if one could get that, don't you think?"

"Marvellous. Did you say you were going out tonight?"

"Yes."

"I suppose you couldn't do with a crew? I'd adore to come."

"Brave of you, under the circumstances. You'd not be afraid to crew for me?"

"Not in the least, I'd love it. You mean I may? What time are you going?"

If he had accepted the offer I'm not sure what I'd have done; broken an ankle at least, I expect. But he said:

"Of course you may, some day soon, but you've got me wrong, I didn't mean I was going out with the boat tonight. Actually, I'm going by car to visit friends."

"Oh, I'm sorry, I must have got hold of the wrong end of the stick. A pity, I was getting all excited.'

He smiled. "I tell you what; I'll take you sailing soon— Friday, perhaps? or Saturday? We'll go round to Lake Kalikio-poulos and look for the place—one of the places, I should say— where Odysseus is supposed to have stepped ashore into the arms of Nausicaa. Would that be classical enough for you?"

"It would be marvellous."

"Then I'll look forward to it . . . Look, there's the ferry."

"Ferry?" It came out in a startled croak, and I cleared my throat. "What ferry?"

"The mainland boat. She crosses to Igoumenitsa and back.

176

There, see? It's not easy to see her against the glitter. She'll be in in about twenty minutes." He looked at his watch, and pushed back his chair. "Hm, she's late. Well, shall we go?"

"I'd like to go upstairs, please, if they have one."

The owner of the hotel, who was at Godfrey's elbow with the check, interpreted this remark with no difficulty, and led me up an outside stair and along a scrubbed corridor to an enormous room which had been made into a bathroom. It was spotlessly clean, and furnished, apart from the usual offices, with a whole gallery of devotional pictures. Perhaps others before me had fled to this sanctuary to think . . .

But it was Baedeker I had come to study. I whipped it open and ran a finger down the page. The print was hideously small, and danced under my eyes. *One drachma a day for the drago-man is ample . . . valets-de-place, 5 dr. per day, may be dis-pensed with . . .*

Ah, here was something that might be expected to appeal to an avid classicist like myself. *The tomb of Menecrates, dating from the 6th or 7th Century B.C. . . . .* And bang on the way home, at that. Now, if only I could persuade Godfrey that my day would be blighted if I didn't visit this tomb, whatever it was . . .

I could; and it was a winner, for the simple reason that nobody knew where it was. We asked everybody we met, and were directed in turn, with the utmost eagerness and goodwill, to a prison, a football ground, the site of a Venetian fort, and a pond; and I could have felt sorry for Godfrey if I hadn't seen quite clearly that he thought that I was trying desperately to spin out my afternoon with him. The man's armour was com-plete. In his vocabulary, God was short for Godfrey.

I was paid out when we did finally run Menecrates to earth in the garden of the police station, and the custodian, welcoming us as if the last tourist to visit it had been Herr Karl Baedeker himself in 1909, pressed on me a faded document to read, and thereafter solemnly walked me round the thing three times, while Godfrey sat on the wall and smoked, and the lovely dusk fell, and the hands of my watch slid imperceptibly round, and into the clear . . .

"After six o'clock," said Godfrey, rising. "Well, I hope you've time to have a drink with me before I take you home? The Astir has a very nice terrace overlooking the harbour."

"That would be wonderful," I said.

CHAPTER FIFTEEN

I prithee now lead the way without any more talking.

II. 2.

IT was quite dark when Godfrey finally drove me back to the Villa Forli. I said good-bye at the front door, waited till the car had vanished among the trees, then turned and hurried indoors.

A light from the kitchen showed that either Miranda or her mother was there; but the *salotto* was empty in its cool, grey dusk, and no light showed from Phyl's bedroom door. In a moment I knew why: I had made straight for the telephone, and just before I lifted the receiver I saw the pale oblong of a note left on the table beside it. I switched on the table-lamp, to find a note from Phyl.

"Lucy dear (it ran), *Got a wire this afternoon to say that Leo and the kids are coming on Saturday, and he can stay two whole weeks. Calloo, callay! Anyway, I've gone into Corfu to lay in a few things. Don't wait for me if you're hungry. There's plenty for G. too, if he wants to stay. Love, Phyl."*

As I finished reading this, Miranda came into the hall.

"Oh, it's you, Miss Lucy! I thought I heard a car. Did you see the letter from the Signora?"

"Yes, thank you. Look, Miranda, there's no need for you to stay. Mr. Manning's gone home, and my sister may be late, so if there's something cold I can get——"

"I came to tell you. She telephoned just a few minutes ago. She has met friends in Corfu—Italian friends who are spending one night only—and is having dinner with them. She said if you wanted to go, to get a taxi and join them at the Corfu Palace, but"—a dimple showed—"none of them speaks any English, so she thinks you would rather stay here, yes?"

I laughed. "But definitely yes. Well, in that case, I'll have a bath, and then have supper as soon as you like. But I can easily look after myself, you know. If you'll tell me what there is, you can go home if you want to."

"No, no, I shall stay. There is a cold lobster, and salad, but I am making soup." She gave her wide, flashing smile. "I make good soup, Miss Lucy. You will like it."

"I'm sure I shall. Thank you."

She didn't go, but lingered at the edge of the light thrown by the little lamp, her hands busily, almost nervously, pleating the skirt of the red dress. I realised, then, suddenly, what my preoccupation hadn't let me notice till now; this was not the subdued and tear-bleached Miranda of the last week. Some of the gloss was back on her, and there was a sort of eagerness in her face, as if she was on the edge of speech.

But all she said was: "Of course I will stay. I had a day off this afternoon. A day off? Is that what the Signora calls it?"

"Yes, that's right. The afternoon off. What do you do when you get an afternoon off?"

She hesitated again, and I saw her skin darken and glow. "Sometimes also Adoni has the afternoon off."

"I see." I couldn't quite keep the uneasiness out of my voice. So she had spent the afternoon with Adoni. It might be that fact alone which had set her shining again, but I wondered if anyone as young as Adoni could possibly be trusted not to have told her about Spiro. Even for myself, the temptation to break the news to the girl and her mother had been very strong, while for the nineteen-year-old Adoni, longing, like anyone of his age, to boast of his own share in last night's exploits, the urge must have been overwhelming. I added: "No, don't go for a moment, Miranda; I want to make a phone call in rather a hurry, and I don't know how to ask for the number. The Castello, please; Mr. Max."

"But he is not there, he is away."

"I know, but he was to be back before six."

She shook her head. "He will not be here till late, Adoni told me so. Mr. Max rang up at five o'clock. He said he would be home tonight, but late, and not to expect him to dinner."

"Oh." I found that I had sat down rather heavily in the chair beside the telephone, as if the news was in actual physical fact a let-down. I did not think then of the effort that had been wasted, but simply of the empty spaces of the evening that stretched ahead, without news ... and without him. "Did he say anything else?"

"Only that 'nothing had changed'." She gave the words inverted commas, and there was something puzzled and inquiring in her look that told me what I had wanted to know. Adoni had after all kept his word: the girl had no idea that there was anything afoot.

Meanwhile I must make do with what crumbs I had. 'Nothing had changed.' We could presumably expect him on the late ferry, but if nothing had changed, it didn't sound as if a police escort was likely, so he might not bring Spiro back with him, either. More I could not guess, but my part in the affair was decidedly over for the day; I couldn't have kept Godfrey any longer, and it didn't seem now as if it was going to matter.

"Where was Mr. Max speaking from?"

"I don't know. From Athens, I suppose."

"From *Athens*? At five o'clock? But if he was planning to come back tonight——"

"I forgot. It couldn't have been Athens, could it? Adoni didn't say, just that it was the mainland." She waved a hand largely. "Somewhere over there, that's all." And, her tone implied, it didn't matter much one way or the other. Outside Corfu, all places were the same, and not worth visiting anyway.

I laughed, and she laughed with me, the first spontaneous sound of pleasure that I had heard from her since the news of her brother's loss. I said: "What is it, Miranda? You seem excited tonight. Has something nice happened?"

She was opening her lips to answer, when some sound from the kitchen made her whisk round. "The soup! I must go! Excuse me!" And she vanished towards the kitchen door.

I went to have my bath, then made my way to the dining-room, where Miranda was just setting the contents of a large tray out in lonely state at one end of the table. She showed no desire to leave me, but hovered anxiously as I tasted the soup, and glowed again at my praise. We talked cooking all through the soup, and while I helped myself to the lobster salad. I asked no more questions, but ate, and listened, and wondered again what magic the 'afternoon off' with young Adoni had done for her. (I should say here that Miranda's English, unlike Adoni's, was not nearly as good as I have reported it; but it was rapid enough, and perfectly understandable, so for the sake of clarity I have translated it fairly freely.)

"This is a dressing from the Signora's book," she told me, handing a dish. "She does not like the Greek dressing, so I have tried it from the French book. Is it good? You had a nice day, Miss Lucy?"

"Lovely, thanks. We went to the Achilleion."

"I have been there once. It is very wonderful, is it not?"

"Very. Then we had tea at Benitses."

180

"Benitses? Why did you go there? There is nothing at Benitses! In Corfu it is better."

"I wanted to see it, and to drive back along the sea. Besides, I was longing for some tea, and Corfu was too far, and I wanted to look at some antiquities on the way home."

She knitted her brows. "Antiquities? Oh, you mean statues, like the ones on the Esplanade, the fine English ones."

"In a way, though those aren't old enough. It really means things many hundreds of years old, like the things in the Museum in Corfu."

"Are they valuable, these antiquities?"

"Very. I don't know if you could say what they were worth in terms of money, but I'd say they're beyond price. Have you seen them?"

She shook her head. She said nothing, but that was because she was biting her lips together as if forcibly to prevent speech. Her eyes were brilliant.

I stopped with my glass half-way to my mouth. "Miranda, what is it? Something *has* happened—you can't pretend—you look as if you'd been given a present. Can't you tell me?"

She took in her breath with something of a gulp. Her fingers were once again pleating and unpleating a fold of her skirt. "It is something . . . something Adoni has found."

I put down the glass. It clattered against the table. I waited.

A silence, then she said, with a rush: "Adoni and I, we found it together, this afternoon. When I got the afternoon off, I went over to the Castello . . ." She sent me a sideways glance. "Sometimes, you see, Adoni works in the garden while Sir Gale sleeps, and then we talk. But today, Mr. Karithis was visiting with Sir Gale, and they told me Adoni had gone to swim. So I went down to the bay."

"Yes?" She had my attention now, every scrap of it.

"I could not find him, so after a bit I walked along the path, round the rocks towards the Villa Rotha. Then I saw him. He was up the cliff, coming out of a bush."

"Coming out of a *bush*?"

"It was really a cave," explained Miranda. "Everybody knows that there are caves in the rock under the Castello, they used to use them for wine; and Adoni told me that he had seen down through a crack, and heard water, so he knew that there must be more caves below. This island is full of caves. Why, over near Ermones——"

"Adoni had found a new cave?"

She nodded. "He had not been on that part of the cliff before. I did not know he was interested in—I don't know the word— exploring? Thank you. But today he said he wanted to find out where the water was that lay under the Castello, and he knew that Mr. Manning was away with you, so it was all right. I think"—here she dimpled—"that he was not very pleased to see me. I think he had heard me, and thought it was Mr. Manning come back. He looked quite frightened."

And well he might, I thought. My heart was bumping a bit. "Go on, what had he found?"

Her face went all at once solemn, and lighted. "He had found proof."

I jumped. "*Proof?*"

"That is what he said. Myself, I do not think that proof is needed, but that is what he said."

"*Miranda!*" I heard my voice rise sharply on the word, and controlled it. "Please explain. I have no idea what you're talking about. What proof had Adoni found?"

"Proof of St. Spiridion and his miracles."

I sat back in my chair. She stared at me solemnly, and as the silence drew out I felt my heart-beats slowing down to normal. I had a near-hysterical desire to laugh, but managed to stop myself. After a while I said gently: "Well, go on. Tell me . . . no, don't hover there, I've finished, thank you. Look, would you like to bring the coffee, and then sit down here and have some with me and tell me all about it?"

She hurried out, but when she came back with the coffee, she refused to take any with me, or to sit down, but stood gripping a chair-back, obviously bursting to get on with her story.

I poured coffee. "Go on. What's this about the Saint?"

"You were at the procession on Palm Sunday."

"Yes."

"Then perhaps you know about the Saint, the patron of this island?"

"Yes, I know about him. I read a lot about the island before I came here. He was Bishop of Cyprus, wasn't he, who was tortured by the Romans, and after he died his body was em- balmed, and carried from place to place until it came to Corfu. We have a Saint like that in England, too, called Cuthbert. There are lots of stories about him, and about the miracles his body did."

182

"In England also?" It was plain that she had never credited that cold and misty land with anything as heart-warming as a real Saint. "Then you understand that we of Corfu are taught all about our Saint as children, and many stories of the miracles and marvels. And they are true. I know this."

"Of course."

She swallowed. "But there are other stories—stories that Sir Gale has told me of the Saint, that I have never heard before. He—my *koumbàros*—told us many tales when we were children, Spiro and me. He is a very learned man, as learned as the *papàs* (the priest), and he knows very many stories about Greece, the stories of our history that we learn in school, Pericles and Alexander and Odysseus and Agamemnon, and also stories of our Saint, things that happened long, long ago, in this very place, things that the *papàs* never told us, and that I have not heard before."

She paused. I said: "Yes?" but I knew what was coming now.

"He has told us how the Saint lived here, in a cave, and had his daughter with him, a princess she was, very beautiful. He had angels and devils to do his bidding, and worked much magic, raising storms and stilling them, and saving the ship-wrecked sailors."

She paused doubtfully. "I do not believe, me, about the daughter. The Saint was a bishop, and they do not have daughters. Perhaps she was a holy nun ... It is possible that Sir Gale has got the story a little bit wrong?"

"Very possible," I said. "Was the daughter called Miranda?"

"Yes! It was after this holy woman, a Corfiote, that I was called! Then you know this story too?"

"In a way." I was wondering, in some apprehension, what rich and strange confusion Sir Julian's Shakespearian theories might have created. "In the English story we call him Prospero, and he was a magician—but he wasn't a bishop; he was a Duke, and he came from Milan, in Italy. So you see, it's only a——"

"He lived in a cave behind the grove of lime-trees along the cliff." She waved northwards, and I recognised Sir Julian's cheerfully arbitrary placing of the scene of *The Tempest*. "And there he did all his magic, but when he became old he turned to God, and drowned his books and his magic staff."

"But, Miranda ..." I began, then stopped. This wasn't the time to try to point out the discrepancies between this story and that of the Bishop of Cyprus, who (for one thing) had already been with God for some thousand years when his body arrived at the island. I hoped there was some way of explaining how legends grew round some central figure like alum crystals round a thread. "Yes?" I said again.

She leaned forward over the chair-back. "Well, Adoni says that Mr. Max is making a play out of this story, like ... like ..." She searched her mind, and then, being a Greek, came up with the best there is ... "like *Oedipus* (that is a play of the old gods; they do it in Athens). I asked Sir Gale about this play, and when he told me the story I said that the priests should know of this, because I had not heard it, and the *papàs* in my village has not heard it either, and he must be told, so that he can ask the Bishop. Why do you smile, Miss Lucy?"

"Nothing." I was thinking that I need hardly have worried. The Greeks invented cynicism, after all; and every Greek is born with an inquiring mind, just as every foxhound is born with a nose. "Go on; what did Sir Julian say?"

"He laughed, and said that his story—of the magic and the books—is not true, or perhaps it is only a little true, and changed with time, and that the poet who wrote the story added things from other stories and from his own mind, to make it more beautiful." She looked earnestly at me. "This happens. My *koumbàros* said it was like the story of Odysseus—that is another story of this island that we have in our schools, but you will not know it."

"I do know the story."

She stared. "You know this, too? Are all English so learned, Miss Lucy?"

I laughed. "It's a very famous story. We have it in our schools, too."

She gaped. This was fame indeed.

"We learn all your Greek stories," I said. "Well, Sir Julian's story of the magician may have some tiny fragment of truth in it, like the legends about Odysseus, but I honestly think not much more. I'm sure he didn't mean you to believe it word for word. The story he told you, that Mr. Max is making a film play out of, is just something that a poet invented, and probably nothing to do with the real St. Spiridion at all. And you must see for yourself that the bit about the cave and the princess can't possibly be true——"

"But it is!"

184

"But look, Miranda, when the Saint was brought here in 1489, he was already——"

"Dead many years, I know that! But there is *something* that is true in Sir Gale's story, and the priests must be told of it. We can prove it, Adoni and I! I told you, we found the proof today!"

"Proof that *The Tempest* is true?" It was my turn to stare blankly. Somehow, after the mounting excitement of Miranda's narrative, this came as a climax of the most stunning irrelevance.

"I don't know about any tempest, but today we found them, in the cave behind the lime-trees. There's a passage, and a cave, very deep in the cliff, with water, and that is where he drowned his books." She leaned forward over the chair-back. "That is what Adoni found today, and he took me in and showed me. They are there in the water, plain to see, in the very same place where Sir Gale told us—the magic books of the Saint!"

Her voice rose to a dramatic stop that Edith Evans might have envied. Her face was shining, lighted and full of awe. For a full half-minute all I could do was sit there, gazing blankly back at her, framing kind little sentences which might explain and question without too cruel a disillusionment. Adoni had been with her, I thought impatiently; what in the world had Adoni been thinking about to allow this fantasy to go on breeding? Certainly he would not share her beliefs, and she would have accepted an explanation from him, whereas from me, now . . .

Adoni. The name stabbed through the haze in my mind like a spearpoint going through butter-muslin. What Adoni did, he usually had a good reason for. I sat up, demanding sharply: "Adoni found these—things—in a cave in the cliff? Where's the entrance?"

"Round the point, half-way up the cliff, above the boat-house."

"Ah. Could it be seen from the bay—our bay?"

She shook her head. "You go half-way up the path to the Villa Rotha. Then it is above the path, in the rocks, behind bushes."

"I see." My heart was bumping again. "Now, when Adoni saw it was you, what did he say? Try to remember exactly."

"I told you, he was angry at first, and would have hurried me away, because we should not have been there. Then he stopped

185

and thought, and said no, I must come into the cave, and see what he had found. He took me in; it was a steep passage, and long, going right down, but he had a torch, and it was dry. At the bottom was a big cave, full of water, very deep, but clear. Under a ledge, hidden with pebbles, we saw the books."

"A moment. What made you think they were books?"

"They looked like books," said Miranda reasonably. "Old, old books, coloured. The corners showed from under the pebbles. You could see the writing on them."

"Writing?"

She nodded. "Yes, in a foreign tongue, and pictures and magical signs."

"But, my dear girl, *books*? In sea-water? They'd be pulp in a couple of hours!"

She said simply: "You forget. They are holy books. They would not perish."

I let that one pass. "Didn't Adoni try to get at them?"

"It was too deep, and very cold, and besides there was an eel." She shivered. "And he said they must not be disturbed; he would tell Sir Gale, he said, and Mr. Max, and they would come. He said that I was his witness that he had found them there, and that I was to tell nobody about them, except you, Miss Lucy."

I put my hands flat on the table and held them there, hard. I could feel the blood pumping in the finger-tips.

"He told you to tell me?"

"Yes."

"Miranda. You told me earlier that Adoni had said these books were 'proof'. Did he say proof of what?"

She knitted her brows, "What could he have meant, but proof of the story?"

"I see," I said. "Well, that's marvellous, and thank you for telling me. I can hardly wait to see them, but you won't tell anyone else, will you, anyone at all, even your mother? If—if it turns out to be a mistake, it would be dreadful to have raised people's hopes."

"I won't tell. I promised Adoni. It is our secret, his and mine."

"Of course. But I'd love to ask him about it. I think I'll go over to the Castello now. D'you think you could get him on the phone for me?"

She glanced at the clock. "There will be nobody there now.

Sir Gale was going back to Corfu with Mr. Karithis for dinner, and Adoni went with them."

"But Max has the car. Adoni didn't have to drive them, surely?"

"No, Mr. Karithis brought his car. But Adoni wanted to go into Corfu, so he went with them, and he said he would come back with Mr. Max later."

Of course he would. Whatever he had found in the cave by the Villa Rotha, whatever 'proof' he had now got, Adoni would get it to Max at the first possible moment, and if he was right about his discovery—and I had no doubt he was—then tonight the hounds would close in, and the end I had wanted this afternoon to hasten, would come.

I glanced at my watch. If the ferry docked at ten-forty-five ... give Max an hour at most to hear Adoni's story and possibly collect police help in Corfu ... half an hour more for the drive ... at the outside that made it a quarter past midnight. Even if Godfrey had got back from his date, whatever it was, he might be in bed by that time, not where he would hear or see explorers probing the secrets of the cliff ...

My hands moved of their own accord to the edge of the table, and gripped it. My thoughts till now formlessly spinning, settled and stood.

Godfrey had said he was going out tonight; and there was the impression I had had of urgent business to be done and a clear field needed to do it in. Was it not conceivable that the objects so mysteriously hidden under his house were part of this same night's business? That in fact by the time Max and the police were led to the cave in the small hours, the 'proof' would have gone? And even with Adoni's word and that of his witness there would be nothing to show what had been there, or where it had gone? We would be back where we were, possibly with Godfrey's business finished, and himself in the clear ...

Reluctantly, I worked it out. Reluctantly, I reached the obvious, the only conclusion. I stood up.

"Will you show me this cave and the books? Now?"

She had started to stack the supper things back on the tray. She paused, startled. "Now, Miss?"

"Yes, now. It may be important. I'd like to see them myself."

"But—it's so dark. You wouldn't want to go along there in the dark. In the morning, when Adoni's back——"

"Don't ask me to explain, Miranda, but I must go now, it

187

might be important. If you'll just show me the cave, the entrance, that's all."

"Well, of course, Miss." But the words dragged doubtfully. "What would happen if Mr Manning came down?"

"He won't. He's out, away somewhere in his car, he told me so, so he's not likely to be using the cliff path. But we'll make sure he's out, we'll ring up the house ... I can pretend I left something in the car. Will you get me the number, please?"

Somewhere in Godfrey's empty house the telephone bell shrilled on and on, while I waited, and Miranda hung over me, uneasy, but obviously flattered by my interest in her story.

At length I put the receiver back. "That's that. He's out, so it's all right." I looked at her. "Will you, Miranda? Please? Just show me where the cave is, and you can come straight back."

"Well, of course, if you really want to ... If Kyrios Manning is away I don't mind at all. Shall I get the torch, Miss Lucy?"

"Yes, please. Give me five minutes to get a coat, and some other shoes," I said, "and have you got a coat here, or something extra to put on?" I didn't bother to ask if it was something dark; by the saint's mercy the Corfiote peasants never wore anything else.

Three minutes later I was dressed in light rubber-soled shoes and a dark coat, and was rummaging through Leo's dressing-table drawer for the gun I knew he kept there.

CHAPTER SIXTEEN

This is the mouth o' th' Cell: no noise, and enter.
IV. 1.

THE bay was dark and silent: no sound, no point of light. It was easy enough to see our way across the pale sand without using the torch we had brought; and once we had scrambled up under the shadow of the pines where the dolphin had lain, and gained the rocky path along the foot of the southern headland, we found that we could again make our way without a betraying light.

We turned off the track into the bushes some way before reaching the zigzag path that led up towards the Villa Rotha.

Miranda led the way, plunging steeply uphill, apparently straight into the thickest tangle of bushes that masked the cliff. Above us the limes leaned out, densely black and silent. Not a leaf stirred. You could hardly hear the sea. Even after we had switched the torch on to help us, our stealthy progress through the bushes sounded like the charge of a couple of healthy buffaloes.

Fortunately it wasn't far. Miranda stopped where a clump of evergreens—junipers, by the scent—lay back apparently right against the cliff.

"Here," she whispered, and pulled the bushes back. I shone the torchlight through.

It showed a narrow gap, scarcely more than a fissure, giving on a passage that sloped sharply downwards for perhaps four yards to be apparently blocked by a wall of rock. The floor of the passage looked smooth, and the walls were dry.

I hesitated. A puff of breeze brought a murmur from the trees, and the bushes rustled. I could feel the same breeze—or was it the same?—run cold along my skin.

"The passage goes to the left there"—Miranda's whisper betrayed nothing but pleased excitement—"and then down again, quite a long way, but it is easy. Will you go first, or shall I?"

I had originally intended merely to stay hidden where I could watch the cave's entrance until Adoni brought the men down, and to send Miranda home out of harm's way. But now it occurred to me that if Godfrey did come to remove the 'books' before Max arrived, I, too, should need a witness. This was to put it at its highest. To put it at its lowest, I wanted company. And even if Godfrey found us (which seemed unlikely in this tangle of darkness), there was no risk of our meeting with Yanni's fate. I was prepared, and there was the gun—the gun, and the simple fact that two people were more than twice as hard to dispose of as one.

But still I hesitated. Now that we were here, in the quiet dark, with the sounds and gentle air of the night so normal around us, I wanted nothing so much as to see for myself what it was Adoni had found. If Godfrey did come tonight to remove it, if I should be unable to get a look at it, or to follow him, then we were back at the post, and no better off than before . . .

Three parts bravado, three parts revenge for these people I had come so quickly to love and admire, and three parts sheer blazing human curiosity—it was no very creditable mixture of

189

emotions that made me say with a briskness that might pass for bravery in the dark: "Is there anywhere to hide once you get inside the cave?"

I saw the glint of her eyes, but she answered simply: "Yes, a lot of places, other caves, with fallen rocks, and passages——"

"Fair enough. Let's go. You lead the way."

Behind us, the juniper rustled back into its place across the gap.

The passage led steadily downwards, as sharply right-angled as a maze; I guessed that the mass of rock had weathered into great rectangular blocks, and that the passage led down the cracks between them. Here and there side-cracks led off, but the main route was as unmistakable as a highway running through a labyrinth of country lanes.

Miranda led the way without faltering; left, then right, then straight on for thirty feet or so, then right again, and along . . . well into the heart of the promontory, I supposed. At the end of the last stretch it looked as if the floor of the passage dropped sheer away into black depths.

She paused, pointing. "The cave is down there. You can climb down quite easily, it is like steps."

A few moments later we were at the edge of the drop, with before us a sort of subterranean Giants' Staircase—a vast natural stairway of weathered rock leading down block by block on to a ledge that ran the length of a long, lozenge-shaped cave floored with black water. The ledge was some four feet above the level of the water, overhanging the smooth, scooped-out sides of the pool.

We clambered down the stairway, and I shone the light forward into the cave.

This was large, but not awesomely so. At the end where we stood the roof was not so very high—perhaps twenty feet; but as the torchlight travelled further, it was lost in the shadows where the roof arched upwards into darkness. There, I suppose, would be the funnelled cracks or chimneys which carried the fresh air into the upper caves, and through which Adoni had first detected the existence of the one where we now stood. Further along the ledge there were recesses and tunnels leading off the main cave, which promised a good choice of bolt-hole should the need arise. The walls were of pale limestone, scoured and damp, so that I guessed that with the wind on shore the sea must find its way in through more of the cracks and crevices.

Now the deep vat of sea-water at our feet lay still and dead, and the place smelt of salt and wet stone.

Miranda gripped my arm. "Down there! Shine the light. Down there!"

I turned the torch downwards. At first I could see nothing but the rich dazzle as the water threw back the beam, then the light seemed to soak down through the water like a stain through silk, and I saw the bottom, a jumble of smooth, round pebbles, their colours all drained by the torchlight to bone-white and washed green and pearl. Something moved across them, a whip of shadow flicking out of sight into a crevice.

"See?" Miranda crouched, pointing. "In under the ledge, where the stones have been moved. There!"

I saw it then, a corner like the corner of a big book, or box, jutting out from among the pebbles. It looked as if the object, whatever it was, had been thrust well under the ledge where we stood, and the stones piled roughly over it.

I kneeled beside Miranda, peering intently down. Some stray movement of the sea outside had communicated itself to the pool, and the water shifted, shadows and reflections breaking and coalescing through the rocking torchbeam. The thing was coloured, I thought, and smooth-surfaced; a simple mind conditioned by Sir Julian's stories might well have thought it was a book: myself, I took it for the corner of a box with some sort of a label. Vaguely, I could see what might be lettering.

"You see?" Miranda's whisper echoed in the cave.

"Yes, I see." Any thoughts I might have had of braving the eel and the icy water to get at the object died a natural and unregretted death. Even if I could have dived for the thing, and lifted it, I couldn't have climbed the four smooth feet of overhang out of the pool without a rope.

"It is a book, yes?"

"It could be. But if it is, I don't think you'll find it's a very old one. The only way it could be kept down there is if it was wrapped in polythene or something, and that means——"

I broke off. Something had made a noise, some new noise that wasn't part of the cave's echo, or the faint whispers of the night that reached us through the invisible fissures in the cliff. I switched the light out, and the darkness came down like a candle-snuffer, thick as black wool. I put a hand on the girl's arm.

"Keep very still. I heard something. Listen."

191

Through the drip of water on limestone it came again; the sound of a careful footstep somewhere in the passage above.

Here he came. Dear God, here he came.

Miranda stirred. "Someone coming. It must be Adoni back already. Perhaps——"

I stopped her with a touch, my lips at her ear. "That won't be Adoni. We mustn't be found here, we've got to hide. Quickly . . ."

I took her arm, pulling her deeper into the cave. She came without question. We kept close to the wall, feeling our way inch by inch till we came to a corner, and rounded it safely.

"Wait." I dared a single brief flash of the torch, and breathed relief. We were in a deep recess or blocked tunnel, low-roofed, and filled with long-since-fallen debris, that burrowed its way back into the cliff above the water-level.

I put the light out. Slowly, carefully, and almost without a sound, we slithered our way into cover, deep into a crevice under a wedged block of limestone, flattening ourselves back into it like starfish hiding from the pronged hooks of the bait-fishers.

Not a moment too soon. Light spread, and warmed the cave. I was too deeply tucked back into the cleft to be able to see more than a curved section of the roof and far side of the main cave, but of course I could hear very clearly, as the cave and the water magnified every sound; the tread of boots on rock; the chink as the powerful torch was put down somewhere and the light steadied; the man's breathing. Then the splash of something—whether his body or something else I couldn't tell—was let down into the pool.

A pause, while the water lapped and sucked, and the breathing sounded loud and urgent with some sort of effort. Then a different splashing noise, a sucking and slapping of water, as if something had been withdrawn from the pool. Another pause, filled now with the sounds of dripping, streaming water. Then at last the light moved, the slow footsteps retreated, and the sea-sounds of the disturbed pool, slowly diminishing, held the cave.

I felt Miranda stir beside me.

"He has taken the book. *Could* it not be Adoni, Miss Lucy? Perhaps he has come back to get the book for Sir Gale? Who else would know? Shall I go——?"

"*No!*" My whisper was as urgent as I could make it. "It's not Adoni, I'm sure of that. This is something else, Miranda . . .

192

I can't tell you now, but trust me, please. Stay here. Don't move. I'm going to take a look."

I slid out of the cleft and switched on the torch, but kept a hand over the glass, so that the light came in dimmed slits between my fingers. I caught the gleam of her eyes watching me, but she neither moved again nor spoke. I inched my cautious way forward to the main cave, to pause at the corner of the ledge, switch off the torch, and listen yet again. There was no sound but the steady drip of water, and the faint residual murmur from the pool.

Flashing the light full on, I knelt at the edge, and looked down.

As I expected, the pile of stones had been rudely disturbed, and, as far as I could judge, had dwindled in height. But there must have been more than one of the rectangular objects there, for I could see another corner jutting from the cobbles at a different angle from the one that had been visible before. And there on the ledge leaning against the wall as if waiting for him to come back, was an iron grapple, a long hooked shaft which dripped sluggishly on to the limestone.

I stood up, thinking furiously. So much for that. Adoni had been right; here was the key we were wanting, the clue to Godfrey's murderous business. And it was surely simple enough to see what I ought to do next. I had no means of telling what proportion of his cache Godfrey had taken, or if he would come back tonight for the rest; but in either case, nothing would be gained by taking the appalling risk of following him now. If he came back, we might meet in the passage. If he didn't—well, the rest of the 'proof' would still be safely there for Max when he arrived at last.

And so, let's face it, would I . . .

I was hardly back in my niche before we heard him coming back, the light growing and brightening before him up the limestone walls. The performance was repeated almost exactly; the plunge of the grapple, the grating haul through the pebbles, the withdrawal, the pause while the water drained . . . then once more the light retreated, and we were left in blackness, with the hollow sucking of the troubled pool.

"Wait," I whispered again.

As soon as I got to the main cave I saw that the grapple had gone. I crouched once more on the streaming rock and peered down. As I expected, the pile of pebbles had settled lower, spreading level as what it had hidden had been dragged away. The pool was empty of its treasure.

No need, this time, to stop and think. The decision was, unhappily, as clear as before. I would have to follow him now. And I had better hurry.

In a matter of seconds I was back beside Miranda. "You can come out now. Quick!"

She materialised beside me. Her breathing was fast and shallow, and she was shivering. She was still taut and bright-eyed, but the quality of her excitement had changed. She looked scared.

"What is it, Miss? What is it?"

I tried to sound calm and sure. "The 'books' have gone, and it was Mr. Manning who took them, I'm sure it was. I have to see where he puts them, but he mustn't see us. D'you understand, *he mustn't see us* ... I'll explain it all later, but we'll have to hurry now. Come on."

We heaved ourselves up the last of the Giants' Staircase, and crept from angle to angle of the passage, lighting the way warily, and stopping at each corner to listen ahead. But nothing disturbed us, and soon we were at the mouth of the cleft, cautiously parting the junipers. The air smelt warm and sweet after the cave, full of flower-scents and the tang of bruised herbs; and a breeze had got up and was moving the bushes, ready to mask what sounds we made.

We edged down, feeling our way, through the tangle of bushes and young trees. Although no moon was visible, the sky was alight with stars, and we went quickly enough. I dared not make for the path, but pushed a cautious way, bent double, above one arm of the zigzag from which I thought we should be able to see the boat-house, and at length we came to the end of the ridge where honeysuckle and (less happily) brambles made thick cover between the young limes.

We were just above the boat-house. Its roof was silhouetted like a black wedge against the paler sea beyond. I thought, but could not quite make out, that the landward door stood open.

Next moment it shut, softly, but with the definite *chunk* of a spring-locking door. A shadow moved along the boat-house wall, and then he came quietly up the path. We lay mouse-still, hardly breathing. He rounded the corner below us, and came on up, with a quick, stealthy stride whose grace I recognised, and next moment, as he passed within feet of us, I saw him clearly.

He had changed from the light clothes of the afternoon, and now wore dark trousers, and a heavy dark jersey. He carried nothing in his hands. He went straight on past us, and his light tread was lost in the movements of the breeze.

In the heavy shadow where we lay I couldn't see Miranda, but I felt her turn to look at me, and presently she put out a hand and touched my arm. The hand was trembling.

"Miss—Miss, what *is* it?"

I put a hand over hers, and held it. "You're quite right, it's not just a case of being caught trespassing, it's something much more serious, and it might be dangerous. I'm sorry you're in it, too, but I want your help."

She said nothing. I took a breath, and tightened my hand over hers.

"Listen. I can't tell you it all now, but there have been ... things have been happening, and we think ... Mr. Max and I ... that they have something to do with your brother's accident. Adoni thinks so, too. We want to find out. Will you just trust me and do as I say?"

There was a pause. Still she didn't speak, but this time the air between us was so charged that I felt it vibrate like a bow-string after the shaft has gone.

"Yes."

"You saw who it was?"

"Of course. It was Mr. Manning."

"Good. You may be asked ... what is it?"

"Look there." She had moved sharply, pointing past me up the cliff to where, above the black trees, a light had just flashed on. The Villa Rotha.

I felt my breath go out. "Then he's safe there for a bit, thank God. I wish I knew the time."

"We dare not shine the torch?"

"No. I should have looked before. Never mind. It looks as if he's put those things in the boat-house; I wish to heaven I dared go down and take a look at them ... he did say he was going out tonight, and *not* with the boat, but he might only have been putting me off so that he'd be able to go to the cave. He may hang around here all night ... or he may have been lying, and he'll come down again and take the boat, and that will be that." I stirred restlessly, watching that steady square of light with hatred. "In any case, the damned thing's locked. Even if ..."

195

"I know where the key is."

I jerked round to peer at her. "*You do?*"

"Spiro told me. There was an extra key which was kept underneath the floor, where the house reaches the water. I know the place; he showed me."

I swallowed. "It's probably not there now, and in any case . . ."

I stopped abruptly. The light had gone out.

Minutes later, we heard the car. That it was Godfrey's car there could be no manner of doubt; he switched on her lights, and they swept round in a wide curve, lancing through the trees and out into space, to move on and vanish in the blackness over the headland as the engine's note receded through the woods. There was a brief, distant thrumming as he accelerated, then the sound died, and there was darkness.

"He's gone," said Miranda, unnecessarily.

I sat up. I was furious to find that my teeth were chattering, and clenched them hard, pushing a hand down into the pocket where Leo's gun hung heavy and awkward against my thigh. Two things were quite certain; I did not want to go anywhere near Godfrey Manning's boat-house; and if I didn't, I should despise myself for a coward as long as I lived. I had a gun. There was probably a key. I had at least to try it.

"Come on, then," I said, and pushed my way out of cover and dropped to the path, Miranda behind me. As we ran down-hill I gasped out instructions. "You must get straight back to the house. Can you get into the Castello?"

"Yes."

"Then go there. That way, you'll see them as soon as they get home. But try to telephone Adoni first . . . Do you know where he might be?"

"Sometimes he eats at Chrisomalis', or the Corfu Bar."

"Then try them. If he's not there, some of his friends may know where he'll be. He may have gone down to the harbour to wait, or even to the police . . . Try, anyway."

We had reached the boat-house. I stopped at the door, trying it . . . futilely, of course: it was fast locked. Miranda thrust past me, and I heard her fumbling in the shadows round the side of the building, then she was beside me, pushing the cold shape of a Yale key into my hand.

"Here. What shall I tell Adoni?"

"Don't tell him what's happened. Mr. Manning may get back

196

to the house, and pick the phone up, you never know. Just say he must come straight back here, it's urgent, Miss Lucy says so ... He'll understand. If he doesn't, tell him anything you like— tell him I'm ill, and you have to have help—anything to get him back here. He's not to tell Sir Julian. Then you wait for him ... Don't leave the Castello, and don't open the door to anyone else except Max or the police ... or me. If I'm not back by the time he comes, tell him everything that's happened, and that I'm down here. Okay?"

"Yes." She was an ally in a million. Confused and frightened though she must have been, she obeyed as unquestioningly as before. I heard her say, "The Saint be with you, Miss," and then she was gone, running at a fair speed along the shore path to the Castello's bay.

With one more glance up at the lightless headland, and a prayer on my own account, I prodded around the lock with a shamefully shaky key, until at last I got it home.

The catch gave, stiffly, and I slipped inside.

CHAPTER SEVENTEEN

No tongue: all eyes: be silent.
IV. 1.

THE boat-house was a vast structure with a high roof lost in shadows, where the sea-sounds echoed hollowly, as in a cave. Running round the three walls was a narrow platform of planks set above the water, and along the near side of this lay the sloop. The rapidly dimming light of my torch showed me the lovely, powerful lines, and the name painted along the bows: *Aleister.* It also showed me, propped against the wall by the door, the grapple from the cave.

There was no hiding-place in the boat-house other than the boat itself. I clicked the lock shut behind me, then stepped in over the cockpit coaming, to try the cabin door.

It was unlocked, but I didn't go straight in. There was a window in the back of the boat-house, facing the cliff, which showed a section of the path, then the black looming mass of cliff and tree, and—at the top—a paler section of sky where stars burned. With eyes now adjusted to the darkness, I could just make out the sharp angle of some part of the Villa Rotha's roof. So far, excellent. If Godfrey did come back too soon, I should have the warning of the car or house lights.

Inside the cabin, I let the torchlight move round once, twice . . .

The layout was much as I remembered in Leo's boat. Big, curtained windows to either side, under which were settee berths with cushions in bright chintz; between these a fixed drop-leaf table above which swung a lamp. A curtain was drawn over the doorway in the forward bulkhead, but no doubt beyond it I would find another berth, the W.C., and the usual sail bags, ropes, and spare anchor stowed in the bows. Immediately to my right, just inside the door, was the galley, and opposite this the quarter berth—a space-saving berth with half its length in the cabin, and the other half burrowing, as it were, into the space beyond the after bulkhead, under the port cockpit seat. The quarter berth was heaped with blankets, and was separated from the settee berth by a small table with a cupboard underneath.

And everywhere, lockers and cupboards . . .

I started, methodically, along the starboard side.

Nothing in the galley; the oven empty, the cupboards stocked with cooking equipment so compact as to leave no hiding-place. In the lockers, crockery, photographic stuff, tins of food, card-board boxes full of an innocent miscellany of gear. In the ward-robe cupboards, coats, oilskins, sweaters and a shelf holding sea-boots, and shoes neatly racked, all as well polished and slick as Godfrey himself . . .

It was the same everywhere; everything was open to the searcher, all the contents normal and innocent—clothing, spare blankets, photographic equipment, tools. The only place not open to the prying eye was the cupboard at the end of the quarter berth, which was locked. But—from its shallow shape, and my memory of Leo's boat—I imagined that this was only because it held the liquor; there was none elsewhere, and it was hardly big enough to store the packages I was looking for. I left it, and went on, even prodding the mattresses and feeling under the piled blankets, but all that came to light was a paper-backed copy of *Tropic of Cancer*, which I pushed back, rearranging the blankets as they had been before. Then I started on the floor.

Here there would be, I knew, a couple of 'traps', or sections of the flooring which were made to lift out and give access to the bilges. Sure enough, under the table, and set in the boards, my eye caught the gleam of a sunken ring which, when pulled, lifted an eighteen-inch square of the planking, like a small trap-door. But there was no treasure cave below, only the gleam of bilge-water shifting between the frames with the boat's motion, and a faint smell of gas. And the same with the trap in the fo'c'sle.

The engine hatchway under the cabin steps was hardly a likely place for a cache; all the same, I looked there, and even lifted the inspection cover off the fresh-water tank, to see nothing but the ghostly reflection of the torchlight and my own shadow shivering on the surface of the full forty-gallon complement of water. Not here . . .

I screwed the cover down with hands that sweated now, and shook, then I put the torch out and fled up the steps and on to the deck.

The window first . . . No lights showed outside, but I had to make sure. I ran aft, ducked under the boom, and climbed on the stern seat to peer anxiously out.

All was dark and still. I could—I must—allow myself a little longer.

I started over the cockpit, using the torch again, but keeping a wary eye on the boat-house window. Here, too, all seemed innocent. Under the starboard seat was the space occupied by the Calor gas cylinders, and nothing else. Under the stern seat was nothing but folded tarpaulins and skin-diving equipment. The port seat merely hid the end of the quarter berth. Nothing. Nor were there any strange objects fastened overside, or trailing under the *Aleister* in the sea; that bright idea was disposed of in a very few seconds. I straightened up finally from my inspection, and stood there, hovering, miserably undecided, and trying hard to think through the tension that gripped me.

He must have brought the packages here. He had not had time to take them up to his house, and he would hardly have cached them somewhere outside when he had the *Aleister* handy, and, moreover, no idea that he was even suspected. He might, of course, have handed them to some accomplice there and then, and merely have been returning the grapple to the boat-house, but the accomplice would have had to have some means of transport, which meant either a donkey or a boat; if a donkey, Miranda and I must surely have heard it; we might not have heard a rowing-boat, but why should Godfrey use one, when the *Aleister* and her dinghy lay ready to his own hand? No, it was obvious that there could be no innocent explanation of his use of the hidden cave.

But I had looked everywhere. They were not in the boat, or tied under the boat; they were not on the platform, or on the single shelf above it. Where in the world could he, in this scoured-out space, have hidden those bulky and dripping objects so quickly and effectively?

An answer came then—so obvious as to be insulting. In the water. He had moved them merely from the bottom of the cave to the bottom of the bay. They must be under the *Aleister*, right under, and if I could only see them, there was the grapple ready to hand, with the water still dripping off it to make a pool on the boards.

I was actually up on the cockpit coaming, making for the grapple, when I saw the real answer, the obvious, easy answer which I should have seen straight away; which would have saved me all those precious minutes, and how much more besides; the trail of drops leading in through the boat-house door and along the platform; the trail left by the dripping packages, as obvious to the intelligent eye as footprints in fresh snow. I had no excuse, except fear and haste, and (I thought bitterly) Nemesis armed with a nice, heavy gun had no business to be afraid at all.

And the trail was already drying. I was calling myself names that I hadn't even known I knew, as I shone the yellow and flickering torchlight over the boards of the platform.

Yes, there they were, the footprints in the snow; the two faint, irregular trails, interweaving like the track of bicycle wheels, leading in through the door, along the platform, over the edge . . .

But not into the water after all. They went in over the side of the *Aleister* and across her deck and straight in through the cabin door.

I was in after them in a flash. Down the steps, to the table . . . I had never even glanced at the bare table top, but now I saw on the Formica surface the still damp square where he had laid the packages down.

And there the trail stopped. But this time there was only one answer. The trail had stopped simply because all Godfrey had had to do from there was to open the trap-door under the table, and lift the things straight down.

I had the trap open again in seconds. I laid it aside. The square hole gaped.

I ran back to the steps and peered up at the window. No light showed. I dropped on my knees beside the trap, clicked on the torch and sent the small yellow eye which was all it had left skidding over the greasy water in the *Aleister*'s bilges.

Nothing. No sign. But now I knew they had to be there . . .

And they were there. I had gone flat down on the floor, and was hanging half inside the trap-door before I saw them, but they were there; not in the bottom, but tucked, as neatly as could be, right up under the floorboards, in what were obviously racks made specially to carry them. They were clear of the water, and well back from the edges of the hatch, so that you would have had—like me—to be half in the bilges yourself before you saw them.

I ducked back, checked on the window again, then dived once more into the bilges.

Two sweating minutes, and I had it, a big, heavy square package wrapped in polythene. I heaved it out on deck, spreading the skirts of my coat for it so that I in my turn would leave no trail, then turned the light on it.

The torch was shaking now in my hand. The yellow glow-worm crawled and prodded over the surface of the package, but the glossy wrapping almost defeated the miserable light, and all I got, in the three seconds' look I allowed myself, was the impression of a jumble of faint colours, something looking like a picture, a badge, even (Miranda had been right) a couple of words . . . LEKE, I read, and in front of this something that could be—but surely wasn't—NJEMIJE.

Somewhere something slammed, nearly frightening me out of what wits I still had. The torch dropped with a rattle, rolling in a wide semicircle that missed the trap by millimetres. I grabbed it back again, and whirled to look. There was nothing there. Only darkness.

Which was just as well, I thought, recovering my senses rather wryly. Even if I had reacted properly, and grabbed for the gun instead of the torch, I couldn't have got it. Prospero's damned book, or whatever the package was, was sitting right on top of it, on the skirts of my coat. I had a long way to go, I reflected bitterly, before I got into the James Bond class.

The wind must be rising fast. The big seaward doors shook again, as if someone was pulling at the padlock, and the other door bumped and rattled. The water ran hissing and lapping along the walls, and shadows, thrown by some faint reflection of starlight, shivered up into the rafters.

The window was still dark, but I had had my warning, and enough was enough. The trap-door went snugly back into place, my torch dropped into my other pocket, and, clasping the package to me with both hands, I clambered carefully out of the *Aleister*.

At the same instant as I gained the platform, I saw the movement on the path outside the window. Only a shadow, but as before there was no mistaking the way he moved. No light, no nothing, but here he was, just above the boat-house, and coming fast.

And here was I, stuck with my arms full of his precious package for which he had almost certainly tried to do double murder. And I couldn't get out of the place if I tried.

*   *   *

The first thing was to get rid of the package.

I crouched and let the thing slide down between the platform and the boat. The boat was moored close, and for a panic-stricken moment I thought there wasn't enough room there; the package was tangled in my coat, then it jammed in the gap, and I couldn't move it either way, and when I tried to grab it back I couldn't, it was slippery and I couldn't get a grip on it again . . .

I flung myself down, got a shoulder to the *Aleister*, and shoved. She moved the inch or so I needed, and with a brief, sharp struggle I managed to ram the package through and down.

It vanished with a faint splash. And then, like an echo, came the fainter but quite final splash of Leo's gun slipping from the pocket of my coat, to vanish in its turn under the water.

For one wild, crazy moment of fear I thought of swinging myself down to follow gun and package and hide under the platform, but I couldn't get down here, and there was no time to run the length of the boat. In any case he would have heard me. He was at the door. His key scraped the lock.

There was only one place big enough to hide, and that was right bang in the target area. The boat itself. It did cross my mind that I could stand still and try to bluff it out, but even had the *Aleister* been innocent, and Godfrey found me here at this hour, inside a locked door, no bluff would have worked.

With the boat literally loaded, I hadn't a hope. It was the cabin or nothing.

I was already over the side, and letting myself as quietly as a ghost into the cabin, as his key went home in the lock and turned with a click. I didn't hear the door open. I was already, like a hunted mouse, holed up in the covered end of the quarter berth, with the pile of blankets pulled up as best I could to hide me.

The blankets smelt of dust, and carbolic soap. They covered me with a thick, stuffy darkness that at least felt a bit like security. The trouble was that they deprived me of my hearing, the only sense that was left to tell what Godfrey was up to. Strain as I might through the thudding of my own heart-beats, I could only get the vaguest impression of where he was and what he was doing. All I could do was lie still and pray he wouldn't come into the cabin.

The boat rocked sharply, and for a moment I thought he was already in her, but again it was only the wind. This seemed to be rising still, in sharper gusts which sent little waves slapping hard along the hull, and sucking up and down the piles on which the platform stood. I could feel the jerking motion as the *Aleister* tugged at her rope, then she bucked, sharply and unmistakably; Godfrey had jumped into her.

Minutes passed, filled with the muffled night-noises, but I could feel, rather than hear, his weight moving about the boat, and strained my senses, trying to judge where he was and what he was doing. The boat was steadier now, swaying gently to the small ripples passing under her keel. A draught moved through the cabin, smelling freshly of the sea-wind, so that I guessed he must have left the boat-house door open, and this might mean he didn't mean to stay long . . .

The wind must be quite strong now. The boat swayed under me, and a hissing wave ran right along beside my head. The *Aleister* lifted to it with a creak of timber, and I heard the unmistakable sound of straining rope and the rattle of metal.

Then I knew what had happened. There was no mistaking it, rope and metal and timber active and moving—the boat was alive, and out in the living sea. He must have swung the big doors open without my hearing him, then poled her gently out, and now she was alive, under sail, slipping silently along shore, away from the bay.

I couldn't move. I simply lay there, shivering under my load of blankets, every muscle knotted and tense with the effort of keeping my head, and trying to think . . .

Max would surely be back by now; and even if he was still in Corfu, Adoni was probably already on his way home . . . and he would have left Miranda's message for Max, so Max wouldn't linger in Corfu, but would come straight here, and probably bring the police. When they got down to the boat-house and found the boat gone, and me with it, they would guess what had happened. There wasn't—I knew this—much hope of their finding the *Aleister* in the darkness, but at least I might have a card or two I could play if Godfrey found me. Under the circumstances he could hardly expect to get away with my disappearance as well.

Or so I hoped. I knew that if he discovered about the missing package he would probably search the sloop, and find me. But since there was nothing I could do about that, my only course was to stay hidden there, and pray for a choppy sea that would keep him on deck looking after the *Aleister*. Why, he might not even come below at all . . .

Just three minutes later, he opened the cabin door.

CHAPTER EIGHTEEN

What shall I do? say what? what shall I do?
I. 2.

I HEARD the click, and felt the sudden swirl of fresh air, cut off as the door shut again.

There was the rasp of a match; the sharp tang of it pierced right up into my hidden corner, and with it the first smoke of a newly-lighted cigarette. He must have come in out of the wind for this, and now he would go . . .

But he didn't. No movement followed. He must be very near me; I could feel, like an animal in the presence of danger, the hair brushing up along my skin. Now I was thankful for the chop and hiss of water, and for the hundred creaking, straining noises of the *Aleister* scudding on her way through the darkness. Without them, I thought he would have heard my heartbeats.

He can only have stood there for a few seconds, though for

me it was a pause prolonged almost to screaming-point. But it seemed he had only waited to get his cigarette properly alight: he struck another match, dropped it and the box after it on the table, and then went out and shut the door behind him.

Relief left me weak and sweating. The closed end of the berth seemed like an oven, so I pushed the blanket folds back a little, to let the air in, and cautiously peered over them, out into the cabin.

A weapon; that was the first thing ... I had the torch, but it was not a heavy one, and would hardly count as adequate armament against a murderer. Not that it was easy in the circumstances to think of anything (short of Leo's gun) that would have been 'adequate', though I would have settled for a good, loaded bottle, if only the damned cupboard had been open. But bottles there were none. I cast my mind furiously back over the cabin's contents ... The galley? Surely the galley must be packed with implements? Pans were too clumsy; it must be something I could conceal ... a knife? I hadn't opened the shallow drawers during my search, but one of them was bound to hold a knife. Or there was the starting handle for the engine, if I could get the engine hatch opened silently, and then station myself on the galley side, behind the door, and wait for him ...

Cautiously, one eye on the door, I reached down to push the blanket aside, ready to slide out of the quarter berth.

Then froze, staring with horror at the foot of the berth.

Even in the almost-darkness I could see it, and Godfrey, in the matchlight, must have seen it quite clearly—my toe, clad in a light yellow canvas shoe, protruding from the huddle of blankets. I was about as well hidden as an ostrich beak deep in sand.

Now I knew what had happened. He had come in quickly out of the wind to light his cigarette, had seen what he thought was a foot, had struck another match to make sure—and, having made sure, had done what?

I was answered immediately. The boat had levelled and steadied, as if she were losing way. Now, seemingly just beside me, the engine fired with a jerk and a brief, coughing roar that nearly sent me straight through the bulkhead; then it was throttled quickly back to a murmur, the merest throb and quiver of the boards, as the *Aleister* moved sedately forward on an even keel. He had merely turned the boat head to wind without taking in the mainsail, and started the engine, so that she would hold herself steady without attention. I didn't have to guess why. His quick step was already at the cabin door.

I whisked off the berth, dropped my wet coat, and straightened my dress. There wasn't even time to dive across the cabin and open the knife-drawer. As Godfrey opened the door I was heading for the table and the box of matches, apparently intent on nothing more deadly than lighting the lamp.

I threw a gay greeting at him over my shoulder.

"Hullo, there. I hope you don't mind a stowaway?"

The wick caught, and the light spread. I got the globe fitted back at the third try, but perhaps he hadn't noticed my shaking hands. He had moved to draw the curtains.

"Naturally I'm delighted. How did you know I'd decided to come out after all?"

"Oh, I didn't, but I was hoping!" I added, with what I'm sure was a ghastly archness: "You saw me, didn't you? You were coming in to unmask me. What's the penalty for stowing away in these seas?"

"We'll arrange that later," said Godfrey.

His voice and manner were pleasant as ever, but after that first bright glance I didn't dare let him see my eyes; not yet. There was a mirror set in a cupboard door: I turned to this and made the gestures of tidying my hair.

"What brought you down?" he asked.

"Well, I wanted a walk after supper, and—*have* you a comb, Godfrey? I look like a mouses's nest!"

Without a word he took one from a pocket and handed it to me. I began, rather elaborately, to fuss with my hair.

"I went down to the beach; I had a sort of vague idea the dolphin might come back—they do, I believe. Anyway, I went to look, but it wasn't there. I walked along the path a bit, listening to the sea, and wishing you *had* been going out. Then I heard you—I knew it must be you—over at the boat-house, so I hurried . . . You know, just hoping."

He had moved so that he was directly behind me. He stood very close, watching my face in the glass. I smiled at him, but got no response; the light eyes were like stones.

"You heard me at the boat-house?"

"Yes. I heard the door."

"When was this?"

"Oh, goodness knows, half an hour ago? Less? I'm no good

over times. I'd have called out, but you seemed to be in a hurry, so——"

"You saw me?"

His breath on the back of my neck brought panic, just a flash of it, like a heart-spasm. I turned away quickly, handed him his comb, and sat down on the settee berth, curling my legs up under me with an assumption of ease.

"I did. You were just coming out of the boat-house, and you went rushing off up the path to the house."

I saw the slightest relaxation as he registered that I hadn't seen him coming down from the cave with the packages. He drew on his cigarette, blowing out a long jet of grey smoke into a haze round the lamp. "And then?"

I smiled up at him—I hoped provocatively. "Oh, I was going to call after you, but then I saw you had a sweater and things on, so you probably *were* going out after all. I thought if I just stuck around you'd be back, and I could ask you."

"Why didn't you?"

"Why didn't I what?"

"Ask me."

I looked embarrassed and fidgeted with a bit of blanket. "Well, I'm sorry, I know I should have, but you were quite a time, and I got bored and tried the door, and it was open, so——"

"The door was open?"

"Yes."

"That's not possible. I locked it."

I nodded. "I know. I heard you. But it hadn't quite caught, or something, you know how those spring locks are. I'd only tried it for something to do—you know how one fidgets about— and when it opened I was quite surprised."

There was no way of knowing whether he believed me or not, but according to Spiro the catch had been stiff, and Godfrey had no idea I could have known that. I didn't think he could have changed the lock as he had threatened, for I had heard him myself wrestling with it on Monday; but that was a chance I had to take.

He tapped ash into a bowl on the liquor cupboard, and waited. He looked very tall; the slightly swaying lamp was on a level with his eyes. I toyed with the idea of giving it a sudden shove that would knock his head in, but doubted if I could get there quickly enough. Later, perhaps. Now I smiled at him instead, letting a touch of uncertainty, even of distress, appear.

"I—I'm sorry. I suppose it was awful of me, and I should have waited, but I was *sure* you wouldn't mind my looking at the boat——"

"Then why did you hide when I came down?"

"I don't know!" The note of exasperated honesty came out exactly right. "I honestly don't know! But I was *in* the boat, you see, in here, actually, poking about in the cupboards and the ga—kitchen and everything——"

"What for?"

"What *for*?" Every bit of technique I'd ever had went into it. "Well, what does a woman usually poke around in other people's houses for? And a boat's so much more fun than a house; I wanted to see how it was fitted, and the cooking arrangements, and—well, everything!" I laughed, wooing him back to good temper with all I had, playing the ignorant; it might be as well not to let him know how much I knew about the sloop's lay-out. "And it really is smashing, Godfrey! I'd no idea!" I faltered then, biting my lip. "You're annoyed with me. You *do* mind. I—I suppose it *was* the hell of a nerve ... In fact, I *knew* it was, and I suppose that's why I hid when I heard you at the door ... I suddenly thought how it must look, and you might be furious, so I got in a panic and hid. I had a vague idea that if you weren't going sailing after all I could slip out after you had gone. That's all."

I sat back, wondering if tears at this point would be too much, and deciding that they probably would. Instead, I looked at him meltingly through my lashes—at least, that's what I tried to do, but I shall never believe the romantic novelists again; it's a physical impossibility. Godfrey, at any rate, remained unmelted, so I abandoned the attempt, and made do with a quivering little smile, and a hand, genuinely none too steady, brushing my eyes. "I'm sorry," I said, "I truly am. Please don't be angry."

"I'm not angry." For the first time he took his eyes off me. He mounted a step to pull the door open, and looked out into the blackness. What he saw appeared to satisfy him, but when he turned back he didn't shut the door.

"Well, now you are here you might as well enjoy it. I can't leave the tiller much longer, so come along out. That's not a very thick coat, is it? Try this." And he pulled open the cupboard and produced a heavy navy duffel coat, which he held for me.

"Don't bother, mine will do." I stood up and reached for my own coat, with the torch in the pocket, then remembered how wet it was. For the life of me I couldn't think offhand of any reason for the soaked skirt where I had knelt in the puddles of water. I dropped the coat back on the bunk. "Well, thanks awfully, yours'll be warmer, I suppose. It sounds like quite a windy night now."

As he held it for me to put on, I smiled up at him over my shoulder. "Have you forgiven me? It was a silly thing to do, and you've a right to be furious."

"I wasn't furious," said Godfrey, and smiled. Then he turned me round and kissed me.

Well, I had asked for it, and now I was getting it. I shut my eyes. If I pretended it was Max ... no, that wasn't possible. Well, then, someone who didn't matter—for instance that rather nice boy I'd once had an abortive affair with but hadn't cared about when it came to the push ... But that wouldn't work either. Whatever Godfrey was or wasn't, he didn't kiss like a rather nice boy ...

I opened my eyes and watched, over his shoulder, the lovely, heavy lamp swinging about a foot away from his head. If I could manoeuvre him into its orbit ... I supposed there were circumstances in which it was correct, even praiseworthy, for a girl to bash a man's head in with a lamp while he was kissing her ...

The *Aleister* gave a sudden lurch, and yawed sharply. Godfrey dropped me as if I had bitten him.

"Put the lamp out, will you?"

"Of course."

He ran up the steps. I blew the lamp out, and had the glass back in a matter of seconds, but already the *Aleister* was steady again, and Godfrey paused in the doorway without leaving the cabin, and turned back to hold a hand down to me.

"Come out and see the stars."

"Just a moment."

His voice sharpened a fraction. He wasn't as calm as he made out. "What is it?"

"My hankie. It's in my own coat pocket." I was fumbling in the dimness of the quarter berth among the folds of coat and blanket. The torch dropped sweetly into the pocket of the duffel coat; I snatched the handkerchief, then ran up the steps and put a hand into his.

Outside was a lovely windswept night, stars and spray, and black sea glinting as it rushed up to burst in great fans of spindrift. Dimly on our left I could see the coast outlined black against the sky, a mass of high land blocking out the stars. Low down there were lights, small and few, and seemingly not too far away.

"Where are we?"

"About half a mile out from Glyfa."

"Where's that?"

"You know how the coast curves eastwards here along the foot of Mount Pantokrator, towards the mainland? We're about halfway along the curve . . ."

"So we're running east?"

"For the moment. Off Kouloura we turn up into the strait."

("*I reckoned we were about half-way over,*" Spiro had said, "in the strait between Kouloura and the mainland.")

"You'll feel the wind a bit more when we get out of the lee of Pantokrator," said Godfrey. "It's rising quite strongly now." He slipped an arm round me, friendly, inexorable. "Come and sit by me. She won't look after herself for ever. Do you know anything about sailing?"

"Not a thing." As he urged me towards the stern seat, my eyes were busily searching the dimly seen cockpit. Only too well did I know there was no handy weapon lying about, even if that lover-like arm would have allowed me to reach for it. But I looked all the same. It had occurred to me that he probably carried a gun, and I had already found out that there was nothing in the pocket nearest me, the left; if he got amorous again it might be possible to find out if it were in the other pocket . . . As he drew me down beside him on the stern seat I pulled the duffel coat round me for protection against his hands, at the same time relaxing right into the curve of his shoulder. I was thinking that if he wore a shoulder holster he would hardly have cuddled me so blithely to his left side, and I was right. There was no gun there. I leaned cosily back, and set myself to show him how little I knew about sailing. "How fast will it go?"

"About eight knots."

"Oh?" I let it be heard that I had no idea what a knot was, but didn't want to expose my ignorance. He didn't enlighten me. He settled the arm round me, threw his cigarette overside, and added:

"Under sail, that is. Six or seven under power.'

"Oh?" I had another shot at the same intonation, and was apparently successful, because he laughed indulgently as he turned to kiss me again.

The *Aleister* tilted and swung up to a cross-sea, and the boom came over above us with the mainsail cracking like a rifle shot. It supplied me with an excuse for the instinctive recoil I gave as his mouth, fastened on mine, but next moment I had hold of myself, and responded with a sort of guarded enthusiasm while my open eyes watched the boom's pendulum movements above our heads, and I tried to detach my mind from Godfrey, and think.

What he was doing was obvious enough: not being sure yet of my innocence, he hadn't wanted to risk leaving me unguarded while he got the mainsail in and took the *Aleister* along under power. All he could do was hold her as she was, head to the wind, the engine ticking over, the idle mainsail weathercocking her along, until he had decided what to do with me. It was just my luck, I thought sourly, stroking his cheek with a caressing hand, that the wind was more or less in the direction he wanted. If he was aiming (as I supposed he was) for the same place as on the night he had tried to drown Spiro, then he must still be pretty well on course.

A sudden gust on the beam sent the *Aleister*'s bows rearing up at an angle that brought the boom back again overhead with a creak and a thud, and Godfrey released me abruptly, his right hand going to the tiller. And as he moved, leaning forward momentarily, I saw my weapon.

Just beyond him, hanging on its hooks behind the stern cockpit seat, was the sloop's lifebelt, and attached to this by a length of rope was the smoke flare ... a metal tube about a foot long, with a drum-shaped float of hollow metal about two-thirds of the way up its length. It was heavy enough, and deadly enough in shape, to make a formidable weapon if I could only manage to reach it down from the hook where it hung a foot to my side of the lifebelt. The rope attaching it was coiled lightly over the hook, and would be some ten or fifteen feet long—ample play for such a weapon. It only remained to get hold of it. I could hardly reach past him for it, and would certainly get no chance to use it if I did. If I could only get him to his feet for a moment, away from me ...

211

"Why do you leave the sail up?" I asked. "I'd have thought it ought to come down if the engine was going."

"Not necessarily. I'll want to take her in under sail soon, and in the meantime she'll take care of herself this way."

"I see." It was all I could do, this time, to sound as if I didn't. I saw, all right. He would take her in under sail for the same reason that he had taken her out: for silence. And it was pretty obvious where we were heading. We were making for the Albanian coast with our cargo; and 'in the meantime' I, no doubt, would be shed as Spiro had been shed. After I had gone he could spare both hands for the *Aleister*.

I took a deep breath of the salt air, and leaned my head confidingly against his shoulder. "Heavenly, isn't it? I'm so glad I stowed away, and that you're not really angry with me about it. Look at those stars . . . that's a thing one misses terribly in London now; no night sky; only that horrible dirty glare from five million sodium lamps. Oughtn't you to have a light, Godfrey?"

"I ought, but I don't. As long as I don't meet anyone else breaking the law, *we* see *them*, so there's no harm done."

"Breaking the law?"

I thought he was smiling. "Running without lights."

"Oh. You're taking photographs, then? Of the dawn?" I giggled. "What'll Phyl say *this* time, I wonder, when I land home with the milk?"

"Where is she tonight? Did she know you'd come out?"

"She's out with friends at the Corfu Palace. I got a note from her when I got in, and it was too late to join them, so I just stayed home. I . . . felt kind of blue. We'd had such a lovely day, you and I, I just couldn't stay in the house, somehow."

"Poor Lucy. And then I was foul to you, I'm so sorry. Anybody know where you are?"

The question was casual, almost caressing, and it went off like a fire alarm. I hesitated perhaps a second too long. "Miranda was in the house. I told her I was coming out."

"To the boat-house?"

"Well, no. I didn't know that myself, did I?"

He did not reply. I had no way of knowing whether my wretched bluff had worked. The cool uncommitted tone—pleasant enough—and the cold sensuality of his love-making, gave no clue at all to what he felt, or planned to do. It was a personality from which normal human guesses simply glanced

212

off. But whether or not he had accepted my innocence, I had reckoned that nothing I could say would make any difference to my fate. The only weapon I held so far against him was the knowledge I possessed: that Spiro was alive, that Godfrey might be accused of Yanni's murder, that Adoni and Miranda had seen the packages, and that Miranda had watched him carrying them to the boat-house, and must know where I was now. And finally, that Godfrey on his return would certainly be met by Max, Adoni and (by now) the police, who this time would not be prepared to accept easily any story he might dream up. In plain words, whether he killed me or not, his game was up.

The trouble was, it worked both ways. If it made no difference what he did with me, then obviously his best course would be to kill me, and make his getaway (surely already planned for) without going back at all into the waiting hands of Max and the Greek police.

So silence was the only course. It was faintly possible that, if he believed me innocent he might abandon his mission and take me home, or that I might be able to persuade him to relax his watch on me for long enough to let me get hold of the more tangible weapon that hung beyond his right shoulder . . .

I said quickly: "Listen. What's the matter with the engine? Did you hear that?"

He turned his head. "What? It sounds all right to me."

"I don't know . . . I thought it made a queer noise, a sort of knocking."

He listened for a moment, while the engine purred smoothly on, then shook his head. "You must be hearing that other boat —there's one over there, see, north-east of us, out from Kentroma. You can hear it in the gusts of the wind." His arm tightened as I twisted to look, pulling away as if to get to my feet. "It's nothing. Some clapped-out old scow from Kentroma with a pre-war engine. Sit still."

I strained my eyes over the black and tossing water to where the light, dim and rocking, appeared and disappeared with the heaving sea. Up-wind of us, I was thinking; they'd never hear anything: and if they did, they'd never catch the *Aleister* with her lovely lines and silken engine.

Suddenly, only a short way from us, a flash caught my eye, a curve and splash of light where some big fish cut a phosphorescent track like a line of green fire.

213

"Godfrey! Look!"

He glanced across sharply. "What?"

I was half out of my seat. "Light, lovely green light, just there in the sea! Honestly, it was just *there* . . ."

"A school of fish or some such thing." His tone was barely patient, and I realised with a jerk of fear that his mind was moving towards some goal of its own. "You often see phosphorescence at night hereabouts."

"There it is again! Could it be photographed? Oh, look! Let me go a moment, Godfrey, please, I——"

"No. Stay here." The arm was like an iron bar. "I want to ask you something."

"What?"

"I've had the answer to one question already. But that leaves me with another. Why did you come?"

"I told you——"

"I know what you told me. Do you expect me to believe you?"

"I don't understand what you——"

"I've kissed women before. Don't ask me to believe you came along because you wanted to be with me."

"Well," I said, "I admit I wasn't expecting it to be quite like that."

"Like what?"

"You know quite well."

"I believe I do. But if you follow a man round and hide in his bed and play Cleopatra wrapped in a rug you can hardly expect him to say it with lace-edged Valentines."

It was like acid spilling over a polished surface, to show the stripped wood, coarse and ugly. There had been splashes of the same corrosive this afternoon. If there had been light enough to see by, he would have caught me staring.

"Do you have to be so offensive? I know you were annoyed, but I thought you'd get over that, and if you want the truth I can't see why you should mind so damned much if someone *does* have a look at your boat. I've told you exactly what happened, and if you don't believe me, or if you think I should fall straight into bed with you here and now, you can just think again. It's not a habit of mine."

"Then why did you behave as if it were?"

"Now, look——!" I broke off, and then laughed. At all costs I mustn't let him force a showdown on me yet. I would have to let anger go, and try a bit more sweet apology. "Look, Godfrey, forget it! I'm sorry, it's silly to blame you, I did ask for it . . . and I *was* putting on a bit of an act in the cabin, I admit it. That was silly, too. But when a woman gets in a jam, and finds herself faced with an angry male, it's an instinct to use her sex to get her out of it. I haven't shown up a bit well tonight, have I? But I never thought you would be quite so furious, or quite so . . . well, quick off the mark."

"Sexually? How little you know."

"Well, you've had your revenge. I haven't felt so idiotic and miserable since I remember. And you needn't worry that I'll follow you around again . . . I'll never face you by daylight again as long as I live!"

He did not answer, but to my stretching senses it was as if he had laughed aloud. I could feel the irony of my words ring and bite in the windy air. A little way to starboard the trail of green fire curved and flashed again, and was gone. I said: "Well, after that, I suppose I must ask you to ruin your trip finally and completely, and take me home."

"No use, my dear." The words were brisk, the tone quite different. I felt a quiver run through me. "Here you are, and here you stay. You're coming the whole way."

"But you can't want me——"

"I don't. You came because you wanted to—or so you say—and now you'll stay because I say you have to. I've no time to take you back, even if I wished to. You've wasted too much of my time as it is. I'm on an urgent trip tonight and I'm running to schedule——"

"Godfrey——"

"—taking a load of forged currency across to the Albanian coast. It's under the cabin floor. Seven hundred thousand leks, slightly used, in small denominations; and damned good ones too. If I'm caught, I'll be shot. Get it?"

"I . . . I don't believe you, you're ribbing me."

"Far from it. Want to see them?"

"*No.* No. I'll believe you if you like, but I don't understand. Why? What would you do a thing like that for?"

Kentroma was abeam of us now, about the same distance away. I thought I saw the faint outline of ghostly foam very near, and the loom of land, and my heart leapt; but it vanished. A small rocky islet at most, lightless, and scoured by the wind. As we ran clear of it I felt the sudden freshening kick of the wind, no longer steady from the east but veering and gusting as the mountains to either side of the strait caught and volleyed the currents of air.

And there, not so far off now, were the lights of Kouloura, where the land ended and the strait began . . .

I dragged my mind back to what he was saying.

". . . And at the moment the situation in Albania is that anything could happen, and it's to certain interests—I'm sure you follow me?—to see that it does. The Balkan pot can always be made to boil, if you apply heat in the right place. You've got Yugoslavia, and Greece, and Bulgaria, all at daggers drawn, all sitting round on the Albanian frontier, prepared for trouble, but none of them daring to make it."

"Or wanting to," I said sharply. "Don't give me that! The last thing Greece wants is any sort of frontier trouble that she can be blamed for . . . oh!"

"Yes, I thought you might see it. Dead easy, isn't it? A lovely set-up. Communist China sitting pretty in Albania, with a nice little base in Europe, the sort of foothold that Big Brother over there'd give his eye teeth to have. And if the present pro-Chinese Government fell, and the fall was attributed to Greece, there'd be a nice almighty Balkan blow-up, and the Chinese would be out and Russia in. And maybe into Greece as well. Get it now?"

"Oh, God, yes. It's an old dodge, Hitler tried it in the last war. Flood a country with forged currency and down goes the Government like a house of cards. How long has this been going on?"

"Ferrying the currency? For some time now. This is the last load. D-Day is Good Friday; it's to filter as from then, and believe you me, after that the bang comes in a matter of days." He laughed. "They'll see the mushroom cloud right from Washington."

"And you? Where will you see it from?"

"Oh, I'll have a ringside seat, don't worry—but it won't be the Villa Rotha. 'G. Manning, Esq.' will be vanishing almost immediately . . . You wouldn't have got your trip out with me on Saturday after all, my dear. A pity, I thought so at the time. I enjoyed our day out; we've a lot in common."

"Do you have to be so insulting?"

It didn't even register. He was staring into the darkness to the north. "The thing I really regret is that I'll never be able to use

216

the photographs. Poor Spiro won't even get that memorial. We'll soon be reaching the place where I threw him in."

There had been no change of tone. He was still holding me, his arm about as personal as a steel fetter; which was just as well; the touch of his body jammed against mine was making my skin crawl. The cracking of the sail as the boom moved overhead made me jump as if he had laid a whip to me.

"Nervy, aren't you?" said Godfrey, and laughed.

"Who's paying you?"

"Shall we just leave it that it isn't Greece?"

"I hardly supposed that it was. Who is it?"

"What would you say if I told you I was being paid twice?"

"I'd say it was a pity you couldn't be shot twice."

"Sweet girl." The smooth voice mocked. "That's the least of what the Greeks would do to me if they caught me!"

"Where's the currency made? I can't believe anyone in Corfu..."

"Oh, God, no. There's a clever little chap who lives out near Ciampino ... I've been getting my photographic supplies from him for a long time now. He used to work in the local branch of Leo's Bank. It was through him I was brought in on this ... and, of course, because I knew Leo."

I must have gone white: I felt the blood leave my face, and the skin round my mouth was cold and rigid. "*Leo?* I will not believe that Leo even *begins to know* about this!"

He hesitated fractionally. I could almost feel the cruel impulse to lie; then he must have decided it would be more amusing after all to keep the credit ."No, no. Pure as the driven snow, our Leo. I only meant because I had an 'in' with him to get the house, a perfect situation for this job, and of course with that boat-house, which is ideal. And then there's my own cover, being next door to the Forlis themselves ... If anything had gone wrong and inquiries had been made, where do you suppose the official eye would have gone first? Where but the Villa Forli, where the Director of the Bank lived? And by the time they got round to the Villa Rotha, it would be empty of evidence, and possibly—if things were really bad—of me."

"And when the 'mushroom cloud' goes up? I take it that part of the plan is to have the currency traceable to Greece?"

"Of course. Eventually, as far back as Corfu, but with luck, no further."

"I see. I suppose Spiro had found out?"

He lifted his shoulders. "I doubt it. But there was a chance he'd seen a sample I was carrying in my wallet."

"So you murdered him on the off-chance." I drew in my breath. "And you don't even care, do you? It's almost funny to think what fuss I made about the dolphin ... you must have shot at him for sheer jolly fun, since you were leaving in a few days anyway." I peered at him in the darkness. "How do people *get* like you? You simply don't care who or what you wreck, do you? You're a traitor to your own country, and the one you're a guest in, and not only that, you wreck God knows how many people into the bargain. I don't only mean Spiro, I mean Phyl and Leo and the children. You know what it will do to them."

"Don't be sentimental. There's no room for that sort of talk in a man's world."

"Funny, isn't it, how often that so-called 'man's world' works out as a sort of juvenile delinquents' playground? Bombs and lies and cloak-and-dagger nonsense and uniforms and loud voices. All right, have it your own way, but remember I'm an actress, and I'm interested in how people work, even sawn-off morons like you. Just tell me *why*?"

I felt it at last, the movement of anger through his body. His arm had slackened.

"Do you do it for the money?" My voice nagged sharply at him. "But surely you've got money. And you've got a talent of a sort with a camera, so it can't be frustration—unless that turn-of-the-century technique of yours can't get you any sex that's willing. And you can't be committed politically, since you bragged you were working for two sides. Why, then? I'd love to know, just for the record, what makes a horror-comic like you tick over."

"You've got a poisonous tongue, haven't you?"

"It's the company I keep. Well? Just a wrecker, is that it? You do it for kicks?"

I heard his breath go in, then he laughed, an ugly little sound. I suppose he could afford to. He must have found, back there in the cabin, that I had no weapon on me, and he knew I couldn't escape him now. His hold was loose on me, but he could still have grabbed me if I had moved. I sat still.

"Just exactly that," he said.

"I thought as much. It measures up. Is that why you called your boat *Aleister*?"

218

"What a well-read little girl it is, to be sure! Of course. His motto was the same as mine, '*Fais ce que veult*'."

" 'Do what thou wilt'?" I said. "Well, Rabelais had it first. I doubt if you'll ever be anything but third-hand, Godfrey. Throwing people overboard hardly gets you into the master class."

He made no reply. The lights of Kouloura were coming abeam of us. The wind backed in a sudden squall, leaping the black waves from the north. His hand moved on the tiller, and the *Aleister* bucked and rose to meet it. The stars swung behind the mast, tilted. The wind sang in the ropes. The deck heeled steeply as the starboard rail lifted against the rush of stars. The boom crashed over.

"Is that what you're going to do with me?" I asked. "Throw me overboard?"

The *Aleister* came back head to wind, and steadied sweetly. Godfrey's hand left the tiller.

"By the time I do, by God," he said, "you'll be glad to go."

Then he was out of his seat, and swinging round on me, his hands reaching for my throat.

I flinched back as far as I could from the brutal hands, dragging the torch from my pocket as I went. My back came up hard against the port coaming. Then he was on me. The boat lurched; the boom thudded to starboard with the sail cracking like a whip; a glistening fan of water burst over the rail so that his foot slipped and the wet hands slithered, missing their grip on my throat.

The *Aleister* was turning into the seas; the boom was coming back. His hands had found their hold, the thumbs digging in. I braced my back against the coaming, wrenched my left hand free and smashed a blow with the torch at his face.

It wasn't much of a blow. He didn't let go, but he jerked back from it instinctively, straightening his body, dragging me with him . . .

I kicked upwards with my right foot past his body, jammed the foot against the tiller with all my strength, and shoved it hard over.

The *Aleister*, already starting the swing, came round like a boomerang, heeling so steeply into the starboard tack that the rail went under.

And the boom slammed over with the force of a ramjet, straight at Godfrey's head.

CHAPTER NINETEEN

*Swum ashore, man, like a duck: I can swim like a duck I'll
be sworn.*

II. 2.

IF I had been able to take him completely by surprise, it would
have ended the business then and there. But he had felt my foot
go lashing past his body, and the sudden heeling of the *Aleister*
gave him a split second's warning of what must happen. His
yachtsman's instinct did the rest.

He ducked forward over me, one arm flying up to protect his
head—but I was in his way, hitting at his face, struggling to
thrust him back and up into the path of the boom as it came
over with a whistle and a crash that could have felled a bull.

It struck him with appalling force, but a glancing blow, the
upflung arm taking the force of the smash. He was flung
sprawling right across me, a dead weight bearing me back helplessly against the seat.

I had no idea if he were still conscious, or even alive. The seat
was wet and slippery; my hands scrabbled for a hold to drag
myself free, but before I could do this the *Aleister*, caught now
with the wind on her beam, swung hard into the other tack.
Godfrey's body was flung back off mine. He went to the deck all
anyhow, and I with him, helplessly tangled in the loose folds of
the duffel coat. The two of us slithered together across the
streaming boards, to fetch up hard against the starboard side of
the cockpit.

The *Aleister* kicked her way upwards, shuddered, hung
poised for the next perilous swing. I tore myself free of the
tangling coat and managed somehow to claw my way to my
feet, bent double to avoid the murderous boom, staggering and
sprawling as the deck went up like a lift, and the boom came
back again to port with a force that threatened to take the whole
mast overside. I threw myself at the wildly swinging tiller,
grabbed it somehow and clung there, fighting to steady the
sloop and trying, through the bursting fans of spray, to see.

At first I thought he was dead. His body sprawled in a slack
heap where it had been thrown back to the port side by the last
violent tack. His head rolled, and I could see the blur of his
face, not the pale oval that had been visible before, but half an

oval ... half his face must be black with blood. Then the *Aleister* shipped another wave, and the cold salt must have brought him sharply to his senses, for the head moved, lifting this time from the deck, and a hand went with terrifying precision to the edge of the cockpit seat, groping for a hold to pull his body up ...

I thrust the tiller hard to starboard again and laid the sloop right over. His hand slipped, and he was thrown violently back across the deck. It was now or never. I let go the tiller and tore the smoke flare down from its hook behind me. I could only pray that its rope was long enough to let me reach Godfrey where he lay against the side, his left hand now strongly grasping the seat, his right dragging at something in his pocket.

I lifted the metal flare and lurched forward.

Too late: the gun was in his hand. He was shouting something: words that were lost in the noise of wind and cracking spars and the hammering of the boom. But the message was unmistakable. I dropped the smoke flare, and leapt back for the stern seat.

The pale half-face turned with me. The gun's eye lifted.

I yanked wildly at the lifebelt hanging there on its hooks. It came free suddenly, and I went staggering against the side with it clutched to me like a shield. As I gripped the coaming and hauled myself up, the engine controls were just beside my feet. I kicked the throttle full open, and jumped for the rail.

The *Aleister* surged forward with a roar. I saw Godfrey let go his hold, dash the blood from his eyes with his free hand, jerk the muzzle of the gun after me, and fire.

I heard no shot. I saw the tiny jet of smoke spurt and vanish in the wind. I put a hand to my stomach, doubled up and pitched headlong into the sea.

*　　　*　　　*

I was coughing, swallowing salt water, gasping with lungs that hurt vilely, fighting the black weight of the sea with a wild instinct that brought me at last to the surface. My eyes opened wide, stinging, on pitch blackness. My arms flailed the water; my legs kicked like those of a hanging man; then I went out of control, lurching forward again and down, down ...

The cold water closing over me for the second time struck me back to full consciousness. Godfrey. The shot which—fired at a dim target on a wildly bucking boat—had missed me completely. The lifebelt which had been torn from me as I fell, its rope pulled tight on the hooks by my own hasty action with the smoke flare. The *Aleister*, which I had sent swerving away fast at full throttle from the place where I went in, but whose master would have her under control again, searching for me to make sure...

I fought my panic down, as I had fought the sea. I surfaced easily enough, and this time the thick blackness was reassuring. I felt a shoe go, and even this little load lightened me. I trod water, retching and gasping, and tried to look about me.

Darkness. Nothing but darkness, and the noises of wind and sea. Then I heard the engine, I couldn't judge how far from me, but in the pauses of the wind it seemed to be coming nearer. He would come back to look for me; of course he would. I hoped he would think I had been hit and couldn't possibly survive, but he could hardly take the risk. He would stay here, beating the sea between me and the land, until he found me.

A mounting hill of a wave caught and lifted me. As I reached its crest I saw him; he had a light on, and the *Aleister*, now bare of canvas, was slipping along at half-throttle, searching the waves. She was still a good way off, and moving away from me at a slant, but she would be back...

What was more, she was between me and the land. I saw this now, dimly, a black mass studded with faint points of light. It seemed a lot further away than it had from the deck of the *Aleister*.

Half a mile, he had said. I could never swim half a mile; not in this sea. The water was very buoyant, and I was lightly clad, but I wasn't in Spiro's class as a swimmer, and could hardly hope for his luck. I dared do no other than swim straight towards the nearest land, and if Godfrey hunted about long enough he would be bound to see me.

He had turned, and was beating back on a long tack, still between me and the shore. All around me the crests of the seas were creaming and blowing. I was carried up climbing slopes of glass, their tops streaming off against the black sky till the whole night seemed a windy race of wet stars. Foam blew into my eyes, my mouth. My body was no longer mine, but a thing of unfamiliar action, cold and buoyant. I could do little more than stay afloat, try to swim in the right direction, and let the seas take me.

As I swam up the next mounting wave I caught, clearly, the

reek of petrol in the wind, and saw a light not two hundred yards away. The engine was throttled back to the merest throb, and the boat circled slowly round the beam, which was directed downwards into the water. I even thought I saw him stooping over the side, reaching for something—my shoe, perhaps, kept floating by its rubber sole. He might take it as evidence that I was drowned; on the other hand, he might beat in widening circles round the place until he found me . . .

Then not far away I saw another light, dimmer than the *Aleister*'s, and riding high. The *Aleister*'s light went out. I heard the beat of another engine, and the second light bobbed closer. Faintly, a hail sounded. The clapped-out old scow from Kentroma was coming to take a look at the odd light on her fishing pitch . . .

The *Aleister*'s throttle opened with a roar, and I heard it dwindling away until the wind took all sound.

Then I shouted.

The sound came out as little more than a gasping cry, a feeble yell that was picked up by the wind and thrown away like the cry of a gull. The Kentroma boat may have attempted to go in the track of the *Aleister*, I do not know, but I had lost sight of her yellow light, and the sound of her engine, long before I gave up from sheer exhaustion, and concentrated on swimming rather than merely keeping afloat.

It was then that I realised that the sea was dropping. I was well into the lee of the great curve of Corfu, where Pantokrator broke the winds and held the Gulf quiet. And the lights of Kouloura were a long way to my right. I had been drifting westwards, far faster than I could have swum.

The discovery was like a shot of Benzedrine. My brain cleared. Of course. We had been still some distance from the east-bound current that had carried Spiro to the Albanian coast. And tonight it was an east wind. Where I had gone in the drift must be strongly to the south-west. He had thrown Yanni's body in in the Gulf, and Yanni's body had fetched up at the Villa Rotha. I doubted if St. Spiridion would take me quite so neatly home, but at least, if I could stay afloat, and make some progress, I might hope to stay alive.

So I swam, and prayed, and if St. Spiridion got muddled up in my wordless prayers with Poseidon and Prosper, and even Max, no doubt it would come to the right ears in the end.

Twenty minutes, in a sea that was little more than choppy,

223

and with the roar of the rocky shore barely a hundred yards ahead, I knew I couldn't make it. What had been chance for Spiro was none at all for me. Under the lee of the cliff, some freak current was setting hard off shore, probably only the backwash of the main stream that had brought me here, striking the coast at an angle and being volleyed back to the open water, but where I had till now been able to keep afloat and even angle my course slightly north across the current, I no longer had strength to fight any sea that wasn't going my way: my arms felt like cotton-wool, my body like lead; I gulped and floundered as the cross-waves met me, and every little slapping crest threatened to submerge me.

Eventually, one did. I swallowed more water, and in my panic began to struggle again. I burst free of the water, my eyes wide and sore, arms flapping feebly now, failing to drive me on or even to keep me above water. The roar of the breakers came to me oddly muffled, as if they were far away, or as if their noise came only through the water that was filling my ears ... I was being carried back, down, down, like a sackful of lead, like a body already drowned, to be tumbled with the other sea-wrack on the rocks in the bright morning ...

It was bright morning now. It was silly to struggle and fight my way up into darkness, when I could just let myself drift down like this, when in a moment or two if I put my feet down I would find sand, golden sand, and sweet air, sweet airs that give delight and hurt not ... no, that was music, and this was a dream ... how silly of me to panic so about a dream ... I had had a thousand dreams like this, floating and flying away in darkness. In a few moments I would wake, and the sun would be out, and Max would be here ...

He was here now. He was lifting me. He thrust and shoved at me, up, up, out of the nightmare of choking blackness, into the air.

I could breathe. I was at the surface, thrown there by a strength I hadn't believed a man could command outside his own element. As I floundered forward, spewing the sea from burning lungs, his body turned beside me in a rolling dive that half-lifted, half-threw me across the current; then before the sea could lay hold on me again to whirl me back and away, I was struck and butted forward, brutally, right into the white surge and confusion of the breakers, rolling over slack and jointless as a rag in the wind.

A huge wave lifted me forward, tumbled me over helpless in its breaking foam, then dropped me hard in its wake. I went down like a stone, hit something, and went flat on the bottom ... pancaked on the sand of a sloping beach, with the sea recoiling past me, my hands already driven in to the land, like hooks to hold me there against the drag and suck of the retreating wave. The sea tore and pulled and streamed back past me. Sobbing and retching, I crawled and humped myself up the slope, while wave after wave, diminishing, broke over me and then drew back, combing the sand where I clung. And then I was crawling through the creaming shallows, on to the firm dry beach.

I have a half memory, just as I collapsed, of looking back for my rescuer and of seeing him rear up from the waves as if to see me safe home, his body gleaming black through the phosphorescence, the witches' oils of his track burning green and white on the water. The starlight caught the cusp of the dorsal fin, glittered there briefly, then he was gone, with a triumphant smack of the tail that echoed right up the rocks.

Then I went out flat on the sand, barely a foot above the edge of the sea.

CHAPTER TWENTY

Though the seas threaten they are merciful.
I have curs'd them without cause.

v. 1.

THERE was a light, hanging seemingly in the sky far above me.

When this resolved itself into a lamp set in a cottage window, high up near the head of the cliffs, it still seemed as remote as the moon. I cannot even remember now what it cost me to drag myself in my dripping, icy clothes up the path that clung to the rock face, but I suppose I was lucky that there was a path at all. Eventually I made it, stopping to lean—collapse—against the trunk of an ancient olive that stood where a stream cut through the path to fall sharply seawards under a rough bridge.

Here a shallow valley ran back through a gap in the cliff. Dimly I could see the stretches of smoothed ground between the olive trees, painfully cultivated with beans and corn. Here and there among the trees were the scattered lights of the cottages, each with its own grove and its grazing for goats and sheep. The groves were old; the immense heads of the trees stirred and whispered even in that sheltered spot, and the small hard fruit pattered to the ground like rain. The twisted boughs stood out black against the light from the nearest window.

I forced my shivering, lead-weight limbs to move. Under my feet the rubbery olives rolled and squashed. The stems of camomile caught between my bare toes, and I stubbed my foot on a stone and cried out. Immediately there was a volley of barking, and a dog—one of the vicious, half-wild dogs that are a hazard of the Greek countryside—hurled itself towards me through the trees. I took no notice of it, except to speak as I limped forward, and the dog, every hair on end, circled behind me, growling. I felt the touch of his nose, cold on the cold flesh of my leg, but he didn't snap. Next moment the cottage door opened, loosing a shaft of light across the grass. A man, in thickset silhouette, peered out.

I stumbled into the light. "Please," I said breathlessly, in English, "please . . . can you help me?"

There was a startled moment of silence, while he stared at me, coming ghostlike out of the night, soaked and filthy with sand and dust, with the dog circling at my heels. Then he shouted something at the dog which sent it swerving away, and fired some sharp question at me. I didn't know what it was; didn't even recognise the language, but in any case I doubt if I could have spoken again. I just went forward blindly towards the light and the human warmth of the house, my hands stretched out like those of the traditional suppliant, and came heavily to my knees over the threshold, right at his feet.

The blackout cannot have lasted more than a couple of seconds. I heard him call out, then there came a woman's voice, questioning shrilly, and hands were on me, half-lifting, half-dragging me in to the light and warmth of a room where the embers of a wood fire still burned red. The man said something rough and urgent to his wife, and then went quickly out, slamming the door. For a dazed, frightened moment I wondered where he had gone, then as the woman, chattering in some undistinguishable gutturals, began to fumble with my soaked and clinging clothes, I realised that her husband had merely left the cottage's single room while I undressed.

I struggled out of the sopping clothes. I suppose the old woman was asking questions, but I couldn't understand, and in fact hardly heard. My brain was as numb as my body with the dreadful cold and shivering of exhaustion and shock. But presently I was stripped and dried—on a fine linen towel so stiff and yellowed that I imagine it must have been part of the woman's dowry, never used till now, and then a rough blanket was wrapped round me, I was pushed gently into a wooden chair near the fire, logs were thrown on, a pot shoved down into the leaping flames, and only when my discarded clothes were carefully hung up above the fireplace—with much interested fingering of the nylon—did the old woman go to the door and call her man back.

He came in, an elderly, villainous-looking peasant, with a ferocious moustache, and a dirty home-made cigarette drooping from his lips. He was followed, inevitably, by two others, shortish, tough-bodied men out of the same mould, with dark, fierce faces. They came into the light, staring at me. My host asked a question.

I shook my head, but the thing that mattered most to me at that moment was easy enough. I put an arm out of my blanket to make a gesture embracing my surroundings. "Kerkyra?" I asked. "This—Kerkyra?"

The storm of nods and assenting 'ne's' that this provoked broke over me with a physical sense of relief. To open human communications, to know where one was on the map ... of such is sanity. Heaven knows what I had expected the answer to be; I suppose that shreds of nightmare still clung to me, and it needed the spoken assurance to bring me finally out of the bad dream—the isolated near-death of the sea, the prison of the *Aleister* with Godfrey, the unknown black cliff I had been climbing. This was Corfu, and these were Greeks. I was safe.

I said: "I'm English. Do you speak English?"

This time heads were shaken, but I heard the word go round, '*Anglitha*', so they had understood.

I tried again. "Villa Forli? Castello dei Fiori?"

Again they understood. Another fire of talk where I caught a word I knew, '*thàlassa*', which means the sea.

I nodded, with another gesture. "Me," I said, indicating my swaddled person, "*thàlassa* ... boat ..." A pantomime, rather hampered by the blanket ... "swim ... drown."

Exclamations, while the woman thrust a bowl into my hands,

with words of invitation and sympathy. It was soup of some kind—beans, I think—and rather thick and tasteless, but it was hot and filling, and under the circumstances delicious. The men looked the other way politely while I ate, talking in quickfire undertones among themselves.

As I finished, and gave the bowl back to the woman, one of them—not my host—came forward a pace, clearing his throat. He spoke in very bad German.

"You are from the Castello dei Fiori?"

"*Ja.*" My German was very little better than his, but even a smattering might see us through. I said slowly, picking the words: "To go to Castello, how far?"

More muttering. "Ten." He held up his fingers. "*Ja*, ten."

"Ten kilometres?"

"*Ja.*"

"Is—a road?"

"*Ja, ja.*"

"Is—a car?"

"No." He was too polite to say so, but the impression that the single syllable gave was that of course there was no car. There never had been a car. What would they want with a car? They had the donkeys and the women.

I swallowed. So I wasn't yet free of the nightmare; I still had the long frustrations of the impossible journey ahead of me. I tried, not very coherently, to think what Godfrey would do.

He was bound to discover at his rendezvous that the package was missing, and would know that I must have taken it, and where I must have hidden it. But I hoped he would decide that as yet no one else could have reason to suspect him: he might well reckon that if there had been any suspicion of him, his journey would have been intercepted. No, it was to be hoped that he would think I had made a chance discovery—possibly that I had seen him carrying the packages, had hunted for them out of curiosity, and having seen them, had realised that something big was afoot, and had been frightened into hiding and carrying out the elaborate pantomime of innocence on the *Aleister* to save my skin. I was sure that he wouldn't even give Miranda a thought.

Well, he had got rid of me. My disappearance would provoke a hue and cry which he might well find embarrassing after what had happened to Spiro and Yanni, and this might decide him to cut his losses here and now, but the sudden absence of 'G.

228

Manning, Esq.' would naturally focus official attention on his house, and the boat-house, so (since it was unlikely that any official alarm had been raised for me yet) I felt sure that he would have to risk going back tonight to find and remove the last package of forged currency.

And this was where I had to come in. Even if Max were there to receive him, it would take evidence to hold him—hard evidence, not just the hearsay of Adoni and Miranda or even Spiro, which I was sure Godfrey could cut his way through without much trouble. Once they had taken their hands off him for five minutes, 'G. Manning, Esq.', with his prepared getaway, could vanish without trace, for good and all.

I looked up at the ring of men.

"Is—a telephone?" I asked it without much hope, but they all brightened. Yes, of course there was a telephone, up in the village, further up the hill, where the road started. (This came in Greek from everybody at once, with gestures, and was surprisingly easy to understand.) Did I want the telephone now? They would take me there . . .

I nodded and smiled and thanked them, and then, indicating my clothes, turned an inquiring look on the woman. In a moment the men had melted from the room, and she began to take my things off the line. The nylon was dry, but the cotton dress was still damp and unpleasant. I threw the blanket off thankfully—it smelt of what I tried charitably to imagine was goat—and began to dress. But when I tried to put on my frock the old woman restrained me.

"No, no, no, *this* . . . it is an honour for me. You are welcome . . ." The words couldn't have been plainer if she had said them in English. '*This*' was a blouse of white lawn, beautifully embroidered in scarlet and green and gold, and with it a full black skirt, gay with the same colours at the hem—the Corfiote national dress, worn for high days and holidays. Either this also had been part of her trousseau as a young bride, or else it was her daughter's. It fitted, too . . . I put it on. The skirt was of thick, handwoven stuff, and there was a warm jacket to go over the blouse. She hovered round me, delighted, stroking and praising, and then called the men in to see.

They were all waiting outside, not three now, but—I counted —sixteen. On an impulse I stooped and kissed the wrinkled cheek of the old woman, and she caught my hand in both of hers. There were tears in her eyes.

"You are welcome," she said. "English. You are welcome."

Then I was outside, swept up by the band of men and escorted royally up the stony track through the groves to the tiny village, to knock up the sleeping owner of the shop where stood the telephone.

*　　*　　*

No reply from the Castello. I hesitated, then tried the Villa Forli.

The bell had hardly sounded before Phyl was on the line, alert and anxious.

"*Lucy!* Where in the world——?"

"It's all right, Phyl, don't worry. I'm sorry I couldn't ring you up before, but I'm quite okay."

"Where *are* you? I tried Godfrey, but——"

"When?"

"An hour ago—three-quarters, perhaps. He wasn't in, so I thought you might be out with him. Are you?"

"No. Listen, Phyl, will you do something for me?"

"What? What *is* all this?"

"I'll tell you when I see you, but there's no time now. Just don't ask any questions, but will you ring up Godfrey's house again now? If he answers, tell him I'm not home yet, and ask if I'm still with him—just as you would if you hadn't heard from me, and were worried. It's terribly important not to let him know I rang up. Will you do that? It's *terribly* important, Phyl."

"Yes, but——"

"Then please do it, there's an angel. I promise you I'll be home soon and tell you all about it. But I must know if he's got home. As soon as you've rung him, ring me back here." I gave her the number.

"How in the world did you get *there*? Did you go out with him again? I know you were in to supper, because it wasn't washed up; Miranda seems to have just walked out and left everything."

"That was my fault. I sent her on a message."

"You did? Look, just what *is* going on? What with all the supper things just left lying, and you half-way up Pantokrator in the middle of the night——"

"You might say Godfrey ditched me. You know, the long walk home."

230

"*Lucy!* You mean he tried something on?"

"You might say so," I said. "I don't like your Godfrey, Phyl, but just in case he's home by now, I'll ring off and wait to hear from you. But please do just as I say, it's important."

"My God, I will. Let him worry," said Phyl, viciously. "Okay, sweetie, hang on, I'll ring you back. D'you want me to come for you?"

"I might at that."

"Stinking twerp," said my sister, but presumably not to me, and rang off.

* * *

There were twenty-three men now in the village shop, and something had happened. There were smiles all round. As I put down the receiver, my German-speaking friend was at my elbow.

"*Fräulein*, come and see." He gestured proudly to the door of the shop. "For you, at your service."

Outside in the starlight stood a motor-cycle, a magnificent, almost new two-stroke affair, straddled proudly but shyly by a youth of about twenty. Round this now crowded the men, delighted that they had been able to help.

"He comes from Spartylas," said my friend, pointing behind the shop up the towering side of Pantokrator where, a few miles away, I could see a couple of vague lights which must mark another village. "He has been visiting in Kouloura, at the house of his uncle, and we heard him coming, and stopped him. See? It is a very good machine, as good as a car. You cannot stay here, this village is not good enough for a foreigner. But he will take you home."

I felt the tears of emotion, brought on by anxiety and sheer exhaustion, sting my eyes. "You are too good. You are too good. Thank you, thank you all."

It was all I could say, and it seemed to be all they could desire. The kindness and goodwill that surrounded me was as palpable as light and fire; it warmed the night.

Someone was bringing a cushion; it looked like the best one his house could offer. Someone else strapped it on. A third man thrust the bundle containing my damp frock into a carrier behind the saddle. The youth stood smiling, eyeing me sideways, curiously.

The telephone rang once, briefly, and I ran back.

"Yes?"

"Lucy. I got the Villa Rotha, but he's not there."

"No reply?"

"Well, of course not. Look, can't you tell me what all this is about?"

"Darling, I can't, not just now ... I'll be home soon. Don't worry. But don't tell anyone I rang you up. *Anyone*. Not even Max."

"Not *even* Max? Since when did——?"

"And don't bother to come for me, I've got transport. Be seeing you."

The shopkeeper refused to take money for the telephone. It was a pleasure, I gathered, a pleasure to be roused from his bed in the middle of the night by a half-drowned, incoherent stranger. And the men who had helped me would not even take my thanks; it was a privilege to help me, indeed it was. They sat me on the pillion, showed me where to put my feet and how to hang on to the young man's waist, wished me God-speed, and stood back as my new friend kicked the engine into an un-silenced roar that slashed through the village like Pandemonium itself. It must have woken every sleeper within miles. No doubt they would count this, also, as a privilege ...

We roared off with a jerk and a cloud of smoke. The road was rutted, surfaced with loose gravel, and twisted like a snake through the olive-groves that skirted the steep cliffs, some three hundred feet above the sea. Not a fast road, one would have said—but we took it fast, heeling over on the bends as the *Aleister* had heeled to the seas, with gravel spurting out under our front wheel like a bow wave, and behind us a wake of dust half a mile long. I didn't care. The feel of the wind in my hair, and the bouncing, roaring speed between my thighs was at once exciting and satisfying after the terrors and frustrations of the night. And I couldn't be afraid. This was—quite literally—the 'god in the machine' who had come to the rescue, and he couldn't fail me. I clung grimly to his leather-clad back as we roared along, the shadowy groves flicking past us in a blue of speed, and down—way down—on our left the hollow darkness of the sea.

The god turned his curly head and shouted something cheer-fully. We shot round a bend, through a small stream, up some-thing remarkably like a rough flight of steps, and met the blessed smooth camber of a metalled road.

Not that this was really an improvement; it swooped clean down the side of Pantokrator in a series of tight-packed hairpin bends which I suppose were steep and dangerous, but which we took at a speed that carried us each time to the very verge, where a tuft or so of daisies or a small stone would catch us and cannon us back on to the metal. The tyres screeched, the god shouted gaily, the smell of burning rubber filled the night, and down we went, in a series of bird-like swoops which carried us at last to the foot of the mountain and the level of the sea.

The road straightened. I saw the god's hand move hopefully to the throttle.

"Okay?" he yelled over his shoulder.

"Okay!" I screamed, clinging like a monkey in a hurricane.

The hand moved. The night, the flying trees, the hedgerows ghostly with apple blossom, accelerated past us into a streaming blur . . .

All at once we were running through a village I knew, and he was slowing down. We ran gently between walls of black cypress, past the cottage in the lemon-grove, past the little tea-garden with its deserted tables under the pine, and up to the Castello gate, to stop almost between the pillars.

The youth put his feet down and turned inquiringly, jerking a thumb towards the drive, but I shook my head. It was a long walk up through the grounds of the Castello, but until I knew what was going on I certainly wasn't going to advertise my homecoming by roaring right up to the front door.

So I loosed my limpet-clutch from the leather jacket, and got rather stiffly off my perch, shaking out the pretty embroidered skirt, and pulling my own bedraggled cotton dress from the carrier.

When I tried to thank my rescuer, he smiled and shook his head, wheeling the machine back to face the way we had come, and shouting something which, of course, must mean: "It was a pleasure."

As his hand moved on the controls I put mine out quickly to touch it.

"Your name?" I knew the Greek for that. "Your name, please?"

I saw him grin and bob his head. "Spiridion," he said. "God with you."

Next second he was nothing but a receding roar in the darkness, and a cloud of dust swirling to settle in the road.

233

CHAPTER TWENTY-ONE

Thou dost here usurp
The name thou ow'st not, and hast put thyself
Upon this Island, as a spy . . .

I. 2.

THERE was no light in the Castello. The house loomed huge in
the starlight, turreted and embattled and almost as romantic-
looking as its builder had intended. I walked round it to the
terrace, treading softly on the mossed tiles. No light there either,
no movement, nothing. The long windows were blank and curtained, and—when I tried them—locked.

Keeping to the deepest shadows, I skirted the terrace till I
reached the balustrade overhanging the cliff and the bay. The
invisible sea whispered, and all round me was the dark, peppery
smell of the cypresses. I could smell the roses, too, and there
were bats about, cutting the silence with their thin, knife-
edge cries. A movement caught my eye and made me turn
quickly—a small slither of pale colour vanishing like ectoplasm
through the stone balustrade, and drifting downhill. The white
cat, out on his wild lone.

Then I caught a glimpse of light. This came from somewhere
beyond the trees to the right, where the Villa Rotha must lie. As
softly as the white cat, and almost as silently as the ghost from
the sea that I was, I crept off the terrace and padded down
through the woods towards the light.

I nearly fell over the XK 150, parked among the trees. He
must simply have driven her away from the house, so that a
chance caller would assume he was out with the car, and look
no further.

A few minutes later I was edging my way through the thicket
of myrtle that overhung the bungalow.

This was, as I have said before, the twin of the Forli house.
The main door, facing the woods, had a cleared sweep of drive-
way in front of it, and from this a paved path led round the
house to the wide terrace overlooking the sea. A light burned
over the door. I parted the leaves and peered through.

Two cars stood on the sweep, Max's big, shabby black Buick,
and a small car I didn't know.

So he was back, and it was battle-stations. I wondered if the other car was the police.

My borrowed rope soles made no sound as I crept round towards the terrace, hugging the house wall.

The terrace, too, was the twin of Phyllida's, except that the pergola was covered with a vine instead of wistaria, and there was no dining-table, only a couple of large chairs and a low table which held a tray with bottles and glasses. I by-passed these quietly, making for the french windows.

All three were shut and curtained, but the centre one showed a gap between the curtains some three inches wide through which I could see the room; and as I reached it I realised that I would be able to hear as well . . . In the glass beside the window-catch gaped a big, starred hole where someone had smashed a way in . . .

The first person I saw was Godfrey, near the window and to one side of it, sitting very much at his ease in a chair beside the big elm-wood desk, with a glass of whisky in his hand. He was still dressed in the jersey and dark trousers, and over the back of his chair hung the navy duffel coat which I had torn free of before I went into the sea. I was delighted to see that one side of his face bore a really classic bruise, smeared liberally with dried blood, and that the good-looking mouth appeared to hurt him when he drank. He was dabbing at a swollen lip with his hand-kerchief.

The room had seemed at that first glance full of people, but the crowd now resolved itself into a fairly simple pattern. A couple of yards from Godfrey, in the middle of the floor and half turned away from me, stood Max. I couldn't see his face. Adoni was over beside the door, facing towards the windows, but with his attention also riveted on Godfrey. Near me and just to one side of my window was Spiro, sitting rather on the edge of a low chair, with the injured leg in its new white cast thrust out awkwardly in front of him, and Miranda crouched on the floor beside his chair, hugging its arm against her breast as (it seemed) she would have liked to hug Spiro's. The two faces were amazingly alike, even allowing for the difference of male from female; and at the moment the likeness was made more striking still by the expression that both faces shared; a pure, uncomplicated hatred, directed unwinkingly at Godfrey. On the floor beside the boy's chair lay a rifle, and from the way his hand hung near it, twitching from time to time, I guessed that only a forcible order from the police had made him lay it down.

For the police were here. Across the width of the room from Godfrey, and near the door, sat a man I recognised as the Inspector (I didn't know the Greek equivalent) from Corfu who had been in charge of the inquiry into Yanni's death. This was a stoutish, grey-haired man with a thick moustache and black, intelligent eyes. His clothes were untidy, and had obviously been hastily put on, and in spite of the deadpan face and calm, steady stare I sensed that he was not quite sure of his ground, even ill at ease.

Godfrey was speaking in that light, cool voice that I knew so well, so very well.

"As you wish, Mr. Papadopoulos. But I warn you that I'm not prepared to overlook what happened down in my boat-house, or the fact that these two men have apparently broken into my house. As for the girl, I'm not quite sure what it is that I'm supposed to have done with her, but I have given you a complete account of our movements this afternoon, and I'm sure you can find any number of people who will bear me out."

"It's your movements tonight that we're interested in." Max's voice was rough, and only precariously controlled. "For a start, what happened to your face?"

"An accident with the main-boom," said Godfrey shortly.

"Another? Rather too common, these accidents, wouldn't you say? How did it happen?"

"Are you a yachtsman?"

"No."

"Then don't ask stupid questions." Godfrey gave him a brief, cold look. "You've had your turn, damn you. Back down. You've no more right to question me than you had to man-handle me or break in here to ransack the place. If you hadn't telephoned for the police, you can be very sure I'd have done so myself. We'll talk about your methods later."

Papadopoulos said heavily: "If you please, Max. Now, Mr. Manning, you have told us that you have not seen Miss Lucy Waring since shortly after seven this last evening, when you took her home?"

"That is so." To the Inspector his tone was one of tired but patient courtesy. He was playing his part to perfection. All his dislike of Max was there, patent through tonight's more im-mediate outrage, with weariness and puzzlement and a nice touch of worry about me. "I took her home before dinner. I myself had to go out again."

"And you have not seen her since?"

"How often must I——? I'm sorry, Inspector, I'm a little tired. No, I have not seen her since."

"You have given us an account of your movements after you took Miss Waring home. Now, when you finally went down to take out your boat you found the boat-house still locked, and as far as you are aware there was nobody there?"

"That is so."

"There was nothing to indicate that anyone—Miss Waring or anyone else—had been there, and gone again?"

I thought Godfrey hesitated, but it was barely perceptible. He must be very sure that he had sunk me without trace. "No."

"You heard what this girl had to say?"

"Miranda?" Godfrey's tone was not even contemptuous, merely lightly dismissive. "She'd say anything. She's got some bee in her bonnet over her brother, and she'd invent any tale to see me in trouble. Heaven knows why, or where the boy's got this incredible idea of his from. I've never been happier about anything in my life than I was to see him here tonight."

Spiro said something in Greek, one short, vicious-sounding phrase whose import there was no mistaking, and which drew a shocked glance from his sister. He made it clear. "I spit," he said, and did so.

"Spiro!" said Max sharply, and Godfrey raised an eyebrow— a very civilised eyebrow—at the Inspector, and laughed.

"Satan rebuking sin? Always an amusing sight, don't you think?"

"I'm sorry," said Papadopoulos. "You will control yourself, Spiro, or you will go. Let us go back, Mr. Manning. You must excuse me, my English is not so very good; I do not follow this about Satan, and bees, was it? Bees in the bonnet?" He glanced up at Max, who hesitated, and Adoni snapped out some phrase in Greek. "I see." The stout man sat back. "You were saying?" to Godfrey.

"I was saying that whatever Miranda accuses me of, the fact remains that she did not see Lucy Waring enter my boat-house or go near my boat. There is nothing to show that she did either."

"No. Well, Mr. Manning, we'll leave that for the moment . . . Yes, Max, I know, but there is nothing more we can do until

237

Petros gets up here from the boat-house and reports on his search there. He will be here before long. Meanwhile, Mr. Manning, with your permission, there are a few other questions I want to ask you."

"Well?"

"Forgetting about Miss Waring's movements for the moment, I should like to hear about yours ... after you went down to your boat-house. When Mr. Gale met you on your return, and accused you——"

"Attacked me, you mean."

"As you wish. When he asked you where you had been, you told him this was a 'normal trip'. What do you mean by a 'normal trip', Mr. Manning? Fishing, perhaps?"

Adoni said, without expression: "His cameras were in the Cabin."

"So you were out taking photographs, Mr. Manning? May one know where?"

There was a short silence. Godfrey took a sip of whisky, then sat for a moment staring down at the glass, swirling the spirit round gently. Then he looked up, meeting the policeman's eyes, and gave a faint smile that had the effect of a shrug.

"I can see that I'll have to make a clean breast of it. I never thought you'd get on to me. If it hadn't been for this misunderstanding about the girl, I doubt if you would have ... Or were you tipped off?"

There was no change in the Inspector's expression, but I saw Max stiffen, and Adoni was staring. Capitulation, when they hadn't even brought up a gun?

"If you please," said Papadopoulos courteously, "I do not understand. If you would use simpler English——"

"More idioms," said Adoni. "He means that he knows you've been told about him, so he's going to confess."

"I meant no such thing. Keep your pretty mouth shut, if you can. This is between men." Godfrey flung it at him without even a glance, indifferently, as one might swat a midge. Adoni's eyes went back to him, and his expression did not change, but I thought, with a queer jump of the heart: Your mistake, Godfrey ...

"Please," said Papadopoulos. "Let us not waste time. Well, Mr. Manning?"

Godfrey leaned back in his chair, regarding him coolly. You'd have thought there was nobody else in the room. "With your

238

man down there searching my boat it's not much use pretending I have been taking photographs, is it? You have only to look at the cameras ... No, as a matter of cold truth, I had business over the other side."

If the room had been still before, it was stiller now. I thought dazedly: He can't just confess like that ... Why? Why? Then I saw. Miranda had told the police what she knew, and Godfrey realised now that she had been with me on the shore. I did not think that the cave or the packages had been mentioned yet in front of him, but he could guess that she had seen as much as I, and must have told the police about the packages. Moreover, a police constable was now searching the *Aleister*, and, if he was even half good at his job, he would find the cache under the cabin floor. I guessed that Godfrey was intent on getting some relatively harmless explanation in before the inevitable discovery was made.

"Whereabouts on the other side?" asked Papadopoulos.

"Albania."

"And the business?"

"Shall we call it 'importing'?"

"What you call it does not matter. This, I understand perfectly." The Greek regarded him for a moment in silence. "So you admit this?"

Godfrey moved impatiently. "I have admitted it. Surely you aren't going to pretend you didn't know that this went on? I know you've shut your eyes to the way Yanni Zoulas was killed, but between ourselves——"

"Yanni Zoulas?" I saw Papadopoulos flash a glance at Max. Godfrey was taking the wind out of this sail, too, before it had even been hoisted.

"Ah," said Godfrey, "I see you understand me. I thought you would."

"You know something about Zoulas's death that you didn't tell the police?"

"Not a thing. I'm only guessing, from my own experiences with the coastguard system the other side. It's quite remarkably efficient."

"So you think he ran into trouble there?"

"I think nothing. I was only guessing. But guesses aren't evidence, are they?" The grey eyes touched Max's briefly. "I only mean that if one runs the gauntlet of those coasts often enough, it's not surprising if one gets hurt. What was surprising

239

was that the police made so little of it. You must have known what he was doing."

"What was Zoulas's connection with you?"

"With me? None at all. I didn't know the man."

"Then how do you know this about him?"

Godfrey smiled. "In the trade, word goes round."

"He was not connected with you?"

"I've answered that. Not in any way."

Papadopoulos said: "It has been suggested that Spiro here, and after him Yanni Zoulas, discovered something about your business . . ."

I missed the rest. From somewhere behind me, below the terrace, came the moving flicker of a torch, and the sound of footsteps. This would be the constable coming up from his search of the boat-house. I drew away from the lighted window, wondering if I should approach him now and tell him about the package I had sunk in the boat-house; then I remembered that he probably spoke no English. He passed below the end of the terrace, and trod gently round the house.

I tiptoed back to the window. It was just possible that the man had found the package, and if so, I might as well wait a little longer, and hear what Godfrey's defence would be, before I went in to blow it apart.

He had changed his ground, and was now giving a fine rendering of an angry man who has got himself in hand, but only just. He said, with controlled violence: "And perhaps you will tell me what in hell's name I could be doing that would drive me to wholesale murder?"

"I cannot," said Papadopoulos regretfully. "From what you are telling me of the type of goods you 'trade in', I cannot. Radio parts, tobacco, antibiotics? And so on and so on . . . The usual list, Mr. Manning. One wonders merely why it should have paid you . . . The rent of this house, your boat, the trouble to make the contacts, the risks . . . You are not a poor man. Why do you do it?"

"Christ," said Godfrey, "is it so hard to understand? I was stuck here working on my damned book, and I was bored. Of course I don't need the money. But I was bored, and there was the boat, and the promise of a bit of fun with her . . ." He broke off, turning up a hand. "But do you really want all that tonight? Say I do it for kicks, and leave it at that. Apollo will translate."

240

Adoni said gently: "He means that he likes risks and violence for their own sakes. It is a phrase that irresponsible criminals use, and adolescents."

Max laughed. Godfrey's hand whitened on his glass. "Why, you little——"

"Markos!" Max broke across it, swinging round on the Greek. I saw his face for the first time. "None of this matters just now! I'm sorry, I realise that if this man's smuggling across the border it's very much your affair, but all that really matters here and now is the girl. If he insists that——"

"A moment," said Papadopoulos, and turned his head. Adoni put a hand to the door beside him and pulled it open, and the constable came into the room.

He had obviously not found the package, and apparently nothing else either, for when his superior barked a question at him he spread empty hands and shrugged, answering with a swift spate of Greek. Max asked another question in Greek, and the man turned to him, speaking volubly and with many gestures. But I no longer paid him any heed. As I had craned forward to see if the package was in his hands, I must have made some movement that caught Adoni's attention. I found myself meeting his eyes, clear across the room.

Nobody was looking at him; all eyes were for the new-comer, except Spiro's, whose flick-knife gaze never left Godfrey. Nobody seemed to notice as Adoni slipped quietly out through the open door, pulling it shut behind him.

I backed quickly away from the window, out of the fringe of light, and soft-footed my way back round the corner of the house.

A light step beside me in the darkness, and a whisper:

"*Miss Lucy!* Miss Lucy! I thought—I could not be sure—in those clothes ... But it is you! We thought you must be dead!" Somehow his arms were round me, quite unselfconsciously hugging me to him. It was amazingly comforting. "Oh, Miss Lucy, we thought you had gone with that devil in his boat, and been killed!"

I found myself clinging to him. "I did. I did go with him ... and he did try to kill me, but I got away. I went overboard, like Spiro, and he left me to drown, but—*Adoni!* You mustn't say things like that! Where *did* you learn them? No, hush, they'll hear you ..."

"We've got to get him now. We've got to make sure of him."

241

"We will, I promise you we will. I know all about it now, Adoni. It's not just Spiro and Yanni and me—he's a traitor and a paid spy, and I can prove it."

"So?" He let me go. "Come in now, Miss Lucy, there's no need to be afraid of him. Come in straight away. Max is half crazy, I thought he would kill him."

"Not for a minute ... No, wait, I *must* know what's happened. Can you tell me, very quickly? Those are the Corfu police, aren't they? Didn't anyone come from Athens?"

"No. The Athens people said that Max must bring Spiro home, and go to the Corfu police in the morning. They said they would look into it, but I don't think they were much interested—they had their hands full after that Communist demonstration on Tuesday, and this is the affair of the Corfu people, anyway. So Max and Spiro came back alone, and I met the ferry. I told Max about the cave and the boxes that were hidden there, and he was afraid to waste more time by going to the police then—it was eleven o'clock, and only the night man on duty—so he decided to drive home quickly and go to the cave himself."

"Then you hadn't had my message from Miranda?"

"No. She telephoned the Corfu Bar, but I hadn't been in there. I'd gone to Dionysios's house, a friend of mine, and had supper there, and then we went to the Mimosa on the harbour, to wait for the ferry. They sent a boy running to look for me from the Corfu Bar, but he didn't find me. When we got to the Castello, Miranda was waiting for us, and after a time she remembered, and told us about you."

"After a time?"

I heard the smile even through the whisper. "There was Spiro."

"Oh, Lord, yes, of course! She'd forget everything else. Well, I don't blame her ... Go on. She told you about me."

"Yes. I have never seen Max like that before. We ran down to the boat-house, he and I, but the boat was gone, and you. We searched there, and along the shore, and then went up to the Villa Rotha. It was locked, so Max broke the window, and we looked for you, but found nothing. So he got to the telephone, and got Mr. Papadopoulos at his home, and told him everything very quickly, and told him to bring Spiro and Miranda from the Castello as he came. Then Max and I went back to the boat-house to wait for Mr. Manning."

"Yes?"

"We waited for some time. Then we saw him coming, no engine, just the sail, very quiet. We stood in the shadow, just inside the doors, waiting. He did not come in through the doors, but just to the end of the jetty, and he berthed the boat facing the sea, then got out very quietly and tied her up, so we knew he meant to leave again soon. Then he came back along the jetty and into the boat-house." He stirred. "We took him, Max and I. He fought, but we had him. Then Max sent me to look in the boat for you, and when I got back Mr. Manning was pretending to be surprised and very angry, but Max just said, 'Where is she? Where's my girl?' and had him by the throat, and I thought he was going to kill him, and when Mr. Manning said he knew nothing Max said to me, 'Hurry up, Adoni, before the police get here. They won't like it.' "

"Won't like what?"

"What we would have done to make him talk," said Adoni simply. "But the police came then. Mr. Manning was very angry, and complained, and one could see that Mr. Papadopoulos was uncomfortable. We had to come up to the house. The other man stayed to search the boat. You saw him come back just now? He hasn't found anything, only the place under the deck where Mr. Manning had hidden the boxes ... But you heard all that, didn't you?"

"Guessed it. It was in Greek."

"Of course. I forgot. Well, that was all. Wait a moment ..." He vanished round the house wall, and in a few seconds materialised again beside me. A glass was pushed into my hand. "Drink this. There was some whisky on the terrace. You're cold?"

"No. Excited. But thanks all the same." I drank the spirit, and handed back the glass. I saw him stoop to put it down somewhere, then he straightened, and his hand closed over my arm. "What now, Miss Lucy? You said we could get him. Is this true?"

"Quite true. There's not time enough to tell you it all now, but I must tell you some of it—enough—just in case anything happens to me ... Listen." In a few brief sentences I gave him the gist of what Godfrey had told me. "So that's it. Athens can follow up his contacts, I suppose, and it should be possible to work out roughly where he'd go ashore, in the time it took him. They'll have to get on to Tirana straight away and find some

243

way of stopping the stuff circulating. But that's not our concern. What we have to do now is to get the police to hold him, and hold him good and hard."

"What's your proof you said you had? Enough to make them listen?"

"Yes. I've got one of the boxes of currency. Yes, really. I dumped it off the platform in the boat-house, about half-way along the left side. I want you to go down and get it."

"Of course. But I'll go in with you first."

"There's no need. I'd rather you got the box safe. He knows I took it—he must know—and he'll have a good idea where I hid it. He's a dangerous man, Adoni, and if this should go wrong ... I don't want to run any risks at all of his getting down there somehow and getting away, or of his having another shot at killing me, if he thinks I'm the only one who knows where the box is. So we'd better not both be exposed to him at once. You must go and get it straight away."

"All right. Be careful of yourself."

"I'll do that. The swine had a gun. I suppose you took it?"

"Yes. And the police took it from us."

"Well, here we go." I took a shaky little breath. "Oh, Adoni ..."

"You are afraid?"

"Afraid?" I said. "It'll be the entrance of my life. Come on."

*   *   *

The scene was unchanged except that the constable now stood in Adoni's place by the door. Godfrey had lit a cigarette, and looked once more at his ease, but still ruffled and irritated, like a man who has been caught out in some misdemeanour for which he will now have to pay a stiff fine. They had apparently got to the cave and the packages which were, according to Godfrey, radio sets. He was explaining, wearily yet civilly, how the 'sets' had been packed and stored.

I put a cautious hand in through the broken pane, and began to ease the window-catch open. It moved stiffly, but without noise.

... "But surely this can wait till morning? I've admitted to an offence, and I'm perfectly willing to tell you more, but not now—and certainly not in front of a bunch of amateurs and children who seem to be trying to pin a mass murder on me."

He paused, adding in a reasonable voice: "Look, Inspector, if you insist, I'll come in to Corfu with you now, but if Miss Waring is genuinely missing, I really do think you should concentrate on her, and leave my small sins till morning."

The Inspector and Max started to speak together, the former stolidly, the latter with passion and anger, but Miranda cried out suddenly for the first time, on a piercing note that drowned them both.

"He knows where she is! He has killed her! Do not listen to him! He has killed her! I know she went to the boat! He took her and killed her, as he tried to kill Spiro my brother!"

"It is true," said Spiro violently. "As God watches me now, it is true."

"Oh, for God's sake," said Godfrey. He got abruptly to his feet, a man whose patience has suddenly given way. "I think this has gone on long enough. I've answered your questions civilly, Papadopoulos, but it's time this scene came to an end! This is my house, and I'll put up with you and your man if I have to, but I'm damned if I sit here any longer being yapped at by the local peasants. I suggest you clear them out of here, now, please, this minute, and Gale with them."

The catch was off. As the window yielded softly to my hand, I heard Max say, in a voice I hardly knew was his:

"Markos, I beg of you. The girl ... there's no time. Give me five minutes alone with him. Just five minutes. You'll not regret it."

Papadopoulos' reply was cut off by a crash as Godfrey slammed the flat of his hand down on the desk, and exploded.

"This is beyond anything! It's more, it's a criminal conspiracy! By God, Inspector, you'll have to answer for this! What the hell are you trying to do, the lot of you? Papadopoulos, you'll clear these people out of my house immediately, do you hear me? I've told you all I'm going to tell you tonight, and as for Lucy Waring, how often do I have to repeat that I took the damned girl home at seven, and I haven't seen her since? That's the truth, I swear to God!"

No actress ever had a better cue. I pulled the window open, and went in.

CHAPTER TWENTY-TWO

Let us not burthen our remembrances, with
A heaviness that's gone.

v. 1.

FOR a moment no one moved. I was watching Godfrey, and Godfrey alone, so I was only conscious of that moment's desperate stillness, then of exclamations and confused movement as Max started forward, and Papadopoulos jerked out a restraining hand and gripped his sleeve.

I said: "I suppose you weren't expecting me, Godfrey?"

He didn't speak. His face had drained, visibly, of colour, and he took a step backwards, his hand seeking the edge of the desk. Down beside me I caught the flutter of a hand as Miranda crossed herself.

"Lucy," said Max hoarsely, "Lucy—my dear——"

The Inspector had recovered from his surprise. He sat back. "It is Miss Waring, is not? I did not know you for the moment. We have been wondering where you were." I noticed suddenly that Petros, the constable, had a gun in his hand.

I said: "I know. I'm afraid I've been listening, but I wanted to hear what Mr. Manning had to say; and I wanted to know what had happened since I left him an hour or so ago."

"By God," said Max, "we were right. Markos——"

"An hour ago, Miss Waring? He was out in his boat an hour ago."

"Oh, yes. I was with him. I must have gone overboard some way to the east of Kouloura, beyond the island."

"Ah ..." said Spiro, his face blazing with excitement and satisfaction. There were exclamations, and I saw Petros move forward from the door, gun in hand. Godfrey hadn't spoken or moved. He was leaning on the desk now as if for support. He was very pale, and the bruised side of his face stood out blacker as the blood ebbed from the rest.

"Are we to understand——?" began Papadopoulos.

Max said: "Look at his face. He tried to kill you?"

I nodded.

"*Max!*" cried Papadopoulos warningly. "Petros? Ah ... Now, Miss Waring, your story, please, and quickly."

"Yes, of course, but there's something—something urgent—that I've got to tell you first."

"Well?" demanded the Inspector.

I opened my mouth to answer, but what I had to say was drowned by the sudden, strident ringing of the telephone. The sound seemed to rip the quiet room. I know I jumped, and I suppose everyone's attention flicked to the instrument for a split second. The constable, who held the gun, made an automatic move towards it as if to answer it.

It was enough. I hardly even saw Godfrey move, but in one lightning movement the hand that leaned on the edge of the desk had flashed an inch lower, flicked open a drawer, jerked a gun up, and fired, all in one movement as swift and fluid as the rake of a cat's paw. Like an echo, Petros' gun answered, but fractionally too late. His bullet smacked into the wall behind the desk, and then his gun spun smoking to the floor and skidded, scoring the polish, out of sight under the desk. Petros made some sound, clapped a hand to his right arm, and reeled back a pace, right into Max's path as the latter jumped forward.

Simultaneously with the crack of the gun Godfrey had leaped for the open window where I stood, two paces from him. I felt my arm seized and twisted up behind my back in a brutal grip, as he dragged my body back against him as a shield. And a hostage. The gun was digging into my side.

"Keep back!"

Max, who was half-way across the room, stopped dead. Papadopoulos froze in the act of rising, his hands clamped to the arms of his chair. The constable leaned against the wall where Max's thrust had sent him, blood oozing between his fingers. The twins never moved, but I heard a little sobbing moan from Miranda.

I felt myself sway as my knees loosened, and the gun jabbed cruelly. "Keep on your feet, bitch-eyes," said Godfrey, "or I'll shoot you here and now. The rest of you listen. I'm going now, and the girl with me. If I'm followed, I don't have to tell you what'll happen to her. You've shown me how little I've got to lose ... Oh, no, I'm not taking her with me ... She's a damned uncomfortable companion on a boat. You can come down for her as soon as you hear me leave—not before. Understand? Do it before, and..." a movement with the gun completed the sentence, so that I cried out, and Max moved uncontrollably. "Keep your distance!" snapped Godfrey.

247

He had been slowly pulling me backwards towards the window as he spoke. I didn't dare fight, but I tried to hang against him like a dead weight.

Max said hoarsely: "He won't leave her alive, Markos. He'll kill her."

"It won't help him." I managed to gasp it somehow. "I told ... everything ... to Adoni. Adoni knows ..."

"Shut your God-damned mouth," said Godfrey.

"You heard that?" said Max. "Let her go, blast your soul. You don't imagine you can get away with this, do you? Let her go!"

Papadopoulos said quickly: "If you do not hurt the girl, perhaps we will——"

"It will give me great pleasure," said Godfrey, "to hurt her very much." He jerked hard on my arm, and took a step towards the window. "Come along, you. Where's the pretty-boy, eh? Where did he go?"

He stopped. We were full in the window. For a moment I felt his body grow still and rigid against mine, then he pulled me out of the shaft of light, backing up sharply against the window frame, with me swung round to cover him, and the gun thrust forward now beside my waist, and nosing round in a half circle. Behind us, out on the dark terrace, something had moved.

Adoni ... It was Adoni with the package, delivering it and himself neatly into the muzzle of Godfrey's gun.

The next second I knew I was wrong. There was the tinkle of glass, the splashing of liquid, and the sound of someone humming a tune. *"Come where the booze is cheaper,"* sang Sir Julian happily, helping himself to Godfrey's whisky. Then he saw us. The slurred and beautiful voice said, cheerfully: "Hullo, Manning. Hope you don't mind my coming over? Saw the light ... thought Max might be here. Why, Lucy, m'dear ..."

I think I must have been half fainting. I have only the haziest recollection of the next minute or so. Sir Julian came forward blinking amiably, with a slopping glass in one hand, and the bottle still grasped in the other. His face had the gentle, foolish smile of someone already very drunk, and he waved the bottle at Godfrey.

"Helped myself, my dear Manning. Hope you don't mind?"

"You're welcome," said Godfrey shortly, and jerked his head. "Into the room."

248

Sir Julian seemed to have noticed nothing amiss. I tried to speak and couldn't. Dimly, I wondered why Max had made no sound. Then his father saw him. "Why, Max ..." He paused, as if a vague sense of something wrong was filtering through the fog of alcohol. His eyes came uncertainly back to Godfrey, peering through the shaft of light thrown by the window. "There's the telephone. Someone's ringing up." He frowned. "Can't be me. I thought of it, but came instead."

"Inside, you drunken old fool," said Godfrey, and dragged at my arm to pull me out past him.

Sir Julian merely smiled stupidly, raised the bottle in a wavering salute, and then hurled it straight at the light.

It missed, but only just. It caught the flex, and the light careened wildly up to the ceiling and swung down again, sending wild shadows lurching and flying up the walls so that the ensuing maelstrom of action seemed like something from an old film, flickering drunkenly, and far too fast ...

Something white scraped along the floor ... Spiro's cast, thrust hard against Godfrey's legs. Godfrey staggered, recovered as his shoulder met the window frame, and with an obscene little grunt in my ear, fired down at the boy. I felt the jerk of the gun against my waist and smelt the acrid tang of singeing cloth. He may have been aiming at Spiro, but the light still reeled as if in an earthquake, and, off balance as I was, I spoiled his aim. The bullet hit the cast, which shattered. It must have been like a blow right across the broken leg. The boy screamed, rolling aside, with Miranda shrieking something as she threw herself down beside him.

I don't know whether I tore myself away, or whether Godfrey flung me aside, but suddenly I was free, my arm dropping, half-broken, to my side. As I fell he fired again, and then something hit me, hurling me down and to the floor. Max, going past me in a silent, murderous dive for Godfrey's gun-hand.

I went down heavily into the wreckage of the plaster cast. The place stank of whisky and cordite. The telephone still screeched. I was deafened, blinded, sobbing with pain. The two men hurtled backwards out on to the terrace, locked together in a struggle of grunting breaths and stamping feet. One of them trod on my hand as he passed. Papadopoulos thudded past, and out, and Petros was on his knees near by, cursing and groping under the desk for his gun.

Then someone's arms came round me, and held me tightly.

249

Sir Julian reeked of whisky, but his voice was quite sober. "Are you all right, dear child?"

I nodded. I couldn't speak. I clung to him, flinching and shaking as the sound of the fight crashed round the terrace. It was impossible, in that diffused and rocking light, to see which man was which. I saw Papadopoulos standing near me, legs apart, the gun in his hand moving irresolutely as the locked bodies stamped and wrestled past him. Godfrey's gun spat again, and the metal table whanged. Papadopoulos yelled something, and the injured constable lurched to his feet and ran to the windows, dragging the curtains wide, so that the light poured out.

But already they were beyond the reach of it, hurtling back against the balustrade that edged the steep and tree-hung cliff. I saw them, dimly silhouetted against the sky. One of them had the other rammed back across the stone. There was a crack, a sound of pain. Sir Julian's breath whistled in my ear and he said "*Christ Almighty*", and I saw that the man over the stone was Max.

Beside us was a scraping sound and a harshly-drawn breath. Spiro's voice said urgently: "*Koumbàre . . .*" and a hand thrust Sir Julian aside. The boy had dragged himself through the welter of broken plaster to the window, and lay on his belly, with the levelled rifle hugged to his cheek. I cried out, and Sir Julian shot a hand down and thrust the barrel lower. "*No! Wait!*"

From the locked and straining bodies over the balustrade came a curse, a sudden flurry of movement, a grunt. Max kicked up savagely, twisted with surprising force, and tore sideways and free. He lost his grip of Godfrey's gun-hand, but before the latter could collect himself to use it Max smashed a blow at the bad side of his face, a cruel blow which sent Godfrey spinning back, to lose his balance and fall in his turn violently against the stone.

For two long seconds the men were feet apart. Beside me, Spiro jerked the rifle up, and fired. I heard the bullet chip stone. Max, flinching back, checked for a vital instant, and in that instant Godfrey had rolled over the wide stone parapet in a sideways, kicking vault, and had dropped down into the bushes out of sight.

By all the laws he should have broken his back, or at least a leg, but he must have been unhurt. There was a series of slithering crashes as he hurled himself downhill, and then a thud as he jumped to the track.

I don't even remember moving, but I beat Papadopoulos and Miranda to Max's side as he hung, gasping, over the parapet.

"Are you hurt?"

"No." It was hardly a word. He had already thrust himself upright and was making for the shallow steps that led down from the terrace to the zigzag path.

Godfrey was visible below, a shadow racing from patch to patch of starlight downhill between the trees. Papadopoulos levelled his pistol across the parapet, then put it up again with an exclamation. For a moment I couldn't see why, then I realised that Adoni was on the branch of the zigzag path below Godfrey, and more or less in line with him. Godfrey hadn't seen him for the bushes in between.

But the boy must have heard the shots and the fracas up above, and now the thudding of Godfrey's racing steps must have warned him what was happening. He stopped. One moment he was there in the path, standing rigid, head up, listening, then the next he had melted into the shadow of the trees. Godfrey, unaware or uncaring, ran on and down.

Beside me, Miranda caught her breath. Papadopoulos was craning to see. Max had stopped dead at the head of the steps.

Godfrey turned the corner and ran down past the place where Adoni stood waiting.

Ran down ... and past ... and was lost to sight beyond the lower thicket of lime trees.

Miranda cried out shrilly, and Papadopoulos said, incredulously: "He let him go ..."

I said quickly: "He has the evidence I sent him for. He had to keep it safely."

"He is a coward!" cried Miranda passionately, and ran for the steps.

Next moment Adoni emerged from the trees. I couldn't see if he had the package, but he was coming fast uphill. Max had started down the steps in what was now obviously a futile attempt to catch the fugitive, but Miranda flew past him, shrieking, and met Adoni head on, her fists beating furiously against his chest.

"Coward! Coward! Coward! To be afraid of that Bulgar swine! After what he did to your brother, to let him go?

251

Coward! Woman! I spit on you, I spit! If I were a man I would eat his heart out!"

She tried with the last words to tear away and past him, but he caught and held her with one arm, whirling her aside with an almost absent-minded ease as he stepped full into Max's way and thrust the other arm across his chest, barring his path. As I ran down the steps and came up to them I heard, through Miranda's breathless and sobbing abuse, Adoni saying, quick and low: "No. No, Max. Wait. Wait and see."

Where there had been pandemonium before, now quite suddenly there was stillness. Max, at the boy's words, had stopped dead. The three of them looked like some group of statuary, the two men still, staring into each other's eyes, Adoni full in Max's path, looking in the starlight like Michael barring the gates of Paradise; the girl collapsed now and weeping against his side. At some time the telephone must have stopped ringing. Papadopoulos had run back to it and could be heard shouting urgently into it. Sir Julian must have gone to Spiro. The constable was starting down the steps, but slowly, because of his wound, and because it was so obviously too late . . .

The last of the wind had died, and the air was still with the hush before dawn. We heard it all quite clearly, the slam of the boat-house door, and the quick thud of running feet along the wooden platform. The pause, as he reached the *Aleister* and tore her loose from her rope. He would be thrusting her hard away from the jetty . . .

The sudden stutter of her motor was as loud as gun-fire. There was a brief, racing crescendo as the *Aleister* leaped towards the open sea and freedom.

Then the sound was swallowed, shattered, blanked out in the great sheeted roar of flame as the sloop exploded. The blast hit us where we stood. The flames licked and flared over the water, and were gone. The echo of the blast ran up the cliff and beat from rock to rock, humming, before it died into the rustle of the trees.

Sir Julian was saying: "What happened? What happened?" and I heard a flood of breathless Greek from Spiro. Papadopoulos had dropped the telephone and ran forward above us to the parapet.

"Max? What in hell's name happened?"

Max tore his eyes from Adoni. He cleared his throat, hesitating. I said shakenly: "I think I know. When I was on board I smelled gas ... It's a terribly easy thing to do ... leave a gas tap on by mistake in the galley, and then the gas leaks down and builds up under the deck boards. You don't notice it, but as soon as the engine fires, up she goes. I—I once saw it happen on the Norfolk Broads."

"Spiro was saying something about gas." He mopped his face. "My God, what a night. My God. I suppose it must have been ... Had he been using the galley?"

"Not on the way out. It stands to reason, anyway, he'd have noticed the smell when he took the boxes out from under the deck, if it had been really bad. No, he must have used it on the way home. When I took a box out myself the smell was pretty faint. Did you get the box, Adoni?"

"Yes."

"You got a box?" The Inspector's attention sharpened, diverted for a moment. "This is what you were going to tell us, eh? Is it a radio set?"

"It is not. It's a batch of forged currency, Inspector Papadopoulos, part of a cargo of seven hundred thousand Albanian leks that he took across tonight. I managed to steal one package, and hide it in the boat-house before he—he took me. That's where Adoni's been; I sent him to collect it." I added: "I think that you may find that this—accident—has saved everybody a lot of trouble. I mean, if the Greeks had had to shoot him ..."

I let the sentence hang. Beside me, Max and Adoni stood very still. The Inspector surveyed us for a moment, then he nodded.

"You may be right. Well, Miss Waring, I'll be with you again in a minute or two, and I'll be very glad to listen to you then. You have the box safe, young Adoni? Good. Bring it up, will you? Now we'd better get down there and see if there's anything to pick up. Are you still on your feet, Petros?"

The two police vanished down the track. There was another silence. Everyone turned, as if impelled, and looked at Adoni. He met our eyes levelly, and smiled. He looked very beautiful. Miranda said, on a long, whispered note: "It was you. It was you ..." and sank down to the ground beside him, with his hand to her cheek and a face of shining worship lifted to his.

He looked down at her, and said something in Greek, a sentence spoken very tenderly. I heard Max take in a sharp little breath, and then he came to me and took me in his arms and kissed me.

*　　*　　*

253

Sir Julian was waiting for us on the terrace. We need not have been afraid that he would comment on what had just passed between his son and me. He was basking in a warm bath of self-congratulation.

"The performance of my life," he said complacently.

"It certainly was. It fooled me. Did you know he wasn't drunk?" I asked Max.

"Yes. I wasn't quite sure what he'd try on, but I thought it might break the situation our way. Which it did—but only just. You're a lousy shot, father."

"It was the waste of good whisky. It put me off my stroke," said his father. "However, there was enough left in the glass to put Spiro under; I've got the poor child strapped up again, and flat out on the sofa in there. That'll be another trip to hospital as soon as it's light, I'm afraid. Oh, and I telephoned your sister, Lucy. I reassured her quite successfully. It's been quite a night, as they say."

"And not over yet by a damned long way," said Max, a little grimly. "I shan't get any rest till I've heard Lucy's story ... No, it's all right, darling, we'll leave it till Markos gets back. You won't want to go through it all again for him. You must be exhausted."

"I think I've gone beyond that. I feel more or less all right ... floating a bit, that's all." I went slowly to the parapet, and leaned there, gazing out over the dark sea. The dawn was coming; the faintest glimmer touched the far Albanian snows. "Do you suppose there'll be—anything—for them to find?"

"I'm sure there won't." He came to my side and slipped an arm round me. "Forget it. Don't let it haunt you. It was better this way."

"I know."

Sir Julian, at my other side, quoted:

> "'Let us not burthen our remembrances, with
> A heaviness that's gone ...'

And I may say, Max, that I have come to the conclusion that Prospero is not for me. A waste of talent. I shall set my sights at Stephano for this film of ours. I shall write and tell Sandy so today."

"Then you're coming back to us?" I said.

"I shall hate it," said Sir Julian, "but I shall do it. Who

254

wants to leave an enchanted island for the icy, damp, and glorious lights of London? I think I might try don't you?"

Max said nothing, but I felt his arm tighten. Adoni and Miranda came softly up the terrace steps, heads bent, whispering, and vanished in through the french windows.

"Beatrice and Benedick," said Sir Julian softly. "I never thought to hear that magnificently Shakespearian outburst actually in the flesh, as it were. *'O God, that I were a man! I would eat his heart in the market-place.'* Did you catch it, Lucy?"

"I didn't understand the Greek. Was that it? What did she actually say?" When he told me, I asked: "And Adoni? What was it he said when she was kissing his hand?"

"I didn't hear that."

Max glanced down at me, hesitated, and then quoted, rather dryly:

"'You wanted to eat his heart, little sister. I have cooked it for you.'"

"Dear Heaven," I said.

Sir Julian smiled. "You've seen the other face of the enchanted isle tonight, haven't you, my poor child? It's a rough sort of magic for such as we are—a mere musician, and a couple of players . . ."

"Much as I adore being bracketed with you," I said, "it's putting me too high."

"Then could you bear to be bracketed with me instead?" asked Max.

"Well, that is rather going to the other end of the scale," said his father, "but I'd be delighted if she'd give the matter some thought. Do you think, my dear, that you could ever consider dwindling as far as a musician's wife?"

I laughed. "I'm not at all sure who this proposal's coming from," I said, "but to either, or to both of you, yes."

Far out in the bay a curve of blue fire melted, rolled in a silver wheel, and was lost under the light of day.

MORE BESTSELLING
MARY STEWART TITLES

☐	01361 3	The Moonspinners	£2.50
☐	02219 1	Thunder On The Right	£2.50
☐	01439 3	Nine Coaches Waiting	£2.50
☐	01945 X	Wildfire At Midnight	£2.50
☐	18611 9	The Hollow Hills	£2.50
☐	15133 1	The Crystal Cave	£2.50
☐	21984 X	Touch Not The Cat	£2.50
☐	01395 8	My Brother Michael	£2.50
☐	35214 0	The Wicked Day	£2.95
☐	25829 2	The Last Enchantment	£2.95
☐	02458 5	Airs Above The Ground	£2.50
☐	04353 9	The Gabriel Hounds	£2.50
☐	01115 7	The Ivy Tree	£2.50
☐	01262 5	Madam, Will You Talk?	£2.25

All these books are available at your local bookshop or newsagent, or can be ordered direct from the publisher. Just tick the titles you want and fill in the form below.

Prices and availability subject to change without notice.

Hodder & Stoughton Paperbacks, P.O. Box 11, Falmouth, Cornwall

Please send cheque or postal order, and allow the following for postage and packing:

U.K.—55p for one book, plus 22p for the second book, and 14p for each additional book ordered up to a £1.75 maximum.

B.F.P.O. and EIRE—55p for the first book, plus 22p for the second book, and 14p per copy for the next 7 books, 8p per book thereafter.

OTHER OVERSEAS CUSTOMERS—£1.00 for the first book, plus 25p per copy for each additional book.

Name ....

Address ....